Listen for the Mourning Dove

Listen for the Mourning Dove

F.C. Pearce

A NOVEL

Book Leaf Press
New Mexico

LISTEN FOR THE MOURNING DOVE
Copyright ©2016 by F.C. Pearce

First Edition
Published in the United States of America by
Book Leaf Press
New Mexico
www.bookleafpress.com

Library of Congress Control Number: 2015919435
ISBN: 978-0-9969819-0-3
eBook ISBN: 978-0-9969819-1-0
Printed in the United States of America

Cover Art: front and back covers from original watercolors
Mourning Dove in Sycamore and *Leaves and Buttonballs*
by Texas artist Susan Mansell, used with the artist's explicit written permission.

Cover and Interior Design/Production: John Tollett

For Skeet

Prologue

~

It seemed impossible that forty years had passed since she'd seen No. 8 Bobwhite Lane, but the enormity of the live oak tree offered solid proof. It had grown from a spindly five feet tall to at least thirty-five. In contrast, the neighborhood seemed to have withered, emptied of the spirits that had once given it life.

The only things that looked the same were the green and red tiles that framed the front door and its one step. She'd sat there with her father that long-gone October evening, just before the rain came. She remembered the crop of stars that had slipped in and out of view from behind the storm clouds, and she remembered the music.

Part One

1

Concho City, Texas—October 2, 1953

That Friday evening would have been entirely unremarkable had it not been that it was storming for the first time since spring, and that an unfathomable event would be taking place in the wee hours that would mark the 3rd of October unforgettable. But as far as anyone knew, the next morning would be like most other Saturday mornings on Bobwhite Lane: sun shining, dogs barking, kids yelling, and mothers shouting at them above the noisy weekend traffic up on Old Oak Road.

In the nearby countryside, lightning flashed on endless miles of gnarly mesquite. In town, from his wobbly lean-to of weathered boards and tar paper, the young dog on the corner whimpered, then growled at every roll of thunder. The only other sounds breaking the usual after-supper quiet on the lane had been a couple of cars splashing through puddles on their way somewhere else. In picture windows families could be seen milling about, gesturing to one another, getting children ready for bed, or gathering around the neighborhood's few television sets to watch the Friday night fare of *Beat the Clock* or *Ted Mack's Amateur Hour*.

It was almost 9:00, and sprinkling again, when the music started at Alice Bock's tiny frame house on the corner of Bobwhite Lane and Angelus Street. On a Friday night, three years before, Alice's husband Ernest had disappeared, never to be seen or heard from again. Every Friday night since, she'd paid homage to him with her music, convinced that it would eventually lure him home to her. Her 78 record crackled and wobbled under the phonograph needle and, with what seemed like a hundred violins, a crooner's voice drifted out the front windows, past their red shutters, and into the empty street.

She had kept the 1926 recording of "Always" in the top left drawer of her chiffonier since marrying Ernest Bock the same year. Between uses, the record had been wrapped in its overused tissue, then tucked into the folds of a silk bed jacket that had been her mother's. Other than a small brown stain on the edge of one sleeve, the jacket was in pristine condition. Not even the fine silt of the wicked West Texas dust storms, known to steal into the best-built homes, had ever found a way into the sanctified contents of that drawer.

Alice, who looked far older than her forty-six years, had once been pretty with an easy smile, dancing eyes, and lustrous copper-colored hair coiled loosely at the nape of her neck. But when Ernest left, her smile went with him, her eyes went dull, and her shiny locks went gray and brittle. She'd had her hair "hacked off," as one neighbor lady described it, to just below her ears, as though serving some sort of penance. She'd rarely left the house. The only time anyone could count on seeing her was on those Friday evenings when she'd dance past her front windows, her arm positioned high on her phantom partner's shoulder (Ernest was a tall man), wearing the once-white dress and silk gardenia pinned behind one ear that she'd worn the night they married. The same neighbor lady had described Alice's displays as "downright pitiful," and the elderly man next door said that her Friday ritual gave him the "willies."

Diagonally across the way, young Sweezer Riley, just hours away from turning thirteen, had come out on his front porch to listen to the music. The porch overhang was just wide enough to keep him dry. He'd never met Alice Bock, but he figured they had something important in common—his mother, Faithful Abbott Riley, had died the same year that Alice's husband had disappeared. Sweezer had overheard a couple of the old ladies in the neighborhood talking about how Ernest had taken off and left Alice the summer of '50 for some other woman. Sweezer believed that the words of "Always" held a message for him from his departed mother—that even though he couldn't see her, she was always with him.

He nestled into the metal fan-backed chair that had been hers. It was badly in need of a fresh coat of light green, but he didn't want to paint it because doing so would be like painting the last of her away. The only other personal items surviving her were a flowered apron with a handkerchief in the pocket, and a diary titled *The Day Carl Abbott 'Sweezer' Riley Was Born*. Her apron remained on the hook in the kitchen where she'd left it. Joe Riley, Sweezer's father, had forbid him to touch it. Sweezer had kept his mother's diary hidden. Joe remained inside that night keeping company with the only thing he honestly cared about—a good stiff drink. By that time, any night of the week, he'd be three sheets to the wind. That Friday night was no different.

Sweezer remembered the day his mother died. On that very day, she'd repeated the story of how she'd derived the name Sweezer from his given name of Carl: he was born sweet and innocent, but wise like old geezers often were, hence the nickname Sweezer. He remembered the old man Ray Tubbs who had lived down the road from them. Ray had taught him how to fish, to feed four or five lambs at the same time, and to hunt for arrowheads. After Ray passed, Sweezer overheard the old men at the store talking about how much they missed the "old geezer." Sweezer left the store that day feeling proud.

Running his fingers through his mop of sand-colored hair, Sweezer shut his eyes and rested his head on the back of his mama's chair just as giggling and muffled conversation began coming from the yard next door. Annoyed at being disturbed, yet more curious, he got up from his comfortable position to creep through waist-high weeds, to sneak a look over the hedge that separated his house from the Randolph house next door.

Six-year-old Cady Frances Randolph was perched on the tops of her father's shoes as he waltzed her down the sidewalk to the music coming from the Bock house. He was being careful to avoid the mound of dirt that was piled high at the end of the walk. A good-sized hole waited for the live oak shade tree that was scheduled to be planted the next morning. They sang "Always" together.

It was fascinating to Sweezer that a child as young as Cady would know the words to such a song, and that she could carry a tune so well. Dr. Jonas Randolph's voice was entirely drowned out by his daughter's enthusiastic warbling, yet he smiled patiently down at her, twirling her round and round. Watching them had left Sweezer aching for his mama.

He thought back to the time he had met Cady and her father seven months before, when his house was delivered on a flatbed trailer to the lot next door. Cady had stood outside all day that day watching the two-story, yellow frame house get planted on the corner. When he asked her what she was so curious about, she shrugged her shoulders and said, "I think 'cause your house is like in the *Wizard of Oz* . . . came from somewhere else. That's all I guess. I'm gonna go find that wizard man someday. Yep, I sure am."

The house had actually been Sweezer's mother's country place, left to her when her father, Sweezer's grandfather Abbott, died in '39. Sweezer had grown up there. His parents had raised chickens and goats, and had worked the land into pretty good alfalfa crops. Faithful had been an unusually graceful woman for having been raised poor in the country. Her father's death had left her both penniless and motherless when, soon after the funeral, her mother left town with a new man. Faithful dropped out of high school at sixteen and married Joe. All she knew about him was that he was a good dancer, had a steady job as a welder, and promised to take care of her forever. On the day Sweezer was born, a year later, she wrote in her diary: *My beloved son, Carl Abbott 'Sweezer' Riley, my second chance in life and my only hero.* It was her only entry.

A couple of years after Faithful died, Abbott relatives sold the land on which her house sat. With part of the small amount of money that she had squirreled away and left behind, Joe had the house ripped up from its roots and moved, along with twelve-year-old Sweezer, the twenty-some-odd miles into Concho City. That's how the house came to live on Bobwhite Lane's last empty lot. Had there been a tree, a patch of grass, even a bush around it, the place might have seemed more to belong.

Afraid of being seen, Sweezer stole back through the weeds to his position on the chair. He'd had a strange feeling watching Cady and her father dance. He'd had strange feelings before, like the time he dreamt about his mama drowning in a swirling area of Salt Brush Creek right below the big boulder from which she loved to fish in real life. When she was found floating face-down in the exact spot that Sweezer had seen her in his dream, Joe took seriously to the bottle and accused Sweezer of being the devil incarnate.

Alice played "Always" a full four times in a row that night, and danced alone to every play. But when she played "Goodnight, Wherever You Are," popular during the war, it signaled the end of the music for the night. She didn't dance to that one. She sat motionless until nothing could be heard but the scratch and thump of the needle at the end of the record. And then, like clockwork, the house went dark.

Sweezer listened to the rain on the overhang for a little while longer, stretched his gangly arms over his head, and peeked out to catch some raindrops on his face. The porch light was out at the Randolph house. He locked the front door and walked toward the light from the kitchen that formed a yellow triangle on the hall's wood floor. He could see Joe's head on the table, his outstretched arm on the checkered oil cloth, and a glass turned over by his hand. The only thing standing was a vodka bottle, almost empty.

Joe spat and snorted while Sweezer put the glass in the sink and wiped up the few drops of liquor that had beaded up on the cloth. He knew from experience not to disturb his father; it never turned out well. Climbing the stairs to his room, he stepped carefully on each, to avoid the creaks that could stir Joe.

Still dressed, he stretched out on his bed and imagined his mama downstairs baking a cake for him; he could even smell it. When the phone began ringing, he sprang off the bed, ran into the hall, and managed to pick up the receiver before the third ring, and before it awakened Joe.

2

An hour earlier

Dr. Jonas Randolph had left the paperwork spread out on the dining table to keep his promise to his young daughter that he'd spend some time with her that evening. With no school the next morning, she'd be able to stay up well past 9:00 that night. He pushed the paperwork aside and thought about how impossible it seemed that an entire year had passed since he'd moved his family to Concho City. He'd bought No. 8 Bobwhite Lane because it was the right price. He hadn't much liked it otherwise, particularly the tiles around the front door.

Except for Sweezer's house next door, most of the other houses on Bobwhite Lane had been built post-World War II with the requisite picture window in front. The other exception was the Bock house where Alice lived. Ernest Bock's father had built the place with his bare hands around 1912, and had planted the three now-huge pecan trees at the same time; two flanked the front, the third in back. After Ernest's father died not long after, Ernest's mother lived on there until her death in 1926 when newlyweds Alice and Ernest moved in. When Ernest vanished twenty-four years later, hearsay was that Alice had only managed to remain in the house with a small inheritance from her parents.

Bobwhite Lane, one of a number of streets in Concho City named after indigenous birds, was wedged between Old Oak Road and Angelus Street. The small front yards were separated one from another by long rows of neatly trimmed hedges. Bobwhite was home to at least three veterans of World War II; one of them had also served in Korea. The three of them had created a boom of kids with wives from whom they'd been separated for too long. Jonas Randolph was one of them.

Five months earlier, Jonas had arrived with Renata and Cady just in time for them to be counted among the 50,000 or so Concho City residents still reeling from the damage caused by the monster tornado that had turned the area on its ear. The twister, more than a mile across, had blown away most of the northern end of town claiming ninety souls in the melee, leaving a couple hundred others seriously injured. Despite that horror, with the exception of Jonas's wife, the townsfolk still welcomed even a potentially deadly storm if it might drop its liquid manna onto the drought-cracked earth that formed fissures wide enough, and deep enough, to hide small animals.

Renata argued against the move to Texas, particularly moving so close to Jonas's parents. She examined the words engraved on the inside of her wedding ring: *Wither thou goest, I will go.* Before leaving New Orleans, she'd told Jonas that she was willing to keep that promise unless it meant following him into "the valley of the shadow of death." He had assured her that moving to Texas would result in no such end. It was precisely because his parents lived only an hour away that he had accepted the position at the small Surgeons' Clinic Hospital in Concho City. He could no longer work, handle Renata, and care for young Cady without help.

Having become accustomed to her all-night forays into the French Quarter, it hadn't taken Renata long to grow restless with the deathly quiet of Concho City. The tornado hitting on the heels of their arrival had given her the excuse she'd needed to return to New Orleans regularly. "I'm somewhere between terrified and bored to death in this place," she'd told Jonas. It wasn't unusual for him to return home from work to find her gone and Cady playing alone in her room.

Jonas looked back at the paperwork spread out on the table. Unable to tackle it, he stood, stretched, and walked through the living room to the front door. He was tired.

"Cady, come outside with Daddy," he called down the hall.

"Okay, Poppy . . . one more minute. I'm putting my doll to bed," she called back.

He walked outside to examine the large hole in the front yard. The men were scheduled to bring the live oak tree the next morning. He looked back at the house and the glow from the living room's picture window. The light reminded him of a painting he'd seen in a New Orleans gallery of a bayou house at dusk. He'd regretted not buying it. "Next trip," he mumbled to himself.

The house was low slung, small, and typical of those built post-war in Concho City: frame stucco, painted white, with a green slate roof. The bedroom windows were high and small. The living room led to the kitchen, then to the family room, and out the sliding doors to a small concrete patio. The back yard was long and narrow leading to the alley lined with garbage cans. A couple of mesquite trees alongside some thick bushes offered little shade from the blistering West Texas sun.

Cady's room was painted lavender, her favorite color. It was at the end of the hall, beyond her parents' room, with a small bathroom attached. There was a larger bath in the hallway, opposite her parents' room, with a tub that had been the home for an alligator that Renata had brought back from one of her frequent trips to New Orleans. It had been quite small on arrival, only a couple of feet long. When the reptile grew large enough to snap at Cady, Jonas took a day off, hired a man with a pickup, and with the man's help, released the alligator into a swampy area outside Houston. Transporting it had been a nightmare.

Renata had brought back other exotic animals too: a small monkey she had tied to a clothes line in the back yard, who had tragically hung himself while jumping into a nearby mesquite tree, and two tropical birds she'd brought back from a trip to Florida who were given residence in the garage. Jonas was trying to find homes for them when Renata, leaving the car idling in the garage, asphyxiated both. Despite Jonas's pleadings to her to end the practice of dragging any other poor creatures home, she said she couldn't promise. "I'm saving them from a worse fate," she'd insisted.

It was no wonder that Cady, a sensitive child, had begun an animal rescue operation that added to Jonas's already-heavy patient load. There was the time Jonas and Cady were driving back from Pecan Valley and had come upon an injured skunk still alive in the road. At Cady's pleadings, Jonas took it home and operated on it. It recovered fully. Seeing the smile on her face as the creature scurried off into the alfalfa field, near where they'd found it, had more than made up for the odor that, weeks later, still permeated the trunk of Jonas's car.

He saw that smile reappear after he helped Cady care for a mourning dove down in a bush in the back yard a few weeks later. Together they had nursed the plump gray bird back to health. Jonas figured it had been stunned by a hit to the head, reassuring Cady that he thought it would be fine given a little time and their attention. After a couple of days feeding the bird various concoctions with a syringe, it had miraculously flown up to the top of the garage, puffed up its pinkish chest, and cooed its five-note song.

Cady had been full of questions about what would happen to the bird. Jonas explained to her that mourning doves mated for life and that it would likely be returning to its mate. "Like the two doves in my book?" she had asked. There was only one book that was *her* book—*The Little Prince*. Jonas had not remembered mention of doves in the book. He continued explaining to her that the dove had gotten its name, not because of the time of day, but because of the mournful sound it made. He remembered the conversation they'd had:

"Some people think the bird sounds sad, but to me it's the most soothing sound in the world," he'd told her. He carefully printed the words 'mourning dove' on a piece of paper. "And guess what? Jonas means dove in the Hebrew language!"

"So the Hebrews will call you Dove instead of Jonas?" Cady asked.

"Kind of, sweetheart," he'd chuckled, too weary to explain. She'd have asked a thousand questions. "Cady, my dear, just remember that wherever you are, in all the years to come, even when you're as old as me, listen for the mourning dove, and when you hear one, you'll know that everything's all right . . . exactly as it should be. Okay?"

"Uh huh . . . will it be *our* mourning dove?" she asked, as she tucked the piece of paper on which he'd spelled the bird's name into her doll's pocket.

Jonas thought before answering. He'd have to choose his words carefully. "Well, I know if our bird can't be wherever you are, then his brother or sister, or maybe a favorite cousin, aunt or uncle will be. You see, honey, all the mourning doves belong to the same family . . . just like we belong to ours." He was relieved when she didn't question him further on the subject. That was rare.

He took a long look at her. She was graceful, tall for her age, but not a pretty child. His mother, Frances, had frequently mentioned the great blessing it had been that Cady had at least been born with delicate hands and wrists, long fingers, and most important of all—slender ankles that were coveted as much by Frances as by the South.

It had pleased Frances Harrington Randolph that her granddaughter had been given the middle name of Frances, although a disappointment that she would be called Cady. It was a name with no tradition in either the Randolph or Collins families. Renata had chosen Cady, she claimed, as phonetic for a long-departed aunt's initials K.D. "How strange," Frances had told Jonas. Had Jonas not insisted on the middle name of Frances, Renata would have named the child Cady Rose. It hadn't endeared Renata to either of Jonas's parents.

Over the previous year, Cady's hair had darkened to a light brown from the towheaded blonde she'd been since birth. She was a pale child with an unusually wide mouth and big ears, but her deep-set green eyes, full of mischief and sparkle, had made up in large measure for her less pretty features. Despite her odd looks, Jonas was convinced that a real beauty would someday emerge from what he called his "chrysalis-of-a-girl."

~

It had been awhile since Jonas had called Cady to come outside. He turned off the porch light and settled himself down on the one-step landing at the front door of the house. Cady pushed the screen door playfully against his back. With a little grin, he leaned forward to let her pass through.

"Look up there in the sky, honey," he said. He held her around the knees, pointing up to the canopy of fast-moving clouds. Intermittently, the stars would slide into view and then disappear back into the haze. "Watch how the clouds move away so you can see a mess of stars every once in awhile, honey. See?"

Cady stood at Jonas's side staring upwards before she settled down on his lap. His long, thin legs were stretched out in front of him on the sidewalk. She leaned back into his chest, rested her hands on the backs of his, and traced with her finger the bas-relief carving of the leaping deer on the signet ring given him by his Grandfather Randolph. His grandfather had actually dipped the ring in wax to seal important letters. Until he married, Jonas had worn the ring on his left hand where it had been a little less tight. It was a manly ring, in a simple gold setting, holding the rectangle of carved black obsidian.

"Just look at all those stars," Jonas whispered.

"Uh huh, Papa, I see 'em," she said, rooting back harder against his chest.

"Did you remember to wish on the first star you saw tonight?" he asked.

"Uh huh . . . I wished just you and me could go away somewhere special, Daddy . . . just you and me and nobody else."

"Honey, that's you and I, not you and me," he said, kissing the top of her head.

She threw her head back to smile at him. Her hair was impossibly straight and flyaway. Renata had often remarked what a shame it had been that Cady hadn't inherited her father's thick, lustrous hair. A strong breeze lifted her bangs from her forehead.

"You know, sweetheart, I was thinking that we could go on a train ride sometime real soon. What do you think about that?" he asked, tucking the sides of her short bob behind each ear.

"Just us . . . okay?"

"Uh huh, sugar, just us."

"Promise?"

"Absolutely, sweetheart, I promise." They both looked up at the sky. "You know, honey . . . I think hiding the stars every now and then is nature's way of reminding us how lucky we are when we have a whole sky full."

Cady yelped as the stars slipped in and out of view, and pulled his arms around her tighter. "The stars are giggling because we can't find them."

"Uh huh," he said, resting his chin on top of her head. He knew that she was thinking of *The Little Prince*.

She chattered away about how wonderful their train trip was going to be. They'd pass through Pecan Valley where Jonas's parents lived, but they wouldn't stop; they'd go straight to Greenwood, have barbecue at the famous smokehouse there, and then return to Concho City on the late afternoon train. Jonas was just about to take her into the house, to get her ready for bed, when the music started from Alice Bock's house across the way.

"Oh, Daddy, listen, it's the always song. Can we dance and sing . . . please, please, please?"

"You betcha, sugar . . . but for just a little while. Climb on."

Cady stepped carefully, one foot at a time, onto the toes of Jonas's shoes. He waltzed her carefully down the front walk. They'd started dancing together before Cady was old enough to walk, back in New Orleans, on the levee near their house. The nights he wasn't at the hospital working, he'd sung "Always" to her like a lullaby. By the time she was four, she knew every word.

Alice started the record over again, and after singing and dancing along with it a second time, Jonas picked Cady up, despite her pleadings to continue dancing, and carried her into the house. Not only was it beginning to rain, but he knew it would take awhile to get her into bed and asleep.

The next morning promised to find Cady running to the front door, her daily habit, at precisely 6:00 a.m., to get the paper that always landed on the front step. She'd wait patiently for her father to get up, and they'd read together while listening to the hits on the radio. But, the next morning would be different: they'd also be getting ready for the surprise party they had planned to celebrate Sweezer Riley's thirteenth birthday. Cady had wrapped a present for him, and Jonas had bought cupcakes from a local bakery so that the boy would have something akin to a cake. They'd surprise Sweezer a little before noon. Cady could hardly wait.

3

An hour later—Friday, October 2

Cady was still awake. Jonas looked at the stack of bills and other paperwork spread out on the table. He planned to drive over to St. Joseph's with Cady the next day, after Sweezer's party, to check on Renata. Their sixth wedding anniversary was coming up and although it was still a few months away, she had ranted to the nurses earlier in the day about how coldhearted Jonas was to have "incarcerated" her just before such an important event. During and after a binge, she'd have no concept of time. The nurses had found it necessary to restrain her the night before.

Jonas was exceptionally tired, with a heavier-than-usual patient load, but he couldn't risk leaving Cady alone with Renata again until he was sure it would be safe—not after Renata had come close to drowning the child while attempting to wash her hair. Fortunately, Renata was so drunk that Cady had been able to slip from her grip. Jonas had found Cady naked, hiding behind a garbage can in the alley when he arrived home a couple of hours later. Renata had passed out on the bathroom floor by a tub full of water. It wasn't the only time young Cady had managed to escape harm in her father's absence. Jonas admitted Renata to the Pavilion, a euphemism for psychiatric ward, at St. Joseph's Hospital a couple of days later.

He'd kept the issue hidden from his parents. They hadn't wanted Jonas to marry Renata in the first place. He hadn't wanted to give them reason to dislike her more, but he knew the day was coming, and soon, that he'd have to tell them the truth.

Jonas called out to Cady as he made his way to her room. "Okay, darlin', time for you to get into bed." She didn't answer. He found her wrapping bandages around her doll's head. Watching her, he wondered if she would end up choosing medicine as a profession. He'd inscribed his *Pathology in General Surgery* with the following: *Cady R., an unusually smart young lady and future Phi Beta Kappa, of course, and future Alpha Omega Alpha if she chooses the medical field.* Though only six, Cady sensed that he was troubled. Without a word, she reached up and pushed back the errant strands of hair from his forehead.

"Hop up now, honey, and get your pajamas on. I'll be in to tuck you in as soon as you're ready."

"Oh Poppy, can't I stay up a little longer? There's no school in the morning. *Please?*"

"No ma'am. It's late. If you don't get to sleep, you won't be up to get my paper on time, or to watch the men plant our oak tree, or to help me get ready for Sweezer's party. You and I won't like that, now will we?"

"No," she said, in a barely audible voice.

He promised her one Fig Newton before she brushed her teeth.

⁓

Jonas sat at the dining table and began sorting through the pile of bills he'd have a hard time paying, including the monthly fixed amount he owed the clinic group. He'd been notorious for allowing his patients, many of whom were farmers, to pay him in farm-grown produce, or whatever amount they could afford. He'd figured that if his patients didn't pay after the first bill was sent out, then it would be foolish to waste money on a stamp to send a second. "Besides," he'd told himself, "there are enough well-heeled patients to help me make up the deficit."

On the other hand, Jonas's businessman father, Jonas Sr., had his own way of collecting debt: When a patron's payment was overdue, he merely added a zero to their bill. If Mr. Smith, for instance, owed him $10.00, the bill would read $100.00. Mr. Smith would then come in waving the bill in Jonas Sr.'s face, highly indignant about the overcharge. Jonas Sr. would then apologize and collect the full amount owed from a victorious, yet clueless, Mr. Smith. "Brilliant," some had said of Jonas Sr.'s tactics.

He'd grown impatient with his son's lack of business acumen, particularly since he'd had to help Jonas and Renata with living expenses in New Orleans, and with some rather large debt that Renata had incurred while there. Jonas Jr. revered his parents and would do whatever he had to do to put things right with them.

Staring at the bills, Jonas struck a familiar pose: his chin between his thumb and middle finger, his index finger curled over his upper lip. He smiled, remembering how Cady had described the humidity in New Orleans: "the trees tinklin' on ya," she'd giggle. He missed New Orleans but, in the year before he'd moved Renata and Cady from there, he'd seen the necessity to leave. It was not a good town for Renata—too many opportunities, in too many bars, to bring out the devil in her. Her intense dislike of Texas, she had claimed, had made her want to return to Louisiana as often as possible. Her favorite description of West Texas: "a chicken-fried clump of caliche." She had never let Jonas forget how much she despised being there. He'd never imagined, when he'd met his fun-loving nymph in Atlanta nine years earlier, that she would end up threatening everything he held dear. But he loved her and it was too late to turn back.

When Surgeons' Clinic Hospital in Concho City offered him a partnership, he took it, forfeiting some fine opportunities in New Orleans and other large cities. The family situation had taken precedence. He had soothed himself by imagining that, despite his lost opportunities elsewhere, he'd be able to sway a couple of his medical school friends to join him in creating a Mayo-like clinic that would serve the entire western part of Texas, and increase service to the city's burgeoning oil boom population.

He turned on the radio to a local station playing "How Much Is That Doggie In The Window." Cady ran into the kitchen just in time to bark along at the right spots. Laughing, she sat down at the table to eat her Fig Newton, nibbling it around the edges to make it last longer. Jonas then remembered the box of cabbage he'd left on the back seat of the car—payment from a patient from whom he'd removed an ailing gall bladder.

The garage was barely big enough for their one car, especially with yet unpacked boxes lining the walls. The back door of the Plymouth screeched loudly when he opened it. He chuckled when he spotted the stuffed brown bear Cady had put on the back seat when they moved to Concho City. She'd had it since she was born, a gift from Jonas's mother. The bear had fallen over; he set it upright against the arm rest and straightened out the note that Cady had pinned to it with one of her old diaper pins. In child's scribble, it read: *J's gard bear.* She had told him that it was to stay on the back seat to remind him to slow down when she wasn't in the car to remind him herself. He carried the box of cabbage into the kitchen, and set it down on the counter.

Patti Page had finished singing, and the radio announcer was forecasting heavy rain overnight. Just as Cady got up from the table to shut the door to the garage, she heard the sound she dreaded most—the telephone ringing. A call that late could only come from the hospital. It was so seldom that she had her dad to herself. Any interruption was unwelcome. She worried when he was gone. When he picked up the receiver, she wrapped her arms around his leg.

"Dr. Randolph here," he answered, his face dropping when the caller spoke. He looked down at Cady looking up at him. "No, Daddy, no," she whispered.

Jonas listened. His face turned from tired to a grimace. "For cryin' out loud, Ren, why can't you just eat what they've got out there? I'm sure it's perfectly good food. It's late. Where am I going to find a hamburger at this hour . . . and besides, I've got Cady."

"You can just bring her with you," Renata said.

"She's in her pajamas and should have been in bed an hour ago."

"So? There's no school tomorrow, and she'd like getting out with you."

"I'm not dragging her out on a night like this," he said, an uncharacteristic anger in his voice.

"Go get me a hamburger, damn it. I deserve one after what you've put me through. It won't take you long in this one-horse-sorry-excuse-for-a-town.

Burney's is open until midnight."

Cady tugged at Jonas's pant leg, still shaking her head "no."

"If I can rouse Sweezer Riley to come over and babysit, I'll go get your hamburger. But if not, that's that. Now try to relax, honey."

Cady stomped her foot hard against the wood floor and said, "No, Daddy, don't go. You promised to be with me."

Renata yelled into Jonas's ear. "If you let that little brat get her way, there'll be hell to pay when I get home. You can't let a six-year-old rule the roost."

"Ren honey, I'll come if I reach the Riley boy, all right?"

Renata hung up without saying goodbye. Reaching down, Jonas picked Cady up and gently turned her chin toward his face. "Punkin', listen to me. Look at me. It's going to be okay."

She put her head on his shoulder as he dialed the Riley house next door. It was late to be calling, but he took the chance that Sweezer might be up. He was the only boy in the neighborhood who all the mothers used for babysitting. He was reliable and patient with children, and Cady was thoroughly taken with him. The phone rang only twice.

"Riley residence, Sweezer speaking," he said, out of breath.

"Hi Sweezer, this is Dr. Randolph. I apologize for calling so late. I hope I didn't wake you or your dad."

"Oh, no sir, I was just drifting off, and Dad hardly ever hears the phone. What can I do for you, sir?"

"I've got a little emergency and wonder if you could come over and sit with Cady while I take care of it. Could you do that? It ought not to be more than an hour, an hour and a half at the most."

"Well, sir, I guess I could do that all right. You think you'd be back around midnight then?"

"I would sure hope so, but any problem if it runs over?"

"Uh, no sir, I don't think that ought to be a problem. I'm still dressed, so I'll be right over."

Cady, lifted her head near Jonas's ear and whispered, "Please don't go."

"Honey, I won't be gone long, promise, and I'll even give Sweezer permission to let you stay up for a little while longer. You'd like that, wouldn't you?" She didn't answer.

When Sweezer arrived a few minutes later, she ran into her room and shut the door.

"Sweezer, Cady's ready for bed, but I told her she could stay up with you a little while, so maybe you could read something together? She's awful upset about my leaving." He cracked open the door to Cady's room. "Sweezer's here, honey."

She was standing by her bed, arms folded in defiance, hoping that sheer stubbornness would keep Jonas home. Sweezer tapped Jonas on the shoulder, tossed his head toward the living room, and signaled Jonas to leave.

"Cady?" Sweezer said, reaching his hand out to her. "Do you want to come show me how you walk on the back of the couch?"

Jonas hurried away. Cady slipped by Sweezer to run after him, knocking over Renata's prized vase, chipping the cloisonné piece near another chip that Renata had caused when she'd thrown it against the wall in a rage. A new crack in the enamel had formed, and the mouth of the vase was slightly dented. Sweezer ran after Cady.

Cady called out to Jonas in one last effort to stop him before he escaped through the garage door. "Wait, Daddy! Please, just one more minute . . . Wait!" She struggled from Sweezer's hold until the familiar sound of the car's motor was lost in the distance.

Still sobbing, she finally went limp as if to say "no use." She let Sweezer read to her from *The Little Prince* until exhaustion from the tirade overcame her. He covered her with a blanket he'd found on a nearby chair, and settled down on the other end of the couch. He'd leave it to Dr. Randolph to carry her to her bed when he got home.

He put the vase back on its stand and turned the defects toward the wall. In case there was a call, he pulled the side table, with the phone on it, close to the couch. In the unlikely event that Joe stirred, Sweezer had left a note under the vodka bottle telling Joe where he was. Joe had staggered out of the house late at night before, yelling for Sweezer. The boy didn't want to risk another disturbance like that.

Leaving a lamp on in the corner of the living room for Dr. Randolph's return, he wriggled around on the couch until he was comfortable. He thought about how his mother used to celebrate his birthdays with fireworks she'd collected every 4th of July.

Cady was sound asleep, and in a few minutes he would be too. But before he allowed himself to drift off, he thought of his mother's laugh, the way she used to muss up his hair, the way she smelled like fresh talc and lilac water, and most of all, the way he would miss her and the fireworks on his birthday the next day. At least he'd have some babysitting money to take himself to a matinee at the Park Theatre, and enough left over to buy a nickel candy bar. He shut his eyes and smiled when the words to "Always" came back to him.

4

Atlanta—nine years earlier, August 1944

There hadn't been any other event in Jonas's life that had matched in importance his meeting Renata Rose Collins one steamy summer day in '44. He'd been assigned to Fort McPherson in Atlanta just a month before, to await orders for deployment. He'd be leaving in three days.

Walking alongside the pool at the Officers' Club, Jonas had made eye contact with a dark-haired beauty pulling herself out of the water by the pool's shiny side rails, her hair in dripping wet braids. Her dimples deepened as her smile opened widely to the most handsome man she'd ever seen. He smiled back, instantly smitten.

By age twenty-six, he had completed his internship in Chicago. He was immediately inducted into the Army Medical Corps, sent to Walter Reed to study tropical medicine, and then sent to Atlanta. After four years of medical school in New Orleans, he knew the South and felt thoroughly at home there. Although his home state of Texas bridged the Deep South and the Desert Southwest, Jonas believed Texas was considerably more southern than southwestern.

"Stunningly handsome," people said of him—Robert Taylor, Jimmy Stewart, and Tyrone Power, all rolled into one. Throughout medical school, Jonas had been a sought-after escort at every debutante ball in New Orleans. Becoming fast friends with a sixth-generation New Orleanian classmate had given him entrée to that otherwise tightly closed society. The classmate's mother thought Jonas's manners were impeccable and made a point of bringing it up in front of her son regularly. Jonas knew that his mother would be proud to know that her hard work had not gone unnoticed.

He walked past Renata with every intention of asking if she'd be staying awhile, in which case he'd go change into his swim trunks and join her. But before he could make that move, this stranger, for whom he was willing to act a fool, had flung herself back in the water. At the top of her lungs she bellowed, "Save me! Save me!" Jonas, in a moment of pure abandon, tore off his tie and shoes, dove into the water in full uniform, and joined in the charade. It would be the beginning of the wildest three days of his life.

She screamed with delight when he swam over to her, slipped his arm around her, grabbed the waist of her suit, and hurled her onto the side of the pool. He was amazed at how feather-light she was. With a face full of water, laughing out loud, she pushed her hair back from her face.

"I can't believe you *did* that!" she laughed.

"I can't believe you *made* me do that," he chuckled, pulling himself up out of the water to sit beside her. "How about we talk about it over a drink this evening?"

"Sure, why not? I have to work tomorrow, but I'm always ready for a good time," she said.

"Well, why let a little something like work interfere, right?"

"Uh huh."

"So where *do* you work?" he asked, taking the liberty of lifting a strand of wet hair she'd missed.

"Bell in Marietta."

"Bell Aircraft?"

"Yes, that's right."

"They produced that Air Cobra, right?"

"Uh huh, that's right."

"So whadaya do out there?"

"Office work, enough to make ends meet."

"Well, if you'll do me the honor, I'll make sure you get there in time to punch the clock in the morning."

Renata grinned. Jonas couldn't believe his good fortune. For the first time in his life he hadn't asked the questions his mother would have expected him to ask. He was in full agreement with his Army buddies that they should all make hay while the sun was shining.

He suddenly remembered that, even though he was a Captain, he was front and center for a major reprimand if he didn't get out of there and changed. He and Renata agreed to meet at the fort's front entrance that evening.

Jonas didn't have a military mind, having not been in the Army long enough to be fully indoctrinated. That wouldn't matter to a superior if he got caught. He grabbed his shoes and tie amid raucous laughter from onlookers, and sloshed back to the dressing rooms to wring out his uniform before sneaking back into his quarters for a change. It was 4:00 p.m., and they'd agreed to meet at 8:00. He'd have just enough time to finish a letter to his parents, take a snooze, and get himself ready for the evening. He was almost too excited to sleep.

At precisely five minutes of eight, Jonas arrived at the stand of trees outside the front entrance of the fort. He'd snatched a floating gardenia from one of the tables in the Officers' Club dining room and noticed, as he stood waiting for her, that his hand was sweating. He switched hands and rubbed his palm against his trouser leg under his jacket to hide any tell-tale sign of moisture. The taxi drove up, and out stepped the most beautiful creature he'd ever seen.

She wore a short white dress printed with a multitude of colorful floral bouquets. Her hair, out of the braids, was piled loosely on top of her head. He thought she walked like a goddess despite a slight wobble in her high heels. The dress showed off a beautiful pair of legs; slender at the ankle with just enough muscle in the calf to create a nice silhouette. As she came closer, he noticed her deep-set dark eyes. They were blazing and intense. She reached for Jonas's hand. He took hers, pulled her close to him, and kissed her. It was like no other kiss he'd ever experienced. It was deep and strong and sent waves of feeling to a place in him he never knew existed. He placed the stolen gardenia behind her ear and kissed her again.

"My dear man . . . the taxi driver," she said, motioning with her eyes toward the waiting cabbie.

Jonas reluctantly pulled away to give the taxi driver, who was trying to appear uninterested, a five-dollar bill, the biggest tip he'd ever given anyone. "Thank you, kind sir, for delivering the woman of my dreams to me," he said.

"Happy to oblige, sir," the taxi driver replied.

"Say, can you wait while I ask my girl where she'd like to go?"

"Sure, I'll just pull up out of the way," he said, motioning to the right.

Jonas found Renata leaning up against one of the enormous trees flanking the two-lane entrance drive to the fort. She looked like some dream he'd never before had the good fortune to have. "I asked the taxi driver to wait a bit," he said.

"Oh, I just want to stay here for a little. Can you ask him to come back in a little while?"

"Anything for you, my dear," Jonas said, winking at her.

Looking at the five-dollar bill Jonas had tipped him, the taxi driver agreed to return for them. He'd likely make as much on this one ride than he would the entire evening.

Renata was sitting in the grass when Jonas returned to her. He sank down beside her. It was still light out, but they were in a shadow, and clouds had rolled in making it darker than usual that late day. An occasional car passed, but being some distance off the road no one would notice them.

"This tree will mark the spot of the most important event of my life," Renata said, as Jonas ran his finger along her slim arm.

"Oh really and what event would that be?" he asked.

She tugged gently at his lapel. A shiny Caduceus was pinned tightly to it. She knew exactly what it signified—that he was a medical doctor. She pulled Jonas to her and they collapsed into each other's arms onto the grass. He didn't think twice about making love to her then and there, figuring that anyone who might see them, even God, would have to sanction something so wonderful. He felt as much abandon in that moment as he had earlier in the day when he jumped into the pool, uniform and all. He was in love, and nothing could change that—nothing.

They pulled themselves together just before the taxi returned. The taxi driver, no stranger to opportunities taken liberally during the war, and often in the back seat of his cab, recognized that Renata and Jonas had just taken one. He turned off his headlights and waited patiently for the lovers to slip into the back seat.

They hit every bar on Peachtree that night, Renata running barefoot down the famous street trying to get Jonas to follow suit. He laughed and enjoyed her antics but couldn't bring himself to run barefoot, especially in uniform. He'd already tempted fate twice that day, and figured he couldn't remain lucky enough to get away with it again.

When it started raining, they slipped into a little nightspot called the Choo Choo Club. She slipped her heels back on at the door and Jonas held her up by one elbow, both of them a little tipsy from a few cocktails. The trio was on break, but they'd have one more drink and wait to hear a little more music before calling it a night. Their table was in a corner near the piano. When she took a seat on the piano bench, no one noticed but Jonas.

"Are you going to play something for me, darlin'?"

"Do you have a request?"

"Anything you decide is okay by me."

Renata adjusted the piano stool, leaned over toward Jonas, and said, "This one's for us."

She began playing "Always." The room became quiet. The entire keyboard came to life. It was the most beautiful thing Jonas had ever heard. He followed her hands as they swept across the keys. He stared at her profile. She was lost in the music. He was bewitched. When she brought the piece to an end, a man in the back shouted "More, more!" There were a couple of "Bravos!"

"It will be our song forever," Jonas whispered in her ear. "Thank you for making me the happiest man on the turning earth tonight."

When last call was announced, Jonas was told that the drinks were on the house. They ordered Cuba Libres and left half-full glasses as they made their way back onto the street. The rain had stopped. They walked for a little while, looking for a place to get a bite to eat, ending up in a quiet little Italian place at 4:00 that morning. Renata's hair had fallen out of its up-do. The gardenia, a little brown around the edges, was floating in the bowl of water that Jonas had ordered for that purpose.

He had learned little about her, only that she had grown up in Florida, and had moved with her family to Atlanta when her father lost his business during the Depression. She had attended a couple of years of college in New York. Most important of all, she had lost her young husband in the war and was making the best of it working at Bell, helping her parents out when she could. She told him that she was engaged in a fledgling import business with a wily partner she'd met in New York. Renata's history seemed unimportant to Jonas. It was as if their lives had begun the moment they met.

"Do you realize, my love, that I don't even know your name?" he asked.

"I hadn't even thought of it. You'll never guess what it is. Try."

"Whatever means beautiful," he said.

"Well, it's Renata. Renata Rose Collins, and Renata means reborn."

"Perfect!" he said, pulling her over to him to kiss her on the forehead. "And I'm Jonas. Jonas H. Randolph, as my nametag says."

"What's the H stand for?"

"Harrington. It's my mother's maiden name."

"Well, I don't know if my name's perfect as you say. I never understood why I was named Renata when nobody else in the family had the name. It's so, well, exotic . . . and the Collins bunch is so lily white, even though they claim we're part Seminole where they say I get my high cheekbones and all. Oh well, in any case, I've learned to live with the name."

"Well I think that when they named you, they must have known you'd be meeting *me* someday and that you'd be reborn when you did! I love that name. Maybe I'll call you Ren. How would you like that?"

"I'd like that. And is there a meaning for Jonas?"

"My mother told me that it means dove in Hebrew. That's all I know about that, but I also know that we better get you home . . . you've got to be at work in a couple of hours."

The waiter called a taxi. They hadn't been waiting long when one arrived. They held hands the whole way to Marietta, the tiredness finally settling in. Renata was asleep on his shoulder, a tiny snoring sound vibrating in his ear.

When the cab pulled up at the entrance to the bungalows where she lived, Jonas shook her gently awake. The dawn's light cast a haunting glow over her face. Jonas paid the cabbie, and the two of them slid off the back seat onto the concrete walk that led to Renata's bungalow. It was the third down on the left, No. 3 it said on the sign. It belonged to a cluster of twenty or so that were detached, connected only by walkways, neatly edged with flowers. The air held that refreshing cool of a new morning.

A Chinese vase sat regally on a small half-moon shaped table in her tiny entry. He was aware of the art of cloisonné and saw that the vase was a fine example. It seemed out of place in her simple cottage. It must have, he thought, come from an easier time in her life. Renata excused herself while Jonas sank down to the springs of a slightly stained, green divan in the small living room. There was only one other piece of furniture in the room—a chair upholstered in an odd print of fern fronds and dark pink feathers. There was a small wood dining table with two chairs by the lone window on the opposite wall. A tiny kitchen was visible; a cast iron skillet sat on a narrow gas stove.

"Jonas?" she called out from her bedroom.

"Yes, I can hear you. What do you need, m'dear?"

"Turn out the light and come back here with me."

Jonas followed Renata's voice into the small bedroom where she was patting the bed beside her. He crawled in next to her, fully dressed. She was wearing pajamas printed all over with monkeys swinging from tree limbs. "Only a truly alluring woman like you could get away with wearing those things," he told her. She laughed. Everything about her was a wonder to him. She kissed him lightly on the forehead; he responded with light kisses to her eyelids.

When she awoke at noon, she was in his arms. He had a pass from the base, but she was clearly late for work. She called in sick. The plant accepted her excuse. They spent the next two days in the bungalow. Before Jonas reported back for duty, they had promised each other that they would never again be parted—at least not for long.

The night before his deployment, Renata said goodbye to him under the same tree where they'd made love just three days before. Jonas joked about the patch of grass where they'd been, saying that it would no doubt grow extra well after their anointing of it. When the moment came, he gave her a ten-dollar bill for cab fare. She watched him walk away, already scheming about how to keep him in her life. Jonas looked back at her, envisioning a house they'd have someday that would be plenty big enough for a piano. He didn't wave. It seemed a goodbye too inadequate and too painful.

Getting back to his quarters, he finished packing. Memories of the previous few days whirled in his head. He wondered if he should tell his parents and his old buddies about Renata, if they'd be as happy as he was, and if it had all been a dream from which he'd awaken disappointed. He'd be leaving for San Juan that morning at 3:30 sharp, and it would come all too soon. Closing his eyes, he fell asleep thinking about what he'd write in his first letter to her.

Renata's bungalow was particularly hot and humid that night. She was fidgety. The restlessness wasn't so much because she had lied to Jonas about her young husband dying in the war, but because she hated being alone. When Max Aronson called, she was relieved.

"Hey baby, how's it going? It's Max."

"Oh, hi, Max, all right I guess. What's the occasion?"

"I started calling early, but you never answered. Want to go for a drink?"

"Kind of late, isn't it?"

"Not for us night owls. Come on, I'll pick you up in a few. Whadaya say? Besides, gotta little business to discuss with you anyway."

Renata was pulling at her hair, an old nervous habit, already feeling like she was cheating on Jonas, but never one to turn down the chance to escape being solo. "Besides," she thought to herself, "I'm not married to Jonas, not even engaged . . . can't really hurt."

"Oh, all right, Max. Just give me a few minutes to freshen up . . . where we goin'?"

"How 'bout we head over to that joint near your place? The Dixie is it?"

"Okay, that'll do. See you in a few."

"You got it, baby. Be there in a flash," Max answered. He wasted no time getting out the door to pick up Renata.

The Dixie was crowded that night and they shoved their way to a back table. Renata had been annoyed with Max's wild driving on the way over, and was still riled. He'd already had a few too many when he picked her up, and was weaving through the crowd of mostly women, a few men in uniform, and a sprinkling of men too old to go to war. His thick cigarette breath mixed with alcohol had sickened her when he attempted to kiss her, and she was going to make sure he didn't get that close again. When he tried talking business with her, she changed the subject. He wouldn't have remembered the conversation anyway.

He'd fallen hard for her the moment he met her in a bar in Atlanta earlier that year. They'd talked enough for him to learn that she was as prideful and stubborn as she was attractive, but clearly in need of money. She had also made it clear that she had no interest in him romantically, and that's when he made the offer: he'd bring her in as a partner in his new business. He would ship old railroad track from South America, over to Cuba, and eventually to the States. "There's, after all, a serious shortage of steel in America with most going to the war effort," he'd told Renata. "So I'll make a mint, and I'll give you half of everything I make, and you can go to Havana and schmooze with my contacts there. All you have to do is sleep with me when I want, no strings attached. You'll be free as a bird with no affection required." It was understood that if she stopped sleeping with him, the deal would be off. She agreed to the terms.

"Max, you're not going to remember this, but I met a man a few days ago that I think might be the one. He's crazy about me, and he's a doctor of all things . . . a more handsome man you'll never see. Can you imagine that?"

Max said nothing, but motioned to the waitress to bring him another drink. Though he'd tried to win Renata's affection, she'd given him only the required sex. He'd given her one excuse after another about why the money was slow in coming in. It was part of the agreement that the sex would start immediately, before the big money started rolling in, to prove her good faith. He'd paid her rent for a couple of months, plus a small amount of cash, to keep her interested.

He was a short man, not ugly, but she thought he had bad eyes, beady eyes, too close together. His fingers were stubby, and that annoyed her almost as much as the fact that he wasn't a southerner.

"Hey, baby, let's dance."

"No, Max, don't feel like it. It's late, let's go."

"Go? Are you nuts? We just got here. I'm not going anywhere."

"I'm leaving, Max."

He glared at Renata with an angry-red face before turning away to grab the arm of a jolly and inebriated woman a table over. Renata asked the bartender to call a cab.

The cabbie was especially talkative, but she didn't hear much of what he was saying, grunting "uh huh" here and there. The clean breeze in her face through the open back window of the cab was a welcome relief from the stench of the smoky, dank bar. Jonas came to mind, and she thought about how she could never let him know that she'd lied about her husband Lewis. He wasn't really dead, except to her. Their divorce was not yet final.

She left the cabbie a good tip and went straight to her bedroom. She'd have to punch in at 8:00 a.m. She left the bedroom window open that night, remembered Jonas in her bed, and pulled the pillow he had slept on under her. The days and nights with him had left her spent. She was asleep within minutes.

5

Close to midnight—October 2, 1953

From the time he'd left the house, Jonas thought about the day that he and Renata had met in Atlanta: their playfulness in the pool at the Officers' Club, their tenderness under the tree at the fort's entrance, and their wild night on Peachtree.

He'd been gone more than an hour when he pulled into his space at St. Joseph's. It was 11:30 p.m. There'd been an unanticipated forty-five minute wait for the burger at Burney's due to a rush of football fans after a high school game that had been played out between rains.

He turned off the engine to the sound of heavy rain pelting the roof of his Plymouth. A policeman, standing inside the glass door of the hospital staff entrance, saw Jonas pull up. He ran out with an umbrella. Jonas rolled down the window just enough to be heard through the roar of the deluge.

"Hey doc, need some help getting in?" the officer shouted through the crack of the window.

"Yeah, sure would appreciate that," he shouted back, heavy wind blowing the rain into the car.

"Well, come on. No time like the present!"

Jonas quickly grabbed the sack off the floorboard, with the barely warm hamburger inside, and placed the greasy bag under his suit jacket before opening the door to the onslaught. In the short sprint to the back door of the hospital, his jacket got soaked, and his shoes filled with water from the lake of water rushing over the parking lot. Once inside he was relieved to see that the bag was dry, but the grease from the burger had seeped into the lining of his coat.

"Thanks, officer," he said, out of breath, shaking the man's hand.

"You bet. I'll be here a little while longer doin' some paperwork . . . had to bring in one of my ole drunks . . . so if you need an umbrella gettin' back out to the car, just holler."

Jonas smiled the smile that one of the nurses said could light up a dark cave, and made his way to the linen closet where he kept an extra heavily starched white coat. He exchanged his jacket for his hospital coat. His stethoscope was curled up in a hip pocket where he'd left it. His name was embroidered in black on the left chest pocket of his coat—Jonas H. Randolph, M.D.

Walking down the hall toward Renata's room, cargo in hand, he cut the same handsome figure he always had: six-foot-two, slender, with almost-black, thick, wavy hair. His calm and assured manner, his patients claimed, had as much to do with their healing as his surgical technique. Hospital staff knew that if he needed to be located, they'd most likely find him sitting on the side of a recovering patient's bed, the patient holding his stitches, laughing heartily at one of Jonas's corny jokes. Jonas was affectionately known as Dr. J to the nurses. Seeing his smile and his lanky frame striding down a hospital corridor was a highlight in their day.

He rounded the corner into the bright corridor toward Renata's room hearing laughter coming from the nurses' station. Seeing a white coat approaching, the women sat up rigidly, but then broke into smiles of relief when they saw it was Jonas.

"Good evening, Dr. J. How ya doin'?"

"Oh, fine, ladies. Just here to check on Mrs. Randolph."

"Uh, yes sir," one of the nurses said, clearing her throat.

"Anything I should be aware of?" he asked.

"No sir, except that maybe she's been a little more agitated than usual this evening."

"Oh well, I think we can fix that," he said, smiling.

He took Renata's chart and walked slowly away, reading it as he went. The two nurses looked at each other and shook their heads. "Poor Dr. J. That man's had not one minute of peace since she's been in here. It's a cryin' shame. And that little girl of theirs . . . it's just not right."

The door to Renata's room was closed. Weary from the day, the long wait at Burney's, and the battle with the rain, Jonas stopped in the hallway and leaned against the wall to prepare for what would no doubt be a difficult exchange. When he opened the door, he found her in the dark, her forearm shielding her eyes from the hallway's bright light. She sat up in bed and glared at him with eyes once bright and alluring, now stabbing him with anger.

"Well, it's about time you got here. God*damn*, that light's bright."

Jonas moved closer to her, placing the bag on the bedside table, "Hello, dear. How ya feelin'?" he asked, bending down to kiss her.

"How the hell do you *think* I'm feeling having to wait on you all this time?"

"Ren, I know it's not hot, but I did the best I could," he said, pulling the burger from the sack. He handed it to her with a familiar sense of dread.

She took a bite and spit it out onto the paper. "This thing tastes like shit. Here, dump it. I can't eat it."

Jonas took it from her calmly and put it in the trash can next to her bed. "Okay. I can see that I'm not going to be of any comfort to you, so I'd best leave and get home to Cady. Sorry the burger was cold." He kissed her goodbye and she began to cry. He took both her hands in his. "Oh, Ren, what is it?" he asked.

"Jonas, you never understand how hard it is for me."

"Sweetheart, I know it's hard for you, and I'm doing what I can to help you. Don't you know that?"

Rubbing the tears away from her face, she asked Jonas to fish the burger out of the trash can.

"You don't really want me to *do* that, do you, Ren?"

"Yes, I do."

"Okay then," he said, handing her the trash can instead.

She carefully lifted the burger from its resting place on the bottom and began nibbling it. "Um, it actually tastes good," she said, taking another bite.

Jonas sat quietly, feeling as though he would implode. While she ate the burger, he thought about how he would finally tell his parents what was going on, for his daughter's sake. There were all those times that he'd come home to find Renata gone. There would be no communication from her for sometimes as long as two weeks. When she'd finally reappear, she'd chide him for making such a fuss over her absence.

After eating most of the burger, Renata asked Jonas to brush her hair. He looked at his watch. Renata turned on the light by her bed and put on some lipstick. Her skin was flawless. There was never any need for her to wear makeup, not even cheek color with her light olive skin. Like Cady, her individual features were not outstanding but, in concert, they worked. She had maintained her slender figure. She had a bone structure quite fine, with extremely high cheekbones. Cady had inherited her bone structure, but not her mother's skin color. Cady's skin was transparent, like porcelain. No one else, on either side of the family, was fair.

Jonas brushed Renata's hair away from her face and behind her ears in long, slow strokes. She began telling him all about the day, how the nurses had ignored her calls, how the doctor on call had been rude and dismissive, and how the food was unfit to eat. The more she talked, the less Jonas listened.

"Jonas? Jonas? Have you heard anything I've said?"

"I'm sorry, Ren, I'm damned tired. It's been a long day, honey, and I really do have to get home to Cady."

"All right, but first we have to talk about something really important to me."

"Okay, honey, what is it?"

"Well, remember how you said I could go to Cuba when I got better? Well, I need to meet some people down there at the Nacional next month, and I need to make sure there'll be enough money in the bank to cover it, okay?"

"Renata, Cuba's out, honey. We don't have the money. You know that."

Her face fell, and her eyes began spitting fire. "I hate this place, and I hate it when you call me Renata. You promised if I came here, I could get out of here when I wanted. You lied. And on top of it, you're weak. I've got to get away from you, and this sorry excuse for a town, or I'll go insane."

"What you've got to do right now is get some rest, and I've got to get home so, please, let's discuss this later," he said.

When he stood up and turned to leave the room, she threw a pillow at him, hitting the backs of his legs. He stopped, picked it up, and gently placed it on her lap.

"Goodnight, Ren of my heart. I love you."

"See what I mean about you? I just insulted the hell out of you and you tell me you *love* me? Jesus, what's wrong with you, man?"

He managed a smile before leaving the room. He closed her door quietly behind him and paused in the hall long enough to gather his wits about him before he reached the nurses' station. He felt a deep ache in his back. "It's time to call the Rector at the Episcopal Church for a little talk," he thought. There was no one else in town with whom he could confide.

"How's your wife doing, Dr. Randolph?" a passing nurse asked.

"Oh, fine. She might be a little agitated tonight until she gets a sleeping pill. In fact, I think that might be a good idea sooner than later."

"Yes sir, we'll check with the attending. Don't worry Dr. J. We'll take good care of her."

He touched her arm lightly. "Thank you, kind lady."

"Goodnight, Dr. J. Take care now, hear?"

"Sure will . . . you too."

He stopped to say goodnight to the other nurses and, as he disappeared from view, they giggled. One whispered to the other, "Oh, that smile . . . just melts me into a puddle."

He stopped briefly at one of the large windows near the door and stared at the force of the rain on the glass. In flashes of lightning, he could see the broken branches in the parking lot and the tree tops swaying wildly in the wind. When he pulled his jacket from the coat closet, it was still damp. He could hear a radio down the hall playing the theme song from the Moulin Rouge: "Where Is Your Heart?" He thought it might have been a good question to have asked Renata that night. "I'd rather think about her playing it on the piano," he muttered.

The officer with the umbrella was nowhere to be seen. He'd get drenched running to the car, but he figured he'd be home soon enough, dry soon enough, and asleep soon enough not to worry about it. He made it into the car, started the engine, and turned on the radio; the announcer predicted rain throughout the night, sunny skies by morning. "Better for Sweezer's birthday party," Jonas said out loud, backing out into the rushing waters. He sighed deeply before turning right onto Blanton toward home.

His Plymouth was a reliable car, and a gift from his father right after Cady was born. He often drove too fast. That night, even in the driving rain, he drove faster than usual. Anxious to get home, he plowed through the waters on Blanton. "Vaya Con Dios" was playing on the radio.

He reached down to turn up the volume and began singing along. The wipers could barely keep up with the pounding rain. He was squinting, leaning forward, straining to see when, suddenly, a blinding light flashed before him with a noise and impact so enormous that, in one split second, he and his entire world became suspended within the midst of it. Then in utter silence, bits and pieces of metal, and glass, and other debris floated through space in slow motion all around him.

When the Plymouth settled to a stop at the bottom of the Blanton Street underpass, the last verse of "Vaya Con Dios" was echoing off its concrete walls. Jonas sat motionless, staring straight ahead, one tiny trickle of blood dripping from his left ear onto his collar.

6

A few minutes later—1:10 a.m.

The standing water at the bottom of the underpass reflected wavy ribbons of red from the spinning light on top of the police car. It was safe to say that most people in Concho City, and certainly on Bob-white Lane, were sound asleep, unaware of the tragedy that would be stunning news on the front page of the Concho City Times when they awoke. The bars had closed an hour before, and there was no *good* reason for anyone to be out on such a night.

Jonas was sitting upright and rigid in the Plymouth. His left eye was wide open, staring straight ahead, his right eye partially out of its socket. Bright blood trailed down from his left cheek and ear, dissolving into the collar of his shirt. Bits of glass filled his hair; some larger shards pierced his scalp. His forehead appeared sunken and dark blue with bits of curly flesh protruding through, oozing clear liquid mixed with blood and debris. On the passenger seat next to him his eyeglasses and his neatly folded necktie were somehow undisturbed. His hands made tight fists at his sides.

The roof of the car had been completely separated from what had been the front windshield. It was pushed beyond the back seat area, completely exposing him. A loose piece of metal, swinging back and forth, made an unearthly clanging noise. The back seat was covered in glass.

Passengers in a car coming from the opposite direction on Blanton had seen Jonas's car careening and spinning around once and a half, coming to a stop, with the hood pointed off to the right, not quite broached.

For a brief moment in time, a profound sense of loneliness settled over Blanton Street. The song on the radio was the last vestige of the life and world left behind.

The rain had let up, and Bill Armand, breathless, had left his shaken wife in the car to proceed cautiously to the bottom of the underpass. He had gotten to Jonas just as the loose piece of metal disengaged, splashing into the considerable amount of rainwater collecting around the car's tires. Seeing Jonas's bloodied face, Armand's mouth turned to cotton. He had trouble speaking. He walked in circles, kicked frantically through the ankle-deep water, rubbed his forehead equally frantically, and finally forced himself to look into Jonas's frozen stare.

"Sir, oh my God, sir, are you okay?" he whispered, moving closer. He tried to lick his lips, but still not a drop of moisture to do so. "Sir, just a minute," he said to Jonas, clearing his throat, his hands up to his eyes, rubbing them, rubbing his hands together, all in an effort to return to some kind of normalcy, to keep from fainting with a heart racing out of control. When he cleared his throat again, he thankfully felt a little saliva return to his mouth and tongue.

"Sir, my name's Bill, Bill Armand. I'm right here with ya. Can you hear the sirens? They're coming for ya, to take care of ya. I'll be here right by your side . . . promise. Nothin's gonna happen to ya, sir. You're gonna be all right. Can ya hear me, sir?"

There was no response, not even a blink of Jonas's one eye that seemed unharmed. Its gaze was fixed straight ahead.

Sirens wailed in the distance. The wailing seemed to be getting closer, but muffled by the thickness of the wet night air. Never taken to praying, Armand squeezed his eyes shut, clutched his hands together, and said out loud, "Oh God, if you really exist, please save this man. Don't let him die. Jesus, I can't stand this. Damn, please don't make me watch him die. Amen."

Armand, his eyes still closed, sweat pouring off his head, heard a car door slam, and opened his eyes to see a policeman half sliding down the underpass from the direction of St. Joseph's. The soles of his shoes were slapping the water as he got nearer the bottom.

"Hey, Sir," the policeman shouted. "Did you see what happened here?"

"I just saw his car going out of control, officer. This just happened a few minutes ago. I'm trying to help this poor fella. Can you call for help? He's bad hurt."

"Somebody already has. I was leaving St. Joe's when I heard it from the dispatcher. There's help on the way."

"Boy, I'm glad to hear that. I thought I might be lyin' to the fella when I heard the sirens, not knowin' for sure if they were comin' for him."

The policeman moved in closer and looked at Jonas who had not changed position or uttered a word. His face was badly swollen and there was an unsettling gurgling sound coming from his throat. There was nothing but static on the radio. The policeman reached over Jonas to turn it off.

"Whuda we do, officer? Do ya know what to do?"

"No sir, I don't, but Regional Hospital's sending an ambulance, and the fire department's sending a crew. They'll know what to do. They'll be here any minute."

Afraid to get too close for fear of hurting him, Armand put his hand lightly on Jonas's shoulder. Jonas's white shirt had turned a dark pink. Armand felt faint. He was a big man, middle-aged, with huge hands and a bulbous nose that sat off-center. There were deep furrows in his brow that seemed to disappear into the top of his balding head. His eyes were small, and he had full lips with very large teeth. "There's something about this man that seems familiar," Armand said to himself.

An ambulance, fire truck, and three police cars pulled up in succession. Armand stayed by Jonas and the mutilated car, reassuring him in a heavy West Texas drawl. "It'll be all right, sir . . . help's here." Armand's eyes flashed terror. As the emergency crews grabbed their equipment and hurried toward the car, Armand continued talking to Jonas.

Jonas sat rigid, as if holding on with everything left in him to control his awful moment, to keep himself connected to life. His arms were still by his side, his hands still forming tight fists, his jaw still clinched. Armand and the officer could see that he was likely somewhere in his thirties, dressed like a professional. The officer coming from St. Joe's didn't recognize Jonas or the car.

It suddenly dawned on Armand that this was the man he had sold a hamburger to about an hour and a half before. He was sure of it. He recognized Jonas's suit coat. It had stood out among all the jeans and cowboy hats. He remembered that it was late when the man came into Burney's. The place was packed. He hurried the burger when the man said he was taking it to his sick wife out at St. Joe's. "That poor man musta been on his way home from delivering that burger to his wife," he thought to himself.

Armand spoke once more to Jonas. "I'm sorry, sir. I know ya gotta be hurtin' bad, but I swear you're gonna be fine. See there? Looky there sir, the emergency folks are here, and they're gonna get you the help ya need, and you're gonna be fine. I promise ya gonna be fine."

The gurgling in Jonas's throat grew louder. His face was black.

"Jesus Christ, what happened here?" the ambulance driver yelled out to the policeman as he sloshed through the rainwater toward Jonas.

"Not sure, but it's bad," said the officer. "There's at least one witness, but we don't have the whole story yet."

Armand stepped away when the emergency workers reached Jonas. They shined a flashlight into Jonas's face, so swollen that his eyes were no longer visible. Jonas suddenly went limp, his body sank. Armand, who was leaning against the wall of the underpass, threw up the entire contents of his stomach.

"God, we've got to get this poor guy outta here muy pronto or we're gonna lose him right here and now!" the ambulance driver shouted.

Getting Jonas out of the car took more time than they had expected. When he was finally loaded in the ambulance, they radioed ahead to the hospital to alert staff to prepare for the worst; he was barely breathing. The attendant held an oxygen mask loosely over Jonas's mouth and nose for the two-mile ride to the hospital.

"We're bringing in a male, guessing in his thirties, slender build, tall, severe head trauma, increasing edema, contusions and lacerations about the face, semi-detached eyeball. Some freak auto accident, no determination of cause," the driver told the dispatcher. The ambulance raced to the hospital.

"It happened so quick," Armand told the police officer.

"Where were you headed when you saw the accident?"

"Home, sir."

"Kinda late to be out on a night like this, don't you think?"

"I don't get off work 'til late. My wife picked me up at about 12:45 from Burney's . . . where I cook. We close at midnight but it takes me a while to clean up and lock up. We were driving home, about to turn off, when we saw the car," he said, pointing over to Jonas's vehicle. "It was spinnin' with stuff flyin' everywhere . . . happened real fast. I left my wife in the car up top while I ran down here. The cop, uh, sorry, the officer that came up right after me told me somebody had called the accident in."

"Did you see what caused the accident, sir?"

"No sir. Like I said, I just saw the car spinnin' as I was about to take a right to my house before you get to the underpass. But I have to tell you, I'm pretty sure I sold this man a burger earlier tonight. He said he was taking it out to his wife at St. Joe's. He musta been comin' back from there when this happened."

"Did you notice any other vehicle in the vicinity?"

"No sir, sure didn't."

"You didn't see that truck up the other side of the underpass just sittin' up there loaded up with pipe?"

"No sir, what truck?"

"Well, seein' as how you was comin' from the other direction, I guess you couldn't see the truck up there?"

"No sir. Still there?"

"Yeah, it is, but no driver. Just sittin' up there. Looks like there's some oilfield pipe hangin' cockeyed off the back of that rig, no flags, nothin'. Can't find the driver. Strange."

"Man that *is* strange. Reckon he ran off?"

"Could be . . . we're lookin' around. There's a bar up on the hill there, and I think the owner's the one who called in the accident . . . musta heard the impact. If you can stay a little while longer, we'd like to ask you a few more questions. Could I get your name, sir?"

"Oh, yeah, it's Bill, Bill Armand."

"Okay. And you said you work as a cook at Burney's, Mr. Armand?"

"Yes sir, twenty years this month matter-of-fact."

"Good for you. Burney's definitely got the best burgers in Concho City."

"Uh, thank ya, officer," Armand said. He thought to himself that it didn't seem right to talk about how good the burgers were at a time like that; didn't seem respectful. "Officer, let me tell my wife what's goin' on. She's up top in the car. She's already pretty upset. I'll be right back. Is that Ok?"

"Sure, just come on back down when you're done. We'll be here awhile."

The officer joined the others, taking measurements, looking for any clue about what might have happened, and who the victim was. They combed every inch of the inside of the vehicle and the street, looking for a wallet, anything that would identify him.

On the floor, behind the driver's seat, the officer found a stuffed toy bear covered in debris, a soggy, ink-stained piece of white paper pinned to it. He scooped it up, along with the pair of glasses and the tie from the front seat, and put all three items into a large bag. He tied the bag and wrote the time, date, and location of the accident on the tag, the Louisiana license plate number, and the contents of the bag. In the space designated for the victim's name, he wrote *pending identity*. The bag would be delivered to the hospital along with a sketchy police and eyewitness report.

7

Regional Hospital—a short time later

A steamy fog drifted over the pavement, moving in swirls around the bushes that lined the drive at Regional's emergency entrance. The ambulance attendants' lower legs disappeared into the soupy haze as they raced to pull the gurney out of the back. Two of the emergency room staff ran out to help.

"No ID?" one of them asked.

"Nope, they're searching though," the ambulance attendant answered.

"Ok, let's go."

The gurney was wheeled as fast as it would go down the long hall and through the double doors toward the operating room area. The attending physician ran toward Jonas while two nurses followed closely behind.

"We gotta get goin' now. No time to waste. Got a room ready?"

"Yes sir, all ready to go."

"Anybody know who this man is?" the doctor asked, walking briskly alongside.

"No sir."

"Will somebody go call Dr. Randolph? We need him here to help." The doctor gently pushed Jonas's eye back into its socket, and applied gauze to it and to the open head wound. "Somebody call the eye specialist and get him over here . . . Anybody able to reach Dr. Randolph?" he asked again, as he scrubbed up to perform an emergency tracheotomy.

"No sir, his home line's ringing busy. We've tried over and over."

"Damn. Okay then, we'll do what we can and hope for the best, but keep trying to reach him."

One of the nurses was holding Jonas's head still when his right arm suddenly fell out from under the sheet that covered him. Startled by what she saw, the nurse jumped away from the table, holding her hand over her mouth to keep from screaming.

"Oh my God, no!" she cried out. It's Dr. Randolph!"

"What?" the attending asked.

"This is Dr. Randolph. I recognize his ring."

"Are you certain?"

"Yes, absolutely. I often admired it, and he told me it was his grand-father's and those are . . . they're his hands. Nobody has hands like Dr. Randolph's . . . and his hair. Oh my God, it's Dr. J without a doubt."

"Try to reach his wife," the attending said, through a sudden wave of nausea.

The rest of the staff, at hearing the grim news, shook their heads and offered soothing words to one another, sharing disbelief at what had befallen their friend and colleague.

"He was so young," one young nursing student remarked.

"What do you mean he *was* so young? He's *still* young," another answered.

"Oh, you know what I meant. It's just such a cryin' shame."

The tracheotomy was offering a small reprieve from what they believed would be inevitable by dawn. "If we can just keep him alive until his family gets here," the attending said, examining the area around the tube inserted into Jonas's trachea.

"Do you think he'll make it?" one of the nurses asked.

"Maybe for a few hours . . . but beyond that . . . I don't think there's a cat's chance in hell. His head's a mess. He needs more surgery. I'm afraid he can't tolerate it."

Jonas was lying motionless under the bright operating room lights, one nurse standing by his side, holding his right hand, her starched white cap so white that it made her uniform look beige. Small groups of hospital personnel took turns standing vigil outside the operating room door.

"It's so unfair, so wrong," a nurse said. "One thing's for certain . . . we could sure use him around here about now. Remember just a year ago when he saved that poor fellow who crashed during a polyps removal procedure? I mean he was dead before he could count to ten."

"You bet I remember," another answered. "I was in the O.R. that day. I'd never seen anything like it. Dr. Randolph just slit that guy's chest open, pried back the ribs, and started massaging his heart right then and there. Brought him back, by God, and the guy hadn't been breathing for at least five minutes."

"It was a miracle."

"No. It was no miracle. It was *Dr. Randolph.* And now look at him. It doesn't look like he's going to be anywhere near as lucky as his patient was. It's just not fair."

The policeman entered the hospital carrying the personal items he'd taken from the wrecked car, just as Dr. Stuart Moran, the general surgeon, arrived from St. Joe's. "I left St. Joe's as soon as I got the call," Moran said. "I saw his wife out there earlier. In fact I talked with her just about an hour ago, and she told me that Dr. Randolph had just been in to see her. You know she's a patient out there. Somebody needs to let her know what's happened."

"Why's she hospitalized, do you know?" the attending asked.

"I don't know. What happened to him?" Moran asked the attending, as they hurried toward Jonas.

"Freak auto accident. Looks like he drove head-on into a load of pipe. Don't know how he survived it."

"What's been done?"

"Trach, cleaned up the surface debris a bit, got Doc Evans over here to do the best he could with the eye trauma."

"X-rays?"

"Yeah, fractured skull, bone fragments penetrating pretty deeply into brain substance. The emergency crew said they saw what they thought was brain in the back seat of his car."

Moran closely examined Jonas's head. "Has anyone reached his family?"

"I'll call them, sir. I know Dr. Randolph's father quite well," a young nurse answered. "He paid for my nursing school, along with about five other girls. It's not a call I want to make, but better me than a stranger."

"When you get them on the line, let me know. I'll need to talk with them."

The young nurse disappeared into an office near the trauma room to make the call. She knew that the elder Randolph would be fast asleep and that the news he'd hear would be shocking. She also knew they had one other son and a nephew they had raised. They'd adopted the nephew when his parents were killed. Both of them lived out of town. She hadn't met either of them, and had only seen them a few times in Pecan Valley when they'd come home to visit.

She used the phone at the reception desk, dialing O for the Operator.

"Operator, may I help you?"

"Uh, yes, I need to be connected with Pecan Valley, Texas."

"What party are you trying to reach in Pecan Valley?"

"I need to be connected to the residence of Mr. Jonas Randolph, please. It's an emergency."

"Hold the line, please." A moment passed. "Go ahead with your call for Mr. Randolph, please."

"Mr. Randolph?"

"Yes, who is this?"

"Mr. Randolph, this is Betty Henderson. Remember me?"

"Yes, Betty, of course I remember you," he replied, shaking his head to awaken. "But why on earth are you calling me at this hour?"

"Well, sir, I'm calling from Regional Hospital in Concho City, and I regret to inform you that your son, Dr. Randolph, has been involved in a serious car accident, and is hospitalized here receiving treatment."

He turned on the bedside lamp and sat up straight. "My son . . . *what?* My son is hurt? Is he going to be all right?"

"Dr. Moran wants to talk with you, sir, if you can hold the line while I get him?"

"Yes, of course," he answered, a sweat breaking out on his brow.

"Mr. Randolph, This is Dr. Stuart Moran in Concho City. I am very sorry to tell you that your son was involved in a freak auto accident this morning and has sustained a severe injury to the frontal lobe area of his head. He needs surgery right away. We are unable to reach his wife, so as next of kin do we have your permission to operate? There's not much time to spare."

"Of course, you must do what has to be done."

"Jonas, what is it? What's happened?" Frances asked, turning on the lamp on her side of the bed.

"Dear, now settle down. I'll tell you in a minute," he said, patting her arm while he continued to talk with the surgeon.

"Can you tell us what happened, doctor?"

"No sir, I don't know exactly. The police are working on it. It happened on Blanton Street at the underpass. That's all I know presently."

"We're on our way. Do everything you can for him, and tell him his parents are coming, will you please?"

"Yes of course."

"Thank you, doctor."

"Please drive safely, Mr. Randolph. It's rainin' pretty hard out over here."

Jonas Sr. held his wife in the double bed that they had shared their entire married life. His hand shook as he reached up with a damp palm to smooth his rumpled, thinning white hair. Frances was holding her chest, unable to speak.

They'd rarely been up at that hour—only when their second-born, Cullen Harden Randolph, had come into the world, or when one of their boys had come down sick. Jonas Jr. had come into the world in the bright light of an afternoon the year before Cully. And then there was Parkton, their nephew, who had come to live with them at age twelve when his parents, Jonas Sr.'s brother Gerard and his wife, were both killed in an oil field explosion. Frances and Jonas Sr. adopted Park a year later. Cully, with his brother Jonas off to military school, became deeply embittered about having to share the limelight with the interloper cousin, Park, who was a year younger than him. "My stair-steps," Frances had often called them. Frances and Jonas Sr. spent most of Cully's and Park's youths breaking up their frequent bloody fights.

"Daddy, what on earth has happened?"

"Jonas has been hurt, dear. We need to get dressed and get over to Concho City."

Jonas Sr. reached over and pulled Frances to him. She was shivering, clutching his large arms with all her might. In that moment, she seemed more fragile than he had ever noticed. Her tiny frame had always been a delight to him. He was a large man, big-boned, standing at six feet. Holding Frances had always made him feel invincible. She was a diminutive four feet ten. That she had managed to bear two hefty sons, continued to hold him entirely captive to her.

"What's happened to our boy?"

"He's been in an auto accident. The doctor didn't elaborate, but from the tone of his voice, I—"

Frances pulled away, not wanting to hear the rest. She flew out of bed, threw open the closet door, grabbed the first dress she saw, and her everyday black pumps from the closet floor. Throwing the dress on the bed, she ran over to the dresser to get her girdle and a pair of hose. She returned to the edge of the bed to struggle into both. Jonas Sr. stood frozen in front of his closet door. Throughout all their thirty-six years together, Frances had, more often than not, been the stalwart one, her husband softer and more vulnerable.

"Daddy, what *are* you doing? You have to get dressed!"

At that, Jonas Sr. turned, lowered himself into the wicker rocker at the foot of their bed, and began to sob. Frances went to him. She stood over him, her hand on his shoulder. She stared at the pink-plumed flowered wallpaper that they'd had put up right after Cady's birth six years before. Cady had made a game of standing in front of the wallpaper's plumes, pressing her head into the wall at just the right spot, pretending to be wearing a few of the plumes on her head. Frances continued staring at the wallpaper. It was a reprieve from the present horror.

"We're going to get through this, dearest. Together, we will," she said, bending over to kiss the top of his head. "Now let's get going."

"Yes Frances. I'm sorry," Jonas Sr. said, looking up at her.

"Put on your Eisenhower jacket, Jonas. No need for a suit."

Jonas Sr. wiped his face with his hands, lifted his Stetson from his closet shelf, and his shoes from the shoe rack. He took his grey jacket, brown tie, starched white shirt, and neatly pressed khakis off their hangers to follow his usual routine: blowing lightly on his Stetson, wiping off the tops of his shoes with a cloth used only for that purpose, and laying his clothes out on the bed.

Meanwhile, Frances finished dressing and went to the kitchen. She got the key to the garage out of the drawer, where it was always kept, and took her seat at the kitchen table to write a note to Rachel, their housekeeper of twenty years, to let Rachel know what had happened. The familiar sound of the rock-tick of the water heater in the telephone nook offered some solace. And then she remembered the letter from her son that she kept under a stack of recipes in the miscellaneous drawer by the clothes washer.

She smoothed out the fragile and worn paper from so many readings, and shielding her eyes from the harshness of the ceiling light, began to read what Jonas Jr. had written and sent in a letter to her in '44, right after his induction into the Army. It read: *I miss my old homeland, Pecan Valley—the place I call home—the place others of my blood have called home since 1886—a place that holds its history carefully in its wrinkled old hands—a place where the duet of the mourning dove and the redbird continues, without fail, year after year, after year, after year.* Jonas had written in the letter that this was how he saw what he could really count on in life.

"Oh, my dear child," she said softly. "How I always thought that I couldn't love you more—until this moment." Closing the letter, she slipped it into the pocket of her dress and wept.

"Frances, are you all right?" Jonas asked, as he entered the kitchen, his Stetson in hand.

"Yes, dear," she answered, wiping her tears with an already-damp hanky. She handed him the key to the garage.

"Okay, let's go, shall we?" Jonas said, as he pulled Frances's chair out.

She stood for a moment to get her wits and her balance about her. Her husband helped her with her coat. He then flipped the switch for the driveway light as he and Frances stepped out onto the back screened porch. He fumbled around in his pocket to find the keys to the kitchen door while Frances made her way past the little painted metal cabinet where she kept canned goods, the shoebox where Jonas kept his polishing paraphernalia, and the speckled white metal table upon which old Mr. Penn would leave the groceries he had delivered once a week for more than thirty years. The screen door stayed open for that purpose, and for the gardener's ease in accessing yard supplies that were stored in the porch's small closet.

The air had that heaviness that Frances described as a warm, wet hanky over the nostrils. The pecan tree by the garage spread across the driveway and high above the garage; it was loaded with pecans. Frances stood under its wide canopy waiting for Jonas to back their giant Buick Road Master out of the garage. He'd then ritually close and lock the sliding garage door. That night he left the garage unlocked.

Frances remembered the time, just nine months, before when little Cady, at that very spot, sat under the sprawling pecan and cried inconsolably after stepping squarely into the middle of her sixth birthday cake. The cake had been placed on the back floorboard of the Buick to be transported to Concho City. The child had begged her grandmother to ice it in her favorite color—lavender. Frances had painstakingly mixed blue and red food colorings until her granddaughter approved the hue. She remembered how Jonas, after hearing of his child's heartbreak over the cake's demise, drove over to Pecan Valley to secretly retrieve a spoonful of the icing from the alley garbage can. He took it to a paint store in Concho City to have the color matched. While she slept completely unaware of the happy surprise she would have on her return home from Pecan Valley, he painted her room lavender.

Frances then thought about the sun shining on her roses and hoped that this awful night would disappear into the bright morning of so many other carefree mornings. The cat next door cried out. Frances thought that the old yellow feline, who had often wound through her legs of a morning while she tended the roses, must have sensed something was wrong.

It surprised Jonas Sr. when Frances didn't wait for him to open her car door. She slid across the seat to sit close to him. He backed out the long drive, past the tall sycamore, onto Euless Street, and then right on Baker. It was only six blocks to town.

A lone light was shining in the first-floor window at the fire station. The police dispatcher sat there nightly, waiting dutifully for a very occasional distress call. They drove through the two blinking lights on the main drag and passed not a single other car. There had been only one car parked out front at the all-night Lone Star Café. They then crossed over the Corona River for the forty-two mile drive to Concho City. It was 2:45 in the morning.

They didn't talk. That was something rare to Jonas and Frances in all their years together, but that their firstborn's life could be ending was a conversation neither could have. Frances felt sick, but kept it from Jonas for fear it would interfere with his driving. They had decided not to call Cully or Park until they knew more. Frances closed her eyes and thought about little Cady, remembering all those happy times when Cady stood in front of the mirror that hung on the closet door, turning and turning, admiring herself wearing Frances's hat, purse, and high heels. In that tiny moment of memory, life was as it should have been.

They came into a hard rain about sixteen miles outside of Concho City; Jonas Sr. was forced to pull over. Frances sat erect, straining to see out the Buick's windshield through the thick ribbons of water.

"Do you think this rain will ever let up, dear?" Frances asked matter-of-factly.

"I sure hope so," he answered, straining to catch a glimpse of the road through the wiper blades. I think we'll have to replace these blades next time we get a chance."

"Yes, I suppose so," Frances said, gripping her knees.

"I'm going to go on and take it slow."

"Let's be careful, Jonas. We can't let anything happen to us. I suppose we'll have to see if Renata's been called. I hope little Cady Frances is all right."

"I'm sure she is, Frances. Try not to worry," he said, patting her knee.

He turned the Buick carefully back onto the highway. They'd passed only a couple of trucks, each creeping through the deluge. He hit the high beam, and then the low, settling on the low. It was some sort of purgatory, he thought, being held in that slowness, when his heart was racing ahead to his son's side.

When they pulled into the hospital parking lot, Frances sat up straight, fussed with her hair, and smoothed her dress over her knees. Luckily, the rain had let up. They hadn't thought to bring umbrellas. Jonas Sr. pushed the button of the handle on the passenger door and tugged. The door felt heavier than he had ever remembered. Frances attempted a smile, but it couldn't disguise the pallor of her skin or the fear in her eyes. Taking Jonas Sr.'s hand, her legs trembled as she slid off the seat.

She leaned into her husband, clutching his arm, holding it firmly against her chest as they made their way into the hospital. His steps quickened as he passed the reception desk and pushed through the swinging doors to the operating room area. His throat was so dry that he was having trouble swallowing. He could feel Frances's heart pounding against his arm. As two nurses hurried toward them, Frances's body slipped from his arm. Dropping his Stetson, he managed to get his left hand behind her back just before she hit the hard tile floor.

8

Austin, Texas—a few hours later

The phone conversation with Jonas Sr. had been brief. Park opened the front door of his garage apartment, hoping for a breeze. It was hot and still. He stood out on the landing for a little while before turning on the light to awaken Cully.

"Wake up, man," Park called out, shaking him.

"Wha . . . what the hell?" Cully grumbled, squinting against the bright ceiling light. "Damn . . . what time is it?" he asked, as he swatted at Park.

"It's 4:00 a.m. and Dad just called. Brother J's been in a bad car wreck. We've gotta hurry and get to Concho City . . . so get your ass up."

Cully rolled out of bed, his eyes swollen and half-closed. He and Park had tied one on the night before and, as usual, he had outdone Park by at least four shots.

"Is he gonna die?" Cully asked, yawning.

"I don't know, but Dad said to hurry and get there, so it sounds pretty serious."

"Jesus, man, Mother must be falling apart about to lose the *good* son."

"What a crap thing to say, Cully."

"Aw, come on, you know it's true . . . J's her knight in shining armor."

"Come on, get moving, Cully," Park said, shaking his head.

The humidity was high. It had rained all day in Austin, far more the norm there than in West Texas. Even when it rained, Park opened the windows wide, and kept fans blowing ineffectively in every room. The humidity was inescapable; even the bed sheets stayed damp—rain or shine.

He'd moved into the Midtown Austin garage apartment a few months before, and had established a good rapport with the owners of the Tudor style house that sat just a few yards away. A hazy moon popped out between fast-moving clouds that night. Otherwise, it would have been too dark to see Park's apartment in the tall, thick stand of live oaks that surrounded it.

Cully had been staying with Park the entire time Park had lived there. Luckily, Jonas Sr. was helping Park with the rent since Cully wasn't earning a penny; he'd quit his job at an architectural firm in San Antonio after only two months there. He maintained that they weren't paying him enough. Frances and Jonas hoped he'd go back to university to get his degree, but he'd shown no interest in doing so.

"Come on, hurry it up," Park shouted to Cully through the bathroom door. "Then, go get the car started while I write the landlord a note."

"Screw you," Cully said, giving Park the middle finger as he emerged from the bathroom.

"Grow up, Cully. It's about time don't you think?"

Cully took his time going down the apartment's steps to the driveway. Park tidied up as quickly as he could, turned out the lights, and hoped that they wouldn't wake up his landlords. The rent would be due in a few days and Park wouldn't have it without Jonas Sr.'s help. Park knew his place. Despite Jonas Sr.'s and Frances's insistence that Park was just as much their son as were their other two, Cully never lost an opportunity to remind him that he was nothing more than the orphaned cousin.

Cully waited in the idling '52 Chevy that Jonas Sr. and Frances had given Park as a gift. Cully was tempted to honk the horn, and had it not been that he wanted to impress the landlord's young wife, whom he found enticing, he would have. Waking her up at this hour would nix any chance he would have of getting her attention later on.

Park had wondered why their dad hadn't given the newer '52 car to Jonas; Park hadn't made any offer to switch. He thought that Jonas, being a doctor, would soon be making enough money to afford any car he wanted. And too, Park wasn't above allowing Frances and Jonas Sr. to go overboard with gifts. He was aware that it was their way of trying to make it up to him for the death of his parents. Despite his twinge of guilt at accepting those terms, Park took full advantage.

Cully pulled on the headlights and quickly backed the Chevy out the long gravel drive. Between the headlights on bright and the spinning and grinding of the gravel under the tires, it would be a miracle if the landlords and neighbors didn't awaken with a jolt.

"Man, what the hell's *wrong* with you?" Park asked. "I'll be lucky if there's not an eviction notice on the door when we get back."

"Relax, man." Cully answered, lighting a cigarette as he tore down Rock Lane toward the highway.

"What the hell made you so sorry, Cully?"

Cully jerked the wheel to the shoulder and stopped. "I don't owe you one iota of anything, and I damned sure don't want to spend the next three hours on the road listenin' to your drivel. Got it? You know I'm not gonna change, and you're not gonna win, so drop it," Cully said.

Park stared out the window, gritting his teeth, his knuckles white. "Drive, Cully. At this rate, brother J might be dead by the time we get there. Our brother should be all that matters right now."

"How many times do I have to tell you that you are *not* J's or my brother . . . you're a cousin, and you'll never be anything more."

"I hate you down to your mean bones," Park muttered, grabbing his knees with his hands to keep from slamming a fist into the side of Cully's head.

Cully grinned the same spiteful grin that had driven Park to madness since childhood. It was Park who usually ended up the worse off when the two of them locked horns. Park was short and wiry, and no match for Cully who was tough, thick, and taller. Neither was as tall as Jonas.

"Park . . . Park? You asleep?" Cully asked, jabbing at his side.

"No, of course not. Do you want me to drive?" Park asked.

"Nah, I'm awake. What are you going to do with the folks? I mean they're gonna be emotional, especially Mother, and I hate that crap," Cully said, writhing in the driver's seat.

"Just keep your mouth shut," Park answered. "That's my advice."

"Do we have to look at him? I mean I don't want to see him all banged up."

"He's your brother, Cully. You'll *have* to see him."

They were only an hour and a half from Concho City when Cully slowed the car. He told Park he was slowing to watch for deer, but Park knew why he was delaying. For all his bravado, Cully was a coward. Park was saddled with him, unable to escape Cully's disregard for everything Park cared about. Neither of them had been able to hold a candle to Jonas, but Jonas had always praised each of them for their smallest accomplishments. Though Jonas was only a year older than Cully, and a couple of years older than Park, he had come to feel responsible for the two of them, for the kind of men they'd eventually become.

Park's decision to go to business school instead of medical school had been a disappointment to Jonas, but he never let Park know. Cully dropped out of his third year at the new School of Architecture at the University of Texas, much to Frances and Jonas Sr.'s dismay, promising them, "I'll finish school as soon as I get my wild hairs satisfied." His WWII service, spent safe from the front lines as an Army supply clerk, had taught him nothing of real war. Instead, he parlayed the homefolks' gratitude for his service into an endless round of parties, considering the discipline of university studies too restrictive.

Cully stopped for gas outside the small town of Twig. It was predawn with nothing stirring but the birds greeting a new day. The Texaco station had just opened. The old man who ran it wore a crisply ironed Texaco shirt, and was in the middle of rolling up the single door bay as they drove up. He wiped his hands on a red cloth hanging from his pocket and motioned to his first customers of the day.

"Mornin' young fellas," the old man said, tipping the bill of his hat as he walked to the car.

"Mornin' to *you*, old fella," Cully answered, kicking open the door of the Chevy.

"What can I do for ya?"

"Fill 'er up."

"Yes sir. Need your windshield cleaned?"

"Yep, give it a good goin' over."

"Check that oil?"

"Nah, don't bother."

Park opened the passenger side, leaving the door open as he stretched and walked toward the old red coke case just outside the front door of the station.

"Are they cold, sir?"

"You betcha. Grab ya one. I'll add it to the bill."

"You want one, Cully?"

"Nah, got anything stronger, old man?"

"No sir. I don't run that kinda place . . . county's dry and so am I."

"Too bad," Cully said, laughing.

"Don't pay any attention to him, sir. He's got no upbringing," Park shouted.

"Hmm, I guess he don't," the old man muttered, shaking his head as he finished filling up the car, then turning to Cully.

"That'll be $3.17, includin' the coke."

"That man over there'll pay ya," Cully told the old man, pointing at Park.

Park pulled the fifteen dollars he had left for the month out of his back pocket, counted out four crisp one dollar bills, and followed the old man inside for his change. The neatly kept office smelled of rubber and oil.

"Here ya go, son. That'd be 18, 19, 20," he counted out slowly in pennies, and then in dimes, "30, 40, 50, 60, 70, 80, 90 and one dollar, sir, makin' four."

"Thank you, sir," Park replied, handing the old man a tip of thirty cents.

"That's right kind of ya, son. Thank ya. Ya'll have a nice trip and come on back to see us, hear?"

Park made his way back to the car. Cully was leaning against a tree, his left knee propped up against the trunk, taking a long drag off the

Lucky Strike that he'd taken from Park's stash in the glove compartment. Walking back toward the car, he flicked the butt from between his middle finger and thumb. It landed near the front door of the station, a thin trail of smoke emanating from it as it rolled a little way on the paved drive. The old man, never looking up, shook his head, stubbed it out with the toe of his well-worn boot, and threw it away in a nearby trash can.

The Chevy rumbled on down the highway with about forty-five minutes to go to reach Concho City. The humidity had dropped a good forty percent from Austin's steamy ninety percent. They passed a deer carcass on the side of the road that must have been there a long time; his mouth agape, there was nothing left of him but bones, hide, and hollow eye sockets. Park thought of Jonas at the sight of this poor, unfortunate creature. Just as pressing on his mind was how he was going to ask his father for the rent money. It was going to be tricky in light of the circumstances. Cully began whistling.

"Cully, any chance you can shut that business up? This is no time for whistling."

"Park, you know what your problem is? You never have figured out how to have fun."

~

It was about 6:45 a.m. when Park and Cully arrived at Regional Hospital. They found their father sitting beside their mother in a private room where she was resting from her earlier collapse. She'd lost a kidney twelve years before, on Pearl Harbor Day to be exact, and hadn't been the same since. Jonas's accident had put her into shock, something about her albumin levels the doctors said. She'd been given a course of glucose intravenously.

When Frances saw Park and Cully, she put her arms out to welcome them. Park moved forward into Frances's arms while Cully stood back. Jonas Sr. put an arm around Cully from which he shrank. It was always the same with Cully: even as a child, he had stiffened at any sign of affection.

Park walked toward the recovery area; Cully lagged behind. Two nurses, like sentries, stood on either side of Jonas's bed. Cully stayed in the hall, his hands digging so deeply into the pockets of his pants that he ripped the right one completely open. Park looked in, averted his eyes in horror, and quickly left the area with Cully following closely behind.

"Where's Renata?" Cully asked his father.

"They've put her in a room here," he answered tersely, directing both Park and Cully into the hallway.

"Why?" Cully asked.

"I don't know why, but she was apparently a patient at St. Joe's when this happened, and one of the doctors went out there, got her, and brought her here. I can't even think about her right now."

"So where's the kid?" Cully asked.

"Renata says she's home with a babysitter. One of you needs to go over there later on to check on her."

"Park can go. I'm not good at that sort of thing."

"Well it's high time you *got* good at it because *both* you boys are going to have to help your mother and me with this thing."

Cully took off to find Renata. He was the only one in the family, besides Jonas, who seemed to like her. One of the nurses directed him to a small waiting area near the recovery area where Renata appeared to be asleep on the lounge's well-worn couch. She was still in the St. Joseph's hospital gown.

"Renata?" Cully whispered close to her ear.

"Oh, Cully, when did you get here?" she answered, her eyes half open.

"Just got here. What's happened to you?"

"I was having a little neck work done out at St. Joe's and Jonas had come to check on me. When he left, this horrible thing happened. They wanted to put me in a room here, but I refused."

"Well, that's a hell of a note."

"Have you seen him?" Renata asked.

"No, and I'm not going to. Not my cup of tea."

"Where's Park?"

"He's in there with Mother."

"They hate me, Cully. They blame me for what's happened."

"Oh well, they hated you anyway. They wouldn't need much to hate you more. They told me the kid was with a babysitter."

"Yeah, she's with that Riley boy from next door."

"Anybody gonna go get her?" Cully asked, wincing from the pain in his left leg, the result of an accident during a wartime training exercise. Sitting for long periods brought it on.

"I don't know, but the boy will stay with her until somebody gets over there."

"When are you going to tell her?" Cully asked.

"I'll let the old man tell her. They'll take her for awhile," Renata answered, sitting up straight.

"Well, ole girl, you know you're too damned mean to be down and out for long," Cully said.

"Yeah," Renata said, smiling up at Cully. "Ain't it so? I'm sure glad you're here. Go check on Jonas for me, will you? They won't let me in to see him."

"Sorry, pretty one, but you'll have to recruit someone else for that nasty task, m'dear . . . like I said, not my cuppa tea."

It was fully light outside; the rain had stopped. A completely exhausted Dr. Moran called Jonas Sr. and Park out of Frances's room. Jonas Sr. shut the door so that Frances wouldn't hear.

"As you know, your son made it through the surgery," Moran began, "but the injury to his brain was worse than we thought. He's still very swollen, but his airway's open." Moran pointed to his own throat to show them where they'd inserted the tube after Jonas's tracheotomy. "I removed embedded skull fragments from the frontal lobe portions of his brain," he continued, running his finger from left to right over his own forehead. "I'm sorry to say that his eye will also be permanently damaged. He was given a couple of units of plasma and two pints of whole blood during the operation, and another pint of whole blood on his return to his room."

Jonas Sr. removed his glasses and wiped his eyes with Park standing motionless by his side. "My son's eye was already damaged in a riding accident, torn retina, years ago."

"I see," Moran answered, reaching up to grasp Jonas Sr.'s shoulder in a show of compassion. "We've got a long day ahead of us, and I hope you can get some rest, sir."

"Do you think he'll make it?"

"I think the next twelve to twenty-four hours will tell us more, but I don't anticipate, with damage this extensive, that there'll be a good outcome."

"Thank you, Dr. Moran, for all you've done. When can we see my son?"

"You can go in now for a little while, but he's unconscious," Moran said, looking at his watch. "I'll tell you goodbye for now, Mr. Randolph, but I'll be checking on your son regularly, and I'll report any changes to you immediately."

"Thank you, sir," Jonas Sr. said, shaking the doctor's hand.

He and Park walked toward the nurses' station where a stack of the Concho City Times sat at the end of the counter. The front page read: *Local Surgeon Critically Injured At Blanton Street Underpass.* There was a photo of Jonas Jr. taken just a few weeks before, for the Surgeons' Clinic marketing campaign, and a chilling caption reporting that the thirty-five-year-old doctor was not expected to live. Jonas Sr. took a paper, carefully folded it, and tucked it under his arm. He and Park walked in silence to the recovery area.

9

Bobwhite Lane—6:30 a.m., October 3

When Sweezer awoke, he was startled to find that he was still in the Randolph living room. Cady was no longer on the couch, and the blanket he'd placed over her the night before was in a crumple on the floor. The phone had fallen off the little table. It was off the hook.

He raised the blinds of the picture window behind the couch to see that the sun was shining at intervals, slipping back behind darkish clouds that were left over from the previous night's storms. He sat on the edge of the couch just long enough to shake off the rest of his sleep, and rubbed the matter from his eyes. His first thought was that it was finally his thirteenth birthday and, his second, that something was terribly wrong.

"Cady?" he called out, as he padded down the hall. "Where are you?" There was no answer. He knocked on Dr. Randolph's bedroom door, slowly opening it to find no evidence that Dr. Randolph had been there during the night. Puzzled, he went to the kitchen, to the back room, and then to the garage to find it empty. Alarmed, he continued calling Cady's name, finally opening the front door to find her sitting on the front step, cross-legged, with the newspaper on her lap.

"What are you doing out here, Cady? You scared me half to death." He opened the screen door just enough to slip through without bumping the little girl with it. "Cady, why aren't you answering me?" he asked, moving around in front of her to find her staring down at the paper opened in her lap, her face red and swollen. "Look at me. What are you doing out here?"

"Daddy's dead," she whimpered, looking up at him with frightened eyes.

"What are you talking about? Why are you saying that?"

Cady held the newspaper up so Sweezer could see the picture of Jonas on the front page. His heart began racing and Cady began crying when she saw the look on his face.

"See? I told you. My daddy's dead."

"He's not dead. It says here that he got in some freak accident and that he's in the hospital." His finger was trembling as he traced the small newspaper print. "Someone would have called if he wasn't all right." He suddenly remembered that the phone had been off the hook all night.

Sweezer put his arm around her shoulder and reassured her over and over that everything would be all right, that someone would probably be there soon. She lowered her head, cradling the newspaper in her lap, her small arms wrapped tightly around her knees. Sweezer wondered what to do next. Joe would be in no shape to help and the paper read that Dr. Randolph was not expected to live.

"Daddy got cupcakes for your birthday and your party and he's got to come home . . . oh, where's Daddy?" she cried out, gulping for air.

Sweezer paced up and down the sidewalk, running his hands through his hair. When he attempted to take the paper from her lap, part of it tore away as she grabbed it away from him. The horror on her face turned to relief when he showed her that the photo of Jonas's face had not been torn.

"Let's go in the house, Cady. Come on." He held out his hand to help her up. "I'll find out how your daddy is. He's going to be all right, I promise. Now come on." He took her hand to help her inside. "Listen to me. I'm going to go over to Miss Alice's to see if I can get her to help us, okay?"

"Okay," she said, gasping between sobs.

"Now don't move from this couch, you hear?"

"Okay. Promise you'll come back, promise?"

"Of course I will. Pinky-swear," he said, entwining his little finger around hers.

Sweezer bounded across the street, and in spite of a slight hesitancy to knock on Miss Alice's door so early, he found himself pounding on it instead. It took a long time for the door to open, and when it did, it opened just a crack.

"What is it? What do you want?" she asked, a tremor in her voice.

"Miss Alice, I'm Sweezer Riley from across the street. You don't know me, but I listen to your music every Friday and—"

"You *what*?" she interrupted.

"I listen to your music."

"What on earth do you want, boy? The chickens are barely up."

"Something's happened to Dr. Randolph across the street, and his daughter's alone, and we need help. Can you help us?"

"What on earth can *I* do?" she replied, sounding more annoyed than nervous.

"Can you help us telephone somewhere for help?"

"Where would I telephone, for goodness sake?"

"It's in the paper, Miss Alice."

Her Concho City Times was still rolled up and perched on the edge of her porch. She unrolled it to find the picture of Jonas and the headline. Her expression softened into concern. Though they'd never spoken, she considered Jonas kinder than the others in the neighborhood. He never missed nodding her direction with a wave and a smile those rare times when they were both outside. She had never returned his smile or waved back. She'd only caught glimpses of Renata.

"That little girl is alone you say?"

"Yes ma'am, except for me. I was babysitting her for Dr. Randolph last night . . . and he never came home."

"Oh dear," she said, wringing her hands. "Where's the child's mother?"

"I'm not sure, ma'am, but I think she's sick in the hospital."

"Go on back over there with the child, young man, and I'll be over directly."

"Thank you, ma'am . . . I figured you'd help."

Alice cracked a tiny smile at him, feeling a tenderness come over her that surprised her. She'd only just met this tousle-headed boy, yet felt a kinship with him. She quickly dressed and pulled her hair back with bobby pins to try to make it look more presentable. It wasn't her habit to be seen out in the daytime, other than to go to the store for a few groceries and, even then, she'd hide behind dark glasses and a head covering. The urgency of the moment moved her to dispense with all of that. She dialed the number for Regional Hospital, her hand shaking a little.

"Good evening, Regional Hospital."

"Did you say this is Regional Hospital?" Alice asked.

"Yes, ma'am, may I help you?"

"Uh, yes," she said, clearing her throat. I, uh, am, uh . . . my name is Alice Bock. I'm calling to see if there are any family members at the hospital with Dr. Jonas Randolph. I understand he's been in some kind of car wreck."

"Are you a family member?" the receptionist queried.

"Oh, no, but I am a neighbor, and Dr. Randolph's little girl is over in the house with a young babysitter, and the boy came over here looking for help."

"Hold the line, please," the receptionist said.

It seemed an eternity before anyone came back on the line, and Alice found herself wondering what she was going to do with those children. She'd had none of her own, and hadn't a clue how to minister to them.

"Miss Bock?"

"Yes, this is Alice Bock, and that's *Mrs.* Bock."

"I'm sorry, Mrs. Bock. I understand you were calling about Dr. Randolph's condition?"

"Well, no, I'm calling because his little daughter's alone with a young babysitter who came to me for help."

"Oh dear, I see. Dr. Randolph's parents and brothers are here in the hospital. Can you hold, please, while I locate one of them to speak with you?"

"Yes," Alice answered nervously.

About five minutes had passed. Alice had rehearsed over and over what she would say to any family member who came to the phone. She looked at the front page of the paper again, reading it more carefully. It sounded like Dr. Randolph could die. She started feeling one of her spells coming on when, blessedly, the threat was dispelled by a voice on the other end of the line.

"Hello . . . Mrs.Bock is it?"

"Yes, this is Mrs. Bock."

"My name's Parkton Randolph, Dr. Jonas Randolph's brother. I understand you're calling about my little niece who's alone at home with a babysitter?"

"Yes sir, that's right. I'm just the neighbor across the way. The babysitter boy came over just a little while ago asking for help."

"Thank you for calling about this. I'll be over there as soon as I can, but in the meantime, would you be kind enough to check on the youngsters for us? I tried calling the house last night, but the line was out of order."

"I guess I can go over for a little while, but I'm a stranger to you people and I'm afraid I'll make it worse for the little girl."

"Does she know what happened?" Park asked.

"From what the boy told me, yes, and she's real upset about it."

"Okay, one of us will be over there as soon as possible. Thank you for your help."

When they hung up, before going over to the Randolph house, Alice went through her tiny house, checking the back door lock and the windows with the same precision she would if leaving for an extended trip. She made her way down her front walk, repositioning one of the bobby pins in her hair as she stepped off of her front curb. It had been years since she'd ventured out the front. All comings and goings were from the back, when she'd pull her old De Soto out of the shed to drive from the property unseen. She began feeling woozy again, a feeling all too familiar since Ernest had left. Once, right after he disappeared, she had found herself pulled over to the side of the road in her car, unable to drive, unable to breathe, and unable to see. Since then, she'd been terrified to venture too far from home. The Piggly Wiggly, three blocks away, was as far as she had been in three years, and she'd been known to leave a full cart of groceries behind in moments of distress.

Alice knocked on the Randolph's door. Sweezer opened it immediately. "Come on in, Miss Alice."

"All right, but I can't stay long. The child's family will be here soon." She stepped slowly into the living room, measuring every step. Cady was sitting sideways on the couch, her face buried in a cushion.

"Sit down, Miss Alice. I don't know if there's anything to drink, but I can get you a glass of water," Sweezer offered. "Would you like that?"

"No thank you son. I'll just sit here until the adult gets here. I told the uncle I would."

"Today's my birthday, Miss Alice. I'm thirteen," he told her.

"Oh, well then, I wish you the best, young man," Alice said, fidgeting in the chair.

"Thanks. I think if my mama was alive, she'd have loved that music you were playing last night," Sweezer told her. She didn't reply.

Sweezer was thinking better about bringing up his birthday in front of Cady, who had not said a word since she'd come inside. He made a wish to himself, with his fingers crossed, promising God that if he'd let Dr. Randolph live, he'd never make another birthday wish.

"Cady?" Sweezer asked, as calmly as he could muster. "Do you want to eat one of my birthday cupcakes? You must be hungry."

"No. Not without Daddy," she answered. "They're in the kitchen in the corner by the stove on a plate where Daddy put them last night. And your present's in there too."

Alice was feeling more and more like an intruder. Sweezer went into the kitchen, found the three cupcakes and the small gift wrapped in brown paper and twine. He slipped the gift into his pocket and brought the cupcakes into the living room. The cakes were in a box, iced in white, sprinkled with multi-colored sugar. Each had a candle. Jonas had planned a little party. Setting the plate down on the coffee table in front of the couch, Sweezer signaled Alice to move her chair a little closer to the table.

When Park arrived about forty-five minutes later, Alice and Sweezer had each eaten a cupcake, leaving the third untouched. Cady had refused to eat and had not turned to face the room once. When Park approached her, she buried her face into the tufts of the sofa back.

"Thank you, Sweezer, for staying with Cady, and thank you, Mrs. Bock, for calling us and watching the young folks," Park said.

"Was glad to, Mr. Randolph . . . oh, and I noticed there's a box on the kitchen counter. It's full of cabbage . . . kinda smelly."

"Do me a favor, young fella. Go dump it in the garbage, will you?" Park asked, digging in his pocket for some change to give to the boy.

"Sure I will but, please, just keep the change."

Alice Bock made her way to the front door. When Sweezer opened the door for her, Cady jumped off the couch and ran to him. "You're not leaving me, are you . . . are you, Sweezer?"

"Not yet. I'm going to take the cabbage out to the alley first."

"Daddy won't like it when he finds out you threw away his cabbage."

"Your uncle told me to throw it away."

"That's right, Cady, honey," Park said. "The cabbage is rotting."

Cady stood frozen as Sweezer went out the back door with the box.

"Cady," Park said. "I'll be taking you to Pecan Valley for a few days until your mother gets better."

"I want my daddy. I want to see my daddy. Is he dead?" she asked, remembering all the animals she'd seen dead, not fully understanding where they'd gone, but understanding that they weren't coming back.

"No, he's not dead. You'll see him soon."

"Where's my grandmamma?"

"She's not feeling well," Park answered, noticing Sweezer had come back into the house. "We'll work this thing out, little girl. Now don't worry. Go and get some clothes to take to Pecan Valley now."

"I'll help her, Mr. Randolph," Sweezer broke in. "She probably doesn't know what to get."

"Thanks, you're a good boy. I don't know much about kids."

Sweezer went back to Cady's room and picked out some clean clothes for Cady's time away. She'd only be there for the weekend, and maybe a few days into the next week. Park had Sweezer put the clothes in a large sack that he'd found in the kitchen, and then reached for the remaining cupcake.

"No!" Cady shouted, grabbing the cupcake from Park. "I'm saving it for my daddy." She held it away from him.

"Okay, Cady, honey, okay. Just settle down," he said, holding both of his arms in the air as Sweezer moved toward the front door to leave. "Goodbye, young man . . . thanks for everything. What does Dr. Randolph ordinarily pay you for your services?"

"Oh, no sir, I don't care for any money. I just want Dr. Randolph to be okay, but thank you anyway."

"But we owe you for the babysitting."

"No sir, I don't want any money," Sweezer said firmly, holding his hand out to shake Park's.

"Well, if that's the way you want it, ok, but I'd sure be glad to pay you," Park said, shaking Sweezer's hand.

"Goodbye, sir," Sweezer said, turning toward Cady. "Cady, I'm going now, but I'll see ya later, ok?"

"Will you take Daddy's cupcake and save it for him?"

"The ants'll get it, Cady," Sweezer said.

"Please, please save it for him?"

"Okay," he said, taking it from Cady. "Don't worry, I'll keep it safe."

"Okay. Bye," Cady answered.

"See ya, Cady."

"Thanks again," Park said, saluting the boy.

"Sure sir."

Walking back across the yard to his house, Sweezer wondered where he'd hide the cupcake so that Joe wouldn't find it. He reached into his pocket with his free hand to feel the scratchy brown paper holding the gift from Cady.

He was relieved to find Joe just where he had left him the night before. Through the side window, Sweezer caught sight of Park putting Cady into the Chevy. With the top of her head barely visible in the passenger seat window, the car rolled out of the driveway. He watched it head up to Old Oak Road, disappearing around the corner. He felt abandoned.

He crept upstairs to his room, placed the cupcake on his dresser, and put his birthday gift from Cady next to the cupcake. He opened his dresser drawer and took out the faded brown pajamas printed with cowboys and lariats that were his last gift from his mother. The sleeves were at his elbows now, the bottoms hit mid-calf, and the buttons were missing except for the top one. He put them on.

Joe allowed no photos of Faithful in the house, but Sweezer kept one hidden in his closet that he brought out often. It was a photo of her holding him when he was a baby. Sweezer caught his image in the dresser mirror, and holding his mama's smiling photo next to his face, he looked to see if Joe was right about how he resembled her more and more as each day passed.

He had much lighter hair than hers and a small crop of pimples erupting regularly on his chin, but he had her slightly pointed chin and her thin face, prominent cheekbones, and her high and wide forehead. He also had her wide-set round eyes, the same hazel color, and even a sprinkling of freckles over the exact same spot across his nose as hers. He'd grown tall and bony like her, taller than the other boys in his seventh-grade class. But especially when he smiled, he looked like her. His small mouth widened into a grin, slightly higher on one side, displaying an exact replica of his mama's perfect set of teeth. She'd often told him how glad she was that he got her teeth instead of a mouthful of stained and rotten ones like Joe's. The sun even burned Sweezer's skin like it did hers, though neither of them was particularly fair. She said that their small ears, shaped like question marks, made them look curious; he stared at his in the mirror.

Thinking about where to hide the cupcake, Sweezer ran an index finger all along one ear, carefully tracing its shape. He placed the cupcake, with the unlit candle sunk deep into its frosting, high on a shelf in his closet. He hoped that the ants wouldn't discover it up that high.

He crawled onto his bed's sagging mattress, stared at the noonday orangey-glow of the side window shade, and then slowly untied the twine on Cady's birthday gift to him. He found a white, oval-shaped rock about four inches long. *Happy Birthday, 10/3/53, from Cady* was painted neatly on one side in black. There was a note attached to it with a rubber band. It read: *Cady found this rock down by the Angelus River for your 13th birthday, for you to keep forever. The cupcakes are from me. Happy birthday from your very good friends.* It was signed Cady and Dr. Randolph.

Sweezer turned the rock over several times, examining it carefully, recollecting the strange feeling that had come over him after having watched Dr. Randolph and Cady dancing on the sidewalk just the night before. Folding Dr. Randolph's note once, he tucked it into the breast pocket of his pajamas. His last thought, before curling up and escaping into sleep, was that his birthday, the 3rd of October, could never again be celebrated.

Sweezer was awakened by the creak of the stairs, warning him that Joe was almost to the top. He slid the gift from Cady under his pillow. He'd lost too many things to Joe's rages in the past, and didn't want to risk losing such an important gift.

"Why in the hell didn't you wake me up, you little son of a bitch?" Joe snarled, wiping dried spittle out of the corners of his mouth with the side of his finger.

"I figured you needed your sleep, Pop."

Joe staggered toward Sweezer. "Like you really care," he slurred.

"Pop, why don't you just go on downstairs and I'll be down to fix us something to eat in a little bit."

"What the hell are you doin' wearin' those goddamned sissy-ass kid pajamas again that's three sizes too small for ya, boy? It ain't even night time besides."

"You know Mama gave them to me, and I don't mind they're too small. Nobody sees 'em anyway, 'cept me, and I'm just takin' a nap rememberin' her. It's my birthday."

Joe turned away, raised an eyebrow, and squinted towards Sweezer as he fell off balance into the wall. "You gonna be a man or what? Aw, screw it, what's the point?" he said, flipping a hand into the air as he disappeared around the corner.

More than once, Sweezer had envisioned Joe accidentally slipping down the stairs, cracking his head wide open at the bottom. But then he'd blink his eyes to make the image go away, feeling bad about thinking such thoughts. Somehow, he loved Joe.

10

Same day—to Pecan Valley

Park had been instructed to call the Randolph's trusted housekeeper, Rachel, the moment he got to Pecan Valley with Cady. Rachel would then come over to stay with Cady until the family could get home. The Chevy still had plenty of gas, so there'd be no reason to stop. Park calmed himself by looking out over the alfalfa fields. Cady sat quietly.

"Uncle Park?" she asked timidly.

"Yes, little girl."

"These kids at school said you weren't my uncle. They said you were my cousin . . . but you're too old to be my cousin, aren't you?"

"I'm your uncle same as if I was born your uncle. It's complicated, kid. Just take my word for it."

"Okay . . . Uncle Park?"

"Yes, Cady, what is it?" Park answered, trying to keep his mind on the road.

"If Daddy hadn't gone to take her that hamburger, he wouldn't have had that wreck."

"What are you talking about, little girl?"

"Daddy had to go take her a hamburger. That's why he got hurt. I told him not to go."

"Take *who* a hamburger?"

"Her. My mother."

"Now, Cady . . . accidents just happen. I doubt it had anything to do with a hamburger."

Cady turned her head towards the window, catching her reflection in the car's window, attempting to imitate Jonas's familiar pose. She climbed up on her knees to get a better look.

"Cady, what are you doing?" Park asked, reaching over to gently pull her down onto the seat.

"I was just looking out the window."

"Well, you could fall, so sit down in the seat. We'll be in Pecan Valley soon."

Twenty minutes later, when the Chevy pulled into the driveway at 161 Baker Street, Rachel was waiting on the back steps. Cady ran into Rachel's open arms, holding tight to Rachel's ample middle.

Park stayed only long enough to bring in the sack of Cady's clothes. With Cady still clinging to her, Rachel offered to make a pot of coffee for Park. "No thanks," he said. "I need to head back to the hospital. We'll call here to let you know what's happening, so be sure to answer the phone. They're operating on my brother later this morning," he said in a whisper so Cady wouldn't hear.

"Aw, don't you worry, Mr. Park. I've been answerin' the phone 'round here pretty near twenty years now."

"Take care, pumpkin," Park said. He bent down to give Cady a kiss goodbye.

"I know what operating means and I heard you. That's what my daddy does everyday, Cady said."

"Don't worry about her, Mr. Park," Rachel said, waving him politely away. "She just needs some time with her ole Rachel. You just get on back over to there and give your mama a hug 'roun' the neck from ole Rachel . . . and tell that fine brother of yours that his ole Rachel loves him and that everything's in the Lord God's hands and they's nothin' to fear. Ya'll can bet your last dollar bill on that one."

Very few knew or paid attention to the fact that Rachel Moon Hawkins, who had always referred to herself as old, was in fact the same age as Jonas.

She'd been only fifteen when she began working for the Randolphs back in '33. When she married at sixteen, Jonas Sr. and Frances bought her wedding dress and attended the ceremony at the Three Kings Baptist Church down by the river. The preacher, Rachel's uncle, declared that she was born into this world an "old soul of the Lord's." Her young husband, Jebediah Moses Hawkins, was killed less than a year after they married when he was broadsided by a truck on the Concho City Highway. She had vowed never to remarry, and had told Frances numerous times that "Toady," as he was affectionately known, was her alpha and her omega, that there'd never be another for her. She'd danced once with a man a few years after Toady's death. It had taken her weeks of praying to feel forgiven.

Park hurried out the back door, shaking his head in the affirmative to Rachel's words, hoping she'd just shut the door and let him go. Since his boyhood, it had made him nervous when she started talking about how good God and Jesus were and about praying for their help. He'd questioned the existence of any *good* God who would allow his parents to die and leave him. Frances had argued more than once with Park about Rachel's intentions, and the necessity of believing in God. The only thing stronger than Park's aversion to religion was his love for Frances.

When the engine of the Chevy started up and drove away, Cady finally let go of Rachel long enough to verify that Park was gone. Rachel carried the sack of Cady's clothes to the bedroom at the top of the stairs. It was designated "Cady's room." It had been decorated with quilted, flowered wallpaper that covered the walls and ceiling, with matching lampshades on the dresser—a girl's room. Frances intended to have her granddaughter visit often.

Rachel sat on the edge of the twin bed that was nearest the window. Cady sat beside her, leaning on Rachel's shoulder. Rachel always smelled so good, like sunshine, the same way the clothes smelled when they came in off the clothes line, piled high in the basket that Rachel carried on her hip.

"Rachel?"

"Yes, shuggums . . . what is it, baby?"

"If Daddy hadn't gone out to buy that hamburger, he wouldn't be hurt."

"What you talkin' 'bout, child?"

"He went to buy a hamburger for my mother, and I cried so hard asking him not to go, and he said he'd be back, not to cry."

"Cady-child, hush now and let ole Rachel give you some sugar."

"Will you rock me?" Cady asked.

"Sure will, baby."

Rachel cranked out the casement window to bring in the fresh morning breeze from the back yard, and settled down onto the rocker below the billowing white organza curtains. Cady curled up in her wide, soft lap. It was only a few minutes before she'd fallen soundly asleep to Rachel's humming and rocking. Rachel pulled Cady's thumb gently from her mouth, so as not to awaken the child. The promise that she'd have buck teeth, if she kept up the thumb-sucking, hadn't kept her from relishing every bedtime when she would sneak the warm, sweet-smelling appendage into her mouth as soon as the lights went out. Despite a bad back, Rachel lifted Cady onto the twin bed and turned the swamp cooler on low, a sound that had always been as soothing to the child as Rachel's humming.

Rachel crept downstairs to begin making lunch with the ingredients she'd brought from home for this emergency—collard greens, sweet potatoes with marshmallows, and the stuff for stewing the chicken she'd bought for Sunday lunch. There would be leftovers, along with a couple of slices of Rachel's lemon pie. Such was the nature of emergencies—making do. She wiped away the tears that she'd hidden from Cady, thinking of Dr. Jonas, and wondering if the hamburger story was true, knowing that Cady was taken to great imaginings. Shaking her head, looking upwards, she whispered, "Lord it just don't seem right. No sir, no how, no way. It sure don't."

It was about 11:30 a.m. when, through the vent, Cady awoke to the smell of chicken cooking. She climbed off her bed and stood at the open window, the curtains still waving in a warmer breeze. She was just tall enough, on tiptoe, to see the top of the pecan tree on the drive and the stand of poplars that had been planted along the back rock wall. It was still warm enough for the locusts to continue their vibrating wing chatter, but for the first time in her life, there was not one sound from the backyard resident doves.

Rachel had been calling Cady for a good ten minutes through the swamp cooler's vent. It connected the kitchen and Cady's room and, when open, acted as a microphone between the two.

"Cady child, come on down here . . . and no dilly-dallyin' at that wallpaper neither. Come on and get you something good to eat before it up and gets cold on us."

"I'll be there in a minute," Cady sputtered, pressing her lips against the vent's cold metal.

"Awright then, but no monkeyin' around, girl, you hear?"

The noise it made when Cady snap-closed the vent was a clear sign that she was through communicating with the kitchen. She then checked to make sure the hygiene chart she'd made and hung in her closet was undisturbed, and when she was satisfied that everything was in order, she began the descent downstairs. Instead of bumping down the sixteen carpeted steps on her backside, as she often did, she stood upright and took one slow step at a time, sliding her hand down the polished wood banister. At the bottom, she followed the newel post's concentric circular design with her fingers. It was "smooth as glass," Frances always said.

Hopping off the last step, she climbed onto the settee in the foyer, gazing at the mural on the wall, her chin on folded arms. The hand-painted scene covered the walls from the wainscoting up. A child with a keen imagination, Cady sashayed down the mural's pastel-colored paths, alongside its painted harbor, with the men in top hats and frock coats, the ladies in long dresses with bustles. She'd even named the little dogs that occasional strollers led along the pathways of the late nineteenth-century New England scene. "Blackie, Whitey, Spot," she'd call out, shaking her finger at them lovingly, chiding the little creatures for one thing or another, like any attentive mother would her children.

"Cady, where are you, child?" Rachel called. She walked out of the kitchen, through the dining and living rooms, toward the foyer.

"I'm coming," Cady called back, crawling off the settee, running head-on into an impatient Rachel who was wiping her hands on her apron.

"It's about time, child. That chicken's been waitin' on you so long that it might not let you eat it."

"Aw, Rachel, you better stop making up those stories or I'll tell on you."

"Don't you be sassin' me, little girl. You be goin' to bed early tonight. This whole thing's been happnin' is making you fretty, and Rachel don't like that . . . No, ma'am she don't."

Cady slipped her arm onto Rachel's soft hip and leaned into her as the two of them made their way to the kitchen. Rachel served up bubbling-hot food from the pots on the stove. She asked Cady to give the blessing.

"Bless the Lord this food we are receiving from thy bounty and . . . and, uh, make my daddy okay. His name is Dr. Jonas Randolph in case you forgot. Amen."

"Amen, sugar. You gonna see your daddy just as soon as he gets to feelin' better. Just remember that the good Lord knows everbody's name. He don't ever forget nobody, especially a good-hearted man like your daddy is."

Cady picked at her food and played alone in her room the rest of the afternoon. Other than a neighbor lady bringing over a fresh loaf of bread, the house was quiet. Jonas Sr. called to ask after Cady and to let Rachel know that Park and Cully were planning to drive over to Pecan Valley the next morning to take Cady to church.

Rachel put Cady to bed early that night and, after cleaning up the kitchen, crept upstairs to sleep in the other twin bed. Having not been blessed with a child of her own, Cady had become like her own. Rachel rolled over on her side and stared a long time at the sleeping child. She smiled when she recalled Cady reciting her bedtime prayer for the first time: " . . . and If I should cry before I wake, I pray the Lord to wake me up and tell me a joke." When Rachel chided her for changing the words,

Cady told her, "Little children shouldn't be talking about dyin' in their sleep; it could give 'em nightmares." Rachel drifted off to sleep hoping that the Lord would forgive her for agreeing. She had often thought that Cady was too smart for her own good.

11

Pecan Valley—October 4

It was Sunday morning and the sun was shining brightly. Rachel was standing at the kitchen sink looking out on the rose garden when Park pulled into the driveway. Park and Cully walked on either side of Frances. She was pale. Even with help, climbing the back steps had left her out of breath. Rachel hurried to unlatch the porch door.

"Come on here, Miss Frances, let me help you on in," Rachel said.

Frances took Rachel's outstretched hand. "Oh Rachel, it's awfully good to see you. How's our little Cady?"

"Aw, she's doin' fine, upstairs playin' in her room, Miss Frances."

"I'm so glad to hear that," Frances sighed, as Rachel helped her into the kitchen to her chair by the stove.

"Boys, go make sure the garage door's locked, will you?"

"Okay, Mother," Park answered, going out the kitchen door, Cully following to disappear into the side yard, the acrid smoke from his cigarette billowing over Frances's prized roses.

"Is there enough in the house for lunch today, Rachel?" Frances asked politely. "Mr. Randolph stayed over at the hospital to be there for Jonas in case he awakens, so that'll be one less mouth to feed."

"Yes'um, I think so. I've got some chicken and greens, and enough sweet potatoes to go 'round if that's all right with you, Miss Frances."

"Sounds just fine Rachel. Thank you. I think I need to go lie down now."

"Let me help you, Miss Frances."

"Oh no, Rachel, that's all right. I'll be fine," Frances answered as Rachel gently pulled the chair out for her. "Will you go help Cady get ready for church? I think our family needs to be there today of all days. I want Cady to look nice. I'm sure Reverend Woodley will mention her daddy at the service this morning. I'll send Park and Cully with her."

"All right now, Miss Frances, don't you worry none. Rachel will see to everything. Now come on . . . and let's get you on into the bedroom."

"Oh, Rachel, how I wish I could be by my son's side to let him know that everything's going to be all right."

"Now, Miss Frances, you are as close to your boy right here as you would be there. He's livin' and breathin' in your beatin' heart," Rachel said, pointing directly at Frances's chest.

"Oh, you're so good for my spirits, Rachel. What would I do without you?"

"Now, now, Miss Frances, get on into bed," Rachel said, pulling back the covers. "Rachel's right here, not goin' anywheres . . . an' don't you worry none about that grandbaby . . . and I'll be prayin' hard and loud for Doc 'til the Lord can't help but hear me."

Rachel stayed with Frances until she fell asleep, and then went straight upstairs to get Cady ready for church. She drew Cady's bath and put out the child's favorite towel—the one with the embroidered butterfly. After buttoning Cady's dress, Rachel made her way back downstairs to find Cully having joined Park, the two of them with coffee cups in hand.

"Oh hello, Rachel," Park said, as Rachel entered the kitchen.

"Hello, Mr. Park," she answered. "Hello to you too, Mr. Cully," she said, making her way to the stove.

Cully raised his cup toward her for a refill. He didn't look at her. He'd never engaged in an actual conversation with her.

"Aren't you the gentleman?" Park said, punching Cully lightly in the arm.

"Now don't you two get started," Rachel said. "Not gonna have any fussin' and fightin' on a day like this. I got to get the child ready for church, and you two could use some sprucin' up too. Your mama 'spects ya'll to get Cady on up to church and then on back over to Concho City to hold up that daddy of yours . . . and be there in case brother Jonas wakes up. We don't want neither of 'em to be over there alone too long . . . no sir, we don't."

"No, Ma'am," Park answered, grinning, taking a last gulp of coffee.

Cully ignored her, turned his chair toward the back door, and slapped the heel of one shoe onto his mother's chair at the end of the table.

⁓

They entered a full sanctuary at the little Presbyterian Church where Cully, Cady, and her father had all been christened. Not one more person could squeeze comfortably into any of the pews, but the Randolph pew was left empty, always reserved. Only once had a poor, unaware newcomer made the mistake of sitting there. The Randolph men and Cady entered the pew just as the church organist played an Amen on the pipe organ that had been donated by Cady's great-grandparents many years before. When the rumbling noise of people taking their seats, shuffling bulletins, purses, and children had ceased, the preacher began to speak in a decided southern, not Texas, drawl:

"Members of this congregation, and guests joining us today, I open this service with the sad news that one among us, Dr. Jonas Randolph, whose family has had ties with this church and congregation since its inception, has met with a terrible fate . . ." The preacher paused at the audible shock throughout the sanctuary from those who hadn't yet heard the news about Jonas. Some of the single elderly ladies reached out for each other's hands. There were nods of pity and sympathy directed toward Park and Cully. Those seated in front of and behind the Randolph pew nodded and whispered condolences to them. Cady began scribbling on the church bulletin with a pencil she'd found on the back of the pew in front of her. She wrote over and over: "My name is Cady Frances Randolph and my daddy's gonna come get me." She hunched over the paper, cupping her small left hand over her writing to hide it from any prying eyes. The preacher continued:

"Dr. Randolph was operated on yesterday, in the wee hours, over at Regional in Concho City. It is not known what the outcome will be. May we bow our heads in prayer: Dear Lord, as the sun rises on another day of suffering for so many of this world, and in particular for one of our own, Dr. Jonas Randolph . . ."

Cady, seated between Park and Cully, flinched when one of the elderly ladies of the church reached over the back of the pew and touched her shoulder during the prayer. Park bent over and whispered in her ear. "Cady, be nice."

"No!" she said defiantly.

"You must behave. I mean it."

With her petticoats making a scratching noise against the pew in front, she took quick side-steps on her toes, over Cully's lap to the far end of the pew, by the stained glass window, before either of them could stop her. Cully glared at her as she pushed as hard as she could against the arm of the pew to avoid his grip. She swung her legs back and forth defiantly and, with squinted eyes, wordlessly warned Cully to leave her alone.

When the service ended, Cady wound her way through the crowd of outstretched arms and women's starched crinolines, to the parking lot, where she waited by the Chevy for Park and Cully to emerge from the throng of well-wishers. Cully threatened her all the way home with how much trouble she'd be in. As soon as the Chevy came to a stop in the driveway, Cady flew out of the back seat and into Rachel's arms.

There was hardly any talk around the kitchen table at lunch, except for Park telling a weary Frances what a great service it had been and how a good bit of it had been about Jonas's accident. When Cully began telling Frances about Cady's behavior in church, Rachel began banging dishes to the point of distraction.

"Park, dear, you and Cully go on back to Concho City now and be with your brother and dad," Frances instructed. "We'll be okay here. Dad's getting a room at the Ranch Motel down by the Angelus River tonight. You two stay over there with him."

"Of course, Mother, we'll call you in the morning," Park replied.

Rachel held onto Frances who waved a weak and slow goodbye to Park and Cully at the top of the back steps; Park waved back. Cully made no attempt to return the gesture or the gaze from his mother. That Frances loved Park and Cully equally, as she so often remarked, was a mystery to Park; he believed he was a far better son to her than Cully would ever be.

Pecan Valley's main drag was lined with cars in front of the few eateries in town where many of the Pecan Valley families flocked after church every Sunday. It was a time to show off new frocks or family members from out of town. That Sunday, a good many were talking about Jonas's accident. There wasn't a great deal known, and more than a good bit of gossip, about what had actually happened. There was a story going around that Renata was driving the car, even though the Concho City paper reported that Dr. Randolph was alone in his vehicle. It turned out that someone had seen Renata at Regional in a hospital gown, and had assumed that she was involved in the wreck.

Park crossed the Corona River and drove past the cemetery that held the remains and buried secrets of generations of Pecan Valleyites, including the Randolph ancestors. Cully insisted that Park stop on the shoulder so that he could relieve himself. The highway was busy with families driving back from the popular country steakhouse after Sunday lunch. He pulled the Chevy as far off the road as possible, and turned off the engine. There wasn't even a mesquite tree to hide behind.

"Why didn't you go at home, Cully?"

"Didn't have the urge then," Cully said, his lips pursed tightly around the cigarette he was lighting.

"Figures," Park said.

Park looked out over the countryside, remembering when the family took drives out to the family farm, to check water levels in the creeks or at the country club lake after big rains, or to water at the cemetery to keep the crepe myrtles alive. The conversations were often spirited, with the boys' voices pitched higher and higher, competing for Frances's attention. Jonas was of no temperament to compete with the younger two. If Frances's slight pats on their shoulders, or one of her disarming smiles, didn't calm them down, then their father would pull the car off the road, take them out of their mother's hearing range, and give them hell. With his cigarette dangling from his mouth, Cully zipped up his trousers with one hand,

and waved at a family driving past with the other.

~

Park pulled into the hospital parking lot in Concho City. Cully grabbed the keys out of the ignition the moment Park turned off the engine.

"Give me back those keys!" Park yelled, grabbing for them.

"Not a chance, bro. I'm taking the car . . . I've gotta get outta here. I'll be back after while."

"Damn it, Cully. Dad'll be furious."

"He'll get over it."

"Not a chance," Park blurted back as Cully took off.

It was just after 5:00 p.m. Jonas Sr. was standing outside the door of the recovery room while Dr. Moran talked in low tones with the staff inside.

"Where's Cully?" Jonas Sr. asked Park.

"He took the car, Dad, to go be by himself for a little while, he said. How's Jonas?"

"Son, why did you let Cully take that car?"

"I didn't. He just took it."

"You've got to get some gumption, son, and say no."

"There's no saying no to Cully, Dad. You know that. I didn't raise him. And if I had, I'd have already disowned him."

"Son, you're treading on dangerous ground talking about your brother like that."

"Yes sir, I'm sure I am," Park said, with a sigh of resignation. "By the way, Dad, where's Renata?"

"She left, said she was going home, that she was feeling rocky. It's just as well. She wasn't doing us any good staying up here. I told her I'd be here and that we'd be keeping Cady in Pecan Valley until tomorrow afternoon. She seemed glad about that."

"Yeah, I'll bet," Park said, shaking his head.

"You'll need to go get Cady and bring her back over here tomorrow. She's got to get back to school. Renata's not answering the phone. You can take the Buick, if need be, to go by there in the morning to let Renata know what time you'll be bringing Cady back."

"Okay, dad, I'll do whatever you need me to do."

~

Park and Jonas Sr. sat staring at Jonas. Park reached over to touch Jonas's hand, running his finger over their grandfather's ring, still on Jonas's finger. He resigned himself to the fact that it would not pass to him should Jonas die. Cully would surely get it. Park hated that the ring mattered so much to him. Jonas's death seemed imminent. Jonas Sr. left the room to put in a call to the local funeral home to make preliminary funeral arrangements.

Park, shifting his gaze from the ring to the institutional green wall behind Jonas's bed, saw that the clock read 5:45 p.m. He hoped that Cully would not return in time for dinner. It would give him the opportunity, ill-timed as it was, to discuss with his father the rent coming up, and the added expense of housing Cully. It wouldn't be an easy conversation.

12

Early evening—October 4

Cully drove the Chevy around downtown for awhile before heading over to the house on Bobwhite Lane. When he got there, he stopped across the street and stared at the place. The blinds were closed in the picture window and the Sunday paper lay tightly rolled on the front steps. Deciding to wait for some sign of life, he drove the Chevy into the driveway and turned off the motor.

Except for a couple of kids playing ball a few houses down, it was like any other Sunday to Cully—lifeless. Head back, he rolled down the window, lit a cigarette, and slapped the heel of one shoe onto the dashboard. When the front door opened, and Renata motioned him inside, he threw the cigarette into the yard and hurried to the door; it was left ajar. Picking up the paper from the front step, he rounded the corner to find Renata stretched out on the couch barefoot, her robe tied tightly around her waist.

"What are you doing here, Cully?" she asked with a yawn, her slender arms stretched above her head.

"Better question is what are *you* doing here? Shouldn't you be the long-suffering wife beside her dying husband?" he asked. He pitched the paper onto the sofa.

"If I didn't like you so much, I'd hate you," she said. She threw the newspaper onto a nearby chair, not noticing the front page report of Jonas's condition. "Sit down, Cully, and make yourself comfortable."

"I'll sit down and make myself comfortable after I make myself a little drink. After what I've been through, I need one," he said.

"The liquor's in the kitchen cabinet next to the stove. While you're at it, fix me a vodka rocks."

Cully found a half-empty bottle of vodka, and then cracked open a tray of ice. When he returned with the drinks, Renata was sitting up on one end of the couch patting the cushion beside her. He sat close to her.

"So you got here just in time for cocktail hour. Did you plan it that way?" she asked, taking a sip.

"You remember you told me you were going home today?" he asked.

"No, but I'm glad you're here. I couldn't take one more minute of that hospital. They wouldn't let me in to see Jonas anyway, and the old man and Park completely ignored me." She paused to take another sip. "Anyway, there was no point exposing myself any longer to that Petri dish of a joint, so I took a powder."

"Uh huh . . . felt the same way, sister."

"Just curious, you care anything about ole brother Jonas?" Renata asked.

"Where in the hell did *that* come from?" he asked. "It's not my fault he's up there banged up. He's not so special that nothing should ever happen to him. Crap happens to people everyday. Look at all those people who got it in that tornado last year. There might have been some assholes like you and me who deserved it, but probably most of them didn't."

"What would the old man think if he found out you were here with me? He'd cut you off for sure," she said. She shook the ice against her mouth to get the last sip of vodka.

"The only thing that matters is what *we* think," Cully snapped back, winking at her. "And besides, how's the old man going to find out? Neither of us is going to tell him, and there's for sure not a cat's chance in Hell that *Jonas* will ever know."

"Well, what I know for sure is that I need another drink," she said, handing him her empty glass.

"Your wish is my command, fair lady."

He noticed how fragile her hands were, the antithesis of how he viewed her. She had long, thin fingers and palms no bigger than a child's. He felt himself getting as excited as he had the night he met her in Pecan Valley Christmas of '46. Frances and Jonas Sr. had thrown an engagement party to introduce Renata to their friends. After all the guests had left, and after Jonas and the rest of the family had gone to bed, Cully and Renata had sat talking on the back steps until the wee hours. The rush of excitement he'd felt at getting close to this woman he knew he couldn't have, had made him want her all the more.

They had finished three vodkas each by 6:30 that evening. When Cully reached over, pulled Renata close to him and kissed her, she didn't resist.

"What are we *doing?*" she asked, in a raspy, low voice.

He kissed her again.

"We're doing, fair lady, what we *want* to do."

"But what are you going to tell the old man about where you've been?" she asked, nuzzling into his neck.

"None of his business," he answered, turning off the lamp, pulling her robe wide open.

The next morning, Cully thought he was dreaming when he heard the loud knocking on the door. Shaking off the effects of the vodka, he jumped up from the sofa and shook Renata.

"Renata, wake up. There's someone at the door."

She sat up slowly, parting the drapes just enough to slip a finger under one of the Venetian blinds. Everything looked awash in that surreal pink-yellow color that she'd seen all those times she'd stumbled out of dark bars in New Orleans into the harsh glare of day. Blinking repeatedly, her pupils finally adjusted enough for her to make out the two-tone green color of her father-in-law's Buick.

"Oh my God, it's the old man's car parked out front," she whispered, closing her robe around her. She instructed Cully to run into the back bedroom. Cully pulled on his pants, picked up his shoes, and hurried to the back of the house. Renata ran the glasses to the kitchen sink. After fussing with her hair, she opened the door to find Park standing there holding the puny-sized Monday morning paper.

"Park, is everything all right with Jonas?"

"Here, read all about it, Renata," he said, slapping the paper into her hand. "What's Cully doing here? He took my car last night and Dad's livid." He brushed her shoulder as he moved into the hall entry.

"He just got here a few minutes ago to ask me for some coffee."

"So where is he?" Park asked.

"He's using the bathroom in the back. Come on in."

"No. I'm not staying. I just came over here to tell you that I'm bringing Cady back over here this afternoon."

"Okay, I'll be here. What time do you think you'll get here?"

"I don't know," Park answered, shifting from foot to foot. "Just be here between 1:00 and 5:00."

"Okay, of course. I'll be here," she said. She caught sight of Cully coming up the hall. "Cully," she called out. "I was just telling Park you stopped by for some coffee."

"What are you doing here? Following me around?" Cully asked.

"Dad asked me to let Renata know that the kid would be coming back over to Concho City this afternoon. You better come up with a damned good story about where you were last night before you see him. He's mad as hell at you for running off last night."

"I was out with some friends of mine. We got crocked . . . so I ended up bunking with one of 'em. I just stopped by here to see if Renata had some black coffee, not that it's any of your business."

"I don't believe a word of that cock and bull crap . . . and hopefully Dad won't either."

"Well, I don't give a shit if you believe me or not."

"Yeah, I know, Cully, but you better give a shit if *Dad* does."

Before Park could get out the door, Renata caught him by the arm and asked again about Jonas.

"He's hanging on by a thread, Renata, not that it apparently matters one way or the other to you," he said, yanking his arm up and away from her.

"I'll be up there in a little while to see him."

Park didn't respond and headed out the door. He drove down Angelus Street toward the river. Fall was settling in with a slight chill. He had always liked the tree-lined streets in that part of Concho City, and the way the Angelus River meandered through town. He thought about the big house that Jonas had his sights on, but would now likely never have—an idyllic place on the river, nestled under a canopy of live oaks, with a lush back lawn leading down to a gazebo, a boat ramp, and a perfect view of the City Park's golf course across the river.

Park pulled the car over about halfway down Angelus Street to get his wits about him. Perhaps he shouldn't have been surprised to find Cully with Renata, but he was undone by it. He felt an old anger rising up in him. It was no time to tell his parents about Cully. They wouldn't believe him anyway. He took a deep breath and drove on.

"Renata, I'm going," Cully announced. "It was great while it lasted."

"It'll never happen again," she said.

He reached for her playfully. "Never say never my sweet," he said, flicking a finger under her chin.

"Don't, Cully. I'm no saint, but I feel bad about what happened."

"Why? You know you loved it."

"Oh, go on, get outta here," she said, her southern accent more apparent than usual. "And," kicking at him playfully, "don't you come back."

"Don't worry, old girl, it wasn't *that* good," he said, dodging another play-slap from her. Lighting a cigarette, he threw the blown-out match on the coffee table, grinned at her, and backed out the front door.

With Renata's scent still strong in his nostrils, Cully drove back to the hospital not bothering to put gas in Park's car. He rehearsed what he'd say to his father about where he'd been.

13

Concho City—Christmas Eve

The Angelus River turned a shimmering red, green, gold, and blue from the holiday lights of the large homes situated along its banks. An array of small boats bobbed gently on the colored water, some of them part of the show with decorations of their own. The most popular river display was the larger-than-life Santa commandeering a boat with the reindeer on a barge out front. Multi-colored lights were wound around the rope reins that held the crafts together, and Rudolph's nose blinked bright red.

City Park was the best place to ogle the festive displays, and despite their recent tragedy, her grandparents would drive Cady to the park that night to find the delight in her eyes at seeing the displays. Then after, they'd go to the River House for catfish and hush puppies. But before the reverie, they would stop at the hospital to be with Jonas. He had somehow survived the accident, but hadn't regained full consciousness. Cady would open her gifts at his bedside.

Neither Park nor Cully would be home for Christmas, nor had they been home since Jonas's accident. Park was putting a partnership together with a man who had the money to invest in Park's idea for a string of all-night, drive-up pharmacies across Texas. Overhead would be limited to rent and utilities for the small space, inventory, and a pharmacist who'd sell drugs and a few sundries through a window that they'd install themselves. With no other employees to pay, the inventory could be discounted to give the traditional pharmacies some serious competition. He hoped to get the first store up and running by spring. It would be located near the big new hospital off Highway 183 in Austin. One of his college friends from pharmacy school was poised to be the guinea pig manager for the first store. They had decided to call the enterprise "On the Go Drugs."

Cully had gone skiing in Colorado with some former fraternity brothers, and had gotten one of them to pay for his trip. Park was never sure if it was Cully's wily charm or his pugnacious nature that was more persuasive in getting him what he wanted when he wanted it. He'd used both with equal effectiveness. Park was glad Cully was gone for the holidays. Cully's only real value to Park was the extra rent money he got from Jonas Sr. for putting Cully up. He'd wanted to tell their parents about finding Cully at Renata's, but couldn't risk their not believing him. He needed their financial help too much to take the chance of offending them. They'd likely have made excuses for Cully anyway.

The back seat of the Buick was reserved for Cady and her father's gifts, and for the token gifts Frances and Jonas Sr. would be exchanging with each other that night. They'd been deposited into a large sack that Jonas Sr. had used for former Christmas Eves when he had played Santa for his boys. It would also be the only way to get the gifts into the hospital without having to make several trips. Frances had put together several tins of her homemade Christmas cookies for the doctors and nurses.

They'd be leaving Pecan Valley early enough to get back in time to get Cady to bed at a decent hour. The child was staying with them again. It had become a regular occurrence since Jonas's accident. With Renata in New Orleans, and school out for the holidays, Cady would be on an extended stay with her grandparents until her mother's return. Jonas Sr. had loaded everything in the car, including his wife and Cady.

"Here you are, Frances," he said. He handed her the pillow she used in her rocker to support her back during all those Canasta games they'd played. "Okay, we're off."

Cady sat on a pillow between her grandparents, gripping the stuffed bear that her grandmother had rescued the night of the accident. She had not wanted her grandmother to wash it, worried it would drown. Frances had done her best to get all the tiny bits of glass and muddy debris out of the fur, but the bear looked worse for the wear. There was a new note on it that read simply "guard bear." Rachel had found a little patch of fabric on which to write it, and affixed it to the bear with a large safety pin she'd found in her sewing kit. Cady began singing Christmas songs. Frances joined in.

"Dear, is our singing interfering with your driving?" Frances asked her husband.

"No not at all. You girls have at it."

"Do you think Daddy'll hear me sing?" Cady asked, leaning into Frances.

"Of course he will, dear."

⁓

Jonas's hospital room was dark except for one light over the bed. The small electric Christmas tree that Frances had brought and left on the bedside table was unplugged. Since the accident a little over two-and-a-half months before, Jonas's condition had gone from unconscious to semi-conscious. There was the smell of rubbing alcohol in the air. The overhead light revealed a disturbing pulsation dead center of Jonas's forehead. Frances hurried over to the bed to turn out the light before Cady noticed. Jonas Sr. turned on a lamp in the corner of the room that threw off a softer light.

"Jonas, dear, it's Mother," Frances said softly. She very carefully touched his forehead and lifted a strand of hair that had strayed. His hair was just coarse enough to require a dressing crème. No one would expect the nurses to do more than put a little water on a comb, and Frances couldn't see her way clear to asking them to do more. Jonas Sr. began pulling the presents out of the sack as Cady found the cord to the little tree. On her hands and knees, she began looking for the wall socket.

"Oh, be careful, dear."

Just then the little tree glowed with its multi-colored lights.

"See, I knew how to do it," Cady announced proudly. "I want to sing to him now."

"Let's wait just a minute, dear, until Granddaddy gets all the gifts arranged."

Cady sat quietly on the floor, playing with one of her colorfully wrapped gifts. Her grandparents stood on either side of their son's bed, speaking in low tones, each holding a hand.

"All right dear. Why don't you sing your carol now?"

Cady pulled an envelope out of her small purse, and placed it on the bedside table under the small tree. On tiptoe, she slipped her bear under the sheet next to her father, and began singing the first verse of "Silent Night."

A couple of nurses stopped in the hall to listen. "Oh my God, that's the sweetest thing I've ever heard," one nurse, near tears, said to the other. "Doesn't it look like he's reacting?"

"I do believe he is. Do you suppose we're just seeing things?"

"No, I don't think so."

Frances was applauding, her clapping muffled by the leather gloves she wore. Suddenly Cady stopped singing the carol, slid the chair over to the bed, climbed onto it, and leaned over Jonas. "You're getting well, just like our mourning dove, Daddy," she said, close to his ear. She then began singing "Always" to him in a whisper.

Frances gripped Jonas Sr.'s hand. "I think there's a change on Jonas's face. Look at him. I think he's smiling."

"I don't think so, dear."

"Yes, he *is*. I'm his mother and I know."

"Should we tell a nurse?" he asked.

"Yes, but let's give Cady a little time with him first."

"Cady, dear, would you like to open some of your presents now?" Frances asked.

"Okay, but can I give Daddy's to him first?"

"That's *may* I give Daddy's present to him, dear . . . and yes, you may."

Cady carefully opened the envelope and pulled out the two train tickets to Greenwood that she had fashioned out of stationery that she'd colored with crayon. "Daddy, I'll open this present I made for you since you're a little bit asleep. When you get awake, we'll take our train trip just like you promised, okay? I'll hide the tickets in a secret place until you're all better, okay?"

Frances sank into a chair in the corner and wiped tears away with a hanky before Cady could see. Cady then pulled another envelope from her purse, one she had pilfered from her grandfather's desk drawer. It was one of Jonas Sr.'s business envelopes that Cully had designed, with the Randolph Properties symbol in the upper left corner. It was a drawing of one of the commercial buildings in South Texas that Jonas Sr. owned that he was particularly proud of, surrounded by depictions of an oil derrick and cotton bolls to denote his business diversity.

Ordinarily, Jonas Sr. would have been annoyed at Cady for getting into his desk without permission, but that night he let it go. Frances handed the sealed envelope to him. Inside, there was a remarkably well-executed crayon drawing of their son in a lab coat with Dr. J. Randolph printed on the front; there were black and red xoxoxoxox's drawn across his forehead in place of stitches. Cady had drawn the four of them smiling and holding hands. Renata was not included.

"Grandmamma, Daddy knows we're here. He told me he liked it when I sang my songs to him."

"He did? I didn't hear him say anything, dear."

"Oh, he didn't talk. He squeezed my hand."

"Did you hear that, Jonas? I told you he knew."

Jonas Sr. patted his wife's hand. "Yes, dear," he answered.

Watching Cady tinker with her presents, Frances noticed that the child was looking especially pale, her velvet dress looser on her from the time she'd bought it just before Christmas. She'd also noticed Cady's cuticles torn and raw from chewing them, a habit no child that age should have. Too often her hair wasn't clean, and Renata would send dirty clothes with her on those Fridays after school when they'd pick her up for weekend visits to the house in Pecan Valley. As Sunday afternoons approached, Frances had become more and more reluctant to return Cady to Renata.

Frances's gaze fell back on her son. Could it have been true what Cady continued to insist, that he had gone out to buy a hamburger for Renata the night of the accident? She thought there had to have been a better reason for him to have been out on such a night to meet such an end. She got up from the chair and gave her son a kiss on his forehead. "We wish you a Merry Christmas, my dear. We'll be back to see you very soon."

They left the little tree alight and walked out into the bright hall, stopping at the nurses' station to leave the tins of cookies Frances had baked for them. A couple of the nurses agreed with Frances that Jonas had shown signs of response that evening, the first they'd seen since the accident, that they'd already made note of it for the doctor. The Randolphs made their way to the elevator. A throng of gift-juggling visitors piled out, scattering in all directions, leaving an empty elevator for the Randolphs' slow ride down. Cady turned her head into her grandmother's soft middle and cried.

The lights along the river—especially Santa and the reindeer—hadn't cheered Cady up as much as they'd hoped; after their catfish dinners and ice creams, the child seemed happier.

Frances and Jonas Sr. talked in the car on the way home. Cady leaned forward to listen.

"Did you get everything finalized with the Trust, dear?" Frances asked.

"Yes. The instrument's been drawn up. Everything's fine."

"Well, no time like the present."

"What's a Trust?" Cady asked.

"Oh it's just something we're doing to take care of your daddy and you, to make sure you both always have what you need."

"But *you're* taking care of Daddy and me."

"Well, dear, the Trust is there to help you and him if we can't."

"You can't take care of Daddy and me?"

"Of course we're going to take care of you, dear. Don't worry. A Trust is just an extra bank account. That's all. Now you sit back in the seat, dear. It's safer."

After that conversation, Cady didn't leave Frances's side for a full week.

One week later, on New Year's Eve, with Renata still in New Orleans, the train carrying Jonas Jr. and the private nurse left Ft. Worth's stockyards. It would be an overnight trip to the Mansard Clinic in Topeka, Kansas. He would be admitted there to be assessed and rehabilitated for what was hoped would be an eventual return to some semblance of a normal life. The Texas doctors felt Mansard would be Jonas's best chance at recovery. There was no facility like it in Texas. Frances and Jonas Sr. would fly to meet the train in Topeka when it arrived. Rachel would stay at the house in Pecan Valley with Cady until Renata's return.

Jonas Sr. arranged for a state room on the train that was large enough to accommodate the nurse, the hospital bed, the IV pole, and all of the other supplies necessary for the trip. Going by plane was out of the question. The nurse, Mary O'Malley, had worked for Jonas at the Surgeons' Clinic in Concho City when he first arrived, but she'd taken bereavement leave for a few months after her husband died. She was not only glad to be helping Dr. Randolph, but glad to be making the handsome sum that Jonas Sr. was willing to pay her for staying on with his son at Mansard for at least the first six weeks.

The nurse unpacked the satchel with Jonas's belongings. It contained a muffler, a pair of gloves that had been Christmas presents to Jonas from his parents, several sets of pajamas, a robe, slippers, telephone numbers, and instructions that Jonas Sr. had pecked out with two fingers on his old Royal typewriter. At the very bottom of the instructions, he explained why Cady's toy bear was included with the cargo.

Nurse O'Malley hadn't left Jonas's side other than to use the lavatory. She hadn't eaten or slept until she'd made sure that his catheter, feeding tube, and IV were all firmly in place and clean, and that his urine bag was emptied. He didn't stir the entire trip.

At trip's end, the train's porter, dressed in a crisp white cap and coat, discovered Cady's stuffed bear hidden under a towel on the floor of Jonas's state room. In the chaos of getting her patient safely off the train, she had inadvertently left it behind. It was taken to lost and found at the Topeka Train Depot but, when no one claimed it, it ended up at the house of one of the station employees, on a shelf in his child's room. Cady's note was removed.

14

~

New Orleans—New Year's Eve

Renata hurried along Canal Street, hoping to get to Marvin Gauthier's office before it closed. The pavement, still wet from a heavy rain, was streaked with the bright colors of the blinking neon signs that turned night to day along the city's wide thoroughfare. She ran on the balls of her feet, her heels coming out of the backs of her pumps. Her steps were smaller than usual to avoid slipping. A couple of vodkas had beefed-up her nerve for the meeting.

An influx of tourists milled up and down Canal's wide sidewalks, and as she approached the Jung Hotel, a large group of merrymakers poured out its front doors onto the sidewalk in front of her. She pushed her way through the middle of them, excusing herself as she went. Gauthier's office was still a city block away, and she'd promised him she'd be there no later than 5:00 p.m. It was 5:30.

"Marvin, I know I'm late," Renata said, out of breath. "Can we still meet?"

"Come on in and sit down," he said, pointing to a beat-up leather chair in front of his desk. "I did wanna get outta here early, but this won't take long."

"Yes, and I'm not going to be in town very long this time. I really need to work something out with you before I leave. You know about Jonas, about the wreck. He's in bad shape, and I don't know if or when he'll be able to work again . . . so I'm hoping you can give me some more time to pay you back."

"Renata, I've extended your loan twice now and I can't keep it up," he said, leaning back in his chair, hands behind his balding head. "I've got a business to run here. I decreased the amount of interest you owed me in spite of you puttin' up that piano you didn't even own as collateral. I gotta have that money by no later than the 1st of February, and that's final."

"Come on, Marvin, that's only a month away!"

"What about those rich in-laws of yours? Why don't you hit *them* up?"

"They have no idea I owe this money, and I can't tell them. And if they *did* know, they'd never pay it. They hate me."

"You and Doc are both on that note and they're his next of kin. I'm going to ask them for the money if you don't have it in my hand by the 1st of February . . . and that's a promise, turtle dove."

She rose from her chair, glaring down at Gauthier. "You can't do that!"

"Oh yeah? Just watch me."

"Aw come on, Marvin, you've just *got* to give me a little more time."

"No ma'am. Get that moulah to me by the 1st of February or I call Doc's folks. I'm sorry about Doc. He's a decent fella. For the damned life of me I don't know why in hell he ever got mixed up with the likes of you, but that ain't my problem."

"I despise you, Marvin. Go ahead and do whatever you want, and I hope your greed comes back to haunt you someday."

When she left, Gauthier slammed the door shut behind her. She knew from the sound of it that it would be closed to her permanently.

She walked back over to Royal, and then to the bar on Toulouse that she and Jonas had frequented years before. She took a seat at the far end of the polished oak bar, away from the door. No one else was in the place.

"What'll it be, Miss?" the barkeep asked.

"Double vodka on the rocks."

"You wanna run a tab, good-lookin'?" he asked, speaking in a heavy New Orleans accent.

She looked away. "No, I'll pay as I go."

"That'll be two dollahs, pretty Miss," he said, holding up two fingers. "Say, haven't I seen you in here 'nutha time?"

"Maybe . . . maybe not."

"Uh huh, I been 'roun' a long, long time, baby, and I never forget a pretty face."

Renata dismissed him with a wave of her hand and a smile, and ordered a second round. Being well-seasoned in his profession, the man took the cue and left her alone.

She finished her drink, and left a dollar on the bar. Sliding off the stool, she lost a shoe on the way down. Hopping around on one foot, she struggled to get it back on. "If Jonas were here," she thought, "he'd be scooping up that shoe, slipping it on my foot like I was Cinderella, and flashing that gorgeous smile at me."

Back in the shoe, she made her way onto a much busier street filled with wild-eyed tourists wrapped in last year's Mardi Gras beads, wearing funny hats, and waving all manner of exotic drink in a mass, drunken toast to the new year. The economy of New Orleans depended on, and happily accommodated, a full shedding of inhibition from its guests, and those visitors came prepared to spend large amounts of money for that privilege. Renata often remarked that she felt less oppressed in New Orleans than anywhere on earth.

Her short walk back to the apartment took longer than it should have; she had to negotiate through trouble on the way. Music blared from the open doors of a string of bars. She hesitated along the way, in the shadows, to avoid the bar fights that often spilled out to the sidewalks. It wasn't unusual to come upon a fresh stabbing or shooting.

She finally turned the corner onto Royal, making her way through the gate and across the courtyard, to the second-floor apartment she had rented for the week. Everyone she'd known in the early days, except Marvin Gauthier and Lottie Hebert, who owned the place where she was staying, had left town.

Lottie stood at the door of her first-floor apartment. When she spoke, she whistled through the gap left from a missing front tooth.

"Hey, baby doll, whatcha been out doin'?'

"Aw nuthin' much," Renata answered.

Lottie's frizzy, gray hair was lit up from behind by the bulb dangling from the ceiling of her living room.

"Well, come on in here, sugar, and take a load off. I've got some cheap champagne we can send bad ole '53 out with."

"Oh, all right. I guess I can come in for a little while."

Lottie disappeared into the back, wiping her hands on the front of her cotton print dress. Her thick waist bulged over a cinched, thin belt. She limped from arthritis in both hips.

Renata's plan to get not only her loan extended by Marvin Gauthier, but an extra bit of cash from him to pay Lottie for the room, had failed miserably. She wasn't particularly fond of Lottie, but keeping a friendly rapport with her would be in order, given that she'd have to leave New Orleans owing Lottie money. She'd seen some of Lottie's friends and, if given the nod, they'd have no trouble holding her feet to the fire, or her head in a bucket of water.

Lottie's front parlor smelled of stale cigarette smoke and mold, and the only clean thing in the place was a copy of the previous month's issue of *See* magazine with Marilyn Monroe's photo on the cover. Renata studied the shiny gold halter top the sex goddess wore, her sultry stare, and her white teeth made whiter by her bright red lipstick. Her attention quickly shifted to the upper right corner of the magazine cover: *Is Soviet Russia Collapsing?*

In Havana that past July, Renata had heard a good deal of chatter at the Hotel Nacional bar about the Soviets someday taking control of Cuba. She wondered how Russia might be on the brink of collapse but still able to take control of an island thousands of miles away. The fact that southernmost Florida was only ninety miles from Cuba, and that there'd be some strategic advantage to the Russians getting that close to America, had never crossed her mind. The nightlife at the Nacional, in the company of poets, musicians, writers, and assorted odd-ball outcasts, was all that had held allure for her those halcyon days in Havana.

When she and Jonas moved to New Orleans the summer of '47, she was as happy as she'd ever been. The good times there had at least rivaled those that she'd spent in Cuba, when she and Max Aronson were in business there. It had been ten years since she'd laid eyes on Max, since '44, when she'd left him in the bar the night soon after she'd met Jonas. Max had introduced her to the Cuban culture, the Cuba Libres, and the haunting melodies and rhythms of the music that the all-night bands played at the Nacional. She'd try to find Max. If she played her cards right, he might just set her up again.

Lottie came out of the back with a bottle of Cook's, and splashed the cheap champagne into cloudy water glasses.

"Awright then, here ya go."

Closing her eyes against the ugliness of the glass, Renata took a sip. "Thank you, Miss Lottie."

"You 'magine we'll make it to see '54 come in?" Lottie asked.

"I doubt it," Renata answered, looking down at her watch. It was only 8:30.

"The last time I saw a bran' new year in was back in '46," Lottie said, chuckling.

"For me, it was last year in that godforsaken dirt-trap town in Texas. I told my husband that it would be the last time I'd see in a new year there. Little did I know it might be the last time *he'd* see in a new year *anywhere*. He's awful bad off in the hospital back there."

"That's a cryin' shame, honey. I hate hearin' it . . . you're too damned young to be going through somethin' so terrible."

The women had finished off the bottle by 9:15. Renata said goodnight and climbed the courtyard steps to her room. Hardly feeling the effects of the champagne or the earlier vodkas, she found the lack of inebriation unfortunate. She sprawled out on the bed fully clothed and stared at the moldy-brown water marks on the ceiling. She could hear the crowds outside, but fell off to sleep remembering how disappointed she'd been to find out that Jonas had very little income when they moved to New Orleans in '47. Had it not been for the senior Randolph paying most of their bills, including their rent, she and Jonas, and newborn Cady would have been in worse shape than her family had been during the Depression. Her father had lost a successful lumber business, his well-appointed home on the east coast of Florida, and his will to get back on top. Her mother's lazy days of playing bridge at the country club, wearing pretty frocks, and employing a full-time housekeeper had come to an end.

After, the Collins family became relegated to one side of a small, working-class duplex in Atlanta. Renata's father, Frank Collins, had family there. The job he'd managed to get installing windows provided little in the way of comfort. This had driven Renata's mother to a rage so fever-pitched that she'd ended up waving a loaded gun in her husband's face, threatening to kill him and herself. Young Renata and her sister Miriam watched in horror, hiding in an old trunk in their bedroom. It had left an impression on Renata that entirely supplanted any memory of their privileged and happy days in Florida. When her mother died, Renata had managed to steal away with the last vestige of those better times: a fine Chinese cloisonné enameled vase.

At exactly 11:00 p.m., she awoke and retrieved the last bit of cash she'd hidden under the apartment's stained mattress. She slid the bills into the side pocket of her purse, made her way through the courtyard out onto Royal, and slipped into a sea of revelers heading toward Jackson Square.

The only things of her mother's that remained with her were the black lace mantilla and rosary that she carried in her purse at all times. Despite the fact that she hadn't set foot inside a church since the war years, her mother had instilled in her the need to be ready for mass and confession at a moment's notice. "Such irony," she thought. She remembered her mother's complete inability to adjust to the family's unfortunate change of circumstance. Renata's eyes narrowed in a sarcastic sideways glance. "How cruel and weak my mother was," she whispered into her rosary.

There were only a few bowed heads dotted here and there inside St. Louis Cathedral. Someone's cough, and another's footsteps, echoed throughout the Basilica. Feeling the edges of the mantilla brushing against her cheeks, she lit a candle and prayed for the first time in years for a way out of the predicament she'd found herself in.

She left the cathedral feeling no comfort, and no assurance, that the prayer would be answered. The night sky was ablaze with fireworks exploding over the nearby Mississippi. That it was 1954 inspired nothing but fear in her. She slipped the mantilla and rosary into her purse and made her way back to the bar on Toulouse for another round of vodkas.

～

The airport in New Orleans was crowded the following Sunday, the 3rd of January. A large crowd of hung-over revelers were returning to their respective hometowns across America, leaving their secrets behind in the city that would sweep them away with the rest of the street debris. She told Lottie that she'd send the rest of the rent she owed her as soon as she got back to Concho City. Lottie was agreeable. The schmoozing had been effective, saving her from Lottie's thugs.

There would be a three-hour layover in Houston. A couple of passengers, recovering from overindulgences in food and drink in New Orleans, had used the nausea bags provided in the seat backs with a resulting stench that sickened a number of the other passengers seated nearby. Renata somehow staved off the urge to join them. Staring out the window at the wetlands, she dreaded returning to parched Concho City.

～

On her return, finding Jonas's hospital room empty, she went directly to the nurses' station, decidedly agitated. "Where is my husband, Dr. Randolph?" Her eyes were on fire.

"Ma'am, it would be best for you to speak with Mr. and Mrs. Randolph about that."

"No, you tell me right now! He's my husband and I have a right to know. Where the hell is he?"

"Mrs. Randolph, there's no sense talkin' that way. I can tell you that he's in good hands, but it's not my place to say anything more."

"I'll get a lawyer and sue you all, damn you," she threatened. "Is Dr. Moran in the hospital?"

"No, Ma'am. He's on vacation and isn't due back for another week."

"This is crazy . . . you're all crazy," Renata called back to them, making her way to the elevators.

Back at the house, Renata's hand trembled as she dialed Park's number. "Where is he, Park?" she asked, swallowing the last bit of vodka from a bottle she'd hidden away under the closet trap door for emergencies.

"Well, hello to you too . . . if you're asking about Jonas, he's been sent to a clinic out of town for assessment and treatment," Park said.

"Who the hell else would I be asking about? I'm his wife and should have been told about this."

"Listen here, you told no one where you were or when you'd return. How the hell did you expect us to inform you?"

"I had business of Jonas's and mine to take care of in New Orleans, since Jonas can't, and I won't be persecuted for that."

"No one's persecuting you, but Jonas's health and welfare couldn't wait on you to decide when or *if* you were going to return. Think about *him* for a change. And while we're at it, you might want to know where and how your daughter is?"

"I know that the old ones took her. So where is he?" she asked again, then more subdued.

"Let my parents tell you."

"I'm his wife, Park. I have a right to know where he is."

"Well, I'm not at liberty to tell you."

Renata slammed down the receiver. Sitting in the living room with the drapes closed, she hadn't counted the number of vodkas she'd downed before the knocking on the front door startled her. She opened the door to find Rachel standing there, Cady at her side.

"Hello," Rachel said, holding Cady's hand.

"Come on in. I'm just waking up from a nap."

"Miss Renata, Cady's got school tomorrow, and Miss Frances and Mr.

Jonas asked me to get her back over here. If you need help, I've got a friend over here who's not working right now . . . and well, Miss Frances said they'd see to paying her."

"Where's my husband?"

"You'll have to ask Mr. Jonas and Miss Frances about that."

"What gives with this ask-the-Randolphs crap? You all sound like parrots."

"I'm sorry, Miss Renata, it's not my business to be talkin' 'bout."

Cady grabbed Rachel around the waist and looked up at her pleadingly. "Rachel can't you stay with me, please?"

"No she can't, little girl," Renata said, pulling Cady away from Rachel.

"Cady, honey, Rachel's got to get back over to Pecan Valley, but I'll be checkin' on you, sugar," she said, glaring at Renata.

"I'll let you know if I want help over here. But before you go, you can go put her clothes up and straighten up around here. I've just gotten in from a long trip and I'm tired."

"Okay, but I need to get back on the highway before dark . . . don't see good at night."

"Rachel, can I go back with you?" Cady pleaded. "Please?"

"Child, you gonna be awright. Rachel's not far off. Now go on and get your jammas on. You got school first thing and you need your sleep. I'll come in and tuck you in before I go."

"You heard what Rachel said, now get on back there and get ready for bed," Renata snapped, her eyes shooting fire.

Cady headed back toward the bedroom, looking over her shoulder longingly at Rachel. Though it was getting late, Rachel straightened up and washed a pile of dishes. The child was dead silent back in her bedroom. Even when Rachel hugged her goodnight and tucked her in, Cady said nothing. It was a silence Rachel wasn't used to from the child. She left feeling uneasy. She'd call her friend Beatrice to see about having her stop in to check on Cady, whether Renata liked it or not.

Renata, seeing the Buick disappear around the corner onto Old Oak, went straight to the kitchen to pour another drink. Cady held on tight to a stuffed cat that Frances and Jonas Sr. had given her for Christmas. Rachel had hooked the gold heart-shaped locket, another of Cady's Christmas gifts, around her neck. Cady felt for it to make sure it was hidden beneath her pajama top. If Renata saw it, she'd take it from her like all the other gifts she'd been given. She'd also hidden away the train tickets she'd made for her dad. Her need to stand watch over herself was mercifully relieved when she found Renata passed out on the couch in the living room an hour or so later. She covered her mother with a blanket and pretended she wasn't there.

15

Topeka—January 1954

Jonas stared out the window of his private room at Mansard. The snow was deep and untouched in the open fields. There were drifts at least five feet high. Nurse O'Malley sat by his side, flipping through a magazine. His seizures, both violent and silent, were coming more often, sometimes twice a day, but movement in his arms and legs was improving, and he was sitting up in bed on his own. His body had withered. He was eating, but not enough. The staff hoped that as soon as they could get him on his feet and into physical therapy, he'd regain some appetite and bulk.

Though his facial wounds were healing well, it was obvious that those to his forehead, his ear, and to his eye, mostly blind and drifting off center, would be lifetime reminders of that awful night just three months before. Despite his scars, the nurses at the clinic considered him handsome. Nurse O'Malley had made a point of showing Mansard staff the pre-accident photo of him in the Concho City Times that she had kept ready in her purse. She wanted to make sure that the orderlies and other staff knew just how well regarded he was back home.

"Dr. Randolph? Good morning, sir. My name's Joel Steiner. I'm a doctor on staff here at Mansard and have been following your case. I hope to help you while you're here with us," he continued, as he approached Jonas's bedside. Jonas did not respond. The hospital records from Texas hadn't given Steiner much to go on. No one knew what the long-term effect of Jonas's brain injury would be. Still in the beginning of his career, Steiner was developing treatment techniques for brain injury that were making news. His study and findings into how psychiatry applied to brain injury, particularly frontal lobe injury, had landed him a much sought-after position at Mansard, and financial support for his pioneer research in neuropsychiatry.

Jonas slowly turned his head away from the window and stared at Steiner, blinking rapidly. It was mid-January, and while Jonas was responding to stimuli, he hadn't spoken since he'd arrived—except once, after an experimental injection of Sodium Pentothal. The doctor asked him who he was and if he knew what had happened to him. Jonas answered in a weak voice, "You won't get anything out of me." He hadn't spoken a word since.

Dr. Steiner looked back at one of the nurses and asked for Jonas's chart. The Sodium Pentothal experiment had the entire staff baffled. Jonas had been able to speak with the drug, so why not without it? They would try again later. It was expected that Jonas would need to remain at the clinic for at least six months, maybe as long as a year.

Frances and Jonas Sr. had left Topeka that 15th of January morning to return to Texas after having been in Topeka for close to two weeks. They'd visited Jonas every day for at least three hours, usually through the lunch hour. They'd been able to reach Renata by telephone only twice, and both conversations were strained. Cady had talked into the phone once when Frances held it to Jonas's ear, but she hadn't noticed a change in Jonas's facial expression as she had on Christmas Eve at the hospital in Concho City.

They had left a small photo of Cady by Jonas's bedside, and the envelope containing the drawing that Cady had given him on Christmas Eve. They had intended to return with Cady's stuffed bear, but Mary O'Malley had regretted telling them that when she unpacked Jonas's things at the clinic, the bear was missing. In the chaos of arrival in Topeka, she told them that she must have left it in the state room of the train. Frances hated to think how it would affect Cady. She wouldn't tell her, and hoped that the child wouldn't ask.

~

The Randolphs planned to spend at least two weeks back in Pecan Valley before returning to Topeka. Rachel was to pick them up at the bus station in Pecan Valley later that evening. They'd flown into Concho City and taken a cab to Bobwhite Lane to get Cady. The cabbie put their bags in the small entryway. It was Sunday, Cady's seventh birthday, and they'd take her to the River House for catfish, and get her back home and into bed early for school the next morning. Renata begged off joining them; she was feeling ill.

The River House was busy that night. They were seated by a window so that Cady could stare out at the ducks that were settled in for the night on the river bank. It was her favorite thing to do at the River House. That night, instead, Cady pushed her spoon around in circles on the white tablecloth.

"Cady, honey, how is school going?"

"Okay I guess."

"Why don't you tell me about what you've been studying."

"Just spelling and reading."

The child then stared out the window, her chin in her hand.

"What words have you learned to spell?"

"I like that word *look* the best. My teacher drew eyes in the o's."

"How clever of her . . . don't you think so, dear?" Frances asked Jonas Sr.

"Yes, indeed, that's very clever. Have you two ladies decided what you want to drink?" Sr. asked, hoping to hurry the dinner along so they could get back to Pecan Valley. He was tired.

The child devoured every morsel on her plate, careful to leave the catfish bones intact, a skill she'd learned from Jonas Sr. When the waitress filled her empty glass with more lemonade, she drank the glass dry. She never asked about her father, not once.

"Grandmother, I don't want to go to school tomorrow."

"Why dear? You love school."

"I like my teacher, but I can read better than the other kids, so I won't get behind. Can I go to Pecan Valley with you? Please, can I?"

"That's *may* I go to Pecan Valley, Cady dear, and the answer is no, but you'll be with us next weekend. Okay?"

"I guess so," Cady answered, staring down at her empty plate.

When their taxi arrived back at the house on Bobwhite Lane, Renata met them on the sidewalk all smiles, even hugging Cady, asking her how the meal had been, and if she'd had fun. Cady didn't answer; her head down, she shook her head yes or no. She attempted to hide the little gold bracelet her grandparents had given her for her birthday that evening. It matched her locket.

While the cabbie put their bags into the trunk, Frances watched Cady disappear into the house with Renata. She felt uneasy. Renata had asked nothing about Jonas since they'd told her he was hospitalized out-of-state and that they would be paying all her expenses in his absence.

"I'm worried about Cady," Frances said, patting her husband's knee in the back of the cab.

"Oh now, Frances, stop worrying. She'll be all right."

"The child's not herself."

"Let's just get home and get some rest and things will seem better tomorrow."

"I hope you're right," Frances sighed. She flicked away a piece of lint from her grey wool suit. The velvet-wrapped wire clips of her felt hat had pinched her head so tightly that it had given her a headache. She'd bought the hat at the Gus Mayer store in New Orleans a couple of years before, and it had come out of the hat box for only a couple of hours on Sundays for church, and lunch after. "I'll have to choose a more comfortable hat to wear for the next trip."

Jonas Sr. had fallen asleep in the cab on the short ride to the bus station. When they arrived at the station, he stayed awake just long enough to board. The Greyhound stopped at every little farming community along the way, but stayed a longer time than usual at the station in Rowan. The bus driver apologized for the wait, but there had been some emergency with a passenger sufficient enough to warrant the bus not leaving without him. Frances stared at her husband's face in the light from the bus station. He was ghostly pale.

When the bus finally rolled into the Pecan Valley station an hour late, Rachel was waiting in the Buick. It was close to 9:00 p.m. Frances had to shake Jonas Sr. awake. His Stetson had fallen into the aisle. Someone had stepped on it by mistake. He was furious. Frances dusted it off with her hanky and fixed the crease. It hadn't satisfied him.

Rachel headed the car toward her simple frame house in "Colored Town," as the section was unapologetically called. It was even designated as such in big letters on the Chamber of Commerce City Map. When a couple of Negro men had dueled with guns on the main street a few years before, the police hadn't interfered, nor had anyone else. The men shot each other dead in full view of half the town.

While Jonas Sr. snoozed in the back seat, Rachel and Frances had a lively discussion about what had happened in Pecan Valley while they were away. No one Frances knew in Pecan Valley, or anywhere else for that matter, was more dignified or more intelligent than Rachel was. While it went unspoken that their friendship and high regard for one another couldn't be enjoyed in public, it did not diminish their abiding affection for one another.

While she waited for Rachel to get safely inside, Frances scooted across to the driver's side to take her husband and the enormous Buick home. Barely able to see over the steering wheel, Frances passed the courthouse, the railway station, and a few stores. The Buick would have to remain in the driveway overnight, and the bags left in the trunk. Jonas Sr., too tired to make a fuss about it, ascended the back porch steps, one at a time, gripping the railing with one hand, Frances with the other. For the first time in their lives, the two of them got into bed fully clothed with unbrushed teeth.

16

Concho City—February 1954

Cady stood on an abandoned crate in the back alley. It was the beginning of February, but warm enough to be outside without a coat. She stared up at the strobe lights crossing each other through a soupy sky. She believed they were God's fingers. Visible in the alley that moonless night were the reflective yellow eyes of a cat sitting sphinx-like on the wall across the narrow escarpment. She was comforted by the cat's presence.

She strained on tiptoe to see over the rock alley wall toward Sweezer's kitchen window. There were no lights on. It had been days since Renata had left her there, ordering Cady to stay in the house, and not to answer the door or phone until she got back. The child had followed those orders without question. Having stayed home from school, and having eaten everything she could find, she hoped that Sweezer would discover that she was alone.

Sweezer had just gotten home that night from driving Joe over to a honky-tonk on the other side of town, and had parked the old junk Ford, the one that Joe had wrecked a number of times, on the side of the house. He'd just gotten his beginner's driver's license and as long as a licensed adult was in the car, he could drive legally until he got his full license at fourteen. He was dreading it since Joe had told him he'd have to go to work after school and on weekends as soon as he could legally drive alone. Joe had not worked since Faithful's death. The money she'd left would soon be gone. Sweezer knew it would be up to him to keep them afloat.

He'd been having the feeling that something was not right over at the Randolph house. He hadn't seen any sign of life over there in days, and hadn't seen Cady once. Since they'd met, he'd seen her at least once a day. He hadn't heard anything about how Dr. Randolph was doing either. The newspaper had stopped running updates on his condition.

By the time Sweezer knocked on the Randolphs' front door, Cady was back in the house, sitting in the living room, twirling the gold bracelet around her wrist—the one that her grandparents had given her. There was only one small light on in the kitchen to help her see to get around. She peeked carefully through the blinds to see who was knocking. She opened the door just a crack.

"Sweezer, my mother told me not to open the door, not to talk to anyone, and not to answer the phone until she got back."

"Cady, you need to let me come in. Have you been here alone for a long time?"

"Yes," she answered. "But I can't open the door. I'll get in trouble if anyone sees me."

"Okay, I'll go around back in the alley . . . and you open the gate and let me in, okay?"

"Okay." She ran out to the back gate to wait for Sweezer.

"Okay, I'm here. Open the gate," Sweezer whispered, out of breath. She opened it slowly so none of the neighbors would hear the creak it normally made. "What is going on over here? Where is your mother?"

"I think she went to some place called Cuba," Cady whispered. "Did you see God's fingers up there in the sky?"

Looking up, Sweezer grinned, "Aw no, that's something happenin' in town, like some new store opening or something, and that's how they announce it around town with those big ole lights goin' back and forth. They do that in Hollywood too, for big movies and movie stars."

"That's what *you* think," she said.

"Why'd your mother leave you here all alone?"

"A lady was taking care of me, but my mother told her to leave."

"I haven't seen you leave for school in the morning."

"I don't go now . . . I already know how to read," she said, twisting her hair around her finger.

"You can't stay here alone anymore."

"Yes I can . . . I'll get in trouble if you tell on me. You won't tell on me, will you, Sweezer?"

"I won't get you in trouble, but you have to be with adults. I'll stay over here with you tonight and skip school tomorrow. I'll just write a note to my teacher and sign my pop's name. I do it all the time."

"Okay . . . my tummy hurts, Sweezer. I'm hungry."

"Don't worry, I'll go over to my house and get us some food and be right back."

Cady ate every bite of the peanut butter and jelly sandwich that Sweezer had cut in half and laid out on a napkin. She drank two full glasses of the cold milk he'd brought from his icebox.

He found four bottles of spoiled, unopened milk on the counter, two empty boxes of cereal, and a flame in one of the burners on the stove.

"Cady, did you light this stove?"

"Uh huh. I know how."

"How long has it been on?"

"I don't know," she said, shrugging her shoulders.

"My God, you could have burned the house down or gassed yourself to death!"

Cady started to cry and Sweezer felt bad for scolding her. He found *The Little Prince* and started reading it to her. She slapped at the book and told him to stop, that she hated it and never wanted to read it again, that she was going to throw it away. To distract her, he offered to teach her how to play jacks. She acquiesced. They played on the linoleum floor in the kitchen's dim light until Cady grew frustrated. She could barely hold four jacks in her small hand. Sweezer sat with her until she fell asleep on the couch. He stayed with her all night that night.

The next morning he left to go see if Joe had come home. He told Cady he'd be back with some more food as soon as he could. Not ten minutes after he'd left, Renata opened the front door, tossed her suitcase into the corner of the front entry, and set down a sack of groceries on the floor in the entryway.

"Well, hello there. I see you survived while I was gone," Renata said, poking a finger in Cady's stomach. "Did you do what I told you to do?"

"Yes, ma'am," Cady answered, looking down at her feet.

"Can't say that I'm glad to be back in this hell hole, but back I am. Are you glad to see me?"

Cady backed away. "I guess," she said.

"Whadaya mean, you guess?"

She grabbed for Cady again. Cady backed further away, knowing what her mother was capable of when she got that tone in her voice. There was a knock at the door. Renata opened it to find Sweezer standing there. He had seen the cab drop her off.

"Oh hello Mrs. Randolph."

"Hello, kid. What can I do for ya?"

Thinking fast on his feet, he said, "I just wondered if you wanted to buy some raffle tickets from me to help pay for my science club project at school."

"Sorry, kid, you're barking up the wrong tree. Go ask the other neighbors."

"Okay, thanks anyway. Uh, is Cady at school?"

"No, she's home sick today. And why aren't you in school?"

"Oh I stayed home with my pop today. He's sick."

"What a coincidence, kid. You better get on home then."

⌇

When the phone rang at the Randolph house a few hours later, Cady answered it. She hoped it would be Sweezer.

"Randolph Residence, Cady speaking."

"Cady, dear, this is Mrs. Witter calling."

"Yes ma'am."

"Dear, you've missed several days of school, and I'm concerned that you're getting behind in your work. Are you well?"

"I have a little tummy ache, that's all."

"Well, if it's all right, I'd like to drop off some homework for you during the lunch hour so you won't get too far behind. That will be in about thirty minutes, dear."

"Oh no, ma'am, I don't need it. You know I already know how to read, so I'll just catch up tomorrow when I'm at school."

"I think I'll drop it by anyway, dear."

"Well, okay."

When the doorbell rang, Cady invited Mrs. Witter in and offered her a cup of tea. The first-grade teacher laid a folder of homework on the coffee table. They talked on the couch a little while, Cady making small talk like an adult. Mrs. Witter was amazed that the child could be so calm and collected with her mother square in the middle of the living room floor, passed out under a blanket. Mrs. Witter could detect the smell of alcohol wafting up through the open weave of the covering. Cady had covered Renata believing that Mrs. Witter wouldn't notice the clump on the floor. When the teacher left, she knew she'd have to intervene, to speak to the grandparents, and soon.

Sweezer hadn't returned. When Renata came to, she took a bath, put on a robe, and began cooking the food she'd bought. Cady had been hiding in her room since Mrs. Witter left. Smelling the aroma coming from the kitchen, as hungry as she was, she knew better than to act excited. When the doorbell rang, she heard a man's voice, and then heard her mother talking and laughing with him in the kitchen.

"Hey kid, go wash your hands and get out here for dinner," Renata yelled back towards Cady's bedroom.

"Come on and give me a kiss, baby," the man said to Renata, his speech slurred, obviously drunk.

"Get outta here," she said, pushing him away. "I've got to feed the kid."

"Well, then . . . get on with it."

"Cady, I said get your young ass in here to the table right now or you won't get one bite to eat," Renata shouted.

Cady moved cautiously into the kitchen, overwhelmed by the smell of the food. She sat down at the long table between the kitchen and back room and watched her mother place steaming hot bowls of sliced beef, green peas, and mashed potatoes in the middle of the table. She kept her hands folded in her lap, careful not to show her eagerness to eat; it would assure her not getting a morsel.

"Okay, I've got one more thing to add before we dig in," Renata said, going back into the kitchen, returning with a full bottle of vodka and a couple of glasses of ice.

Cady waited patiently as Renata and her man friend took their places at the table. Ashes fell onto the tablecloth from the man's cigarette. Attempting to wipe them off the table with the side of his hand, he instead left a long, gray smudge on the tablecloth.

Renata splashed vodka into her glass, then into his, and then systematically poured enough of the liquor on each of the steaming dishes of food to soak each cold. Cady clutched her stomach.

"Go ahead and dig in, you little bitch," Renata cackled.

"Damn, woman, that's hard stuff, even for the likes of *you*. What'd that kid ever do to you?"

"What's it to you?" she asked, punching him hard in his shoulder as she rose from her chair to stand threateningly over him.

"Hey, lady, you better watch it," the man said, drawing his hand up.

When a physical struggle ensued between Renata and the man, Cady ran barefoot from the room, out the front door, and through the mess of stickers hidden in the Riley's sea of side-yard weeds. She beat on Sweezer's door as hard as she could. The soles of her feet were on fire. The razor-sharp points on the stickers jabbed into her soft flesh. She rolled her feet painfully onto their sides waiting for Sweezer to answer the door.

"Cady, what's the matter?"

"My mother's mad, and if she finds me, she'll kill me. Hide me!"

"Come on inside . . . quick."

"I stepped on a thousand stickers."

"Aw, now, couldn't be *that* many," he said. Sit down quick and I'll pull 'em out."

She winced and cried out with each extraction. When he'd gotten all he could see, he brushed his hands lightly over the bottoms of both her feet to make sure he hadn't missed any.

"Come on, let's get outta here."

He carried her piggyback across the street to Alice Bock's house. Cady held him tightly around the neck, bobbing up and down as he ran, her feet throbbing from the leftover poison of the stickers.

When Alice turned on the porch light and saw them, she opened the door wide to them, frightened by the look on Sweezer's face, and the fear in Cady's.

"What on earth is going on here?" Alice asked.

"Miss Alice, you've gotta help. Mrs. Randolph's gonna kill Cady sure as my name's Sweezer Riley."

"Get in here, children," Alice said, shooing them in. "What has *happened,* children?"

"If my mother finds me, she'll hurt me," Cady cried, sitting on the floor, squeezing her feet to make them hurt less.

"It's true, Miss Alice. She left Cady alone in the house for a long time—days—and just came back drunk and mean with some man."

Renata was yelling outside. "Cady Randolph, you better show your hide or it'll be mine!"

From Alice's front window, Sweezer watched Renata beating on his front door; her man friend was trying to pull her away. She then started across the street toward Alice's house, the man following close behind.

"Oh Miss Alice, they're headed over here. You better go call the police. Miss Alice? Did you hear me?"

Alice was frozen in fear. Renata was beating on the door. Several neighbors were looking out their front doors to see what all the commotion was about. Sweezer stormed out the front door, pushed Renata off the porch and into Alice's front yard. Renata's man friend backed away into the street.

"Get off this property!" Sweezer threatened with a clinched jaw, his face beet red, his fists in the air.

"Who do you think you are, you skinny little weasel," she screamed at him. "Where is that kid of mine?"

"None of your business . . . now get on outta here."

"Renata, come on," her man friend said.

"Get your hands off of me, you scrawny bastard."

"Don't you come one step closer," Sweezer warned her, one fist pulled back by his ear, poised to strike.

"Come here, you little son of a bitch," she said, lunging at him.

Sweezer hit her square in the jaw, knocking her out cold. She fell backwards, her head just missing the curb. With her man friend trying to revive her, Sweezer ran back into Alice's house, bolting the door behind him. Alice was at the window, shaken and ashen. Cady sat in a corner of the living room, her hands over her ears, the bottoms of her feet still on fire. Then miraculously, as if an entirely different person had emerged, Alice said in a commanding voice, "Come on, we're getting out of here before she comes to." She found an old pair of house slippers to put on Cady's swollen feet.

"Where are we going? Did you call the police?" Sweezer asked.

"We're going to Pecan Valley, to the child's kin over there . . . no time to wait for the police, and no sense getting them involved in this. That's the family's business."

"But what if the family's not *there?*"

"Then we'll go to the police over there. Come on now . . . let's get gone while the gettin's good."

The three of them rushed out back to the barn-like structure that housed Alice's De Soto. Alice's skin turned clammy, a sure sign that she was in danger of going into one of those awful states that she'd get into every now and then. When it happened, she could hardly breathe. "Nervous condition," her doctor had told her.

"I'm not sure if I can drive, boy," she whispered, running her hand over her face and grabbing her arms, pinching herself hard to feel normal again.

"Come on, Miss Alice, give me the keys. I'm a good driver. I got my beginner's license . . . been drivin' since I was ten."

Cady got down on the floorboard in back. Sweezer locked the car doors while Miss Alice insisted on running back to get her purse which she'd forgotten in the terror of the moment. Sweezer, dry-mouthed, started up the car as Alice, purse in hand, fumbled with the keys to get the back door locked.

With Alice finally safe in the passenger seat, he backed the car into the street slowly, and then pushed the gas pedal to the floor toward the big intersection a few blocks away. They had mercifully gotten away just as Renata was being helped to her feet.

Alice knew the way to Pecan Valley and provided navigation to the old Pecan Valley highway. Sweezer had never driven on a highway at night. Miss Alice, looking pale, clutched her upper arms. Sweezer repeatedly reassured her that everything would be all right. He'd have to face his father, Joe, and Renata, later. All he could hope was that neither of them would remember what had happened. Miss Alice reached over and turned on the radio. Patti Page was singing "How Much Is That Doggie In The Window." Having not heard it since the night of Jonas's accident, Cady climbed onto the back seat, rolled over on her stomach, and cried into both hands.

When they arrived in Pecan Valley, Cady directed Sweezer to her grandparents' house. He parked the De Soto on Baker Street, in front, and took Cady to the door. Miss Alice elected to stay in the car. When the porch light came on, Sweezer felt the first relief he had all evening. Cady ran into Rachel's arms.

"What on earth is going on here . . . and child, where are your shoes and socks?" Rachel asked, taking Cady into her arms.

"We had to run away. She was after us," Cady told her.

"Who was after you, child?"

"Her . . . my mother."

Sweezer interrupted. "My name's Sweezer, ma'am . . . me and my dad live next door to the Randolph's house in Concho City."

"That's my dad and I," Cady said, proudly correcting him.

"You must be the boy who babysits Cady some?"

"Yes, ma'am, that's right."

"Well, ya'll get on in here," Rachel said, noticing the woman sitting in the De Soto. "Who's that out in the car?"

"It's Miss Alice, Dr. Randolph's neighbor. Let me go get her out of the car," Sweezer said.

"Miss Alice, come on," Sweezer said, opening the car door.

"Hadn't we better get on back to Concho City, boy? It's getting late."

"We have to go inside for a little, Miss Alice, if it's all right. I need to explain what happened."

"Okay, then, but for just a little while, boy. I need to get on home. It's late and I'm done in by all this business."

~

Sweezer noticed how fancy the Randolph house was, and how sparkling clean the kitchen was. "It would be a dream to live like that," he thought to himself. While Rachel cleaned Cady's feet, applied some ointment, and put a pair of clean socks on the child, Rachel explained to Sweezer and Miss Alice that Mr. and Mrs. Randolph were out of town for a short trip, but would be arriving back in Pecan Valley the next day. She told him that she'd almost gone home that night, but something had told her not to leave. "The Lord musta been talkin' out loud at me," she said.

She served Sweezer and Miss Alice some water with Cady's arms wrapped tightly around her. Cady's feet felt better in the cushion of the fresh socks. "Child, what has happened to you?" Cady just squeezed her tighter.

Sweezer recounted every detail of the evening's drama while Alice sat silent, shaking her head in the affirmative, and wiping her brow and upper lip with a hanky that she'd pulled out of her purse.

"Is that right, child?" Cady shook her head yes. "Well, don't you worry none. You're back home safe with your ole Rachel now. Nothin' and *nobody's* gonna hurt you no more. She turned to Sweezer and Alice. "Listen here, it's gettin' up late now, and Mr. and Mrs. Randolph would have my hide if I didn't make ya'll up some beds . . . they'd 'spect you to stay to thank you fine folks."

"No, ma'am, thank you anyway, but we have to get on back. My daddy doesn't know where I am . . . and Miss Alice, well, she has her own home, and I'm sure she's anxious to get on back."

"That's right, son," Alice said, taking a sip of water. As anxious as she was, she was also feeling more alive and present than she'd felt in years. She gave Rachel her phone number.

"Well, I guess we'll be goin' now, Miss Rachel . . . but, well, I'm a little worried that Cady's mother might show up over here looking for her," Sweezer said.

"Aw, now, don't you worry none about that, son. I've got the Sheriff's number writ down in my head, and I'll get him over here in a cat's blink if there's even a speck more trouble. Thank you for takin' such good care of our little girl . . . nice meetin' you good folks."

"Yes'um, you too," Alice answered.

On the way back, Miss Alice chattered away for the first time in a very long time. She'd had no sustained conversation with anyone since Ernest had disappeared, and felt a kinship with young Sweezer that she'd felt with no one. They talked, even laughed, about their close call that night, about Sweezer's mother, Dr. Randolph's accident, and even Alice's Friday night music. She told him a little bit about Ernest, about how happy they'd once been. But when Sweezer asked where Ernest was, she said that she didn't want to talk about it anymore. It made Sweezer all the more curious. There was no more conversation the rest of the way. The only sound was the whistling around the De Soto's cracked-open wind wing.

It was close to midnight when they got back to Concho City. Alice had fallen asleep, and not even Concho City's bright street lights, flickering over her eyelids through the car window, had stirred her. Sweezer had made a mental note of the route they'd taken so he'd have no trouble reversing the route back to Bobwhite Lane.

When they got back to Bobwhite Lane, he decided to make a couple of surveillance runs, driving up and down the street to make sure that Renata was nowhere in sight. Finally turning the De Soto into its three-sided stall, he made sure all the door locks were pushed down tight before he turned off the engine.

"Miss Alice?" he whispered at first, gently nudging her shoulder. "Miss Alice?" he repeated a little louder, watching her return to consciousness. "We're back at your house. Come on now, wake up. Let's get you on back inside."

"Oh my," she responded, yawning and stretching her arms out in front of her, reaching around to fuss with her hair. "I musta fallen off."

"Yes ma'am. I'll run around and get the door for ya."

She gathered her purse, and the slippers she had loaned Cady, as he slipped his hand under her elbow to help her out. "Oh, wait a minute," she said, opening the glove box. She handed Sweezer the flashlight she kept there for emergencies. Sweezer grew increasingly jittery.

They hurried to the back door. Sweezer shined the flashlight into every shadow. They stood outside, for what seemed an eternity to him, while Alice fidgeted with every key on her ring to unlock the back door. He shined the flashlight on the keyhole until the very last key on the ring blessedly turned the tumbler. He had never felt more relieved.

Safely inside the kitchen, Alice's hand groped along the kitchen wall to find the switch that turned on the light over her sink. It revealed a filthy countertop with at least a week's worth of smelly, unwashed dishes stacked willy-nilly, tumbling over into a badly chipped enamel sink. Sweezer felt sick and disappointed at the same time. He turned his face out the open door to take a deep breath of fresh air. The kitchen smell had been overwhelming.

Alice rummaged through a couple of drawers to find scratch paper on which to exchange their phone numbers. Sweezer said goodnight, assuring Alice that no matter what time, she could call him. Taking a long look around before stealing across the street to his house, he looped around wide to avoid being seen under the street light out front.

The Randolph house was dark. He locked his front door from the inside, something he was never to do if Joe was out. That night, by necessity, was the exception. He inspected every room, opening closet doors, looking behind drapes, even behind the shower curtain in the only bathroom. He was then satisfied that Renata wasn't hiding inside, lying in wait.

In the dark, from the side and front windows of his room, Sweezer looked for any trace of her. The light remained on in Alice's kitchen. He remembered how clean and sweet smelling the kitchen in Pecan Valley had been in comparison to Alice's. On a night it seemed would never end, he also remembered his friends, Cady and Dr. Randolph, and wondered if he'd ever see them again.

17

~

Concho City—March 1954

The shingle on the front lawn was swinging back and forth in an early morning breeze. It read Law Offices of Grafton, Grafton, and Lowell in understated gray lettering. The offices were located in the nineteenth-century, two-story structure that had been the boyhood home of the senior Grafton. His pioneer rancher father had overseen its construction in 1889, and it sat as proudly as then on tree-lined Humboldt Boulevard alongside one of the only two genuine adobe structures built in Concho City around the same time.

Gerta James, the firm's matronly secretary, walked slowly through the tall double doors into what had once been Robert Grafton's father's library. Her eyes were steady on the three porcelain cups she carried on a tray, poured to the brim with steaming-hot coffee. She had acquired, with practice, the ability to walk a good distance, from the kitchen to the library, without spilling a single drop into the saucers. The senior Mr. Grafton preferred not having the coffee poured at the table; he felt it was less dignified. Grafton's son and partner, Robert III, known as Bobby, and their new partner, Bertrand Lowell, were seated at the small conference table getting ready for Frances and Jonas Sr.'s arrival.

Grafton, Sr. stared, as he often had, out one of the tall library windows, remembering the view before the ill-fitting, post-war commercial buildings sprang up along the boulevard. As a child, he'd played quietly in front of the same windows while his father worked. He'd watched finely dressed ladies taking strolls with parasols, waving at the buggies passing by. The milk cart, drawn by his favorite horse, the one he named Brownie, would stop in front so that he could run a carrot out to the hard-working steed. When Brownie dropped dead at the age of twenty-eight, he'd cried for days. Not one day had passed that the aging Grafton hadn't lamented the unfortunate and ruinous modernization of Humboldt Boulevard.

"Thank you, Miss James," Grafton said, nodding his head to the woman who had delivered the coffee with perfectly dry saucers for over thirty years. She was just past sixty, with dyed red hair to mask her considerable amount of gray. Unmarried and in need of employment, she wasn't about to lose her job to some younger woman who was yet to pluck the first wiry, colorless intruder. Fortunately, she knew Grafton's habits so well that he found her indispensable. Knowing that Bobby Jr. didn't hold the same attachment to her, she planned to retire when the senior Grafton did.

"You're welcome, sir, and would any of you gentlemen care for anything else?" she asked, as she carefully removed the empty tray from the table.

"We'll need you to take some shorthand before the Randolphs get here," Grafton answered politely.

She left the room and returned with a steno pad, taking her place on a straight-backed chair near one of the library's tall windows. It was partially opened for the first time since early fall. That March morning's breeze, though refreshing, also hinted at the sweltering heat that was on its way. The mourning doves were thick in that part of town and, between their coos and the rest of the birds' endless chirping, it sounded like full-blown spring on Humboldt Boulevard.

"Boys, wrapping up this Randolph case is gonna be mighty tricky," Grafton said in a gentrified Texas drawl, stuffing some cherry tobacco into his pipe. "We've got the non compos mentis ruling, the custody issue, the suit business, and all of 'em needing to meet up at the finish line. Bobby, what you got from that private dick Ray Harlow?"

"Well, I've got quite a bit," Bobby answered, thumbing through a stack of papers on the table. "There's some interesting information in here about cars parked over at Renata's all hours of the night . . . and there's a couple of letters Mr. Randolph found at the house after the accident from some fella who appears to be her lover boy. We've got testimonials from the Riley boy, the teacher, the maid, and the neighbor lady."

"Does Ray Harlow know to be over here this mornin'?" Grafton asked.

"Yes, sir . . . he ought to be here in a few minutes."

"Okay, let's talk about the paperwork to get over to Harold Jones at county court. You got those papers handy, Bert?"

"Yeah," Bert Lowell answered, pulling out the notes about Jonas's post-accident mental status.

"Looks like everything's in there. How about the accident report and all the hospital reports? Got those?"

"Yeah, it's all here," Bert answered.

Bert Lowell, the newest partner, had just moved to Concho City a couple of months before, from Little Rock, with a wife and three kids in tow. While he had never lived in Concho City, he had grown up in West Texas, the son of another pioneer rancher who had had dealings with Grafton's father. He was somewhere between the Sr. and Jr. Graftons in age. The older Grafton had often commented about the ideal blend of age, schooling, and experience the firm possessed. It added no small amount of prestige that Bertrand Lowell had studied law at Yale.

Continuing his line of questioning, Grafton asked, "Hear anything more from those trucking company lawyers over in Ft. Worth?"

"They're claiming no fault, citing the ole being-hit-from-the-rear ruling for their clients," Bobby answered.

"And they're claiming that there's no proof that Dr. Randolph won't be able to earn big money again," Bert added.

"Yeah, well . . . *we're* claiming no fault because ya-gotta-have-backlights-and-flags-on-that-drill-stem-pipe-stickin'-eight-feet-out-the-ass-end-on-the-truck-abandoned-in-the-middle-of-the-road ruling for *our* client," Grafton spewed out in one breath. Bobby . . . you write up that non compos mentis business, and get it over to Judge Jones this afternoon, hear?"

"Yes sir, will do," he answered, saluting his father as he often did.

"I think we ought to be able to persuade ole Jones to our way of thinking PDQ with what we know about his particular proclivities," Grafton added, peering at Gerta over the tops of his glasses, motioning with his eyes for her to leave the room.

Everyone knew full well what Grafton was intimating regarding Judge Harold Jones's proclivities. Despite the judge's bullet wounds to both legs acquired in a bar room brawl, and his consequent heavy addiction to pain killers, he continued to sit on the bench. He'd taken all manner of bribes from attorneys, and their well-heeled clients, to keep his drug habit fed, and his aberrant behavior in public and in court ignored. He would therefore be putty in Grafton's hands.

"Okay," Grafton said, puffing on the pipe, filling the room with a pleasant aroma. "The non compos mentis ruling is going to take care of getting the Randolphs that guardianship for Dr. Jonas and, with the rest of our plan, getting the Power of Attorney and any insurance claims out of Renata's hands . . . and, by the time we're done, any court'll be hard put to dispute Doc's loss of earning power for the duration. As far as tightening up the child's custody hearing for juvenile court, ya'll got Ray Harlow working on that little idea we had?" Grafton asked.

"Yes sir, by now it's wrapped up. He'll tell us about that when he gets over here," Bert answered.

"We want to have enough time to talk it over with Ray before Mr. and Mrs. Randolph get here. When will they be here, Miss James?"

"Anytime now, sir," she said.

"Go get Ray on the phone and tell him to hightail it over here."

While they waited for the detective Ray Harlow to show up, Bert and Bobby returned calls, and Miss James made another pot of coffee. She then began typing her earlier notes, with two sheets of typing paper and a fresh sheet of carbon paper slipped between. Grafton returned to the large mahogany desk that sat in the same spot it had since his father had it delivered from back East shortly after the house was built. Floor-to-ceiling bookshelves surrounded the room and held a massive number of books, mostly his father's. Miss James's desk sat on the other side of the wide hall, in the front window of what had once been the front parlor, so that she could see visitors as they approached and have a good view during her lunch hour.

Appearing at the arched opening of the parlor, Grafton asked, "Miss James? Could you please come on back to my office?"

"Yes sir, I'll be right there," she answered, just as the Randolphs' Buick pulled up in front.

"Oh dear, Mr. Grafton, looks like the Randolphs are here early," she said, getting up quickly.

"Well, have them take a seat in the waiting area, and tell them we'll be with them shortly." He quickly climbed the stairs to get Bobby and Bert. He'd thought about installing an elevator, but had decided that the stairs were healthier.

Grafton had been the attorney for the Randolphs for a number of years. Though Jonas Sr. had never met Bert Lowell, Lowell's father had done business with his father, and that was enough for Jonas Sr. to trust Bert's participation in the case.

Frances held her husband's arm to steady him. He'd been feeling unwell since January. "Weak in the knees," he'd said. They walked slowly on the long concrete walk, up the steps, and across the wide porch to the beveled glass doors. Miss James's form appeared through the sparkling, colored prisms.

"Good morning, Mr. and Mrs. Randolph," Miss James chirped, as she opened one side of the double doors. "Glorious morning, isn't it?"

Jonas Sr. tipped his Stetson to Miss James and then removed it altogether before he and Frances stepped inside. "Good morning, Miss James," he said. Frances acknowledged her with a smile. If there was one rule of etiquette that Jonas Sr. observed without fail, it was removing his Stetson before entering a room. Miss James and Frances clutched hands.

"Come in and wait right here while I get Mr. Grafton," Miss James said, showing Mr. and Mrs. Randolph to their seats. "He and the others are finishing up their conference, and they'll be with you shortly."

The two of them took their seats on the twin wingback chairs in the front hall. Jonas Sr. flipped through the pages of a hunting magazine that held absolutely no interest for him, while Frances, her feet barely touching the floor, struggled to pull her skirt free from under her on the feather-stuffed cushion. After she felt sufficiently rearranged, she reached over the arm of her chair to pat her husband's shoulder, giving him one of her reassuring smiles.

"Jonas, Mrs. Randolph, good morning," Grafton said, approaching Jonas Sr. with a hearty handshake, lightly touching Frances on the arm. "Come on into the library . . . and how 'bout a nice hot cup o' Joe while we wait for the others?"

Frances smiled widely, exposing her beautiful teeth. She was particularly proud that she'd lost not one of them. "That would be nice," she said. "Dear, would you like a cup?"

Jonas Sr. ran his finger under his heavily starched collar. "No, thank you," he said. "I'd just as soon get on with this thing."

"Come right on back then," Grafton replied, taking Jonas by the arm, signaling to Miss James to bring the coffee. Frances followed behind.

The agreeable tone of Grafton's voice switched to an intimidating bass that he'd used many times against his opponents in the courtroom: "Now, Jonas, I know all this business is exasperating for you, but it takes time to get things right . . . to make a good strong case, we need to mind our Ps and Qs. I know you'll agree?"

Taking a seat at the conference table, Jonas Sr. took a freshly ironed handkerchief out of his pocket to wipe his brow. "Yes, of course I agree, Robert. I'm sorry if I seem impatient . . . it's just that this damn thing's been hard on my wife and me and of course on our granddaughter, not to mention on our son, and we need to get back to some kind of normal living . . . and before I forget, here's another threatening letter from that loan shark Marvin Gauthier in New Orleans, trying to suck money out of me for some debt Renata piled up with him," Jonas Sr. said, handing him the letter.

"Don't worry any more about this, Jonas. I'll make sure he doesn't bother you again," Grafton said, noticing the perspiration on Jonas's forehead. Grafton strained to raise the windows, finally resorting to hitting them with the butt of his hand to loosen them up. "Another coat of paint on these windows and they'll be stuck for good," he said, with beads of sweat forming on his own brow, his hand smarting.

"Yes, indeed," Jonas Sr. answered, unaware of the searing pain Grafton was successfully hiding. "Thank you for getting some fresh air in here. It's awfully hot," Jonas said. Miss James returned with a coffee for Frances; Bert and Bobby followed closely behind.

Ray Harlow left his car on the street and walked down the back drive, stamping out his cigarette just before Miss James opened the back door for him. "Better let me take your hat, Ray," Miss James said, holding her hand out to receive it. "Mr. Randolph is a real stickler about men removing their hats indoors."

"Oh sure, here ya go," Ray answered, handing her his well-worn, dusty fedora.

"Let me take you up front. They're all waiting on you," she said officiously.

The two walked the long hall to the library. Miss James liked Ray even though his manners were sometimes lacking. He had at least always been kind to her and, more than anything else, she admired him for getting his work in on time. He apologized to her for being late, that what he was doing for the case had taken longer than he had expected. When Ray entered the library, Jonas Sr. stood up to greet him as Grafton introduced them.

"Ray, I'd like you to give a report to Mr. and Mrs. Randolph about what you've been up to the last few days. Would you like a cup of coffee?"

"Uh, yes sir, that'd be nice," Ray answered. "Well, sir, and uh, ma'am, I've been, as you know, tailing your daughter-in-law, Renata Randolph, for the last couple of weeks and have been reporting to Mr. Grafton and the other lawyers as I go," Ray said, handing Grafton the most recent notes. "I just completed the last task thirty minutes ago, and, well, pretty sure she'll be in custody by suppertime."

"Mr. Randolph, sir, we don't want to distress you," Grafton carefully interjected, "but you have to know how you figure in."

"Spill the beans. I'm not squeamish," Jonas Sr. said.

"Well, sir," Ray continued. "I acquired the diamond ring from the owner of Holden Jewelers and he knows what to do. I used your key, sir, to enter the rear patio door at the Bobwhite Lane home," he said, digging the keys out of his pocket and handing them to Jonas Sr. "And I deposited the ring in the strong box under that trap door in the bedroom closet with the $900.00 price tag still on it."

"Are you sure nobody saw you entering or leaving the residence?" Jonas Sr. asked.

"I'm real sure, Mr. Randolph. I make a business out of being sure, sir."

"What happens now?"

"Well, sir, you and Holden will tell the police that you called Holden this afternoon to tell him that, while looking for a certain legal document, you discovered a ring with his store name and price tag still on it in the strong box at your son's house. Knowing this would not be an item that either your son or his wife could afford, you were calling to inquire about it. You and Holden would then go to the house and call police to tell them that Holden has a ring of that description missing from his store, and that Renata was in the store that morning trying it on. Are you following me, sir, so far?" Ray asked Jonas Sr.

"Yes, go on," Jonas Sr. answered.

"Then you and Holden wait for the police who will come over and take the report. Renata will be taken in and booked. Holden will be waiting for your call, sir, to meet you over at the house. It's airtight, sir. I'll pay Holden his $300.00 when I get the go-ahead from Mr. Grafton," Ray concluded.

"All right, I think I've got it," Jonas Sr. said. "And you sure this Holden fella's not going to come back and want hush money later?"

"Not unless he wants me to report all the stolen goods he has, sir."

"Oh, I see," Jonas Sr. said, shaking his head in disgust. "Now what about the men you've seen over there the last few weeks?"

"Mr. Grafton and Bert have all that," the detective answered.

"Yes, Jonas, we've got a file with all the license plate numbers of the men who've gone in and out of the residence, and those couple of letters from her lover boy," Grafton replied. "And now with this theft charge almost in the bag . . . and the adultery, I think we've got more than enough of what we need to get rid of her. We also advise, when we get her out of the picture, that you tell her that Doc died. It'll be the easiest and best way for everyone in the long run, believe me."

"All right," Jonas Sr. said, rubbing his hands over his face while Frances sat stoically beside him, unable to finish her coffee.

"Okay, Ray. Is that all ya got?" Grafton asked, lighting up his pipe.

"That's it."

"Okay then, Ray, if we've got her down in county jail tonight, you can stop by here tomorrow to pick up your check."

Holding his lower back as he stood up, Ray shook hands with the Randolphs and the lawyers, nodded to Frances, and told them all goodbye. Miss James escorted him out and handed him his hat to which she'd taken a damp rag.

"Why, thank you, Miss James. This ole hat hasn't looked this good since I bought it, and that was too long ago for me to remember when," Ray said, tipping the brim toward her, pinching the crease between his fingers. "I sure do feel bad for those folks in there having to carry things this far, but they've got a real live mess on their hands, don't they?"

"Yes I'm afraid they do . . . and finer people you won't find anywhere. I know it kills them to have to go this direction, but they've got too much to lose if they don't. Anyway, you have a nice day and we'll see you soon."

She watched Ray lumber down the back drive toward the street. She thought about how, in all her years with the firm, she'd never had a case that had kept her up at night like this one had.

18

Concho City—April 1954

It was nearing dead center of tornado season and already summer-hot, but there hadn't been one sign of a storm all spring. Through her cell window, Renata could see the blooming redbud trees on the clipped lawn outside. Juxtaposed with the drab jail building, their beauty mocked and taunted her. In less than an hour she'd be escorted into the county courtroom for what she was told would be a hearing regarding the first degree theft charge against her.

The jail matron, Ruby was her name, had taken a liking to Renata, and had even secreted in some whiskey to her when she saw the all too familiar signs of alcohol withdrawal. There were long nights' conversations with Renata about the status of her case, Renata holding firm to Ruby that she'd been framed. Ruby talked to her about the criminal theft charges against her, and that she'd do well not to contest the county court and juvenile court rulings finding her unfit to take care of her husband or child, especially since she was confined. Ruby told her the sentence could be lightened, even dropped, if she didn't fight the rulings.

Flipping through a number of magazines that Ruby had brought in, Renata uncovered a worn-out copy of the same *See* magazine, with Marilyn on the front, that she'd perused at Lottie Hebert's in New Orleans just three-and-a-half months earlier. "If only I hadn't come back to this shit hole," she thought to herself. "See that thing about the Russians taking over Cuba?" she asked Ruby, pointing to the magazine cover through the cell bars. "I was just down in Cuba a couple of months ago, and everybody there thinks the Russians will take over and bomb the U.S. I think we better move to Cuba, don't you?" Renata said, grinning.

"No, ma'am, not me," Ruby answered. "I like it just fine right here in good ole Texas. You ain't catchin' me with no commies. Ya wanna get dressed now?" she asked, giving Renata a clean skirt and blouse of her daughter's that she'd brought from home for Renata to wear in court.

Renata had been arrested in her bathrobe. She was told that where she was going she'd have to change into jail clothes anyway, not to bother getting dressed. When she protested, they told her she was in danger of getting slapped with an additional charge of resisting arrest if she didn't comply. She went quietly.

"Sure, why not?" Renata answered, taking the outfit from Ruby through the bars.

"Sorry we don't wear the same shoe size. Those jail-issue lace-ups aren't the purdiest," Ruby said.

"That's all right . . . this sure isn't any fashion show. You believe me when I tell you I didn't steal anything, don't you?"

"Sure, honey, why not?" Ruby answered, considering that Renata was probably lying, but figuring she'd go along with it to keep things calm for what was coming up.

"Got a little shot of something?" Renata asked.

"No ma'am, honey, not with you goin' into court. They'd have my hide. I gotta couple of kids to raise up yet. You'll be all right. Just keep breathin' deep."

After Renata changed into the skirt and blouse that were at least a size too big, Ruby unlocked the cell door. Another attendant walked down the long hall with them that connected the jail to the courthouse. Renata was then led into a locked holding room connected to the courtroom.

"What's going to happen, Ruby?" Renata asked, seeming more vulnerable than Ruby had seen her the whole two weeks she'd been confined. Ruby had been informed ahead of time what was to take place that day in the courtroom. The whole case had the townsfolk intrigued. Fearing a run on the courtroom, the County Clerk's Office had even kept news of the hearing out of the papers, and had closed the hearing to the public.

"You'll just go in there and sit down quiet-like and let the Judge do the talkin'," Ruby answered, in as soothing a tone as she could muster.

"I feel like I'm going to the guillotine," Renata said, shuddering.

"What in tarnation's *that?*" Ruby asked.

"It's a contraption that drops a blade from way up high and chops your head off."

"Aw, honey, nobody's gonna be choppin' no heads off."

"Can you promise me that?" Renata asked, smiling sheepishly.

"You bet I can." Ruby said, winking at Renata.

Only a few people, mostly county employees, were seated toward the back of the courtroom. Ruby told Renata to keep her eyes straight ahead. Renata had refused counsel. "I did nothing that I need a lawyer for," she'd told the authorities. "I can defend myself just fine."

To her left, seated at another long table about ten feet from her, sat Frances and Jonas Randolph, Sr. with Robert Grafton Sr., and Bertrand Lowell. Frances's eyes were cast down; Jonas Sr. looked straight ahead.

Grafton had asked Judge Harold Jones's family member to get him over to the courthouse on time. When Jones entered the room, the bailiff called the courtroom to order and asked all to rise. The judge slowly took his seat on the bench, looking worse for the wear. Motioning impatiently with his hand for all to be seated, he hurriedly read out the charges against Renata, and then asked her to approach the bench. Hesitating, Renata turned and looked over at Frances and Jonas Sr. who both looked away. She stepped up onto a platform. Judge Jones motioned to her to step up closer.

Jones, known for ignoring strict protocol in the courtroom, looked at his scribbled notes and, leaning in toward Renata, spoke in low tones. "Mrs. Randolph, you've been found guilty in criminal court of theft in the first degree, and that carries a sentence of five to ten years. You are confined to county jail for that offense. As a result, together with the presentation of other damning evidence against you gathered by the prosecution, you've been deemed unfit to act as guardian for your husband, who is now infirm and determined to be of unsound mind. Further, juvenile court has determined that your dependent child, Cady Frances Randolph, has suffered abuse and neglect at your hands and, as a result, you are found to be unfit. Your parental rights have therefore been terminated. Do you understand everything I just said to you?"

"I didn't steal anything, your honor. It was all trumped up, and I don't know what you mean by other damning evidence," she answered.

"Mrs. Randolph, you'd do well to just let this thing be," he said, leaning out even closer toward her. "Seeing as how you are presently confined to county jail and will be set free only if you'll agree to leave this jurisdiction today to get that psychiatric help, I'd suggest that is a highly desirable direction for you to consider pursuing with great vigor. What do you say?"

"I say that I don't know much about court procedure or the law, Your Honor, but something seems out of order about all this to me." She felt faint, so she was glad that a fan was blowing across her face.

"Are you suggesting something improper, Mrs. Randolph?"

"I don't know, sir. It's just not what I'd think happens in a court of law."

"I tell you what happens in *this* court of law, young woman—you've got a choice. Go free or stay in jail. Which is it?"

"I guess I have no choice, sir. I'll do whatever you say."

"All right, then, go back and take a seat," he said, looking down at his notes. "Will counsel for the plaintiff please approach the bench?" he continued, casting a glance over toward the Randolphs' table. Grafton approached the bench. "Grafton, go tell your clients that she's agreed to the terms, and that I'll announce the ruling to the courtroom."

"All right, go on ahead," Grafton answered.

Renata looked over toward Ruby who returned her glance, nodding her head in the affirmative. The courtroom was quiet, but Renata could hear some mumbling over at the Randolphs' table. Grafton nodded to Judge Jones who tapped his gavel lightly before speaking, asking Renata to rise. She stared up at the courtroom's ornate crown molding.

"This is a highly unusual case, and one we're proud not to be too well acquainted with in Concho City, or out in the county," he began. "Being the peaceful, God-fearing people we are, this court seeks to do its best for all our law-abiding citizens. Given the rulings in criminal, county, and juvenile courts regarding the defendant, Renata Rose Collins Randolph, and as a convenience to the defendant, the conclusions of said courts are combined today, April 17, 1954. The defendant, Renata Rose Collins Randolph, has been charged in criminal court with theft in the first degree which holds a sentence of five to ten years with an active probation period of ten years. This sentence is hereby suspended on the condition that the defendant leaves this jurisdiction and goes under the care of a pre-appointed psychiatrist in Atlanta, Georgia. If the defendant returns to this jurisdiction within the ten-year probationary period, or ceases to see the psychiatrist before she is released by him, the sentence will be reinstated. Mr. Jonas Randolph Sr., who is named permanent guardian of both the defendant's husband and daughter, has arranged payment to the appointed psychiatrist who will also be required to send monthly reports to this court and to Mr. Randolph regarding the defendant's progress. The defendant's parental rights have been terminated in juvenile court, and she is not permitted to have any future dealings with the dependent child, Cady Frances Randolph, without the express permission of the child's guardian." Glaring at Renata, he continued. "And now, Mrs. Randolph, you may return to the jail to gather your personal effects, after which you'll be escorted to the airport for a 4:00 flight to Dallas this afternoon that continues on to Atlanta, Georgia. Is there anything more you wish to say to this court?"

"No Your Honor," Renata answered, looking over at Ruby.

"So be it," Jones said, tentatively tapping his gavel on the bench. "This court is adjourned."

Frances and Jonas Sr. hurried out of the courtroom, avoiding eye contact with Renata, and talked with Grafton for a little while in the hall before getting into the Buick to head over to Grafton's office for the payment arrangements. Ray Harlow was hired to take Renata to the airport and see to it that she boarded the plane. He was already waiting outside county jail.

"I don't feel well," Renata told Ruby as they walked back to the jail. "I feel sick at my stomach."

"Well, it's no wonder. You'll feel better when you get outta here, honey, and on your way."

"No, I think I'm going to throw up," Renata said, vomiting into a trash can in the hallway. "I feel awful sick."

A doctor was in the building seeing another prisoner; he saw Renata in a makeshift examining room at the jail. She was still reeling with nausea. Ruby was asked to stay in the room with her during the exam.

"How long have you been experiencing this nausea?" The doctor asked, examining her abdomen.

"I don't know, maybe off and on for a few months," she answered.

"I'm going to need to check you internally," he told her, asking her to place her feet up on the table.

"Mrs. Randolph, it's pretty obvious to me that you're expecting. Did you suspect that?" he asked, snapping off his gloves.

"What? Pregnant? Are you sure?" she asked, stunned. "I've been feeling queasy for months, but I thought it was pure nerves with all I've been through since my husband's accident."

"I can see why you might have been confused about your symptoms, but there's no question to me that you're pregnant and, judging from the way your uterus feels, that your pregnancy's well-advanced. I'd guess you're a good twenty-four weeks along. Haven't you missed your monthly periods?"

"I don't know . . . I mean I've never been regular . . . and I was eight months pregnant with my daughter before anyone could tell."

"Well, it looks to me like you're repeating that pattern. You'd better see an obstetrician when you get to wherever you're going, if for no other reason than to help you with that nausea. That baby's lucky to be getting any nutrition at all, considering the size you are."

When Ruby walked Renata to the waiting car, she gave Renata a hug, something Renata hadn't had from a female since one from her sister, Miriam, at least ten years before. It startled Renata, the way it felt. She didn't trust it.

"Goodbye, Ruby. Thanks for not hating me."

"Why would I hate you? You're a good egg if you'll just give yourself a chance to be . . . and now you've got that baby needin' ya. That's excitin'! Now get on outta here and start yourself a brand new life. You'll find somebody. You're still young and pretty and, damn, even expectin', you look like one-a-them models in the magazines."

"Goodbye, Ruby, and good luck," Renata said, waving back as she slid onto the front seat of Ray Harlow's car.

There was no conversation on the ride out to the airport. Ray was all business. His job was to drive her to the airport, give her the $100 bill from Jonas Sr. with a letter of instruction about what to do when she got to Atlanta, and to make sure she was on the plane when it took off. The letter said that her sister Miriam would be at the airport in Atlanta to meet her. There was also the name and number of the psychiatrist with whom Jonas Sr. had made payment arrangements. She watched the small planes circling above in a perfectly clear sky, wondering if she'd spend the whole trip to Atlanta throwing up.

When she arrived late that night, her sister was there to meet her. Renata had mercifully slept the whole trip, including through the stopover in Dallas to pick up passengers for the second leg to Atlanta. Hidden under the baggy skirt and blouse that Ruby had given her to wear, her sister hadn't noticed the slight roundness of Renata's belly. If the doctor in Concho City was right, the baby would be born in three months, sometime in the latter part of July. Her sister would discover the pregnancy soon enough, but for then, she would pretend that everything was fine, that she was back in the big city, and free.

"Renata, I know you've been through hell and back with this whole thing, and I hate having to add more misery, but I just got a call from Mr. Randolph this afternoon that Jonas died last night. I'm so sorry," Miriam said, reaching for Renata's hand.

"What? What do you mean he died? How could that be? They said he was improving." Renata said, pulling her hand away from Miriam.

"I don't know what happened, Renata. Mr. Randolph just said it was sudden."

"Why in the hell didn't they tell me?"

"I don't know, Renata. Mr. Randolph did say that they thought I should be the one to tell you."

As they drove past Fort McPherson, Renata caught sight of the enormous tree under which she'd made love with Jonas the night they'd met. She asked her sister to stop at the nearest bar.

～

The following Saturday in Pecan Valley, young Cady daydreamed from the gabled south window of her bedroom about summer coming. The blue chintz cushion of the window seat was soft under her knees. She ran her fingers back and forth over the quilted wallpaper under the window sill. The window was cranked out just enough to let in a fresh breeze to cool her face. Looking down at Baker Street, she watched the cars and pickup trucks leap over the big bump in front of the distinct, columned house where her friend, Geoffrey, lived with his mother.

April had brought with it plenty enough warmth for Frances's enormous weeping willow to sprout a brand new crop of green buds. Cady remembered the time that she and her father had picnicked next to its sizeable trunk, hidden behind a thick curtain of sweeping tendrils.

There was only one more month left of first grade. The mid-year change over to elementary school in Pecan Valley hadn't been easy, but Geoffrey and her new friend at the church, Dell Wayne, had helped. She suddenly sprang off the window seat and ran to her desk to get a sharpened pencil and her copy of *The Little Prince*. Positioning herself back on the window seat with her stuffed animals and her blonde-haired doll, she pulled out the note that Rachel helped her write. It read:

Hi Sweezer. its me Cady. You read this book to me a lot and so I'm giving it to you. She signed it C.R. in curlicued huge letters. *Rachel says hi to you. She helped me write this. I MISS YOU! Ovwa—That's frinch for goodbye!*

She then pulled out the piece of paper from her doll's apron pocket with the words mourning dove written by her father when he was explaining the difference between the spellings morning and mourning, and she added the following: *O say hi to my mourning dove. ByBy agin,*

C.R. She carefully copied the words of the note onto the front page of the book. She would ask her grandfather to take it to Sweezer his next trip over to Concho City. Bobwhite Lane seemed very far away.

The sky was a blinding blue and all along the street's one-mile stretch of mostly Victorian homes there wasn't a single picture window to be seen. The whistle from the cotton gin had signaled the noon hour; the streets emptied. Most everyone in town was home, seated around kitchen tables for lunch, then taking short naps before returning to the business of the day. Cady answered Frances's call through the vent that their lunch was ready. She bumped down the sixteen carpeted stairs and rounded the corner to make her way to the kitchen. Frances was serving up hamburger patties, summer squash, and green beans from the church lady's, Mrs. Pomeroy's, garden. They ate quietly with the back door open to the serenade of the redbirds and locusts, the occasional hiss of the steam laundry on the other side of town, and the coo of a mourning dove perched on the high wire above the rock wall on the alley. "That's Daddy's and my mourning dove," she told Frances. "It followed me here."

Part Two

19

Eight years later—Pecan Valley, September 1962

The funeral at the little Presbyterian Church in Pecan Valley was attended beyond capacity, and the procession out to the graveyard stretched all the way from the church to the last light in town. Every moving vehicle on both sides of the Concho City Highway pulled off onto the shoulder until the procession passed, a long-observed custom in that part of the world. If a vehicle didn't stop, you could bet it was from north of the Mason-Dixon Line.

No one asked why Jonas Jr. wasn't there for his father's funeral. That Frances and Jonas Sr. had lied to Renata and her sister about his dying eight years before had been a lie designed to protect them from any future intrusion by her into their lives. After three years at Mansard, and three at another facility, Jonas Jr. had been sent to a Veterans' Hospital a few hours drive from Pecan Valley where his father felt he should remain. Frances had decided to wait awhile to break the news to her son of his father's death, fearing the news might bring on a seizure. She would wait to tell him when she felt stronger.

Folks from as far away as Dallas, San Antonio, and further south came to pay their respects. Rachel stayed behind at the house to get the food and the coffee ready for the reception after the burial. People dropped by to swap stories and to eat good food until at least late afternoon. Some old friends of Park's and Cully's came just to see them. The kitchen was loaded with homemade breads, casseroles, fried chicken, sandwiches, and desserts brought by the women of the church and nearby neighbors. The Randolph house, in stark contrast to the death it was mourning, came alive with chatter.

Frances was holding up as well as could be expected for a woman who had just lost her husband of forty-five years. She and Jonas Sr. had planned, since their first year of marriage, to take a second honeymoon to Europe to celebrate their fiftieth. The neatly bundled stack of travel brochures sat undisturbed in the top dresser drawer of their bedroom. On occasion, over the years, they had pulled out the brightly colored enticements to chat excitedly about the adventures ahead. The tulips and dykes of Holland held special appeal for them both, and Frances was anxious to visit the Louvre and Notre Dame in Paris. They had planned to complete the trip by spending a few days in Italy with Frances's favorite cousin Edmond, who had transplanted himself in Rome to live a more open existence with his male paramour. Though Jonas Sr. had never approved of Edmond's proclivities, they had both served in World War I, and that commonality had ridden herd over his temptation to judge Edmond too harshly.

Death had taken Jonas Sr. a week earlier, soon after his return home from a drive out to his farm to talk to the tenant farmer about some fencing that needed repair. It was especially hot that day. Frances maintained that he had never fully recovered from either their son's accident or his heart attack shortly after. The day he died, he complained of being especially tired and had gone to the cool of their bedroom to rest. When Frances went to awaken him for supper that evening, he was unresponsive. He was pronounced dead by old Doc James who came straight over after Frances's call. He determined, without hesitation, that Jonas Sr.'s heart had simply "given out." Luckily, Cady had been at an after-school activity and had been spared the sight of her grandfather's body being transported out of the house and away to the funeral home in Pecan Valley's only ambulance.

"Oh, Rachel," Frances called out from her bedroom. "Will you get the door? I'm not quite ready."

"Yes'um. Take your time, Miss Frances. I'll take care of it."

Rachel was wearing the grey maid's uniform, with the white ruffled apron, that she wore for special occasions only. It hung in Frances's utility closet, cleaned and starched after each use, ready for the next occasion. There might be one or two of those a year.

"Well, hello there, young fella. Come on in here," Rachel said, welcoming Cady's school and church friend, Dell Wayne Wilson, into the living room.

"Boy, howdy, looks like I'm the first one here. It's all right to come on in, Miss Rachel?"

"You betcha. Go on and get yourself somethin' to eat, son, and sit on down in the livin' room. I'll let Cady know you're here. She'll be awful glad to see ya."

"Thank ya ma'am," he said, making his way to the long dining table that was completely covered in the most delicious-looking food he'd ever seen, even better than the fare at the Wednesday night church suppers. He awkwardly juggled his full plate, cup of punch, and silverware to take a seat on the edge of the living room couch. He was relieved to have a coffee table on which to set his cup and plate.

Rachel climbed the stairs to find Cady sitting in the rocker by the window. She reached down to smooth a few stray hairs from Cady's high forehead. "Cady, honey, your li'l friend Dell's come over to see ya."

"Oh, that's good. Would you please tell him I'll be down in a few minutes?"

"Sure will, honey. Now get yourself on downstairs. They's lots of folks linin' up to see ya, and Miss Frances needs you to help her with the vis'tin.'"

Cady looked out the south window to see the first cars pulling up to park along both Euless and Baker Streets. Ladies were straightening their hats and skirts while their husbands gave them a hand up onto the high curbs. She recognized most everyone, but there were strangers who must have come from far away.

She and her grandfather had planned to go out to the farm the next weekend so she could feed the lambs. Now that he was gone, she hoped Dell would take her out there occasionally, or that the tenant farmer and his wife might come and get her as they had before. She pinched her cheeks to bring some color into them, hurried down the stairs, and found Dell sitting on the couch, partially hidden behind a growing crowd of well-wishers.

"Hi, Cady," he said smiling, rising politely from the couch.

"Hey, Dell, come on," she said, motioning with her eyes. "Let's get outta here."

"Where we goin'?"

"Outside . . . follow me."

The yard had just been mowed and still had the fresh-cut smell. The roses were in their third bloom of the season, and the bushes were so loaded that it was hardly noticeable that Rachel had robbed at least three dozen of them for the house that morning. A descendant of the old yellow cat from next door was asleep in the shade by the garage, and if it hadn't been for the cars now parked all the way up and down the street, and an overflow of folks gathered on the side lawn, it would have been a typical lazy summer afternoon on Baker Street.

Cady sat down next to Dell on the steps of the former maid's-house-turned-playhouse next to the garage. The playhouse's porch was set back from the garage, hiding them from view.

"God, Dell, I can't believe my granddaddy's gone forever."

"Yeah, wow, pretty unreal," Dell said, exposing large numbers of doodle bugs as he made circles in a patch of dirt with a stick. They rolled up into hard balls, playing dead.

"Be careful not to hurt them," Cady said, reaching over to take the stick from his hand.

"Don't worry, they're fine."

She began scooping up the unearthed bugs in one hand to carefully cover them back up, averting her eyes from the ones who'd met their premature end under his boot.

"Wanna go make the drag later?" he asked.

"Probably can't. My uncles are in, and I'm sure there'll be a family dinner after everybody leaves today."

He rose from the steps and dusted off the back end of his trousers. "Okay, I better go now but, if you can sneak out, give me a call."

"Okay, I will."

She walked Dell back to his father's old Chevy pickup and they talked a little while more about Dell's deflated ego over losing to another boy the prospects of dating one of the girls in the class below. Cady promised to dance with him at the next school dance to make the girl jealous. They laughed about how she'd let Dell kiss her on the dance floor just as they happened to dance by the other girl and her date.

"Umm, I like the idea of that kiss," Dell said, raising his eyebrows up and down like Groucho Marx.

"Dell Wayne Wilson, you little stinker, remember you're trying to get that other girl jealous."

"I'm serious. You're a whole hell of a lot prettier than her," he said. "And nicer too."

"You better stop talking like that and get on home," she said, not wanting to correct his English. "We're buddies. Buddies don't kiss and carry on, and besides, you're too young for me."

"Just a few months . . . doesn't count for much. Come on, just one little kiss before I go," he said, shutting his eyes and puckering up his lips.

"No, you little mess!" she answered, play-punching him in his well-developed arm, made muscular from working on his uncle's farm most days after school.

"Oh, okay. Still friends?"

"Yeah, still friends, rain or shine, if you stop that kissin' stuff."

Her first year in Pecan Valley, Dell had stood up for her when the other kids called her father retarded, or when they teased her about how she'd be crazy or wild like her mother. She had promised him that she'd be his friend forever. He had promised her the same. She believed, without reservation, that the promises would be kept. She watched Dell's pickup disappear up Baker Street before making her way back into the house.

Park and Cully had just gotten to Pecan Valley the night before, but Cady had seen little of either of them. Cully had driven from Houston, arriving only minutes after Park. Park had not married. Cully was single again. His first marriage in 1959 ended when his bride left him a year later. The girl had written to Frances that she couldn't handle Cully's philandering. The short marriage had been an embarrassment to Frances and Jonas Sr., but Cully had told them that the girl had been unusually jealous, and delusional, and that he'd done nothing to arouse her suspicions. They didn't know the girl well enough to dispute Cully's side of the story, so they dismissed her allegations and hoped that Cully would someday find the right girl and marry for good.

"Hey, Cady," Cully called out, motioning for her to come join his group in the living room.

"Hello," she said, approaching the smiling group of men, all awkwardly balancing delicate teacups on glass plates.

"Hey everybody, this is my niece Cady. Gorgeous, isn't she?"

Cady squirmed and nodded to the men. "Nice to meet you all, but I better go help my grandmother," she said.

She backed away, looking around frantically for Rachel or Frances. She found Frances standing by the kitchen door talking with Rachel. The living and dining areas were full of people, including beautiful Marjorie Lane. Her dark-red hair looked soft and silky in the light of the dining room chandelier.

"Hi, Cady sweetheart," Marjorie said, patting the seat of the empty chair next to her. "Come join us."

"Hello Marjorie."

Marjorie had come alone from Austin for the funeral. She had gone out with Park for a couple of years, but ended up marrying someone else when Park showed no interest in anything more than an occasional dinner out. It had greatly disappointed Frances who maintained that Marjorie was the rare combination of beautiful and kind, and would have made a perfect wife for Park, and daughter-in-law for her.

"Have you seen your Uncle Park?" Marjorie asked.

"No, just at the church, but we didn't really talk."

"Well, I want you to think about visiting us in Austin real soon," she said, reaching for Cady's hand.

"I'd like that," Cady said, excusing herself to answer Frances's call from the kitchen door.

She was glad Marjorie had been invited to stay over. It would help Frances to have her there when the house went quiet again. Despite Park's reluctance to make Marjorie more than a good friend, Marjorie and Frances had remained close. Cully was staying at a friend's house and would more than likely not return that evening. He rarely came home, and when he did, he stayed elsewhere. Park would sleep out in the old maid's house.

After dinner, Cady sat in the dark, in her window seat, glad to be alone. The others had turned in early, exhausted from their long drives and the long day. Rachel was so exhausted that she had, uncharacteristically, left her grey uniform, and stained apron, in a heap at the bottom of the hamper, without rinsing out either.

Cady caught sight of Dell's pickup slowing at the corner. It then made a U-turn, and headed back up Baker Street in the direction of his house. He might have thought about throwing a pebble at her window as he had other times when he'd go around back and climb up the utility pole to sit on the flat roof outside her window. They'd talk for hours through the window. He'd even once brought her what Frances considered contraband: a cheeseburger and a coke from the Dairy Palace. With all the lights off in the house that night, he must have decided not to stop.

She thought about her grandfather in the cemetery. She had worried about him in the same way she had worried about all the little creatures that she and her dad had buried. When she called Dell's house from the kitchen, he answered after the first ring.

"Hi Dell. It's me. What are you doing?"

"Oh nothin.' Just went by your house, but the lights were all off," he said softly. "What are you doin'?"

"Just thinkin' about my granddaddy . . . out there all alone in that cemetery. Will you come get me and take me out there?"

"Aw, now, you sure you wanna do that? It's dern spooky out there in the dark and, besides, he's already gone on to heaven."

"Sounds like you're the one scared, Dell Wayne Wilson."

"Nah, but won't you get in trouble for leavin'?" he asked, hoping she'd change her mind.

"I'll sneak out the back. No one will know I'm gone . . . they're all dead asleep. We won't stay out long. So will ya, please?"

"Oh okay, but promise me you won't get mad at me if you end up sorry you went, okay?"

"Don't worry, I promise."

When Dell pulled up by the driveway on Euless, he turned off his headlights. He could still make out fifteen-year-old Cady's slender five-foot-seven frame swaying gracefully down the drive toward him. She had finally grown into her ears and mouth, had a perfect oval face, and flawless porcelain skin. Her hair had turned a much darker brown, and her thick lashes surrounded deep-set green eyes—"Perfect Irish coloring," Frances had often remarked. Cady tried unsuccessfully to downplay her considerable good looks. Budding at the very young age of nine had left her a target for the unwanted advances from not only boys her own age, but also from a few older men in town. Dell had remarked that the men had taken liberties with her because she had no father to protect her. Cady had overheard her grandfather telling Frances that he was afraid her early development would make her loose like her mother. She began wearing clothes a size too big, and had regularly hunched her shoulders forward to hide her full breasts.

It was only 10:00 that night, but the streets were quiet. Dell and Cady drove through the blinking lights on the main drag, out the Concho City Highway, and to the cemetery. The pickup rolled slowly over the gravel road leading to the Randolph gravesite. Dell backed up and turned the headlights on the large mound of sandy red earth frosted with a thick heap of flowers that hadn't had time to wilt.

"Just give me a minute," Cady said, as she tiptoed away from his truck through the soft sand around the grave. She bent down to pull a yellow rose free from its arrangement. Dell turned the parking lights on at Cady's request.

"Granddaddy," Cady whispered, leaning toward the head of the grave. "I don't know exactly what to say right now . . . I mainly just don't want you to be afraid, or feel like we've all deserted you. I'll come out and check on you often, so try not to worry. I'm . . . uh . . . sorry that you won't be here to see me grow up, but maybe you will, huh? Anyway, I love you and I'll do my best to take care of Grandmamma and Daddy for you. I promise. I have to go now. I snuck out of the house, but you probably already know that since you've always had eyes in the back of your head . . . Well, anyway, I'm going now, but remember there's nothing to be afraid of, okay? And, I'm . . . uh . . . sorry for anything I did that maybe you didn't like. I'll try to do better." She bent over to pat the soft soil before walking back to Dell's truck.

"I couldn't think of a thing to say to him, Dell," she said. She held the yellow rose to her nose and breathed in deeply.

"Well, he knows you were there. Are you satisfied now, pretty girl?" Dell asked, reaching over to touch Cady's cheek in time to catch a huge tear about to splash into the rose. "Aw, Cady, I hate it when you cry," he said, putting his arms around her.

"I'm okay. Let's just go."

There wasn't much moon that night, and even fewer cars on the highway than there had been shortly before. Cady wasn't ready to go home. They stopped at the Lone Star Café. The owner of the Lone Star had the accent mark painted over the e, as the French do, and proudly announced at the Chamber of Commerce ribbon-cutting ceremony, "It gives the place class." She sank the stem of the rose into a glass of water while a middle-aged bleached blonde woman, dressed in western clothes and moccasins, slid out from an adjacent booth to drop a nickel into the jukebox. Cady watched the jukebox arm pick up the 45 record, turn it over, and then plunk it down. Skeeter Davis began singing "The End of the World." The cowgirl sang along, with a surprisingly good voice, serenading the much younger cowboy with her. It left Cady in tears. No one in the place seemed to notice but Dell. When the song ended, everyone in the café clapped.

When he dropped Cady off at the end of her driveway, she made Dell cross his heart and hope to die if he told anyone about their going out to the graveyard that night. He promised, then tried to kiss her. She turned her head, smiled, jumped out of the pickup, and waved goodbye.

Managing to get up to her room undetected, she undressed in the dark. Though it had never taken the place of her lost bear, she nuzzled the worn-out stuffed cat that Frances had given her as a replacement, and slipped under Rachel's freshly ironed sheets. In the soft glow of the back alley light shining on her pillow, she whispered, "Goodnight, Granddaddy. See you when the sun comes up."

20

A year later—Pecan Valley, November 1963

Sixteen-year-old Cady's long legs and slender feet inched their way up the window seat wall until her knees locked. She looked down to watch the yardman giving the lawn its last groom of the season. Her old friend Geoffrey and his mother had moved across town, and all that was left of the weeping willow was a depression in the grass after it had been completely upended in a tornado right after Jonas Sr. died. Those sad events so close together had left Frances feeling as uprooted as her prized tree. The blue chintz on the cushion of the window seat had at least remained the same.

It had been a year since her grandfather's death. It disturbed Cady that life had gone on and left him behind, and that life was going on only eight days after President Kennedy's assassination. At both events, the birds had never stopped singing, the squirrels had never stopped chasing each other in the pecan tree, the sprinklers went on and off on schedule, children laughed on the playground, the mailman delivered the mail, and the lawns got mowed. She considered that the willow's uprooting had been the only show of empathy. She hummed "The End of the World," but stopped to listen when she heard a nearby mourning dove. She never heard a dove that she didn't whisper "Thank you." She wasn't sure why; it just felt right.

The day President Kennedy was shot the week before, she'd walked back to school after lunch with confirmation that the world was not as

safe a place to be as when the young President had gotten them safely
through the Cuban missile crisis. The civil defense drills had proven to
be more scary, even more dangerous, (during one of them, a classmate
had banged his head diving under his desk, requiring stitches) than the
threat that Russian missiles were poised to strike only ninety miles from
America's shores. When Jonas Sr. died right in the middle of the whole
affair, Kennedy, absent her father, had become her father-figure-hero
when the crisis was ended in October of '62.

The Principal announced over the intercom, shortly after 1:00 p.m. on
the 22nd of November, that Kennedy had died. A pall came over the high
school, and the entire town, that intensified with the collective shame and
horror that such an unthinkable crime had been committed on hallowed
Texas soil. It was at least as disturbing to Cady that her father, after ten
long years away in rehabilitation, had come home to live the same week.
She had long ago accepted his absence.

Frances climbed the stairs slowly, one hand on the banister, the other
on her thigh. Nearing the top, she stopped to get her breath.

"Cady dear," she trilled.

"Yes, ma'am," she answered, rolling off the window seat to greet Frances
at the top of the stairs.

"Will you come help me change your daddy's sheets while he's gone,
dear? Rachel's not coming today and my back is just not up to it."

"Sure. I'll be there in a minute."

Jonas had disappeared twice that week, including the day the
President was shot. The whole town had been out looking for him, and
several of the men downtown had agreed that the search for Jonas had
been a welcome distraction from the trauma of the assassination. Jonas
had finally been found late that afternoon on a bench in the park with the
park's seventy-five-year-old caretaker. The caretaker was proudly showing
Jonas the rectangular-shaped red, white, and blue Kennedy-Johnson
campaign pin he'd worn in 1960. "Leadership for the 60's" it read. Jonas
had reacted to seeing the button with an unexpected burst of laughter.
It was the same odd and inappropriate response to sad or serious things

that he'd displayed since the head injury. Few people understood the behaviors, including Cady.

Looking at the back of her head in her three-way mirror, Cady attempted to comb enough hair free to smooth over the bird's nest left from a heavy ratting the day before. It was a painful proposition; long sprays of Aqua Net had left the hair immovable. She was often ordered by Frances, or Rachel, back to her bathroom vanity to do a better job. She was satisfied that morning that she wouldn't have to make a return trip. She hopped downstairs looking for Frances.

"Okay, Grandmamma, I'm ready," she called out.

"I'm in here," Frances answered.

In the small office that had become Jonas's room, Frances had laid out a fresh set of sheets on his twin bed. A freshly ironed sheet billowed up as Cady snapped it down perfectly and evenly on the twin bed.

"Grandmamma, I don't understand Dad. He laughs when he should be serious, and he cries when everyone is laughing," she said, shaking her head.

"I know it's hard to understand, but it's the way the injury left him and we have to be patient . . . it's hard for him to adjust to being home again after being away all these years."

"I feel bad about what I said to him this morning, but he expects me to ask his permission to do things like nothing ever happened, like he hasn't been gone all these years, like he's my boss."

"I think you *should* try to include him in asking his advice and his permission to do things, dear. He is, after all, still your father."

"I'll try, but I really don't know him anymore."

"I know it's difficult, dear, and will take time, but it will mean much to him."

"Is he ever going to stop disappearing?" she asked, tucking the bedspread under her father's pillow, smoothing out the spread, and remembering the night he left her and never returned.

"Oh, he knows where he is, he just doesn't remember how he got there."

"I just hope he won't get lost again."

"Try to be patient dear. We have to help him. Now that your grand-daddy's gone, it's up to us to carry on."

"Yes, I know. Listen, I need to go downtown and get those shoes for gym class. May I take the car?" she asked, to change the subject.

"Of course, but I need you to pick your daddy up while you're down there. It's so hot out. He'll be at the drugstore. Will you do that for me dear?"

"Yes ma'am." She felt heavy after the conversation; she wasn't sure if she felt guiltier about being angry with her father, or angrier about feeling guilty. It was a matter of great confusion to her.

It was a typical Saturday afternoon along Pecan Valley's main drag. Every diagonal parking place was filled on both sides of the street, but she was lucky to get a space right in front of the drugstore when a car pulled out just as she arrived. She went into the dry goods store next door, bought the shoes, and threw them into the front seat of the car before going into the drugstore to get Jonas.

"Hey Cady," the familiar voice behind the counter called out.

"Hey Blanche," Cady answered with a smile.

"Your daddy's in the back booth. Want me to bring you a vanilla coke?"

"Okay," Cady smiled, making her way past booths filled with shoppers taking a break with their kids. His back to her, she spotted the unmis-takable bald spot on the back of his head, the result of a laceration in the accident. She slid into the booth.

"Well, hello there. There's my beautiful daughter," he said with a wide smile. It was a wonder that not one of his perfectly aligned teeth had been broken in that accident, considering what happened to the rest of his face. Despite that, though, he was still considered handsome by most of the townsfolk.

Cady wiggled around uncomfortably. "Grandmother wants me to drive you home since it's so hot."

"I appreciate that very much," he said, with the grin that had never left his face since she'd arrived. "But let me buy you a cuppa Joe before we go. See there? I'm a poet."

"You know by now that I don't drink coffee . . . don't you?"

"Okay," he said, looking over the tops of his glasses. He smiled a half-smile, as if embarrassed. Blanche arrived with a vanilla coke for Cady in one hand, the coffee decanter in the other.

"How's about a little warm up Doc?"

"Yes, thank you, young lady."

"You betcha," she answered with a wink, always pleased to be referred to as a young lady being well past forty.

"Dad, we've gotta hurry. It's a quarter 'til. I swear to God, I've never seen anyone so slow, not even the old folks out at the nursing home."

His face flushed. "Don't rush me," he said.

"If I don't, you'll miss supper and you sure wouldn't like that," she said more softly.

Jonas smiled, shook his head no, and took one last sip. Cady felt guilty for being impatient.

Cady let her father out at the back steps while she drove the car into the garage and pulled the doors shut. The fierce Texas sun, along with the sticky sap from the Pecan tree, and the constant rain of bird droppings from its canopy, made keeping the car in the garage a necessity.

After locking the garage door, she ran through the kitchen and past Frances and Jonas who were already seated at the table. It was close to supper. Dell would be picking her up at 6:30 to go to the Dairy Palace for burgers, and then to the drive-in for a double feature.

Two Elvis movies, both filmed in Hawaii, were set to show back-to-back. One had come out the year before, and the other back in '61. Pecan Valley was often three years behind the bigger towns getting films. No one seemed to care. Cady couldn't wait to take the three-mile drive out to the Western Skies Drive-In, to clamp her speaker on the car window, and to wait for the darkness to bring the huge outdoor screen to life. It would be the last double feature of the season.

Jonas, then forty-four, sat quietly that evening in the chair by his father's old desk staring out through the open blinds beyond the side porch. The lights were on in the large, columned house across the way, where Geoffrey and his mother had once lived, and he could see the three children who lived there running through the home's dining room while their parents pored over papers on the dining room table. Lynn and Bob Simms had both been friends of Jonas's since childhood, and their parents had been friends. Jonas remembered them well. They made sure he got to church every Sunday, and Lynn's cinnamon rolls were a Randolph family favorite.

Jonas remembered everything of his past, but seemingly nothing from the time of his accident forward. Had it not been for the hunger pangs that arrived at precisely 8:00 a.m., noon, and 5:00 p.m. every day, and the accuracy of his Timex, he'd have been lost in time. Every evening near 9:00 p.m., he'd open and shut the blinds a full three times in a row before closing them for the evening to get undressed. It would take a full hour. Every movement had to be repeated and precise: he tugged and pulled at every wrinkle of both his dress shirt and coat jacket that he'd hung on the back of his father's desk chair, until both were in perfect alignment. The whole routine was repeated twice more. He placed his tie directly over the middle of his coat and shirt, and then straightened it the same number of times. His suit pants, put through the same rigorous routine, were laid across the arm of the chair.

His father's desk drawers had been emptied of business papers and replaced with Jonas's socks, underwear, and pajamas. The top drawer held his glasses, comb, handkerchiefs, and other small items. He opened and shut each drawer several times and buttoned each button of his pajamas two or three times until his brain could mercifully find the permission it needed to allow him to slip into bed and go to sleep.

"Jonas, dear, are you ready for bed?" Frances asked sweetly through the closed door.

"Yes, Mother."

"You forgot to leave the door open, son." She opened it a crack.

"Oh yes. Sorry, Mother. I forgot."

"I'll leave it just ajar in case you need anything in the night, dear."

"Thank you, Mother, and goodnight," he said, his Phenobarbital taking effect.

"Goodnight, dear Jonas." She blew him a kiss.

"Tell Cady Frances goodnight for me, will you?"

"She's out for the evening but you'll see her in the morning, dear."

He had pulled up the covers to just under his nose. His voice trailed off into a mumble. "See you when the sun comes up, Mother."

He had experienced two grand mal seizures during the night in the week since he'd come home to live. Frances had found herself lying awake most every night, anticipating a raging return. She'd found him both times halfway out of bed, his torso on the floor, shaking violently, his lips blue. Afterward, the late night calls to Doc James left her assured that Jonas would be okay, that she could go back to sleep. Doc James told her that the adjustment to the changes in his family life, and returning home after so long away, had no doubt contributed.

Already in her pajamas and robe, Frances took a seat in her wicker rocker to read a little and to wait up for Cady who promised to be home before midnight. She thought about that October night in '53 when she and Jonas Sr. had gotten the call from the hospital about the accident, and she shook her head wondering how they had ever lived through that awful event. That she had, provided hope that she'd find a way to live through losing her husband. Rachel would be a great help. She had a fearless way of handling Jonas's seizures and odd behaviors, and having been a widow for many years, she'd help Frances join the ranks.

Frances went to the kitchen, made some milk toast, and sipped soothing spoonfuls of the warm, buttery concoction from her place at the end of the table. It was a favorite late-night treat that she and Jonas Sr. had enjoyed together over the years. Glancing over at his empty chair, she felt heavy, lonely, and disconnected. When Cady came bounding through the kitchen door, the weight lifted.

They talked until 1:00 a.m. about their summer plan to see *My Fair Lady* at the Muny in St. Louis. It would be an early graduation present to Cady, and would be coupled with a trip, the two-hour drive over to Columbia, for a campus tour of the University of Missouri where Cady would be studying journalism. When Frances climbed into bed that night, she felt more connected to the person she'd been, before she was a widow, when she could reach over to take her husband's hand in the middle of the night. It was hard sleeping alone. She swore to Rachel that she could smell his hairdressing crème on his pillow. Rachel had told her: "They's a whole lotta 'memberin' goes on in your nose. I gets to smellin' things too, that's not even there . . . just thinkin' 'bout 'em."

21

Concho City—Spring 1965

It would be Cady's last piano recital before graduating high school, and she was ready for the piano lessons to end. Every chair in the music room at Darnell Houghton's home in Concho City was filled. Park had driven in from Austin to attend. That had pleased Frances. Cady waited in the side room for Houghton to announce her. She was next on the program. That she had played the Brahms piece to perfection earlier in the day hadn't quelled her nervousness as she peeked out at the hand-picked crowd of guests. She was Houghton's lone student from Pecan Valley. The other six of Houghton's students lived in Concho City. He had invited every music teacher that side of the Rio Grande to show off his prowess. The few symphony patrons he'd invited were given front row seats.

Cady and Frances had gone over to Concho City earlier that day to do some shopping when Cady spotted a very tall, well-dressed young man at the department store. They locked eyes. He smiled at her, then hesitated, before disappearing out the huge glass doors of the store. She'd had the strong urge to run after him, but Frances had called to her at the same time. Adrenaline coursed through her chest. "What if that was Sweezer Riley?" she thought to herself. Though she hadn't seen him since the night she'd run away to Pecan Valley with him and Alice Bock eleven years before, he'd come to mind, unbidden it had seemed, at odd intervals. When she was fourteen, she called Sweezer's old number. She had found it in a file box that her grandfather had kept. The woman who answered the phone said she'd never heard of Sweezer or Joe Riley, and that they'd had that number for a long while. Cady had never tried to reach him again.

She played the Brahms Lullaby well that night, managing not to hurry through it, as was her habit. Houghton, who had bitten his lip throughout her performance, had looked around wildly for reactions from the symphony women. During the applause, Jonas shouted "Bravo!" He had tried to stand up, but had lost his balance, falling back into his chair. There were nervous giggles from the younger ones in the audience at his enthusiasm. Frances patted him on the knee to quiet him down. Park paid no mind. Cady had grown used to her father's enthusiastic outbursts, but had never become comfortable with them.

Cady joined Frances, her father, and Park to listen to the final performance of the evening. Houghton himself would be entertaining his guests with a Bach Fugue on his newly acquired late eighteenth-century harpsichord, under which he'd had a special revolving platform built. It was as much to showcase himself as his rare find. He reminded Cady more of Liberace than a strict classicist. When Jonas leaned forward to wink at her with his one good eye, Cady thought she had caught a glimpse of the old Jonas before the accident. She quickly turned her attention back to Houghton, unable to trust that the father she had once known so well could still exist behind his odd and alien gaze.

After the concert, the four of them headed to the Old Ranch Restaurant for a bite to eat before heading back to Pecan Valley. Jonas cracked silly jokes throughout the meal. Cady talked about thinking she might have seen Sweezer. Jonas said he remembered Sweezer, but Cady doubted it. Park recounted the cupcake story, remembering it had been Sweezer's birthday the day of Jonas's accident. Cady was learning more about her father, about how his memory worked. He was able to remember his past in great detail, but from his accident forward, he lived in the moment only, remembering nothing that went before or was to come. He knew his family and old friends. Cady held firm to the hope that he knew more than was apparent, despite the belief the doctors and her elders held that the once-handsome, brilliant, and charming Dr. Jonas Randolph was essentially dead and gone.

On the way back to Pecan Valley, Frances and Jonas slept while Cady drove. A country star sang "Hello Vietnam" on the car's radio. Frances's and Jonas's snores whistled in unison. They were still asleep when she pulled into the driveway at 161. Park had followed behind. He would stay overnight to talk over some business with Frances. He and Frances walked Jonas up the back steps while Cady put the Buick away. Later, Frances found Jonas asleep in his chair partially undressed. Doc James had warned that not getting enough rest could trigger a seizure. He'd been seizure-free for an entire year. Frances helped him get ready for bed.

The next morning, Frances and Jonas stood at the end of the driveway waving goodbye to Park while Cady packed up all her music and theory books for storage in the attic. Eleven years of piano lessons, and the last three with Darnell Houghton, had left her ready to leave music behind. She smiled as she threw the last music book into the box along with a stack of the *Keyboard Quarterly*. "No more music . . . not for awhile," she'd declared to Frances. Graduation from high school was approaching, and the whole town was getting ready.

"Cady," Rachel called through the vent from the kitchen. "Nancy's on the line. Come on down and talk to her."

"Tell her I'm on my way down," Cady answered, snapping the vent cover shut and making double-time down the stairs to the kitchen phone.

"Hi Nancy, whatcha doin'?"

"Aw nuthin," Nancy answered. "What time ya want me to pick you up? I've got the car 'til 10:00."

"That's neat. Pick me up at 6:30 and we'll go get a coke and make the drag, okay?"

"That's a deal. I'll honk out front at 6:30," Nancy said, hanging up the receiver.

Cady was standing on the sidewalk when Nancy pulled up. "My God, you'll never guess what just happened," Cady said, opening the Oldsmobile's heavy door, careful to not catch it on the curb. In the short distance between Nancy's house and Cady's, there hadn't been time for the car's air conditioner to cool off the clear vinyl seat covers. Cady bounced onto the scalding plastic. Nancy took off up Euless.

"What? Tell me!" Nancy shrieked.

"I just talked with my mother," she said, grabbing a dirty towel from the floorboard to slide under her legs.

"What? I thought she was dead!"

"That's what I was told, but I never believed it. Anyway, a long time ago my grandfather told me never to take any collect calls from her, or anyone calling for her, but they'd just left to take a spin, and the phone rang, and it was her."

"And? Tell me, my God, what happened?"

"And I accepted the call."

"Oh Lord, so what did she say?"

"She said she was in Chicago, and that I had a little brother who was eleven . . . and then she asked me if I realized that if I ran into them on the street, we wouldn't recognize one another."

"What? How could you have a little brother?"

"I don't know. It must have happened . . . she must have gotten knocked up just before the accident."

"Did she say what his name was?"

"She called him Turner. If that isn't the strangest name . . . "

Nancy pulled the car over, under a tree, to give her full attention to the conversation.

"So *then* what?"

"Well, she gave me this load of crap about how poor they were, and how they needed money, and would I talk to my grandmother to see if she would help. I told her I certainly would not, and that I didn't care what happened to either one of them."

"Oh my God, you *didn't!* And then what?"

"And then she asked me if I was going to college and I told her yes, of course I was, and she said 'bully for you' and then I hung up on her."

"Wow," was all Nancy could muster.

"Come on, let's just go make the drag and forget about it," Cady said, laughing nervously, turning up the radio.

They stopped at the Dairy Palace for jumbo drinks and were followed by a carload of boys for two complete drags before the boys sped out the Concho City Highway. Two-thirds of Cady's life had been spent in Pecan Valley, and she figured she knew as much about Nancy's life as she did her own. There were twelve girls who referred to themselves as "the group." For such a small school, there were at least four cliques of girls and an equal number for the boys.

There was the strange new territory, and the awkwardness, for the colored students, as they were most often called, who were integrated into Pecan Valley's white schools for the first time that school year of '64-'65. Two of those girls in Cady's class stuck solely and closely together, despite their having been mortal enemies all their years at their segregated Booker T. Washington School. Rachel maintained that integration had been the best thing that had ever happened to them, and proof that God did indeed work in mysterious ways. Cady wasn't so sure she agreed with Rachel's conclusion; she told Rachel that she knew how it felt to be an outsider, how it can scare a person into a corner. Cady had her doubts about whether the girls would remain close after graduation, when they would be free to leave their own sequestered corner.

The second and third-generation, American-born Mexican kids didn't drift outside their own groups, since it was clear that the social divide between them and the Anglos was not to be crossed. But during her junior year, Cady had a mad crush on a boy named Carlos. It had strangely endeared her to the boy's sister, who was normally dead set against outside dating. So that Cady and Carlos could see each other, Carlos's sister had even sneaked Cady into the drive-in on one of the Wednesday nights that was designated by the owner as "Latin American Night." It was destined, however, to be a short-lived affair, with their only other means of contact being the little love notes that were secreted away in books or lockers, or delivered at school, one to the other, by Carlos's sister.

And then there were the country girls and boys, mostly of German or Czech origin, who were the children of enterprising farmers who had immigrated to certain rural areas of Texas in the 1880s. They were bussed to school in Pecan Valley from outlying farming communities. Although they often had Catholicism in common with their Latin American counterparts, it wasn't enough to bridge their cultural gap. Bussed back to their family farms after school every day, the country girls stayed mostly to themselves.

"Nancy ... Cady!" several girls shrieked, pulling into the parking lot at the Dairy Palace.

"Hi ya'll. We're going to the park. Meet us down there?"

Carloads of girls sat in the park by the creek, on the hoods of their cars, and talked about graduation coming up, telling stories about boys, about their escapades through the years, their plans for the future. Five car radios blared in sync, the girls singing along with the Beatles, at the tops of their lungs. An elderly couple driving by, rolled up their windows, and glared disapprovingly at the girls.

"Okay, we all love each other to death, so I hope none of us gets off so far that we don't come back—and I'm talkin' about you, Cady Frances Randolph," Nancy said, pointing at Cady, her throat tightening as she fought back tears. "Anyway, Cady, remember us when you go off into the big world and get famous and marry some highfalutin somebody or other."

At 9:30 that night Cady and Nancy left the group to make the drag a couple more times before heading home. When Cady spotted Dell Wayne's pickup at the Dairy Palace, she left Nancy to get a ride home with him. He drove her home slower than usual that night, and turned off the engine and headlights before he rolled up in front.

"Night, Dell," she said, sliding across the seat to give him a kiss on the cheek.

"G'night beautiful. Don't forget me now."

"I'm not gone yet. There's still graduation, and we have a date after . . . remember?" She reached for his hand.

"Yeah I know, but it feels like you're already gone," he said, running his fingers nervously through his hair, staring solemnly ahead.

"We'll always be friends. Remember that vow?" she asked, pulling his chin around toward her to wink at him as she reached for the door handle. He grabbed her arm and pulled her back toward him, kissing her square on the mouth.

"Dell, why did you *do* that?"

"Cause I've always wanted to."

"Bye, Dell, see ya," she said, removing his hand from her arm, jumping out of the pickup.

"See ya, Cady," he called out to her through the open window.

She waved back to him over her shoulder, never looking back, hurrying up the walk, to disappear through the front door. Dell sat there for a little with a clinched jaw. He changed the radio station and headed for the all-night Texaco station out on the Greenwood highway. He liked the way the inside smelled: of tire rubber and the owner's cherry pipe tobacco. The two boys who worked the night shift there were friends and always ready for a game of five-card stud.

Cady hesitated for a moment at the bottom of the stairs. Listening to Dell's pickup rumble away into the night, she smiled thinking of his kiss. Then thoughts about Renata's call intruded. Nancy was the only other person who knew about the call; Frances would find out soon enough, when the bill came. Cady played the conversation with Renata over again in her head, and wondered if the boy named Turner really existed. She ran up to her room, left that disquieting thought at the bottom of the stairs, and fell to sleep remembering Dell's kiss.

On graduation night, the end of May, 1965, Cady and her classmates, in black caps and gowns, gathered in the third-floor library to line up before descending the three flights of stairs to the packed auditorium below. Frances and Jonas had walked over early to secure good seats closer to the back on the aisle. It would be easier for Jonas to get to the bathroom.

The school band, minus the seniors, played marches in the balcony, and the musicians were grateful that one of the auditorium's six huge fans was directly overhead. The other five rotated at maximum speed and, even with the hall's tall windows wide open, a sea of commencement programs waved furiously in front of flushed faces. A few chattered about how they never remembered a May being so hot. Jonas grumbled under his breath, "They say that every year."

Upstairs, a full box of new pens and pencils sat prominently on a desk near the library's blackboard. Holding up the box, Cady made an announcement to all of her classmates: "If any of you think I stole a pen or pencil from you at any time during our school careers, then grab one now or forever hold your peace." She'd been playfully accused of such thievery since the sixth grade, and she made it clear to her friends that she considered her act of contrition that night to be a vindication for life. There were giggles, hugs, and promises to remain friends forever. The teacher shouted instructions to line up, and a few of the girls grabbed one of Cady's pens or pencils before they jumped in line to head down the steps. They would march to the strains of "Pomp and Circumstance" being played with great enthusiasm on the auditorium piano.

The outside air felt cool on the walk home. Jonas walked behind Frances and Cady, holding Cady's rolled-up diploma in one hand, his cane in the other. The usually empty streets were full of cars and groups walking together, chatting and laughing. Ladies' high heels clicked along the sidewalks. Car horns honked up and down Main Street. Folks were either at the auditorium that night or involved elsewhere with the celebration. Dell would pick up Cady in one hour to go to the dance in the double hangar at the old airfield. She wouldn't be staying out for the traditional graduation breakfast at 4:00 a.m. Frances would be driving her to Concho City bright and early the next morning to catch the 9:15 a.m. Texas International plane that would take her to St. Louis via Dallas, to meet her roommate-to-be, and to attend orientation and summer classes before the fall semester.

Frances got Jonas up extra early the next morning to get him fed before leaving for the airport. She would give him enough money to have lunch downtown at the Lone Star Café. She planned to do a little shopping in Concho City, and to meet up with a friend for lunch after seeing Cady off. It was barely light outside when Cady carried her bags to the bottom of the back steps, ready to load them into the Buick. The air was fresh and cool.

"Jonas?" Frances called through his closed door.

"Yes, Mother," he answered, smiling at her as he opened the door a crack.

"Breakfast is almost ready, but are you ready for *it*?" She asked cheerily.

"I was born hungry," he said in the same voice he used when he talked out loud to himself every morning: "Beat me, Daddy, eight to the baaaar," he'd growl. Cady was certain that his "bizarre jibberish," as she called it, was born of his brain injury.

The smell of Old Spice, wafting out of Jonas's door, signaled Frances to begin cooking his breakfast. He'd then unfailingly be at the table within five minutes. Steam would be rising from his plate when he took his seat.

"It's going to be a hot one today, son. Do you want me to see if Rachel can give you a ride downtown for lunch while we're gone?" Frances asked, as she laid a piece of unbuttered toast on his plate.

"Oh, no, mother, I'll walk. It's all downhill from here."

"Well, all right, dear, but you just stay downtown after lunch, and I'll come and get you when I get back into town . . . walking home uphill in this heat is not good for you."

Jonas was relegated most days to doing nothing more than mailing a letter or two for Frances, or picking up something or other from the drugstore downtown. He shaved, dressed in white shirt, jacket, and tie, and carried out whatever menial task cheerfully. He'd been walking down Baker Street every day, the same five long blocks to town, since he'd been released from the hospital two years before—down to the railroad tracks and another two to the post office, back to the drugstore on the main drag, and then home again for lunch. Almost twelve years had passed since the accident, and hardly a day had gone by that he hadn't sat of an

afternoon to read through one of the stack of medical books that Jonas
Sr. had confiscated from the house on Bobwhite Lane. The one with the
inscription from Renata was the most worn: "Hit the books," it said. It was
signed "Love, Monkey."

Frances sat for a long time on one of the hard plastic chairs inside the
small air terminal in Concho City. Having watched a smiling, waving
Cady ascending the stairs of the airplane had sent a pang of sadness into
her heart as strong as any she'd ever felt. But she smiled through it, waving
back cheerfully while Cady's DC-3 taxied away and lifted off. She kept
waving, in case Cady could see, until the plane was a mere dot in the sky.
It was a Randolph tradition to wave goodbye until the train, or the car, or
the plane, or the bus carrying the loved one away disappeared from sight.
Jonas had stood waving goodbye at the end of the driveway that morning
until the Buick disappeared down Baker. Cady waved back to him feeling
her own pang of sadness at the parting. Frances was thankful that she'd
be meeting a friend for early lunch, and that Jonas would be waiting for
her on her return. She sighed, remembering her words to Cady at their
goodbye: "How can we have any hellos without goodbyes?"

22

〜

Eleven years later—April 29, 1976

As the plane got nearer Texas, Cady remembered when Frances waved goodbye to her at the little Concho Valley airport, the day she left for university. There had been a hundred hellos and goodbyes since. She stared down over the clouds from her window seat, grateful for the mourning doves she'd soon be hearing in the back yard at 161. The plane would be arriving Dallas in less than an hour, and then the Texas International puddle-jumper from Dallas to Concho City would take another forty minutes. And then the last leg home.

She had no idea what was packed for her in New York that morning. Never in her twenty-nine years had she been so rattled. Not even that fearsome night she ran away from Bobwhite Lane had affected her as deeply as when she received the call that morning that Frances had suffered a massive heart attack and had lost consciousness. The news had shocked her into a solid paralysis of body and mind. Richard was forced to pack a bag for her. Their seven years of marriage had taught him no more about what she'd need in her suitcase than what she'd needed from him as a husband. He declared himself too busy with work to accompany her; it signaled her that their marriage was over.

When she climbed down the metal stairs of the plane onto the tarmac in Concho City, her legs were trembling. She could see Nancy waving slowly behind the large glass window of the terminal. It was comforting to see her there. Although they had lived apart, and had led very different lives since their school days in Pecan Valley, Nancy had been one of the few constants in Cady's life. She'd been by Cady's side when Jonas Sr. died, when Jonas Jr. finally came home from years of rehabilitation, and when her dog Blackie died thirteen years before. She was the only person Cady called before leaving New York.

"Oh Cady, honey, I'm so sorry about your grandmother," Nancy said soothingly, giving Cady a strong hug.

"Thanks so much for picking me up. I'm so anxious to get to Pecan Valley to be with Grandmother. Let me go get my bag and let's hurry."

"Cady, come sit down with me a minute while they get the bags off," Nancy said in a motherly way, guiding Cady to a chair, placing her hands over Cady's. "Your grandmother passed on this afternoon."

"What? No, that can't be. She wouldn't...I mean, oh my God, no...when?"

"The hospital said about 3:45."

"I was in the air," Cady sighed, lowering her head. "She was all alone."

"No, Cady, Rachel was with her 'til the end."

"Oh my God, but *I* wasn't . . . oh Grandmamma," she said softly.

"What about Dad?" Cady asked, feeling protective of Jonas in a way she hadn't since the night of his accident.

"Rachel sent him downtown to the drugstore earlier and gave him enough money to get lunch downtown, but he's home now. He doesn't know yet. Rachel thought it was best for you to tell him."

Cady remembered her whole life in the forty-two miles to Pecan Valley, about how her grandmother had told her that there was nothing any more mysterious about dying than about being born. Though she wanted desperately to take solace in Frances's words, she could not.

It had been only a couple of months since Frances had visited her in New York. They'd taken the train down to Washington to spend a day shopping and lunching at a pink-clothed table in the tearoom at Garfinckel's. It had been their favorite place to lunch since the days when Cady lived in D.C. working for the small news agency there. When Richard's work took them to New York, the agency kept her on. She'd travel once a week to D.C. to work and to see her old friend Leigh who lived in suburban Maryland. She and New York had never completely warmed to one another, so she was always glad to get back to the District.

Frances had surprised her at lunch that day by telling her that she could see that Cady was in a loveless marriage. They talked long hours about the likelihood of a divorce and in that case, Frances sensing her own impending death, had urged Cady not to return home. The conversation had been hard enough for Cady to have, but the thought that there would someday be no more hellos between them was unimaginable.

"Can you believe we're almost thirty?" Nancy asked, speaking softly to Cady.

"I feel a hundred right now," Cady answered, staring straight ahead at the highway.

"Seeing Rachel will help," Nancy said, patting Cady's hand.

"Yes it will."

"There's the church steeple in Rowan . . . only a few more miles to go," Nancy said.

Richard had come just in time for the funeral and left to go back East immediately after. Rachel was holding up as well as could be expected for a woman who had just lost her best friend. Cully had announced that he'd be staying just long enough to gather up the objects he wanted. Park would stay the night. Jonas was in his room. Cully called Cady and Park into the dining room for what he described as "a little conference."

Cully pulled a cigarette from an almost-empty pack before turning his attention to Cady. "Park and I . . . well, as you probably know, we're named co-trustees of Jonas's Trust and, in that capacity, we feel that's more than enough responsibility to assume for Jonas. It's high time you step in and figure out what to do with Jonas's living situation now that Mother's gone."

"*What?* What are you *talking* about? Grandmother bought that huge apartment in Houston you live in expressly for Dad and a helper to move into if something happened to her, so you could watch after him. She forked out more than a quarter million for that place . . . in your name, for that purpose . . . and she furnished the place, has maintained it! How could you *do* this?" Her voice was trembling and her mouth so dry that she was having trouble forming words. "You've played her for a fool, taken her money . . . and betrayed her."

"Shut your mouth, woman. You don't know what you're talking about," he said, his lips pinching his cigarette flat, his lighter failing him. "I owe you no explanation, and that's all I'm going to say about it," he added, throwing the lighter across the room.

"If she were here, she'd yank that place out from under you faster than you can light that cigarette. Uncle Park, did you know about this?" she asked, turning to Park. He was standing at the bank of dining room windows, staring out at Frances's prized roses. He didn't answer.

"Since you're so goddamned concerned about Jonas, you can take care of him yourself. He's your father and your responsibility now," Cully said, having found a book of matches to light his cigarette. "He can stay here for at least awhile. We'll pay the house expenses, and ole Rachel's, with money from his trust, as long as the money holds out."

"What do you *mean* Dad can stay here for *awhile*? This is *his* home, for God's sake, not yours . . . and now you're threatening his security here too?" She slumped in her chair and covered her face with her hands. Park remained silent, head down.

"I'm done talking about it," Cully said, with a dismissive wave of his hand.

Park turned away from the window and walked toward the kitchen. Rachel ran away from the kitchen door, where she had been listening through the crack, just as Cully barreled through the door, Park following behind.

"I suppose you better go help your little girl figure out what to do with your precious Jonas," Cully told Rachel. He grabbed the coffee pot off the stove to fill his cup, ash falling onto the stove from the cigarette dangling from his mouth.

"What did you *say* to that child?" Rachel answered, her hands on her hips. "And you know your mama don't allow no smokin' in this house!"

"Don't you order me around old woman . . . I call the shots around here now . . . I'll do *what* I like, *when* I like . . . and by the way, that *child,* as you insist on calling her, is a grown woman, and it's time for her to start acting like one," he said, flipping his spoon into the air.

"Your mama done everything in her power to see to Doc and I know, as the good Lord is my witness, what you promised her. She done spent more money on you than most peoples sees in a whole life to make sure of it . . . and here you done stabbed her in her sweet, lifeless heart," she said, wiping up the cigarette ash from the stove.

"Let's not argue," Park interrupted, unable to look Rachel in the eyes. "You know how upset Mother would be if she could hear all this."

"Long as I'm workin' for Miss Cady, now that Miss Frances is gone, God rest her sweet soul, I'll keep workin' here, but not a day more otherwise," Rachel said indignantly, hanging her apron on the hook by the stove.

She joined Cady in the dining room. They sat holding hands a long while before going in to check on Jonas who was asleep in his chair, seemingly unaware of the conversation about him. A medical book was open on his lap. The rose from Frances's coffin, that he had pressed into its pages, had fallen to the floor. Cady retrieved it, closed the book carefully over it, and left her father to his sleep.

"We'll manage, child . . . somehow, some way . . . don't you worry your sweet head 'bout nothin' . . . not one more minute," Rachel said.

"Yes, we'll manage . . . somehow, some way."

Cady sat on the side porch and watched Cully drive away pulling a small trailer full of Frances's best. Park was nowhere to be seen. She walked around back and found him by the alley, draped over the rock wall.

"What are you doin' back here?" she asked, walking toward him through Frances's soft, thick grass.

"Tryin' to gather my wits about me," he answered, turning toward her, eyes down.

Rachel called from the back door that supper was ready. Park followed Cady inside.

23

Chicago—a week later, May 6, 1976

Renata peered around the corner of the miniscule kitchen in the small apartment she shared with her twenty-two-year-old son, Turner. The phone rang. He answered.

"Who's that on the phone?" she asked.

"It's that Cully guy from Texas," he mouthed.

She yanked the phone from his hand.

"Cully? Is that you?" Renata asked breathlessly, waving Turner away.

"Yep, it's me all right. Long time no talk. I've got some news for you."

"Is it about Jonas?" she asked.

"Nah, it's about your favorite old lady—Frances. I thought you'd like to know that she finally bit the dust."

"When?" she asked. She felt weak.

"A few days ago. I thought you would enjoy knowing about it and gloating over it for awhile. You know that I've always looked out after your best interests."

"The only person you've ever looked out for is your sorry self. Why are you *really* calling me?"

"That kid of yours just asked me a minute ago if I knew his old man. You haven't told him much, have you?" he asked, ignoring her question.

"As if it's any of your business, he knows that his father was a doctor who was badly injured in an accident a long time ago and couldn't take care of us anymore, and that's all he needs to know. What did you say to him?"

"I told him I was his uncle and that it was about time someone came clean with him."

"Well, that's liable to come back and haunt you, but it would serve you right. I know you, Cully. You're up to no good."

"Aw, come on, girl. Have a little faith in your old friend Cully. I wouldn't steer you wrong, now would I? Now that the old lady's gone, I could maybe get that kid of yours included in Jonas's Will. How about if I come to Chicago and see you for old times sake and we can talk it over?"

"Like I said, I know you, Cully. I know what you're after. You'd be sorely disappointed. I'm not the same person. It's been tough out here, and it shows on me, as if you'd care. And besides, I wasn't born yesterday. Park would never go along with doing anything that would benefit any kid of *mine,* and he wouldn't go along with any scheme of *yours* either."

"Park will do whatever gets him more money. His business went belly up, and the old lady felt guilty about him being adopted, so she's let him live off her for years, believing his hogwash about his ship coming in some day."

"If she was gullible enough to believe *your* lies all these years, she'd believe *anything,*" Renata answered flatly.

"Park and I are executors of the old lady's estate and trustees of the retard's Trust. Uh, make that of your beloved husband's Trust. If you play your cards right, maybe I can parlay some dough for you too. Capiche?"

"How stupid do you think I am? Park hates me, so no, I don't capiche. You don't make any more sense now than you ever did, and the last thing I want or need is to get mixed up with you again."

"Haven't we gotten all pristine-clean? I thought you'd appreciate me more. I've got to go now, Renata my sweet, but you mull over what I said. I can handle Park. You know how to reach me when you want to talk about this." He hung up without a goodbye.

Renata sank down on the chair by the phone and tried to make sense out of what she'd heard. She'd often thought about how much easier life would be if Frances weren't in it, but now that it had actually happened, she felt oddly sad. She couldn't remember the last time she'd heard from

Cully, but it had been at least a couple of years, and she hadn't spoken with Frances since '54. She had the same old feeling she always had after contact with Cully—that she wanted to get in a tub and scrub her body clean.

"So, Trixie, what'd that Cully dude want?" Turner asked Renata, using the nickname that he'd called her since he heard a man in a bar call her Trixie years before.

"Don't call me Trixie, mister. You know I hate it. I'm your mother, so call me Mother, and don't call me Renata either. It's disrespectful."

"You? Respectable? What a fuckin' joke," he said, pulling his wavy dark-blonde hair back into a foot-long pony tail, grabbing a jacket off the chair. "You're about as respectable as *I* am."

Turner Mitchell Randolph was born early, on July 5th, 1954 in Marietta, Georgia, a little less than three months after Renata had been let out of jail in Concho City. The $125.00 that Jonas Sr. had sent monthly, after Renata had been banished to Atlanta, was just enough to sustain them. She had to sign an agreement that, in exchange for the monthly stipend, she would not seek any further compensation for herself or for Turner.

The envelopes with photos and scribbles from the young Turner, that she had sent Jonas Sr. over the years, had all been returned. Some had been opened but were taped back shut with contents intact. Park wrote to her at Sr.'s death to tell her that there would be no more money coming, that she would be on her own. By then Turner was eight. Renata took a number of lovers, and a job in a bar in Atlanta playing piano, to get enough cash to survive.

When the boy was ten, she moved them both to the Southside of Chicago to follow a married man she'd met in Atlanta, who promised to set her up there in exchange for favors on the side. The arrangement lasted less than a month. After years of playing dives all over the Southside, she'd finally landed a steady job playing piano six nights a week at the Lonely Tracks Club, a jazz and blues place just off Sixty-Third Street. The pay was slim but, combined with the tips from the regulars, and meals at the club, she made enough to get by.

It had been a rough twelve years in Chicago. Renata had no help raising the boy, and it was an even rougher twelve years for Turner without his Aunt Mims, as he called Renata's sister Miriam. Miriam had taken care of him all those nights Renata was working the clubs in Atlanta. The move to Chicago had put an end to any stability for Turner. Most nights, the boy ended up sleeping in smoke-filled back rooms, then dragged home in the wee hours. He failed every class in school and was held back a year. His life lessons had come from the odd set of unsavory characters that frequented the bars and dives where Renata eked out a living. When he was sixteen, he ran away, robbed a couple of stores, ended up in juvenile detention, and was finally given back into the custody of Renata. He never finished high school. The last four years had been a nightmare for her, trying to keep him out of trouble, and from stealing what was left of the little bit she had managed to save over the years. Despite it all, there was something strangely comforting for Renata about having him around. He was cocky, street-wise, and strong— protection she needed in that part of town.

"Listen, Trixie, that Cully guy said he was my uncle, and he said that he thought I could come into some money sometime if I played my cards right. He said I had a sister and that it wasn't fair that she gets all the old man's money when I'm his blood too . . . so I should get my fair share when he kicks the bucket."

"Stop calling me Trixie, damn it, and don't ever again refer to your father as "the old man." As far as a sister goes, yeah, your father and I had a daughter, but I haven't seen her in many years and well, I don't know her. You and me, believe me, we're on our own, always have been, so don't get your hopes up about getting rich off that Texas bunch. It's never going to happen, I can guarantee you that. Cully's no good and will use you for his benefit. None of those Texas people care anything about you or me and they never will."

"Well, I'm that doctor's kid and that Cully says I have rights and someday I'm gonna get what's mine to get. You just hide and watch, old woman. Now what's in here to eat? I'm hungry," he said, the light of the tiny refrigerator revealing deep pockmarks on his face from earlier acne.

"Don't be stupid, Turner. That's all I'm going to say about it," she said, as she left the room, shutting the door of the bedroom behind her.

She sat on the edge of a smelly foam twin-sized mattress that, with a piece of plywood over it during the day, doubled as a desk and sewing table. She took in sewing on the side, a far cry from her mother's dream that she'd make something of herself one day. The night her mother died, she had cursed Renata, spewing barbs about how she'd messed up the only good thing that she'd ever done—marrying Jonas. Had her father lived, Renata believed that *he'd* have at least helped her with Turner.

The living room was the size of a small bedroom, tripling as the dining room, and Turner's bedroom when he was there. The kitchen was the size of a small closet. There wasn't one thing in the apartment for which she had not bartered, found at the Salvation Army, or pulled out of a dumpster. She justified having become a scavenger by telling herself that she was atoning for the sins of those wasteful people who threw away 'perfectly good things.'

She'd taken some small amount of pride in having at least survived the twenty-two years since she'd been removed from Concho City and from Jonas's life. The one time, eleven years before, that she had called Pecan Valley and had gotten Cady, it had been so upsetting that she declared to herself that she had no daughter, and didn't need one. She had ignored Cady's existence—until Cully's call that day.

Renata heard the front door of the apartment slam shut. Turner probably wouldn't come back that night. He was gone most nights. It was her only night off. She sat in the dark, rocking back and forth on the small bed, to relieve the deep pain in her neck and back, staring out the third-floor window of her bedroom at the cracked cover of the streetlight across the alley. Neither the wailing of the baby next door nor the old man's television down the hall were loud enough to drown out the music coming from the blues club next door. She'd somehow learned to sleep through it all. That night, though, she'd be lucky if she slept at all. She kept seeing Frances's face. She prayed for sleep.

24

New York City—end of May 1976

When Richard wanted to curry favor with Cady, he'd called her Cade with a long A. "You don't have to move now, Cade," he said, as she taped shut the last box in the dining room.

"There's no time like the present. Waiting won't make this any less a divorce, and I'll have to be back in Texas for a while anyway to get Rachel and Dad situated."

"And your work . . . what about it?" Richard asked.

"What about *Dad* is a more important question," she said, staring out the dining room window at the flourishing young pine she had saved from neglect when they bought the place. She didn't want Richard to see her sadness at leaving it.

Their years together had started with a complete renovation of their large second-floor flat in the Village. To survive the hot and sultry days and nights of summer in the city, adding the air conditioning had been the best money they'd spent. Those years in New York had been social and busy ones—parties, weekend getaways upstate, frequent trips to Washington for work, camping expeditions, trips abroad—anything but dull. She had come to know the owners of some of the businesses in the neighborhood—that had made her feel more at home, like she'd felt in her old neighborhood in Washington. Leaving Richard wouldn't be easy. She loved him, but staying was impossible. The trust was gone.

"We could try it again, Cade. I'll say I'm sorry a thousand times. Just give it another chance," he pleaded.

"Richard, please . . . it's done. And please stop calling me Cade. There's no going back. We can't try it again because I'm tried out. If you'd said this to me a year ago, or even when we were in Iran, I'd have probably fallen foolishly, blindly into your arms . . . but it's beyond too late for us. We shouldn't have married in the first place . . . not after I found out about you and that woman the week before our wedding. I was so—"

"Aw, come on now," Richard said, interrupting her. "You've always exaggerated that whole thing way beyond the importance of it, honey."

"And you've always added insult to injury by suggesting that. You flat-out lied to me with that ridiculous story about how she was an old friend helping you pick out my wedding band . . . and that I should be ashamed to think so badly of such a nice person. That was particularly low of you, Richard, considering you were sleeping with her. Some exaggeration . . . "

"That was a long time ago and she meant nothing to me . . . and neither did the others."

"No Richard, I disagree. It was clearly *I* who meant nothing to you. Wasn't it enough that you slept around, but staying behind in New York, shacking up with your secretary under the guise of being too busy to travel with me when Grandmother died? And you actually allowed that woman to lie to me about your whereabouts when you were actually there, because you were sleeping with her too? I've finally pulled my head out of the sand," she said, grabbing for a box, turning away from him to hide her distress.

"Okay, m'dear, have it your way. I can see that there's absolutely nothing I can do or say to change your mind."

"That's right, Richard. There's absolutely nothing you can do or say to change my mind." She took a last look at the chandelier she'd bought at a nearby antique store, the way its rainbow prisms danced around the room in the afternoon sun. "Someday there'll be another chandelier . . . and prisms again," she thought to herself, making her way to the door.

Preparing for the 1,400 mile trip to Pecan Valley, Cady remembered Frances's admonishment to her: "If you divorce, don't return to Pecan

Valley." But Frances could not have known then, nor would she have believed, that Park and Cully would essentially leave their brother behind at her death.

It would take an undetermined amount of time for her to make arrangements for Jonas and Rachel. Her decision to give notice at the news agency had been surprisingly easy to make.

25
~

Pecan Valley—first week of June 1976

A little over a month had passed since Frances's death. Cady would
arrive in Pecan Valley two days before her personal effects would
arrive on the moving truck from New York. On the long drive home,
there had been more than enough to plan for, and to think about, than
to dwell on the humiliation of the past, or the uncertainty of the future
without Richard. She was looking forward to meeting Nancy for dinner
at the Lone Star Café that night. Rachel had kept watch at the window
for Cady's arrival. When the car turned into the driveway, Rachel ran out
to greet her.

"Rachel, it's so wonderful to see you," Cady said, throwing her arms
around Rachel's soft middle. "Aw, just listen to that mourning dove tellin'
me hello. I know I'm home now."

"Aw honey-baby, it's a blessing to have you on home," Rachel said,
burying her head into Cady's shoulder. "Stand back now and let me
take a gander at you. Lawsy, we've got to put some meat on them bones.
You need some of Rachel's good cookin'. Come on, let's get you on in
and settled. Your daddy'll be mighty glad to see you when he gets home
from town."

"Aw, Rachel, it's so good to be here in this old kitchen, except for
Grandmamma not being here. It's not right without her, is it?"

"No ma'am, no how, no way . . . but we gotta make do. That's what Miss
Frances would 'spect."

The Frigidaire was humming away, as if busy chilling up some of Frances's favorite bridge club concoctions, and Cady checked behind it to see if the heart she had drawn on the four leaf clover wallpaper, with a junior high boyfriend's initials, was still there. It was. Frances's chair at the head of the table was pushed tightly under. Rachel had left it reverently vacant since Frances's passing.

"I'll get the bags upstairs. You don't lift a thing. You're not getting any younger, you know," Cady said to Rachel.

"I may look all wore out sugar dumplin', but ole Rachel's got a ways to go before she lays her ole head down," Rachel answered, stretching the word 'ways' out for a full second while looking at Cady out of the corner of a twinkling eye.

"Aw Rachel, you still remember that Frost poem I read to you when I was a kid," Cady said, touching Rachel's hand. "I like your words, the way you understand it."

"Uh huh child. I felt the magic rise on up in me the first time you read that fella's fine words to me. Still give me the chill bumps ever time I say that part about havin' a ways to go before layin' it down . . . that forever kind of layin' it down . . . ain't it so?" she chortled, as she tightened her apron around her waist to prepare lunch. "I got a ways to go to get this lunch on too. We need to get you fed and up to bed for a nap, child. That's a long way to home you come, and you got to be flat tuckered out."

"I'm just so glad to be here. I don't feel a bit tired. And besides, I took a long time to get here, so it wasn't such a bad drive. I'm glad I've got my car here. One less thing to worry about," Cady said, twirling the sides of her long brown hair around her fingers and tucking them behind her ears. She was developing a small shock of gray in the front. "Battle wound," she told Rachel.

She stopped at the bottom of the stairs and stared at the old wallpaper mural in the foyer. The figures seemed much smaller now than in her childhood, but when she drew close she could still manage to step into the scene along the harbor. When Rachel called to her from the kitchen to get away from the wallpaper and get ready for lunch, life felt right for the first time in a long time.

Cady figured that there were only seven people on earth who had really known her, and with Frances gone, six were left, Rachel obviously being one of them. Of the remaining five, Jonas would be home soon for lunch, she'd be seeing Nancy and Dell Wayne soon. She wouldn't be long out of touch with her friend Leigh back in Maryland, and unbeknownst to him, wherever on the earth he was, Sweezer Riley would forever remain a member of that select group. As she lugged her bag up the stairs to her old room, she muttered to herself, "There's just not a thing better in this world, besides hearing a mourning dove, than to have friends like mine. We've actually listened to one another . . . and no matter how many years have passed, we remember exactly what we've told each other." Thinking about Jonas, she sighed. "If we're able to remember, that is."

Luckily, the Lone Star was nearly empty that night. Cady and Nancy took a back booth under a neon-lit clock that advertised a different business every hour.

"Okay, Cady, tell me everything. I'm all ears."

"Well, to start with, I really thought if Richard and I could be together in a fabulous place like Iran, we could find a way to get beyond our troubles . . . but no go."

"Did you tell me you were working over there? I never did get straight on that."

"Yes. I got this really great assignment to conduct interviews with a cross-section of Iranians five years after an extravagant shindig the Shah put on."

The waitress interrupted to take their orders.

"Caution to the winds, I'm going to have one of those famous chicken-fried steaks," Cady said, with Nancy following suit.

"Okay, so finish telling me all about it," Nancy said, leaning forward in anticipation.

"Okay, well, supposedly the Shah spent over 200 million to celebrate 2,500 years of the Persian Monarchy . . . and a huge number of Iranians deeply resented the whole affair, along with some other things he had done to royally piss them off, pun intended." They both laughed. "So, anyway, there we were, in the midst of these ancient ruins at Persepolis, looking out over this vast plain . . . spectacular really . . . and below was the site of the Shah's incredibly opulent party. Royals, presidents, prime ministers, sheikhs, tycoons, you name it, from all over the world attended. Lasted four or five days and ended with this grand dinner for 600. Maxim's catered it."

"What's Maxim's?"

"Oh, no matter, but anyway, the tent city, as it's called, is still being used."

"Hate to sound stupid, but what's Persop-a, uh . . . whatever it's called," Nancy asked.

"It's pronounced Per-SEH-po-lis," Cady said. Nancy repeated it back to her slowly. "It was a palace built for Persian kings 2,500 years ago, took a hundred years to build, and then Alexander the Great and his army came through, pillaged, and burned it, but there are these fabulous remains. I mean it's incredible, Nancy. Apparently Alexander, some time after, regretted the destruction, and if you could see what's left, you'd know why. Anyway, remember studying about the Persian Kings Cyrus, Darius, and Xerxes?"

"Yeah, I sure do."

"Well their tombs are near. Anyway, it's just a grand place, Nancy, full of ghosts, a thrilling place to be . . . really."

"Sounds like a *romantic* place to be too."

"Yes," Cady sighed. "I suppose it should have been, but unless there were Iranian officials around or my Foreign Service Officer friend, Arnold, Richard was cold and distant . . . even at the wonderful little hotel where we stayed in this town called Shiraz, not too far from Persepolis . . . roses everywhere in Shiraz, even more than in Tyler, if you can imagine that."

"Wow, I can't imagine any place with more roses than Tyler . . . It sounds like Richard missed a perfect opportunity to make things right with you."

"Yes, I suppose he did," Cady said, looking down at her empty ring finger. "Truth be known? All the beauty and grandeur in the world couldn't elevate our marriage above the sorry state it had become. And then when Richard stayed in New York, when Grandmother died, so he could carry on with his secretary, well . . . it just seemed pointless and too degrading to stay with him. I got my comeuppance, I suppose."

"What on earth are you talking about, comeuppance?"

"I'm talkin' about Daniel, Daniel Sarnoff. You remember him. I probably could have had a fine life with him, but—"

"Yeah, of course I remember him. I know you were really in love back then." Cady lowered her head and Nancy waited, in deference, to finish her sentence. "But you've still got plenty of time to find the right person, have kids, the whole shebang."

"Don't think that's in the cards for me. Maybe I thought about it with Daniel, but that's impossible now . . . not my destiny I'm afraid. Looks like you and John Earl will have to be the ones to carry out that particular mission in life."

The waitress brought their meals. Watching the steam rise from her plate, Cady thought about how she'd met Daniel: it was in D.C. at a bar on Nineteenth Street, in late '69. He was just starting law school, and she was just starting her first job at the news agency. It was love from the start. She felt for the locket he had given her and smiled over at Nancy who was wolfing down her meal with great gusto. The locket was engraved on the backside with "*Until Forever, D.S. to C.R.*" It held a photo of Daniel and her on a Ferris wheel one summer night in New Jersey when they'd visited his family there. She'd never stopped wearing it. Daniel's mother had joked about Cady's hips being the perfect width for bearing children. Daniel was bereft when she married Richard. He joined the Marines and ended up in Vietnam. She'd learned later from mutual friends that the experience there had hardened and troubled him equally. He'd eventually met a nice woman, married, and settled into a busy law practice in New England. The subject of having children had never come up between Richard and Cady. It had been just as well. She couldn't have imagined having children with anyone but Daniel.

"And so, here we are at the Lone Star eatin' chicken-fries. Sure am glad you're here, but won't you miss all the excitement back in the big city?"

Nancy asked, interrupting Cady's thoughts.

"Oh, I don't know . . . maybe a little, but times have changed, and I have too. Right now I'm focusing on Dad and Rachel . . . that's the way it has to be. Sure am glad you're here, Nancy . . . sure am."

"Oh Cady, don't mind me. I, uh . . . well, I don't know what I'd do if I had the responsibility you have right now, or if John Earl ever cheated on me like Richard did you. I'd die or I'd kill him one . . . don't know which. I know your grandmother would be proud of you for taking up where she left off. I'm proud of you too . . . and I'd be lyin' if I said I wasn't glad you're back home. I've missed you . . . and just one more thing: for the record, your grandmother told me, just a couple of days before she died, that she knew she'd influenced your decision to marry Richard . . . and even though she meant well, wanting you to have a more, you know, "seasoned" man than Daniel was, she wished she'd just left you to follow your heart."

"Thanks for telling me that. It means a lot . . . and don't worry about John Earl ever stepping out on you . . . he's completely devoted to you, loves you to the bone. I envy you that."

They chatted until well after midnight. Nancy listened to Cady intently. She'd learned through the years to let Cady come to her own conclusions. And besides, after Frances, Rachel was the only person whose advice Cady ever took as gospel.

⁓

By the next morning, the road fatigue had finally set in. Cady had stayed up far later than she'd intended talking with Nancy the night before. Park and Cully were due into town to meet her at the low-slung metal building down by the river. It housed one of the only two lawyers in town, the one who was filing Probate for Frances's estate. Halford Palmer, better known as Hal, had grown up with Park and Cully and would cut them a better deal than Frances's attorney in Concho City, or the older lawyer in Pecan Valley who was about to retire.

"Mornin' Cady," Palmer said, extending his hand to shake Cady's. "Are the boys over at the house?"

"I have no idea." She was put off by Palmer referring to Park and Cully as "boys" at their ages of fifty-six and fifty-seven respectively.

"Well, how 'bout a cup of coffee, young lady," he said, picking up a filthy cup from an equally filthy tray by the coffee maker.

"No thanks. I'll just have a seat and wait for them to get here. You go back to whatever you were doing."

She stared out the window at the cotton gin across the street. That Park had called her, and had actually chided her for leaving Richard, had left her uneasy about seeing him. When she told him there was philandering involved, Park had told her: "It's just the way men are, and if you'd had any sense, you'd have overlooked it and stayed put where you had some security. Mother would roll over in her grave if she knew you left your marriage and returned to Pecan Valley with your tail between your legs."

Cady reverted to her old habit of picking at her cuticles while she waited for Cully and Park to arrive. She was comforted in her certainty that Frances's Last Will would protect Jonas and her. She heard the car doors slam outside and watched Park and Cully stride up the sidewalk. Cully was grinning at Park, as if sharing a secret. Park looked annoyed.

"Hal Palmer, you old goat, how are ya?" Cully blurted out, shaking his old friend's hand, slapping him on the back.

"Fine . . . just fine. Good seein' you, and you too, Park," Palmer answered, reaching out to shake Park's hand.

Park stepped off to the side. Cully turned toward Cady.

"Hello there stranger," Cully said.

"Hello." Cady sat down to avoid any close contact with him, a talent she had perfected over the years.

"Okay, well, we've only got a few hours to iron this stuff out, so let's get to it," Cully said. He was disheveled looking, and smelled of cigarettes and unwashed hair.

Palmer showed the three of them to a small conference table in the corner. It was entirely covered with stacks of paper. Cady had never seen the Will itself, but Frances had talked often to her about it, trying to help her adjust to the more practical side of dying. "There's nothing, my dear, any more mysterious about dying than about being born," Frances had told her on more than one occasion. The truth was that they both knew that their final earthly goodbye was coming, and the thought was equally hard for them to bear. Cady remembered the call she had gotten from Frances the night before her death; it was clear that Frances had sensed that the event was imminent. She'd gone over with Cady who was to have what, and that all the instructions were in the notebook in the top drawer of the dining room buffet. She disclosed the locations of her Will, her jewelry, mention that Rachel would be provided a $400.00 per month stipend for life, and that Jonas was to live in Houston.

Cady was jolted back into the present by Palmer clearing his throat loudly. "Well," he said, peering over his horn-rimmed glasses. "It looks like your mother's, and grandmother's, Will is pretty straight forward in its provisions. I've made a copy for each of you in case you haven't already got one so you can follow along as I read it aloud . . . and then I'll tell you folks how Probate works. At the present time, there's not a detailed list of the estate's inventory, but you're going to work on it with Cully and get it to me, Park?"

"Yes, that's right, Hal," Park answered. "But from what Cully tells me, there's really not a large amount left in Mother's estate with all the expensive trips Mother took and all the extras with Jonas at home and, uh— "

"And the $250,000 she spent to buy that apartment you live in, Cully?" Cady interjected.

"That's not germane to this meeting, ma'am," Cully said, anger perceptible in his voice.

"To the contrary, there's nothing more germane to this meeting," she said, rearranging herself on the seat of the cane-backed chair. "She told me that she left a notebook outlining her wishes, her assets, and her plans for Dad's care . . . and she purchased the apartment in your name for that very purpose. Where is it? Do you know, Park?" she asked, turning away from Cully.

"I haven't seen any notebook," Park said. "But she did mention to me that she wanted you to have her diamond engagement ring."

"There's no notebook," Cully broke in. "There were a couple of notes left around here and there, some pretty hard to read . . . you know how hard it is to read her writing. I know that diamond ring is worth a pretty penny."

"What's worth more than a pretty penny is that expensive apartment she bought to shelter my father."

"How absurd you are," Cully said.

"This is getting us nowhere," Park said.

The lawyer interrupted. "I say we just deal with the matter at hand . . . and meanwhile Park, you can go ahead and give Cady the ring. You won't need to list it on the inventory."

Palmer read through Frances's entire Will. Park and Cully were named co-executors of the estate and co-trustees of their brother's Trust. What would have been Jonas's one-third would go directly to Cady, since it was believed that Jonas's sizeable Trust would maintain him nicely for the remainder of his life, and also to avoid that one-third being taxed twice. The other two-thirds would be divided equally between Park and Cully. He explained the Probate phase. There would be no assignment, during or after Probate, of property or sale of property, real or otherwise, without permission of all three legatees, otherwise known as an "undivided estate."

The three men shook hands while Cady stood back against the wall. As Park and Cully were leaving, Cully announced they'd return by the end of the week to "shore things up."

Cady drove home with her copy of the Will open on the seat beside her. Rachel was waiting lunch. Cady looked for the notebook. It was nowhere to be seen. Rachel knew about it, but had never seen it. Something about Park's demeanor at the lawyer's office made it clear that it was Cully who held the reins, and that they both knew about the notebook. She was torn between wishing Frances could see what was happening, to put a divine stop to it, and hoping that she was blissfully unaware of the betrayal.

26

Pecan Valley—October 1976

Cady had needed the few months she'd spent in Pecan Valley to gather her wits about her after the breakup with Richard, and to get things set up for her father's care. The delivery of Rachel's stipend had been arranged at the local bank. She'd receive it at the end of each month, with a little extra for staying on with Jonas. The monthly maintenance of the home would be paid out of the interest from Jonas's Trust. Park had agreed to have a report of expenditures and earnings provided to Cady on a quarterly basis.

She moved the table where old Mr. Gorman used to leave the groceries, and installed a clothes dryer in its place for those days when Rachel's sciatica made it impossible for her to carry the laundry out to the clothes line. It had taken heavy convincing from Cady to get Rachel to accept such a luxury provided solely on her behalf.

Cady had heard that Dell Wayne Wilson was in town, so she wasn't surprised when he called.

"Hey, Dell, what are you doing back in town?" Cady asked.

"Hey, how are you doing, Cady?" Dell answered, audibly excited.

"I'm okay . . . as well as can be expected after losing my grandmother."

"Yeah, I know that must be hard," he said in a softer voice. "You know it's been a long time since I've seen you, kid. Sure would like to come over and visit. Would that be okay?"

"Sure, give me about an hour to finish up what I'm doing."

When Cady answered the door to find Dell standing there, she was speechless. "Are you going to invite me in?" he asked. "Or do we need to shut the door and start all over again?" He was grinning from ear to ear.

"Yes, of course, come on in here. Jesus, Dell, you've changed. You've grown up, uh, well I mean... you're a *man,*" she said, feeling the heat of a blush rising up in her cheeks.

"That's what turning twenty-eight'll do for ya," he said, wrapping his arms around her, making sure he didn't get too close with Rachel nearby. "You about ready?" he asked, with one arm still around her.

"Be back after while, Rachel," Cady called out toward the kitchen just as Jonas stepped out his bedroom door into the foyer. "Daddy, you remember Dell Wayne Wilson, don't you?"

"Sure I do," Jonas grinned, holding his hand out to shake Dell's.

"We're leaving now, so will you tell Rachel I'll be back later?" she asked, knowing full well that he wouldn't.

"Sure," Jonas answered, winking at Cady. "Goodnight, Richard. You and Cady have a good time."

"Sure will, Fred," Dell said, with a wide grin.

"Daddy, you called Dell Richard!"

"Oh, gosh. You're not Richard," Jonas guffawed, his face turning bright red.

"No . . . and *you're* not *Fred!*"

Dell drove slowly out to the lake using the back road. His grandfather had left him the one room cabin that he'd built with his own hands a few years before the Second World War had broken out. The electricity had never been turned off. Dell had the small refrigerator stocked with food. The screened porch had a view of the man-made Pecan Valley Lake, and sat on just enough land to hold the cabin.

"What a sweet place this is, Dell," Cady said, stepping out of the pickup, looking over at the mess of mesquite trees dotting the landscape all the way down to the lake's edge.

"Yeah, I like comin' out here. My grandpa leavin' me this place was the best thing he ever did . . . so I could get away from that asshole son of his when I'm home," he said, carefully guiding Cady around a patch of cactus near the front steps.

"Are you talking about your *father*, Dell?"

"Yep . . . the one and only," he replied. "Now come on out here and get comfy," he said, leading her to the cabin's screened porch. Cady held herself close at the elbows and squinted through the last of the day's sun glinting off the water.

"You ever see anything so peaceful?" Dell asked.

"No, I don't believe I have," she answered, in almost a whisper.

"How about we take a little walk? Are ya up for that?"

"Sure, good idea."

They walked slowly along the hard-baked caliche path alongside the lake. He talked about his company in California manufacturing orthotic backrests for long-distance motorcyclists. The business had been successful enough to afford him the time to take off whenever he pleased and to build a big house on thirty acres outside Chico. Despite his rough-edged surface, Dell was an intelligent man with a curiosity about life and a clever sense of humor that Cady found appealing. That he had come back to check on his mother at intervals before her death was, she thought, honorable. She had found little of those attributes in Richard, but despite that, it was no mystery to her why she had married him: to please Frances. Richard was settled, earning a good living, and bound for success—important things that a parent, with little time left, would want for a child.

Dell spotted a copperhead slithering under the ledge of a big rock along the bank, and the crickets were making so much noise they couldn't hear each other talk. They made their way back to the cabin, chatting and laughing about old times. He told her, "I've had a few girlfriends along the way but I've been holding out for the girl of my dreams—one Cady Frances Randolph." She wanted to trust what she was feeling, but her choices regarding the men in her life had left her gun-shy and uncertain.

"Hungry?" Dell asked, peering into the refrigerator, looking for something to rustle up.

"Maybe a little," Cady answered.

"How 'bout a cold one?"

"Don't mind if I do," she answered, surprising herself. She'd never liked beer.

"I don't wanna pry, but I hear you and Richard split. If you don't mind my asking, is that true?"

"Yeah, afraid so."

"You know I never liked him," Dell said, moving closer to her on the porch couch, pushing a thick piece of bang away from her eye.

"Well, I'm afraid I got what I deserved."

"I'll tell you what you deserve. You deserve the world. He was a fool to let you go."

"It's a long way down from that high pedestal you've put me on, and it hurts to fall from such—" Cady was stopped mid-sentence by Dell's lips on hers. The kiss was long and tender. He cupped his hands around her face and studied it intently. He kissed her again. She felt a levity she'd not felt since the tender nights with Daniel so long before. "Oh Dell," Cady whispered, struggling to stand up, looking down at him.

"Come on back here, honey," he said, reaching up to pull her down to him.

They held each other for a long time, staring at one another in amazement. When she felt his bare arms under her blouse, she relaxed. The night was sweet, and their lovemaking was as close to times with Daniel as any since.

When Dell drove her home the next morning, she jumped out of his pickup without saying a word, then leaned against the door, her head in the window, looking at him.

"Cady, honey, don't hurry off so fast. This reminds me too much of that night you graduated. Remember? When you walked off, I didn't see you again for twelve years. I couldn't stand that happening again."

"Don't worry. You know we'll see each other again. We'll just make a point of it."

He reached over, put his hand behind her neck, and pulled her closer to him. "I love you, Cady. I've always loved you, and I want us to be together. Now there I've said it."

"I've got some things to work out, Dell, and I've taken a job at a newspaper in Florida."

"I'll be there next week if you'll have me."

"We'll talk soon, okay? Safe travels back to California," she said, playfully slapping the side of the pickup door as she turned to walk away.

"Don't forget last night and don't forget me," he called out to her.

"How could I?" she called back, hurrying up the driveway, waving to him over her shoulder, and feeling somewhere between elated and relieved.

Cady sat across from Jonas at the breakfast table watching Rachel serve up a plate of eggs and bacon on Frances's everyday china; her monogram in long thin lines of blue decorated one edge.

"Dad, do you remember seeing Dell last night?"

"Who did you say?" he asked, looking over the tops of his glasses.

"Dell, my old friend from high school," she answered, pushing a forkful of scrambled egg around her plate.

"Oh yes, he seemed like a nice young gentleman."

Rachel stood over Jonas holding the percolator handle with a hot pad. "Doc, want a warm up?"

"You bet I do, thank you, kind lady." He chuckled, the little crinkles around his eyes spreading with his smile.

"Dad, are you going to talk with me this morning?" Cady asked.

"Well, sure I am," he said, turning his attention back to his plate.

"Child, now let your daddy eat his breakfast," Rachel interrupted. "You know how he is about eatin.' Not nothin's gonna take him away."

Cady got up and stood at the sink staring out at Frances's roses. Thoughts about Dell's strong arms around her comforted her from yet another of her father's hopefully unintentional, yet solid dismissals. Dell had left back to California early that morning. She fantasized about having gone with him. It was far more preferable than being relegated to second place by a plate of eggs.

It had been by sheer accident that Cady had found the ledger with a phone number for Renata's sister, Miriam, in Atlanta. She'd been looking through her grandfather's desk for any notes that may have been left by him, or Frances, and for Frances's missing notebook. Cady stared at Miriam's number, feeling at once afraid and excited. It had been the first and only link she'd ever had to a contact with her mother in all the years. She packed the ledger carefully into a zippered compartment of her large bag.

When it came time for her to leave Pecan Valley for Florida, she left most her belongings, and Jonas, behind in the capable hands of Rachel who had moved into 161 Baker Street to take fulltime care of Jonas.

Having got the last bag loaded into her car, she went back upstairs to curl up in her old window seat one more time. She stared over at the columned house across Euless, and into the sky above Baker Street. It was the same blinding blue as always. Tucking her head between her knees, she watched her tears drop and dissolve, one by one, into the blue chintz cushion.

27

⁓

Four years later, Chico—August 1980

Cady had not gone into the office that hot day. After Dell's constant pleas to her to move to California, she felt certain that it had been the right thing to do. In early '78, feeling no hesitation to leave Florida or her job at the paper there, she arranged to have her belongings shipped to Dell's thirty acres outside Chico. Since Frances's death and her divorce from Richard, nothing had seemed more important than giving love another chance.

Dell had welcomed her with an armful of flowers and a group of mariachis singing in Spanish: *Bienvenida, bienvenida . . . feliz de que esté aqui* to the tune of "La Cucaracha." She was delighted by the whimsy and romance of Dell's gesture. They made love for two days straight, stopping only for meals and showers, and to answer an occasional business call.

In the two years she'd been there, Cady had expanded Dell's business beyond anything he'd ever imagined. Ten satellite offices had been established coast to coast with plans to relocate the company's manufacturing plant and headquarters from Chico when a suitable location could be found. With trips to take care of business with Jonas and Rachel becoming more frequent, Cady hoped to move the business closer to Texas. Dell was often overwhelmed with the company's rapid expansion, and Cady sensed more and more that he would have preferred the business had stayed small. They spent considerably less time together between Dell traveling a good part of the time, and Cady returning to Texas often. Their divergent paths had begun to make strangers of them. She had adopted a puppy, after finding him abandoned in a parking lot in Chico. She named him Marlon, after Brando. The little eight-pound mutt, black with a white chest, had become her constant companion, traveling with her to Pecan Valley on every trip. Cady couldn't go home without him. The one time she'd left Marlon with Dell Wayne, Marlon hadn't eaten for three days.

The mail truck arrived on time that morning and she caught the kitchen screen door with her hip as the mailman walked toward her up the drive lined with almond trees.

"Here ya go, Cady," he said with a grin, holding a package with a stack of letters on top with one hand, stroking Marlon's head with the other.

"Thank you, Ralph," Cady said, taking the package.

"Ole Dell gone again?"

"Yeah, but he'll be back tonight."

"You tell that ole boy that he better watch out or I'll steal ya," he called back to her, as he made his way back to the truck.

"I'll make sure he gets the message," Cady called, as he drove away.

She held the package under her arm while she flipped through the stack of letters. There was an envelope postmarked Pecan Valley, Texas, from Halford Palmer, Esquire. She dropped the package and other mail by the door, sat on the nearby rock wall, and tore the envelope open:

August 12, 1980

Dear Cady,

I am in hopes that this letter finds you well and enjoying life out there in sunny California.

After four years in Probate, we are ready to make final disposition of the assets in your grandmother's estate.

Attached is a document for your signature that will release to you your full one-third (1/3) interest as provided in her Last Will and Testament. Your portion is valued, after taxes and other fees, at $90,000. A recent appraisal was completed on the home at 161 Baker Street where your father currently resides. It was appraised at $85,000. In addition, you *will receive a check for $5,000 for your portion of funds that were set aside for incidentals during the Probate Process.*

Please read, sign, and date the document enclosed in the presence of a notary public at your very earliest convenience so that we can bring the matter to a close. As soon as I receive same, your check will be mailed to you along with the deed to the family home.

Should you have any questions, please don't hesitate to contact me.

Yours very truly,

Halford Palmer, Esquire
Enclosed: 1 page document

The enclosed document:

NOW THEREFORE in consideration of the sum of ten dollars and other good and valuable consideration herein contained:

I, Cady Frances Randolph, a legatee of the Frances Randolph Estate, accept the deed to 161 Baker Street located in the town of Pecan Valley, Texas, situated on two city lots, fairly appraised at $85,000 along with the sum of $5,000 as valuable consideration to satisfy my one-third (1/3) undivided interest in said estate valued in total at $270,000,

In consideration of 1.1, I, Cady Frances Randolph, release to Cullen Harden Randolph and Parkton Gerard Randolph the remainder and residue of the Frances Harrington Randolph estate, including but not limited to any and all oil and gas interest, stocks, bonds, and real estate remaining in said estate.

I, Cady Frances Randolph, agree to hold completely harmless from liability, present or future, the co-executors of said estate, Parkton Gerard Randolph and/or Cullen Harden Randolph.

_____
Cady Frances Randolph   Date_____

_____
Notary Public Signature   Date_____

Cady stared at her name printed below the signature line for a long while. Her hand was trembling as she picked up the phone to call Hal Palmer. Marlon was curled up by her feet.

⁓

"Dell, I know you hate it that I'm going to Pecan Valley again, but I have to."

"Do you know how many times you've gone back there this year?" he asked, holding both arms up in frustration.

"You told me that you understood my responsibility to my father, and that you'd always support me . . . and now this?

"I've done plenty to support you, but you're not pulling your weight around here."

"How can you say that? I tripled your business in less than two years and I've loved you on top of it. And you tell me I'm not pulling my weight?"

"All right, Cady Randolph. Go on and go, but don't blame me if I can't keep this up."

"Keep *what* up?"

"Sittin' around here working my ass off . . . giving you money while you go and leave me here to do everything . . . *that's* what."

"*Giving* me money? I can't believe you're saying that! I'm your partner and I've earned every penny of it and then some. Dad's well-being, and from your threats, mine too, forces me more than ever to protect our interests in Texas."

"I'm just saying that I'm sick and tired of you leaving me alone. It's not that I'm threatening you."

"I'm sorry, Dell," she answered with a long, deep sigh. "I have to go. I told you before we ever got together that my dad had to be a priority in my life. You said you understood. I'll be back as soon as possible. I do love you in spite of what I'm hearing."

"Oh God, here we go again," he said, pacing back and forth. "I've been nothin' but good to you, but it's never enough."

Cady pulled her suitcase off the bed and made her way out the door, muttering to herself, "This can't be happening. I can't have heard what I just heard, but hear it I did."

Dell mumbled a pinched goodbye and walked away. He didn't help her out to the car or offer to drive her to the airport. She'd learned well from Richard, and then Dell, how to go it alone.

The plane was late getting into Concho City. It had been a long day. Cady was never so glad to see Nancy who had always been there for her. Frances had maintained that new friends were silver, but old friends, like Nancy, were gold.

Cady met with Halford Palmer the next day in Pecan Valley. To her unpleasant surprise, Cully was there.

"Well, hello there, niece. Hal called to let me know you had questions about the release document so I thought I'd pop on up to meet with you too. We really need to get this estate closed up . . . so what is it you need to know?"

"I'm confused about why I'm signing this document I was sent. How am I supposed to know if what you're telling me is correct? I've never seen a copy of the inventory."

Palmer handed her a one-page listing of Frances's holdings she'd never seen before. "Now Cady," Palmer said in a fatherly tone, "I think you should feel assured that you are receiving your rightful one-third based on the true valuation of the inventory at $270,000. I'm sure you might be disappointed in the amount you are receiving. That often happens I'm afraid."

"Yeah, Park and I were surprised too," Cully interrupted. "Mother spent a lot of money before she died, so naturally there's less left. Park's in trouble financially and you want to make sure Jonas keeps a roof over his head, so if you don't accept these terms, I can guarantee that Park will force the sale of 161 and you'll have to find another place to house Jonas. That won't be easy for you or comfortable for him."

"While the majority of your one-third will be tied up in the house," Palmer continued, "it will no doubt appreciate over the years . . . but we're not considering that future valuation of course. Here's the way to look at it: You're getting a damned good long-term investment, $5,000 cash, and a home for your daddy taboot."

"Looks like you haven't left me much choice in the matter . . . and by the way, did her notebook ever turn up?" she asked Palmer.

"Nope, never turned up," Cully interjected. "She must have done away with it."

"I didn't ask you. I asked Mr. Palmer," she said.

"Well, I can't tell you what to do, young lady, but what Cully's telling you about protecting your dad is mighty compelling I'd say," Palmer said, ignoring her question about the notebook. "In my estimation, it's a fair deal for you. The boys are gonna make sure the expenses for the house are paid out of Jonas's Trust, so you won't have any expenses for upkeep as long as your daddy occupies the property. Isn't that right, Cully?" Palmer asked, winking at Cully.

"Yep, that's right. Man alive, that sounds like a damn better offer than I realized. Maybe we should reconsider this deal," Cully said, grinning at Cady.

"Not amusing Cully. I want to get another appraisal on the house," Cady said.

"What? There's only one agent here in town that does appraisals and he's done it fair and square on 161. You're gonna waste our time, *and* yours, trying to get another one," Cully said, shifting quickly from being patronizing to being angry.

"Uh, yes, young lady, not much point spending the money to get another appraisal," Palmer chimed in. "Any other appraisal's gonna come in damned near to the penny as this one I'd suspect."

"Well, so be it. I still want another appraisal."

"I want this thing done and over today," Cully said, almost shouting.

"Calm down, Cully," Palmer said. "Let her throw away her money if it makes her happy."

Cady called the only realtor in town to find out that there was a man in Concho City who appraised Pecan Valley property regularly. He agreed to come over that afternoon. His appraisal came in ten thousand less at $75,000.

"All right, here's what we'll do," the lawyer said, after conferring with

Cully who was clearly agitated. "We'll meet you in the middle."

"So now you're bargaining with me?" Cady asked.

"I'm afraid that's the way it works, missy."

"Really? You mean that's the way it works with *you.*"

After a few more minutes conferring with Cully in the next room, Cully offered to settle at $80,000 with a cash amount due Cady of $10,000.

"I have a call to make," Cady said. "This will just have to wait until tomorrow."

The men grumbled in unison. Cully complained that he needed to get back to Houston.

"I'll handle this for you," Palmer told him. "Get on back to Houston. I'll call you tomorrow.

"Sorry I've come all the way up here to have you delay this thing, but then you've always been a little stubborn, eh Cady?" Cully glared at her in a way that curdled her blood.

She stuffed the copy of the appraisal into her purse, along with the document, and told Palmer she'd be back the next afternoon. Taking the long way home, she drove to the park, stopped by the creek, and talked out loud to Frances as she often did. There was a symphony of dove calls coming from the bushes along the banks. She listened until a sense of calm settled in. She'd call Park as soon as she got back to the house.

"Rachel?" Cady called softly through Rachel's closed bedroom door.

"Come on in, sugar."

"Aw Rachel," Cady sighed, climbing into bed with Rachel who had taken a nap after lunch with Marlon on the pillow next to her. "I've got to talk with you. I've been thinking about trying to find my mother. I know that seems strange, but it just feels like something I need to do. I've got a number for her sister. Should I?"

Rachel took Cady's hand. "Now you listen here child . . . they's nothin' unnatural 'bout needin' to know where you come from. I see that trouble on your sweet face. Did somethin' happen down there at that lawyer man's this mornin'?"

"Yeah, I want to talk to you about that too. I'm getting the deed to 161. Cully showed up. He made it sound like Park would sell the house off if I didn't take it to keep a roof over Dad's head. And they say its value is the majority of what I'm due from Grandmother's estate. They want me to sign this paper saying I got what I was supposed to get and they get the rest."

"Hmm," Rachel grunted, shaking her head from side to side. "You know how I feel about that Cully, and Miss Frances always did worry she'd been too easy on him, him bein' borned puny and all . . . and that poor orphan boy Park been like a fish outta water since he come here after his mama and daddy got blowed up in that 'splosion. Wudn't that Frances and Mister didn't give him up a rightful place . . . he just never got square with nothin' . . . he got big money troubles too. I've been prayin' for him. Don't you worry none about that Cully . . . just leave it to the good Lord to fix that fella up. We'll make it, child. Don't you worry none."

⁓

"Uncle Park, this is Cady."

"Cady! What a surprise. How's California treating you?"

"I'm in Pecan Valley right now; spent the afternoon down at Hal Palmer's office with Cully. They're telling me that Grandmother's estate is closing and that it's worth $270,000, that I'm entitled to one-third that amount which would be $90,000. My first question to you is . . . is that right?"

There was silence on the other end of the phone.

"Are you there?" Cady asked.

"Yes, I'm here. That sounds close enough to being right. After all the expenses during that long Probate period, I think that's about what would be left.

"Is it true that you're in financial trouble and that you'd just as soon sell off 161 to get the cash? Would you really sell the house out from under my father?"

"Is that what Cully told you?"

"Yes, that's exactly what he told me, and Hal Palmer agreed with him."

"It's a lie. I would never do that. But Cully would sell it in a heartbeat. He's been talking about it for awhile now, but I think Palmer convinced him it would be better for him, he'd get more cash, and be less personally responsible for Jonas if he conveyed the house to you."

"So what about you . . . where do you fit into this?"

"It's a long story, Cady, but to keep it simple, he loaned me some money awhile back so I ended up having to sign over my portion of the estate to him to pay him back."

"Couldn't you have just waited for your inheritance?"

"No, it wasn't possible. I had some pretty nasty debtors breathing down my neck."

"Oh, God," Cady sighed, shaking her head. "I really need to know from you whether I can trust the estate value."

"As far as I know, yes."

"All right then. There's only one more thing I need to know."

"Okay, I'll do my best to shoot straight with you."

"You knew that Grandmother bought that place in Houston for my dad, right?"

"Yes, there was no doubt about that."

"Why didn't you speak up back then?"

"Cady, there would have been nothing I could have said or done to change him. He had me by the short hairs financially, as I told you. I'm sorry I haven't been more help to you or around to see Jonas. Life's been rough for me since Mother died."

"I've really got to go now, but thanks for talking with me. I'm sorry things have been so rough for you. Rachel's been praying for you. Good luck with everything."

"Goodbye, Cady. Please tell Jonas hello for me. And please tell Rachel hello too."

"I will. Goodbye."

Park stared at the phone for a long time. For the first time in his life, he didn't mind hearing that Rachel was praying for him. He was even glad. He regretted that he hadn't stood up for her over the years. So often he'd felt like beating Cully to a pulp for treating her so badly, but he'd shrunk away. His throat ached holding back a torrent of emotion. "Guilt's the best guide to show us the right way," Frances used to say. Her words haunted him.

Part Three

28

Twelve years later—Autumn 1992

It had been sixteen years since Cady had stumbled across Miriam Collins's phone number in Jonas Sr.'s desk drawer. She had often taken the small ledger out to look at it, but every time she was tempted to call the number, she had quickly put it away. There was the chance that if she did reach Miriam, she'd be ill received. She wouldn't necessarily blame her aunt for that. The desire to find out what she could about her mother had grown greater than the fear that she'd be rejected. At Rachel's urging, Cady nervously called the number in the ledger and got Miriam's answering machine. That was all the assurance she needed. She made reservations to fly to Georgia. Marlon would stay with Rachel. He was too old to travel, and Rachel liked his company.

Cady checked into the hotel in downtown Atlanta and took a deep breath before picking up the phone to call Miriam. The phone rang and rang, and just as Cady was about to hang up:

"Hello," a woman answered.

"Hello, uh . . . excuse me, but is this Miriam Collins?"

"Who's calling please?"

"Uh, well, my name's Cady Randolph. Is this Miriam Collins?"

"Yes, it is, but—" Miriam stuttered, stopping mid-sentence.

"I am your sister's daughter," Cady said, the blood draining from her face.

"And that would make me your aunt," Miriam said with a bite in her voice. "After all these years, what is it you could possibly want?"

"I found your number in my grandfather's papers and want to know if there's some way we could meet."

"I don't know, I mean why do you want to meet me now, with all this water under the bridge?"

"I never knew where you were, or really even that you existed. I'd heard bits and pieces about you, and then I finally saw my grandfather's note that you were my mother's sister. I don't want to disturb you or upset you. I just want to know if my mother is still alive."

"Why do you ask such a thing? Why *wouldn't* she be? She's not that old."

"I was told she died. I never fully believed it, and now you tell me that she really is alive."

"Please tell me what you want from her or me. My sister's been through hell with that Randolph bunch. We *all* have, and I don't want to see her get hurt again. She tries to live a peaceful life."

"Please believe me that I have no desire to hurt her or you. I'm just trying to find out more about my background and the brother she told me years ago that I had. Could we meet for a coffee or a meal or something this evening or tomorrow early? I'm here in Atlanta and flew here from the West Coast to meet you."

Miriam reluctantly agreed to meet Cady in the lobby of Cady's hotel that evening. She arrived before Cady did, and when Cady stepped off the elevator, Miriam was dumbfounded. She stood up and called out.

"Over here, Cady."

"Hello. How did you know it was me?" Cady asked, turning toward the voice.

"Are you kidding? You're a dead ringer for my sister."

"Well, I hope that's not a bad thing," Cady said, taking a seat across from Miriam.

"No not at all. I'm surprised though, and find it fascinating . . . and maybe even a little emotional. I haven't seen Renata in years . . . looking at you, well, it's as if she's come back from our youth."

Miriam looked nothing like Renata. She was short and stoutly built with a boyish haircut that framed her round face and her large round eyes. There was a gap between her front teeth. Otherwise, she was quite pleasant looking.

"I know it's shocking for you to have me, a stranger to you, suddenly appear after all these years, and I understand that you want to protect your sister, but she is my mother and I want nothing more than to have the opportunity to learn about her and to see her again. I certainly have no intention of hurting her."

"I'll have to call her and make sure it's all right with her for me to give you her number. I hope you understand."

"Of course I do," Cady replied, resting her chin on the back of her hand.

"My God, my sister used to do exactly what you're doing," Miriam said, tears welling up in her enormous eyes.

"What is it I'm *doing?*"

"You're holding your chin on your hand exactly like she did . . . and your hands and arms are carbon copies of hers." Cady felt a strange sense of connection at that moment. She stared down at her hands. They were small and delicate. She'd always been given compliments about them.

"I'm sorry about your father. It must have been very sad growing up without him," Miriam continued.

"Yes, it was, but as the years have gone by, we are beginning to be close again."

"What? What do you mean you're getting close again? You talk as if he were alive."

"Yes, of course he is. It was a miracle that he lived, but he did," Cady answered, seeing that Miriam had turned pale. "What is it? You seem upset."

"We were told that your father died as a result of his injuries in that car wreck. And all these years I thought he was dead, and my parents did. Does my sister know he's alive?"

"I wouldn't know. I'm sorry you thought he was dead. It must be shocking for you to learn that he's not. Why did you think he was dead?"

Miriam was quiet, staring away, squirming a bit in her chair. She finally answered. "Jonas's parents told us he died a couple of months after he was injured. Mama and Daddy died believing Jonas was gone. It had made them heartsick. It made me heartsick too. We all loved him."

"I'm so sorry, Miriam, I'm not sure why they would tell you such a thing. There's a lot I don't understand. I'm hoping to get some answers. Again, I'm sorry."

"It's not your fault, honey," Miriam said, her voice becoming softer and kinder. "Maybe they felt it was best at the time, that it would be easier on all of us . . . but obviously they didn't want Renata around. I guess I can understand that, but it was a cryin' shame that they never wanted to see their little grandson. It might have made a difference in the boy's life."

"So I *do* have a brother," Cady said, feeling a knot forming in her stomach.

"Yes, you do. His name's Turner . . . Turner Mitchell Randolph. "He's younger than you. I think you were about seven when he was born."

"That would make him about thirty-nine?"

"That seems about right. He was a sweet little boy. I don't know what happened, but he's been a lot of trouble for your mother, a big disappointment. The last time I saw him he was a teenager and had been caught stealing . . . ended up in juvenile detention. He's got no respect for his mother or anyone else for that matter. It's a cryin' shame. My sister always said that she got what she deserved when Turner went bad. I never really understood why she'd say such a thing."

"Where is he now?"

"I don't really know. He's in and out of Chicago, only goes to Renata when he wants to steal her money, or have a place to stay. From what I understand, he hasn't called her or seen her in at least a year."

Cady felt uncomfortable and changed the subject, suggesting they take some time to have dinner, relax, and talk about other things. She wanted to forget about Turner, that he existed at all. She couldn't imagine telling anyone else but Rachel what she had learned about the errant stranger who was of her blood.

"Okay. There's a little place near here. It's not fancy, but they serve good home cooking. I'd be glad to drive us there," Miriam said, still reeling from the news about Jonas.

"That sounds great. What do you say we go now?"

They chatted a little in the car on the way to the restaurant, and Cady learned that her mother's parents had both died at fairly young ages—he of a stroke right after Jonas's accident and she, twenty years later, with cancer of the female organs, as Miriam put it. They lingered in the restaurant until it closed at 11:00 that evening. Miriam told Cady story after story about her relationship with Renata—about their childhood, the unhappiness of their mother when their father lost everything in the Depression, and her belief that Renata had developed a delusional life during those years in order to survive them. Miriam told her that when Renata married Jonas, the family thought she might finally become secure enough to overcome her tendencies to get into trouble. She divulged to Cady her own tendency toward depression, and that she had never married, "much to my parents' chagrin," she'd said.

When Miriam left Cady off at the hotel, they made the plan to have breakfast the next morning. Cady barely slept that night, all the stories swimming in her head, particularly the one about Turner. Cady had been incredibly relieved to hear from Miriam that she and Turner looked nothing alike. She went down to the hotel coffee shop when it opened at 6:00 the next morning and waited for Miriam to arrive.

"Good morning, Miriam," Cady said, as cheerfully as she could muster.

"Good mornin', girl," Miriam responded with a thick Georgia accent. "I've got some good news. I called your mother this morning, woke her up. She was very emotional about your being here looking for her and told me to give you her number."

Cady smiled nervously and got her address book out of her purse. "Okay, I'm ready." Jotting the number down, she recognized the Chicago area code. "Has she lived in Chicago long?"

"Yes, but I don't remember how long. Turner was a child when they moved there. I want you to know, before you call her, that she's sick. She won't tell me what's wrong, but I have a feeling it's more serious than she's letting on. She has a lot of dizziness and headaches. She asked me not to tell you, but I think you should know."

"Oh . . . I don't know what to say about that."

"I think you'll know when the time comes," Miriam assured her. "I didn't tell her that your father is alive. I think it's something you should tell her yourself. I have no idea how it will affect her. Please be careful how you tell her."

"I'd keep quiet about it, but I don't know how I'll be able to avoid telling her."

"Well, I'd say it's high time to get things out in the open."

They ate breakfast quietly. When it was time for her to go, Miriam pulled a small box out of her purse and handed it to Cady. It contained an opal ring set in gold with two very small diamonds.

"I want you to have this, Cady. You are my niece after all, and my sister's child. I think you should have something from this side of the family. It was my mother's and your grandmother's.

Cady felt revulsion at this relative stranger referring to anyone but Frances as her grandmother, but quickly mustered as polite a response as she could. "Thank you, Miriam. I'm speechless." It was all she could think to say. She put the ring in her purse.

"Don't you want to try it on?"

"Oh, yes of course."

Cady fished it out of her bag. It was loose on her finger. Feeling that Miriam was satisfied, she put it back in the box with the excuse that she didn't want to lose it. They said their goodbyes in the lobby. Cady looked out her hotel room window, and watched Miriam drive away from the hotel parking lot. She was relieved to see her go. She wanted to feel closer to this woman, this aunt, who had been more generous than she needed to be, and whose life had been turned totally upside down by her surprise visit. She felt grateful to Miriam, but felt no particular kinship with her. Nevertheless, she would write a note of thanks to her as soon as she got back to California.

Sitting on the edge of her bed in the hotel room, she stared at the piece of paper on which she had carefully printed her mother's phone number. When she picked up the receiver, she understood that her life was about to change forever. The phone rang only twice.

"Hello, Betty Phillips speaking," a soft voice answered.

"Excuse me, I must have the wrong number," Cady said, confused, ready to hang up.

"Who are you trying to reach please?" the woman asked quickly.

"I was given this number for someone named Renata Randolph."

"May I please ask who is calling?"

"My name's Cady Randolph."

There was silence.

"My dear, I'm your mother," she said calmly, without hesitation.

There was more silence.

"Are you all right?" Renata asked, breaking the quiet.

"Yes, I think so. Are you?"

"Yes, I am . . . just a bit overwhelmed. I'm glad that this moment has come. I never dreamed that it would. I'm so grateful that you've sought me out and found me."

"I'm not sure what I feel at this moment. Your sister felt she should tell me that you're ill."

"Yes, I've had some problems, but everything's under control right now . . . life's got a funny way of changing in a hurry, but I'm sure you've probably learned that by now. Listen, I . . . uh . . . I wonder if we could meet. I'm no good on the telephone. Could you possibly consider that?" Renata asked, afraid of what the answer might be.

"Yes, I would more than consider it. I can fly to Chicago today. There are so many questions I have that I hope you'll be able to answer. For starters, why did you answer this call with that other name?"

"It's a long story. I hope I can answer that question when we meet, and any others you may have. I'll do my best."

"Will it work for you if I fly up today or tomorrow?"

"Well, yes. I guess there's no time like the present."

"Okay then, I'll call you as soon as I've made reservations."

"Okay. I'll be waiting to hear from you. And in the meantime, my dear, as much as you probably won't believe me, and I can't blame you for that, I want you to know that you have made a dream come true for me today. To have this chance is something I thought I'd never have. That you want to see me is the most wonderful gift I think I've ever been given. Thank you."

Cady was finding it hard to believe that she felt so much for this woman who had hurt her, hurt her father, and left them both. They talked a little while longer, just long enough for Cady to reiterate that she would be calling Renata back with trip particulars. She booked a flight to Chicago that was to depart at 10:30 that morning. She called Dell, who was surprisingly accepting. That was a relief. She finished packing, tucked her mother's phone number into the zippered pocket of her jacket, and called for a cab.

29

Chicago—later that day

Cady checked into the Palmer House that mid-afternoon. She had stayed there on several occasions with Frances, on trips to visit one of Frances's close cousins. She showered and called room service. The emotions of the day, and the rush to the airport in Atlanta, had left her anxious, brief episodes of which she'd been experiencing more frequently. Dell had tired of trying to help her when they occurred, and it seemed that the less patient he got with the events, the worse and more frequent they became. The most relief Cady got was when she visited home, when she'd hear the doves in the back yard.

Before calling her mother, she ordered up some crackers and a club soda to quell the queasiness in her stomach. They made a plan to meet in the lobby of the hotel at 7:00 that evening. They talked about how to recognize one another. Renata would be wearing a brown jacket and yellow scarf. Cady sipped more soda and ate a few crackers. After requesting a wake-up call, she fell into a dead sleep.

She awakened before the wake-up call came and, with an hour left to meet her mother, she turned on the television to listen to the local news while she dressed. The weather report called for intermittent rain throughout the evening. She wondered if the bad weather would delay her mother's arrival, but Renata was already in the lobby. She hadn't wanted to chance being late for the most important appointment of her life since the one she'd kept with Jonas that hot summer night in 1944.

After one last sip of soda water, Cady made her way to the elevator. It was full of convention-goers. She thought about waiting for the next one, but squeezed in, not wanting to be even a minute late. She felt woozy on the long ride down. The elevator jerked to a stop on every floor. She started picking at the cuticle on her thumb with her third finger. When the elevator door finally opened at the lobby level, she took a deep breath and pulled herself up erect. Turning toward the ornate lobby, with its soaring high ceiling, she began scanning the crowd for a brown jacket and yellow scarf.

"Are you looking for me?" Renata asked, startling Cady from behind.

"Good God, how did you know it was me?"

"I'd know you anywhere . . . you *are* my daughter," she said smiling.

"I, uh, I . . . Oh my God, can we please just sit down somewhere?" Cady asked, shocked at her mother's appearance.

They made their way, Renata following Cady, to a grouping of high back chairs off to one side. Cady was struck by her mother's perfect skin, but equally struck by her outdated Lana Turner hair style. Her clothes, purse, and shoes were equally outdated, and heavily worn.

"You're beautiful, Cady. I wish I looked better, for your sake. I hope I won't embarrass you this evening. It's been a long time since I've been out anywhere as nice as this," Renata said, adjusting her skirt and jacket in an uneasy way.

"No, of course you don't embarrass me. I appreciate your making the effort to come here and meet with me," Cady said politely, hoping that she was successfully hiding the discomfort she was feeling.

A waiter approached and asked if either wanted a cocktail. Cady hadn't realized that she had chosen seating in the lobby bar area. Cady was relieved when her mother asked for nothing but a glass of water.

There was a steely composure on Renata's face when she announced that the evening was on her. That look made it clear to Cady that it would be wrong to argue the point. Her mother displayed a gracefulness and pride that was hard to deny. Her eyes were piercing but, unlike what Cady remembered from her childhood, there was now a softness and intelligence in them that she was surprised to see. Though her hair was a yellowing gray and didn't look clean, her high cheek bones and delicate hands were attractive. She apologized to Cady that she had lost a front tooth; she hadn't had the money to replace it. She held her upper lip taut over the area in an effort to hide, mostly unsuccessfully, the gaping hole.

"I'm sorry you've had such a challenging time, and I do hope things will get better for you. I have so many questions to ask you, I don't know where to start. I guess I'd ask you first to tell me why you answered the phone this morning with that other name," Cady said.

"The short answer is that I got into some trouble once with a man I knew and decided to change my name so it would be harder for him to find me. I don't know if I'll ever be able to fully explain my life, and how I arrived at this moment, but I'll try for your sake."

"Well, that's enough of an answer for now. I wrote down all these questions I had, but now that we're here together, I realize that it's more important to just let questions come as we talk. I think I don't trust my own memories very much," Cady said, thinking about how she was still not sure about the hamburger the night of her father's accident.

"Fair enough . . . I can understand that. You were very young when we were separated, and a lot of water's gone under the bridge. You must be forty-something now?"

"I'm forty-five . . . and you, you're what . . . in your seventies?"

"Yes . . . seventy-two. Hard to believe, but even harder to believe that you're forty-five," Renata said, shaking her head. "Listen, I don't know what people have told you about me but, even though I was an adult when you were taken from me, I might as well have been a child myself. I knew so little and had so little confidence then."

"Well, like you say, a lot of water's gone under the bridge. Speaking of the past, I have some belief, and I'm not sure where it comes from, that you played the piano. Is that true?"

"Yes, it's true. I played in a little group for a number of years here in Chicago. But I also played for you when you were little. Don't you remember?"

"No, I don't remember, but if I can find a piano here in the hotel, will you play?"

"Of course," Renata answered without hesitation.

Cady inquired at the front desk. Both the hotel's pianos were in use. The concierge gave Cady directions to a small piano bar around the corner. She returned to the table where Renata was sitting quietly. Cady couldn't help but notice how erect she sat. It was that pride that she had seen in her mother at first glance.

"There's no piano available here in the hotel, but there's a piano bar around the corner. We could go there and see if there'd be a chance of your playing it. Does that sound okay with you?"

"Sure . . . I'm game. Let's go."

The sidewalk was slick from the rain, and Cady found herself holding her mother's elbow to steady her as they walked along. The bar turned out to be further away than the concierge had indicated, but Renata was managing, complaining only that the soles of her shoes were so worn that she was sliding a bit on the sidewalk. She slipped her arm through Cady's. When the bar's neon sign came into view, Cady began to brace herself for what could turn out to be a great disappointment.

There were two seats left at the bar. The piano was on a platform above the bar, and the act that night was finishing his set as Cady and her mother took their seats. He was a one-man-band act, holding a pair of maracas in one hand, his other playing an electric piano complete with percussion backup, and belting out his version of "Quizas Quizas Quizas." His red shirt, with its multi-colored ruffled sleeves, fluttered to the song's finish. A couple of people clapped unenthusiastically in the back of the room.

Cady approached the entertainer. "Excuse me, sir," she said. "I have a request to make . . . uh, while you're between sets. It's a very special request. I'm here with my mother. That's her over there." Cady pointed to Renata. "We're seeing each other for the first time in almost forty years, and she wants to play a little something on the piano for me. Would that be all right? I mean I don't think anyone in here will even notice, and we'll keep it quiet."

"Oh, honey. What a story! I love it! Sure she can come up and play. No problem."

"Thanks so much. Really appreciate it." Cady moved back toward Renata.

Before Renata could get up from her chair, the entertainer turned a spotlight on the piano, went to the microphone, tapped on it, and with it squealing, spoke into it. "Ladies and Germs," he said, stealing an old-time comedian's line in an attempt to be funny. "May I have your attention? I have a very special treat for all you fine folks. This little lady," he said, pointing toward Cady, "is reuniting with her mother tonight for the first time in forty years, and mama wants to play something special for her daughter on the piano . . . so please put your hands together for, what's your name, darlin'?" he shouted toward Renata. She answered. "Here she is, folks," he said with a sweep of his arm . . . "Renata!"

A couple of people in the back applauded, but most ignored the announcement. Cady's and Renata's very private moment had been violated by this well-meaning buffoon, and Cady was nervous about what she might hear—that she might be disappointed.

Renata rose from her chair, glided up the few steps to the piano, sat down, adjusted the piano stool, and warmed up with a few bars of something that Cady didn't recognize. The musician fellow turned the spotlight blue over the piano. Renata whispered down to Cady that it was a lullaby she'd written for Cady when she was a child. Cady felt faint. It was a moment of reckoning. Renata then said, "This one's for your father. It became our song the night we met."

She began playing "Always." It was the first time Cady could remember hearing the song since it had come from Miss Alice's windows that rainy night in '53. It was beautiful. The room got quiet. Cady dropped her head on the bar, and buried her face in the crook of her arm. Renata never looked up. When she played the last note, the room came alive with applause and more than a few bravos! Renata descended the few stairs, took Cady by the arm, and quickly led her out of the bar. The crowd was still applauding when they went out the door. It was chilly on the walk back. Cady was unable to speak. She wondered why no one had ever mentioned her mother's great talent. They slipped into a little diner along the way to warm up.

Renata looked at the menu, and seeing that it was a place she could more easily afford in that pricier part of town, suggested they have a bite to eat, that Cady looked like she could use some sustenance. Cady remembered their last meal together—the night Renata soaked the food with vodka— the night she ran away. They ate burgers, shared a shake, and eventually made their way back to the hotel. "Burgers," Cady thought to herself. "Of all the meals on earth to be eating tonight, we're eating burgers. You just can't make this stuff up." She shivered.

Cady insisted that her mother stay at the hotel that night. There were two beds in Cady's room. She ordered up a toothbrush, an extra robe and whatever else Renata would need. They were close to the same size, so Renata wore a pair of Cady's pajamas and socks.

Renata had remembered so little, she said, of what had happened back in '53-'54. No matter how Cady phrased a question, it made no difference. Renata didn't remember.

"I loved your father, and he loved me, but I wasn't happy in Texas and Frances, I mean your grandmother didn't care much for me, and I—"

Cady interrupted her. "I think it's time I told you something very important, and I hope it won't be too upsetting to you." She felt dizzy.

"What is it?"

"My dad's not dead."

Renata's face went slack. "I always knew he was still on this earth," she answered, not wishing to divulge to Cady that she'd known all along. "I don't know what to say."

"Are you feeling all right? I know this must be quite a shock. It certainly was to your sister."

"Yes, I'm sure Miriam was shocked. Please, tell me about him," Renata said.

"Well, he's come a long way since the accident. After years of rehabilitation, he returned to live in Pecan Valley in the 60s. After my grandmother died in '76, Rachel Hawkins moved into our home there to take care of him. Do you remember Rachel?"

"Yes, I do . . . I remember her well. I'm sorry to hear about your grandmother," she said, not letting on that Cully had told her about Frances's death. "I know that Rachel was quite devoted to her."

"Yes, they were very close and so are we. Dad's life is simple, but he seems happy. He doesn't remember much from one moment to the next, but remembers everything from the past."

"I hope he doesn't remember *everything*," Renata sighed, thinking about the cruelty of the accident.

"If it makes you feel any better, he's never said a bad word about you."

"That sounds like Jonas. He was always too kind for his own good. Well, I'm glad you told me. I'm happy for you that you didn't lose him, but I know these years must have been hard for you and, of course, for Frances. And, well, I can only imagine what they've been like for Jonas."

"I don't know what to say, but are you glad to hear he's still alive?" Cady asked.

Renata smiled faintly, her face gone pale. "Sure I am."

"Yes, of course you would be . . . I, uh, have some questions, if you feel like answering them."

"Well, fire away. I hope I can answer them to your satisfaction."

"Do you remember sending dad out to get a hamburger for you the night of the accident?"

"No. I don't recall anything like that at all. I do remember that he came to check on me that night in the hospital, and that it was raining cats and dogs."

"I was standing next to him when you called him to ask him to bring you the burger."

"Honey, you were a small child and may have misinterpreted the conversation."

"It's the way I remember it," Cady said.

"Well, I don't remember any such thing, but then again the accident was so traumatizing, I don't have much memory of anything during that awful time."

"That's funny. Neither does dad, but then he had a brain injury. Why don't *you* remember?"

"I don't know." Renata looked away.

"What about this boy named Turner?"

"He's my son," Renata said, visibly upset.

"Is he my brother?"

"Well, yes, of course he's your brother."

"I'm sorry if my asking is hard for you, but surely you can understand why I would want to know."

"Yes, of course. You never knew him, or that he existed. I understand your questions about him. He was a sweet small child, but I guess the absence of a good male figure in his life left him at quite a disadvantage while he was growing up."

"I'll be honest with you, Renata. Miriam told me that Turner had been nothing but trouble for you."

"Well, she's being somewhat protective I suppose. She resents the way he's treated me, but I guess I can't blame him. I played piano with a jazz trio, and he grew up in the back rooms of too many bars because I couldn't afford a babysitter. It was hardly a good life for him." Renata pulled at her hair nervously. "Could we please not talk about him tonight? I don't know where he is and it upsets me to think about him. I can only hope he's safe." Weariness came over her face.

"I can see that you're tired. It's been an emotional meeting. Maybe we should get some shut-eye and pick up the conversation in the morning?"

"Yes, I think that's a good idea," Renata answered, the color completely gone from her face.

Before they fell asleep that night, Cady asked Renata if Frances and Jonas Sr. had known about Turner. She was surprised to find out that they had indeed known about him and had sent money to Renata for the boy. They had never told Cady about Turner. There were secrets, like the other one Frances and Jonas Sr. had kept from Miriam and the rest of Renata's family—that Jonas had lived through the accident; Cady had kept her own—the call from her mother all those years before when her mother told her about the boy Turner. She'd heard Frances complaining to Rachel that a collect call had been mistakenly billed to them.

Renata awoke early the next morning. She stared at her daughter sleeping in the other bed and admired Cady's beauty and her relative youth, yet there was a deep sadness about her to which Renata knew she had contributed. She sat looking at Cady for a good half hour before Cady stirred.

"Good morning," Cady mumbled, rolling over and stretching. "Have you been up long?"

"No . . . just a little while."

"How about we order up some breakfast?"

"It's so expensive, room service."

"Well, this is a special occasion, and I don't want to waste what little private time we have left going downstairs."

While Cady ordered up coffee and a light breakfast, Renata dressed and made ready to leave. Cady followed suit and packed her bag. They ate and made small talk, commenting on the weather and how wonderful it was that the sky was clear for Cady's flight back that day.

"I know we don't have much more time to talk this trip, but I have a few more questions if you don't mind," Cady said.

"No, of course I don't mind. What would you like to know?"

"Well, since you thought my dad was dead, did you ever get involved with anyone else?"

Renata wriggled around uncomfortably before answering. "I was young and hopeful that I could start over, but none of the men I met could ever hold a candle to your father."

"Do you remember calling me in Pecan Valley when I was a teenager, when you told me about Turner?"

"No, can't say that I remember that. Was it a good conversation?"

"I'm afraid not. I was very rude to you."

"Oh, well, I'm sure I deserved it."

"I was impetuous and angry then. I regret having been so rude. I guess I'll have to chalk it up to being a confused teenager."

"It's a long story, Cady, why I left. It wasn't pleasant, and it wasn't my choice, but I wasn't mature enough to fight it."

"You mean the whole court scene . . . being in jail?"

"Yes. I don't know how much you heard about it. I blocked much of it from my memory as it was so painful and confusing. I know that I was accused of something that I didn't do, and I knew that Frances and Sr., as I called him, hired some law firm to concoct some story about me to get rid of me. I just couldn't prove it and no one would have believed me anyway."

"Do you remember the night I ran away?"

"No, I don't. Did you really run away? I thought you were taken away."

"No, I ran away. The neighbor boy, Sweezer Riley, helped me get to Pecan Valley. And the lady across the street in the house with the red shutters helped. You were drunk that night, with some man, and poured vodka all over my supper. When they got me to Pecan Valley, I never returned."

Renata looked away, stood up, and walked to the window of the hotel room. "It's a beautiful sky out there. Good clear flying weather," she said.

"I take it you don't want to talk about this?"

"I don't remember any of it, so I don't see the point. But I do remember one thing besides the fact that I loved your father very much: I remember the times you'd walk on the back of the sofa, balancing like a tightrope walker, and I warned you over and over that you could get hurt. One day, when you were at it again, ignoring my warning, I stood at the end of the sofa and put my arms out to you and told you to jump. You went flying off the end. I dropped my arms and let you fall. You looked up at me with these huge bewildered eyes, and I told you then, as I'll tell you now, you can never trust anything or anyone, not even your mother."

Somehow Cady wasn't shocked by the story, more fascinated by it. She did, however, consider that the incident could very well have affected her every good and bad choice she'd made along the way.

When it was time for Cady to leave for the airport, she made sure her mother had enough cash to get a cab back home. They vowed to stay in touch, and Renata promised that Cady would be notified if anything were to happen to her. Renata had hinted about hoping to see Jonas again. The parting wasn't emotional. They each planned that this would not be their last goodbye.

The long flight back to California gave Cady plenty of time to reflect on the time in Chicago, and especially the night before in the piano bar. There couldn't have been produced, not even by Hollywood, a more poignant scene than the one played out in that bar. It was clear that there was much she'd never know, but relief in no longer having to search for what could not be found.

Staring out the plane window, she thought about her mother's performance, that silly but soft-hearted musician man, the hold her mother had on the crowd, and the song. She remembered her mother so poised, so unruffled in the face of such high expectation. It was important to have finally experienced something good in Renata. There had been such incomprehensible hurt.

30

Mid-January 1993

Cady put her hand around her ear to make sure she was hearing the radio correctly. "Shhh, listen. Did you hear that?" she asked Dell.

"Did I hear what?" Dell answered impatiently.

"The song on the radio . . . that stupid-sounding line that dad recites every morning of his life. You know the one where he says 'beat me daddy, eight to the bar'?"

"Okay . . . so what about it?"

"They're playing it on the radio! All these years I thought he made it up, that it was pure brain injury jibberish. I didn't know that it was a real song! I feel so awful that it never dawned on me he could know something I didn't . . . that I was so skeptical and unkind at times." Her stomach was in knots. Marlon had died in his sleep, of old age, the vet said, just two weeks before. Rachel had tried to console her, but was inconsolable herself. She loved Marlon as much as Cady did. Marlon had left far less a mark on Dell.

"You come up with the damned craziest ideas," he said, squinting through the dirty windshield of his truck, looking for the departure lane at the Albuquerque Airport.

It had been two years since they'd relocated the business from Chico to Santa Fe. When Rachel fell ill in '88, her frequent bouts with an ailing heart had made it necessary for Cady to return to Texas more often to help out; being closer to Texas had made traveling to Pecan Valley far easier.

"Okay, we're here," he sighed in relief, jumping out of the truck to pull Cady's bags from the back end of the truck.

"I'll miss you, Dell Wayne Wilson," she whispered into his neck. "I'll call you when I get in, okay?"

"Yep," he replied, patting her back with a distance in his voice that had grown more pronounced over the last year.

She rubbed his arm tenderly. "I love you," she told him.

"Yeah, me too," he mumbled back, turning to walk away.

Rachel awakened Cady that first night to tell her she thought she was having a heart attack. She insisted that Cady call an ambulance. Jonas couldn't be left alone with no one there in the morning. For the first time in her life, since the accident, Cady would be alone with him. What would she do without Rachel? She was terrified. Dell wasn't answering the phone.

The next morning Cady gave Jonas enough money to eat lunch downtown and instructions to stay at the drugstore until she came to get him. She didn't tell him how gravely ill Rachel was, not wanting to believe it herself. Those last hours Cady spent with Rachel at the hospital were otherworldly. Luckily there was no one sharing the room. There was a soft light coming through the aqua-colored curtains of Rachel's hospital room. Cady opened them slightly to see a jack rabbit scampering through the open field that led out to the highway. "A simple and peaceful scene," she thought.

"Child, come on over here to your ole Rachel," Rachel said, motioning to Cady with a bony hand.

"Aw, Rachel, how do you feel, my dear?" Cady ran her hand lightly over Rachel's white hair. It had the same soft sponginess that Cady remembered feeling as a child. "I love you, Rachel." She bent down to kiss Rachel's forehead.

"And I love you, child . . . will forevermore. Ole Rachel will always be close . . . when you can't see me. Soon gonna see Miss Frances . . . lil' ole pooch, Marlon . . . Blackie too . . . Toady, oh, sweet Toady."

"Toady was your husband's name?"

"Yes," she whispered, her eyes clouding over.

"I envy you, getting to see everyone again, and I envy you getting to see Grandmamma and Marlon, but, please Rachel . . . not just yet. I don't want to say goodbye."

"No worry none, child . . . good Lord's gonna see to you and your daddy."

"How do you know? How can you be sure?"

"Gone all my way now . . . time to lay it down . . . I be watchin' out..." Her voice trailed away.

"Oh Rachel, what can I do for you?"

Rachel lifted one finger to Cady to come closer. Her breathing had become labored. Cady put her ear near Rachel's mouth.

"Watch Doc close," she whispered. "He got powerful lots to teach you . . . your mama done all she knew." She seemed to have fallen asleep. Her breathing was shallow. She suddenly opened her eyes. They seemed brighter. "Let it be, child," she said. Those were her last words. Cady thought she saw a smile.

She sat on the side of Rachel's bed and watched Rachel's chest barely moving. The nurse had come in several times. She felt Rachel's pulse once, and wrote something on the chart she was holding.

"Isn't there anything you all can *do?* The doctor hasn't been in, not once, to see her."

"Yes, ma'am, he has, before you got here, but there's really nothin' we can do now 'cept wait."

"Wait for what?" Cady asked near tears.

"For the inevitable, I'm afraid," the nurse answered, matter-of-factly.

Rachel didn't open her eyes or speak again, but when Cady asked if she was all right, she thought she saw another small smile. At approximately 3:45 that afternoon, the exact same time of day that Frances passed, Rachel took a series of rattled breaths, and then slipped away into eternity. Cady sat with her body for a good hour before slipping the pillow she'd brought from home out from under Rachel's head. It was still warm.

"Sleep well, my dearest friend, and tell Grandmamma that I love and miss her, will you? And when you see Marlon and Blackie tell them too, okay?" She smoothed Rachel's hair. "I promise you that I'll listen to Dad and watch what he does, like you said. I'm going to miss you, Rachel . . . oh my God I'm going to miss you. Please stay near, will you? I love you so much."

Clutching Rachel's pillow against her chest, Cady walked slowly out into the hall of the small hospital, stopping at the nurses' station. Not one nurse looked up.

"Excuse me," Cady said, clearing her throat, wiping the tears from her cheeks. "What will happen with Mrs. Hawkins's body?"

"Don't worry none," one of them answered. "We already called the funeral home. They'll be over to pick her up directly. You gonna be responsible for any extra bills?"

"Yes of course. She's family," Cady answered indignantly, walking away.

Cady sat in her car waiting for the ambulance with her face buried in the pillow that held Rachel's final moment. The beat-up ambulance finally arrived, drove to the side of the building, and stopped by the back door. Cady watched as the gurney bumped over the uneven sidewalk and the men slid Rachel's sheet-covered body into the back of the vehicle. She suddenly remembered that Jonas was waiting for her at the drugstore. She wondered if it was Rachel reminding her.

When she got there, Blanche ran out and said he'd been just fine, that they'd taken good care of him. Cady had never been so glad to see him. She apologized to him for the wait and told him, in the car on the way home, that Rachel was gone. He shook his head slowly in the affirmative and said he was hungry. Cady took a deep breath and remembered what Rachel had said about listening to him—that he had a powerful lot to teach her. She'd just gotten her first lesson.

It was a small funeral at the same little Three Kings Baptist Church where Rachel Moon had been baptized, and where she'd married Jebediah "Toady" Hawkins. Cady and Jonas had been there several times with Rachel. Her body was on view below the altar in a simple wood coffin dressed up with the church's satin, cross-covered banner. Rachel herself had chosen and paid for her coffin ahead of time: it had been locked away in the Randolph garage storage room. All that was visible of her from the pews was the corsage that church members had bought and pinned on the powder blue dress that had been Frances's. Frances had left all her clothes to Rachel. They had been the same dress and shoe size. Cady took the one that Rachel had most often admired, but said she'd never have occasion to wear, up to the mortician. She was sure both Frances and Rachel would be pleased. The two of them, after all, were best friends.

There were only a few cars in the procession out to the cemetery, but as was the custom, cars on the highway pulled onto the shoulder and stopped to pay respect. It was almost hot that day, not unusual for West Texas in January. Rachel was interred at the back of the cemetery, next to her mother, "where the coloreds are buried," the funeral man had told Cady the day before the funeral. Cady told him that if there was a plot left next to Rachel's, she wanted it for herself. "You've lived in the big city way too long, talkin' like that," the funeral man had told her, walking off, shaking his head.

Rachel would like to have been buried next to Toady, but after he died in the car crash, his people took his young corpse away to their home in another state. Rachel never knew where he'd been buried. Her own gravesite was in a straight line back from Frances's. She had chosen it for that reason. She and Frances had often talked about how their spirits would one day meet up for visits at the cemetery's fish pond when no one was looking.

Dell had been late for the funeral and had taken a seat in the back. That night he announced to Cady that he was leaving her. "Cady, honey, might as well just tell it like it is. I've met somebody else."

"What do you mean you've met somebody else?" she asked, her mouth gone dry.

"I mean it's over between us. Like I said, I've met someone else. Fifteen years of you goin' back home, leavin' me to do everything alone? No way I'm gonna go another fifteen like that."

Ironically and mercifully, the profound closeness Cady had shared with Rachel in her final hours had numbed Cady to the hard stab of Dell's announcement. She was unable to speak. He slept in the spare room at 161 that night and left the next morning without a goodbye. She watched numbly from the end of the driveway as his pickup disappeared up Baker Street. There was a deep ache in her chest as she walked up the driveway and up the back porch steps. She stopped to open the small metal cabinet where Frances had kept canned goods. There was one can left of Frances's favorite—Ranch Style Beans. She decided she'd never open it.

She found Jonas seated at the table. She rummaged through the Frigidaire to find a carton of eggs. Jonas waited patiently. She scrambled the eggs, cut off a couple of slices of bread from the half-eaten loaf in the breadbox, and plugged in the percolator. He seemed happy. He ate contentedly.

"We're going to have to figure out some way to go on without Rachel, Dad, and Dell's gone too."

Jonas uttered that half-cry-half-laugh that Cady had come to understand was his only way of showing deep emotion.

"Oh, how we'll miss that fine lady . . . and little ole Marlon too," he said.

"Yes we will. Did you understand what I was telling you about Dell?"

Jonas continued eating, not responding.

"Dad? Did you hear me? Dell and I are finished."

"Who?" Jonas asked.

"Never mind Pop . . . just enjoy your breakfast."

When Jonas began choking, Cady instinctively called out for Rachel. She panicked when she realized that Rachel would not be answering the call. She was never so relieved when he recovered quickly and picked up another forkful of eggs, as though nothing had happened.

"Dad, I have something important to tell you. I think Rachel would want me to tell you."

"All right," Jonas said softly, reaching for his coffee.

"I found my mother, and spent a day with her a few months ago."

Jonas took a sip of coffee, looking over the tops of his glasses. "How was she?" he asked.

"She was fine, Dad."

"That's good. That's very good." He took another bite of food.

"Is that all you've got to say?"

"Sure would like a warm up," he said, holding up his cup.

Cady unplugged the percolator and brought it to the table. He smiled up at her as the coffee splashed into his cup. She watched him relish that first hot sip and wished that, for just a little while, she could be like him—uncomplicated and glad for everything. She tried not to think about Dell. Rachel's words about Jonas came back to her: "He's got powerful lots to teach you."

31

Santa Fe, New Mexico—late March 1993

It was nearing sunset and the Sangre de Cristo Mountains were bathed in that pink glow that gave them their name. Cady would miss the sunsets most of all.

"No thanks. I don't need your help."

"Aw, come on, Cady, your pride's getting in your way as usual," Dell said.

"Okay then, how 'bout *this?* I don't *want* your help."

"That would be the first time, m'dear," he said, rolling his eyes.

"Okay, that's enough, Dell. Goodbye and good luck to you," she said, backing out of the door with the last box.

"Jesus, Cady, I was just kidding."

"Not funny, not in the least," she said, taking a last look at the small place they'd shared on Canyon Road for ten years.

"You know I wish you well," he said, following her out to the car.

"How easy that is to say. Easier than saying thank you."

"Thank you? Thank you for what?" he asked, kicking a rock out from under his boot.

"For being your loyal friend all these years, for taking a chance on us, for listening to your problems, for working beside you and building the business up, for believing in you, for caring about you, for giving you the best of me. I realize that my responsibility to my father was hard for you, and I'm sorry for that, but I couldn't abandon him."

"I never asked you to, did I? Look, I did the best I could for you, but it was never enough."

Cady took a deep breath. "Thanks, Dell. You're making this a lot easier for me."

"Ok . . . just wish you'd said that to *begin* with."

"I wish I had too," she said, sighing at the futility of hoping for a respectful, dignified goodbye.

Driving out of the compound, through the sting of tears, she watched Dell turn to go inside through her rear view mirror. Of all the people who had been important in her life, she took some small amount of comfort in knowing that Dell Wayne Wilson was the only one of them who had actually *chosen* to leave her.

The movers were already on their way to Texas with her belongings, and she'd be meeting them at the house in Pecan Valley the next day, staying in a motel on busy Cerrillos Road that night. It had been two months since Rachel had died and since Dell had left. The new woman was moving in with him, so that meant Cady had to get her things out of the Canyon Road place sooner than later. She'd put it off as long as possible.

She wished she was leaving Santa Fe in September, during Fiestas, when Zozobra, the forty-foot-high papier mache figure, would burn in effigy. The figure's burning would take the gloom and doom away from the few thousand onlookers who for decades had worked themselves into frenzies every Friday night after Labor Day. "Burn, burn, burn!" the crowd would roar. It would have been a symbolic time to leave, to start over, but it was March instead, and spring was arriving with the fierce winds that would whip her all the way out of New Mexico the next morning. She did write a letter to Dell, that a friend promised to throw into the pyre at the next burning of Zozobra, containing her parting words for which there had been no audience.

After calling the church couple who had volunteered to stay with Jonas while she was gone, she fell asleep in the motel room relaxed by their assurance that her father was fine and himself getting ready for bed. The motel wake-up call at 5:30 a.m. the next morning would come too soon for the long drive back to Pecan Valley.

She drove the fifty-five speed limit toward Clines Corners, looking into her rear view mirror at the majesty of the mountains she was leaving behind—the same mountains, in all their glory, that had welcomed her back to Santa Fe on so many returns. She knew that nothing, including her, would be the same again.

She stopped in Santa Rosa at the truck depot on the road to Ft. Sumner. There were vivid memories there of the times she and Dell had filled up, gotten coffee, taken Marlon for walks. Marlon had anointed every tire he could manage to raise a leg on, and had been stroked by more truckers and little kids than Cady could count.

She passed through Ft. Sumner and drove on to Clovis to make her traditional stop for a meal at the Mexican food restaurant there, at the end of town on the road to Muleshoe, Texas. From there, there would be only five or so hours left to Pecan Valley on a long stretch of road with little more to see than cotton fields, an occasional grain silo, and feed lots filled with cattle that had no idea what they were in for. There were abandoned small farmhouses and buzzards feasting on the poor creatures that hadn't made it across the highway—all a far cry from the serenity of the Sangre de Cristo Mountains. Cady turned on the radio. Country-western was all she could get.

It was near 4:00 o'clock in the afternoon when she turned into the driveway at 161. She stopped by the back steps to unload the car. Mr. Hammond from the church came out to help her with her bags and a few boxes while his wife, Ella, stood at the stove stirring a pan of soup she was making for Jonas's supper.

"Thank you, Mr. Hammond, for taking care of my dad."

"Aw, we enjoyed it. He's such a fine fellow and so easy to please. It was a pleasure."

"Well, now, if you and Mrs. Hammond need to get home, please feel free. I can take it from here."

"Are you sure about that?" Mr. Hammond asked. "We're just happy to stay tonight if you'd like. You're probably road-tired, so just leave it to us tonight, and start fresh in the morning."

Cady took the Hammonds up on their offer. She was worn out and feeling like a dark blanket was making its way for her head and face. It was that same feeling she'd had at intervals through the years. It was a smothering feeling. Her heart would race and she'd find it hard to breathe. It would take hours to feel well again. Until she did, she'd stay put wherever she was.

"Hello, Dad," Cady said, kissing her father's cheek as he waited eagerly for his supper.

"Well, look who's here!" he said.

"I'll join you for supper in a little bit, soon as I get the car unloaded and into the garage."

"Well, that'll make it taste all the better," he said, smiling broadly.

It was a quiet night. The Hammonds set up the dominoes on the table for a game with Jonas while Cady went upstairs to her room. She sat on the old window seat for a little while, a cool breeze blowing the organza curtains away from the sill. The lights glowed brightly from the big house across the way. She could hear dogs barking a few blocks over, and she shuddered a bit wondering if she could pull herself together enough to be alone with her father, without Frances, and without Rachel. "Can I possibly be strong enough for this?" she whispered to herself. "How am I going to do this? Holy crap, I'm scared."

She crept down the stairs and into her grandparents' old bedroom, opened the small closet door, and found Rachel's once-a-year uniform hanging there. She took it off the hanger, laid it gently on the other twin bed in her room, and fell to sleep.

When Cady got to the kitchen the next morning, the Hammonds had already fixed Jonas's breakfast and were making their way out of the house with the few things they'd brought for their stay.

"Thank you so much again for helping," Cady said, giving Mrs. Hammond a hug, shaking Mr. Hammond's hand.

"Like I said, young lady, we were happy to help and sure did enjoy our stay with Doc. You call on us anytime we can help out, okay?" he offered with a toothy grin, the few strands of his dark hair combed high across his forehead and plastered down on a shiny bald head. "So long, Doc," Hammond said to Jonas, patting him gently on the back. Jonas smiled and thanked him.

The morning sky was clear, with a light wind, and when the sprinklers in the yard across the street came on, she could feel a light spray on her face. In no time the yards would green up. "Can't believe I'm back here and I won't be leaving this time," she mused to herself, as she watched the Hammonds' car disappear around the corner.

She sat on the back steps for awhile before joining Jonas in the kitchen. She decided that she would leave Frances's chair pushed under the kitchen table, as Rachel had, and would take her place at the opposite end of the table where she'd sat as a child. It wasn't a happy day or an unhappy one, but a new and different one.

"Dad, I want to ask you something," Cady said.

"Shoot," he said.

"How would you like to see Renata again?"

"You mean your mother?"

"Yes, I mean my mother."

"Is she here?" His eyes opened wide, the good one fixed on Cady.

"No, but I can see to it if you like. It might be a little while before she can get here."

"It would be wonderful *any* time."

"Okay, I'll start making plans. You sure it's what you want?"

"You bet I am," he said, winking at her. He then turned his attention back to his breakfast.

The rest of the morning passed uneventfully. Jonas took off on foot for town to make his rounds at the post office and the drugstore. Cady finished the dishes.

32

Pecan Valley—September 1, 1993

Renata's trip from Chicago to Concho City had been a long one. Her headaches had gotten worse and more frequent. She'd had to cancel plans to fly to Texas in May. Not wanting Cady to know about the illness, she'd made up a story about some work contract she had to honor. A new drug she was taking had given her some relief and, not wanting to miss the chance to see Jonas again, she'd scheduled the flight to arrive late into Dallas so she'd have an excuse to rest overnight before flying into Concho City.

Cady had met Renata's flight the next morning, and they'd arrived back in Pecan Valley just in time for Renata to relax a little while before seeing Jonas for the first time in forty years. He'd soon be home for lunch. He hadn't seemed to remember that she was arriving that day. It was just as well. Cady only hoped that seeing her wouldn't be too much a shock for him.

"Renata, let me take your bag upstairs for you. Why don't you just sit and relax here in the kitchen?"

"That would be lovely," she answered, looking around the kitchen. "This kitchen hasn't changed at all in all these years. I remember Frances sat there," Renata said, pointing to the chair that was tightly pushed in at the head of the table. "And the same ugly wallpaper . . . I never liked it."

"Well, we like it just fine," Cady said. "I hope it won't be too unpleasant for you."

"Of course not...to each his own, eh?"

"Yes, I suppose so."

Cady excused herself to take Renata's bag up to the guestroom. Tension was building in her, and she was beginning to wonder if she'd done the right thing bringing Renata back into their lives.

"You're going to put me in that front room upstairs? I remember it had a dizzying number of fleurs-de-lis all over the walls," Renata said.

"It *still* does. Would you prefer sleeping elsewhere?"

"Oh, no, that's fine. It was where your father and I stayed when we were here all those times."

Cady took the bag up quickly and opened the vents which she'd forgotten to do earlier. It was predicted to be a high of ninety-five that day. She'd only briefly considered giving Renata the cooler downstairs master bedroom. Had she, Frances would have shuddered in her grave. Hearing voices, Cady ran downstairs.

"My God, Dad, you're home early," Cady said, shocked to find Renata and Jonas locked in an embrace.

"Oh Monkey darlin', I've missed you so," Jonas said, in almost a cry, kissing Renata all over her face, her hands, and her neck.

"And you, Jonas love, I always knew I'd see you again. You can't imagine how I've missed you."

"And not a day has passed that I haven't missed you." Jonas was stroking her face.

"I love you, Jonas."

"And I love you more than life, Ren."

Cady was dumbfounded by the scene. She had not anticipated such affection between them after all the years, after all that had happened. As they continued to caress one another, Jonas's face flushed with a vibrancy Cady had never seen. She felt embarrassed, like some interloper. She left the kitchen, ran upstairs to her window seat, and mumbled to herself, "Oh my God, how did he live through this, not knowing where she'd gone, why she'd left? He's been so alone with this."

Through the years, Cady had asked him many times how he felt about

Renata. "She was brilliant and beautiful," he'd say. When Cady asked if he loved her, he'd say, "Well, of course. She's your mother." Cady stared out the upstairs window, fighting back tears, the tightness in her throat painful. She waited awhile before returning to the kitchen. When she did, she found Renata opening cabinet doors.

"Can I help you find something?" Cady asked, moving closer.

"I was just looking for cups so we could have a cup of Joe for old time's sake."

"Here, let me get them for you. The coffeemaker's ready to go," she said, nudging her mother away from the cupboard. "Do you mind if I have a cup with you two or would you prefer being alone?"

"Of course, you can join us. Your father and I would like that, wouldn't we dear?"

"Yes, of course," he said, following her with his eyes.

Cady sat and listened to them recount times they'd spent together; they made jokes and winked at each other about some tree in Atlanta the night they'd met—obviously a secret between them. At 8:00 that evening, Cady went to Jonas's bedroom and called Nancy.

She and Nancy sat opposite each other on the twin beds. "Nancy, I really appreciate your coming over. I didn't want to be alone. I think it was crazy bringing my mother here."

"Tell me what's going on, Cady. I've never seen you like this."

"I know. I don't know what I expected when I brought her here. I think maybe I wanted to be more included in this thing." She started picking at her cuticles. "And I didn't think, frankly, that Dad would be so glad to see her, or that it would matter so much to him."

"Cady stop picking at your cuticles . . . and tell me, how long's it been since they separated?"

"Forty years."

"Well, if you ask me, this reunion is downright romantic."

"Romantic? I don't know about that," Cady said, moving over to the window seat.

"I'm sorry, Cady. I think I'm making things worse."

Nancy took off her shoes and nestled back into the two pillows on the twin bed that she considered "hers" after so many sleepovers during their school years. They had become more like sisters. Cady sat in the window seat for a long time.

"Nancy? You asleep?"

"Nah . . . just lollygaggin', enjoyin' the cool air."

"What am I going to do? I think I've unleashed some terrible pestilence on this house."

"Aw, come on, Cady. Don't you think you're being a little hard on yourself and maybe just a tad dramatic?"

"What's wrong with me?"

"Nothing's wrong with you. You haven't been around your parents as a couple in a very long time and it feels strange, that's all. We all have a problem accepting that our parents are people like us. And I think it's as hard for us to be adult in their presence."

"What if I've opened up Pandora's box? What happens to Dad when she leaves? And she *will* leave."

"Maybe she won't. Maybe she'll want to stay with him and take care of him."

"Are you kidding? That'll never happen."

"Well, I'm just saying that maybe . . . ," Nancy muttered, not finishing the sentence.

"Can you imagine my mother coming from Chicago to live in Pecan Valley? She hates Texas and, besides, there are too many people who'd run her out on a rail."

"Like who?"

"Like Cully."

"Why? He doesn't even live here."

"Because he'd be afraid she'd get more than he got."

"Get more what?"

"Money, furniture, stock, power, food, marbles . . . *anything!* Even though he doesn't live here, he keeps his big foot in the door. That's a whole other story I'm afraid."

"I don't see how they have any say about your dad seeing his wife or you seeing your mother, and maybe she loves your dad more than she hates Texas and would stand up to them."

"Oh, Nancy, you don't understand. I really do think I've made a terrible mistake bringing her here."

"It's too late for that now. It'll be all right. Listen, I better get on home. You know how that man of mine gets when I'm away too long. Will you be okay if I go?"

"Of course I will be. You go on home. We can talk tomorrow."

Cady followed Nancy down the stairs to see her out. There was laughter coming from the kitchen.

"Dad, it's time for you to start getting ready for bed," Cady said, pushing open the swinging door. "You know how long it takes you."

"Oh, no, it's early still."

"Jonas, dear, Cady's right. We've got plenty of time. We're not getting any younger, and we need our rest. Go on and get ready for bed and I'll come in and wish you goodnight," she said, kissing Jonas on the cheek.

"Oh, all right, Ren, if you say so."

Cady stood at the door, breathing shallowly. There were little beads of perspiration popping up across her forehead. She excused herself to go upstairs. Neither Jonas nor Renata seemed to have noticed. She cranked out both windows as wide as they'd go, took the screen off the one over the window seat, and leaned out over the gable. She breathed deeply until her pulse slowed. She had never left her father alone after dinner, but there was no place for her downstairs.

33

The next morning—September 2, 1993

Cady was awakened by the sound of the phone ringing through the air vent. She threw on a robe and ran downstairs to grab the closest extension in Jonas's room. She found Renata and Jonas wrapped up in each other's arms on his twin bed. She clinched her teeth and answered the phone, making no effort to keep her voice down.

"Hello, Randolph residence, Cady speaking."

"Cady, it's your Uncle Park. How are you?"

"I'm okay, but . . . I, uh, well . . . it's been so *long*. I mean it's such a surprise after all these years to hear from you. Are you here?" she asked, turning around to see Renata slipping out of the room. Jonas remained fast asleep.

"No, I'm still in Austin, honey. I'm sorry to have been out of touch for so long...it's a long story. I realize it sure must be shocking for you to hear from me, but . . . I've got something important to talk with you about. Is it all right to talk now? I mean *can* you talk?"

"Yes, I can talk. So what's going on?"

"I got a call from Cully a little while ago, and I want to warn you that he's going to be showing up in Pecan Valley . . . probably sooner than later. He said that Renata's there. Is it true?"

"Yes," she answered hesitantly.

"Okay, right off the bat, I want you to know that I don't judge you for having her there, but I would be surprised if Renata isn't in cahoots with Cully. I'm not going to ask you why or how she's there after all these years. That's your business. I should have talked to you about something a long time ago, but I was in such a mess of trouble that I wasn't thinking straight. Forgive me. I haven't been a good uncle. I don't know exactly what's up Cully's sleeve, but I can guarantee it's no good. His buddy Hal Palmer's no saint either. Watch them both."

"Why are you telling me this? What's happened?" Cady asked, closing the door.

"I'm pretty sure Cully's cheated you and that Palmer knows about it. I'll bet my bottom dollar that you weren't included in a large draw from Mother's estate right after she died."

"What are you talking about?"

"That's what I thought. You *didn't* know. I found out a couple of years ago that Cully sold a large tract of land a few months after Mother died. There was no property in that area listed on the inventory."

"Where was it?"

"Down in the Valley. I just found out a couple of years ago and not from Cully. I don't know what he did with the money. I'll explain more when I get up there. Did you receive anything about that time?"

"No, nothing until around '80 when I was told Probate was over and the distribution was being made. I got the deed to the house and $10,000 cash. And you?"

"It's a long story, honey. I was in trouble with some debtors breathing down my neck. Cully gave me $30,000 in '76, right after Mother died, and I had to waive my right to the rest of what I might be due from her estate in order to get it. I didn't know about that land then."

"That's all you got from the estate . . . $30,000?"

"Yes, that's all I got. I always knew I was getting screwed, but I had no choice. I needed cash and I was desperate."

"How much did Cully get for the land? Do you know?"

"In excess of $300,000 . . . I believe there were other interests that weren't listed on the inventory either. And this is the hardest part to tell you—Cully got Jonas's signature to replace you with Renata's son,

Turner, as beneficiary of your dad's life insurance policy. As I remember, it's worth close to half a million."

"How do you know all of this?"

"Cully got drunk and called me one night recently and started mouthing off to me. He was joking about how when you were in Santa Fe, I think, he forged Jonas's signature to delete you as beneficiary. I got a check for a few thousand from Cully a few days later, he said to help me out, but I knew it was his way of paying me off to keep my mouth shut."

"So, it looks like his bribe worked. You kept your mouth shut."

"Yes, I should have told you about the insurance policy when I found out. I don't know why I didn't. I'm so sorry."

"I don't know what to say. I need a little time to let this sink in. I can say this though— I don't understand how it could benefit Cully to make that Turner guy a beneficiary. Do you know?"

"What I'm trying to tell you is that Cully does nothing that won't directly benefit him. I think you and your dad have been cheated in the worst way, by someone Mother expected she'd be able to trust. Mother and Dad could never quite allow themselves to see Cully for who he really is. I know this . . . I'm not much better than him, but I can at least try to put things right now, if it's not too late."

"No one could be as rotten as that man," Cady told him. "I'll see you when you get to town. If you need a place to stay, you can stay at the house."

"That's a very generous offer under the circumstances."

"Before I go, do you know anything at all about that notebook of Grandmother's, the one that listed all her assets and her plans? I know that notebook existed."

"Yes, Cady, it did. Cully took it. I only saw it once, and he said it was how they created the inventory list. I don't know what he did with it for sure, but I think he had it at one time in Houston, filed with a bunch of other stuff."

"I knew it," she said, shaking her head. "You told me you would let me know if it was ever found."

"I'm sorry, Cady. I should have told you, but frankly I was too wrapped up in my own affairs. It's no excuse. It's just that there was so much going on and, I . . . oh, God, I should have told you."

"I wonder why Cully would keep something so incriminating. Grandmother told me that she'd stated very clearly what she paid for Cully's apartment in Houston, and why she bought it. You knew all this then, didn't you?"

"Yes, I did. Mother talked about the $250,000 often." Park felt his pulse quicken.

"Is there any way you can get it?"

"Get what?"

"The notebook."

"I don't know how I would, short of breaking into his apartment."

"You know, this is really the last thing I need to be thinking about right now. Dad's health is my biggest concern."

"Yes, of course. Believe it or not, I'm concerned about him too."

"Okay, I'll tell you goodbye now and plan to see you tomorrow then?"

"Yes . . . thanks for talking with me, and well, I hope this won't further distress you, but I'd rather not see Renata while I'm there."

"That's not a problem. She'll be gone."

No sooner had Cady hung up the phone with Park than the phone rang again.

"Good morning, young lady."

"Who is this please?" Cady asked, never liking it when people didn't identify themselves, expecting her to know who they were.

"It's Hal, Hal Palmer. Hope I'm not disturbing you calling this early in the day."

"What can I do for you?" Cady asked.

"Well, word's out that Renata's in town. Is that right?"

"Why are you calling up here asking me this . . . who told you that?"

"Well, actually, no one you know. I just wanted to let you know that your Uncle Cully called me this morning that he'd gotten a call too. He's not happy about it."

"First of all, get this straight . . . what I do, and with whom, is nobody's business— especially not yours or Cully's."

"Now Cady, I want you to remember what your granddaddy made clear. I'm just tryin' to remind you of that and help you out here."

"Help me out? It's come to my attention that helping me out is the last thing on your mind. What are you *really* getting at?"

"I believe you know exactly what I'm getting at. Your granddaddy made it crystal clear that if you made any gesture toward your mother, aided her in any way, etc., that you would be considered persona non grata. He was a damned good friend of mine, rest his soul, and I think he'd expect me to make this call."

"I repeat . . . my comings and goings are none of your business."

"I'm just here to tell you that your Uncle Cully is concerned about Renata being in town."

"I'm going to hang up now, Hal Palmer. And don't call here again. You can tell your pal Cully the same . . . and to mind his own business."

Cady hung up, trembling. Jonas was still fast asleep. She quietly shut the door.

Coffee was brewing in the kitchen. Cady found Renata sitting in Frances's chair.

"Excuse me, but I have to ask you to sit somewhere else."

Renata cut her eyes sideways at Cady. "Good morning to you too . . . is there a reason why I can't sit here?"

"Yes and a very good one. That's my grandmother's chair, and we don't use it."

"Frances has been gone a long time. Don't you think it's time to move on?"

"I think that's my call, not yours," Cady said, still reeling from the conversations she'd had with Park and Hal Palmer.

"Okay, I'll move. I don't want to upset you," Renata said, getting up, sliding the chair back under the table. "How about a cup of coffee and we'll talk about what's bothering you. Is it that you found me in your father's bed this morning?"

"No, it's not because of that. I don't suppose that's any of my business, now is it?"

"Well, I suppose you could *make* it your business."

"It's true that I could, that I might be concerned about my father's welfare, his health."

"I wouldn't do anything to hurt him . . . and I realize that's an odd statement coming from me, since everyone blames me for what happened to him. Maybe it *is* my fault. I don't know. But I can tell you that I'll never do anything again to hurt him. That's my promise."

"I don't know what to say to you," Cady said, pressing her fingernail so hard into her own palm that she drew blood.

"Why don't we just have a cup of coffee for starters," Renata said, getting up to grab the percolator.

They sat sipping the coffee. Cady opened the back door. She heard the redbirds, but no mourning dove. "It's not a good day," she thought. She ran some cold water over the palm of her hand and found a box of Band-Aids Frances kept in the drawer next to the sink. "Grandmother still to the rescue," she thought to herself.

"I'm sorry if I seemed harsh," Cady told her mother.

"Oh, it's all right. I can't blame you for being a little uptight about my being here."

"It never occurred to me that it would be like this," Cady said, her face hot.

"Like what?"

"I don't know, like no time has passed, like everything was perfect between you and my dad, when it was anything *but.*"

"It may not have seemed perfect to you, my dear, but to us, well, that's a different story."

"You treated him like crap," Cady said, moving toward the open back door.

"Adults have fights, disagreements, Cady. As a child, you probably didn't understand."

"Didn't understand? Are you nuts? I heard what happened the night of his accident. I was there."

"You were a child with a child's brain. What you remember, how you remember it, was probably quite different from reality, my dear."

"You made him go out to get you a hamburger that night, when he was tired, when it was storming, when he was supposed to be home taking care of me. He did what you asked, and look what happened to him."

"I told you that I don't remember any such thing. I really don't." Renata poured fresh coffee into her cup. "Want a warm up?" she asked coolly.

"No, I don't."

"Look, for your father's sake, can we just try to put the past aside for this short time?"

"I'll do my best," Cady said, her jaw aching from being clinched.

The kitchen door swung open.

"Dad, how on earth did you get up and dressed so quickly?"

"Did I?" Jonas replied, with a big smile. "Good morning, glory," he said, moving toward Renata, kissing the top of her head.

"Morning, Jonas dear. How did you sleep?"

"Like a baby, thanks to you."

"Good morning to you too, Dad," Cady said.

"Good morning," he said, nodding her direction. "How 'bout a cup o'Joe?"

"Let me get it for you, Jonas," Renata said, hopping up from her chair.

Cady left the kitchen and ran down the back steps toward the little house where she could be alone. She thought about the day of her grandfather's funeral when she and Dell Wayne had sat out there together. Now she was alone except for the offspring of next door's yellow cat sunning himself on the little house's porch. He raised his head slightly when Cady sat down next to him. In all the years since the accident, Jonas had taken at least an hour to get dressed in the morning, often longer. Less than twenty minutes had passed since she'd gotten the calls from Park and Palmer. It was a miracle that Jonas had gotten up and out to the kitchen in that amount of time. "No, it was no miracle. It was Renata," Cady said out loud. "Aw, please, mourning dove . . . let me hear you . . . please, please, please." The katydids were loud, a few birds chirped, but no mourning dove. Mercifully, the yellow cat moved closer and rubbed his head on Cady's arm.

Cady grabbed the car keys off the hook. "I'm going downtown," she announced. "There's food in the fridge in case I don't get back for lunch. Don't open the door or answer the phone while I'm gone, ok?"

"Is there something I should know?" Renata asked.

"I'll explain later. Just do what I say, please?"

"Don't worry. We'll be fine."

34

A few minutes later—September 2

Other than a couple of elderly ladies walking arm in arm down Main, the sidewalks were empty. Cady took a left just before the river, stopped a half block from Palmer's building, and walked the rest of the way. The front door was open. A noisy fan was spinning overhead.

"Well, well, what can I do for you, young lady?" Palmer asked, tugging on one of his suspenders.

"What you can do for me is to tell that sorry Cully Randolph that he will not be messing with me again . . . and that goes for you too."

"Now just a minute, girl . . . you better calm yourself down. What the hell are you talking about?" Palmer asked

"Listen, mister, it has come to my attention that you and Cully took some mighty big liberties with my grandmother's estate back there during that protracted Probate period . . . and don't think for one minute that you're going to get away with it."

"Get away with *what,* pray tell?" Palmer asked, moving in closer to her.

"I believe you and Cully have cheated my grandmother, my father, and me. Her eyes narrowed. "And I can promise you, those days are over."

"Now listen here, missy," Palmer said, pointing his finger at Cady. "It might be prudent for you to consider the gravity of what you're implying before you go any further."

"Do not call me missy, and it might be prudent for *you,* sir, to consider the gravity of what you have participated in. I am *implying* nothing. I am *telling* you that I now know that Cully cheated me. You knew it *then* and *I* know it now."

"You can take your silly paranoia up with Cully. He'll be in town before long."

"I am hardly paranoid. You can also tell your client that he is not welcome in my home so not to bother coming up there. I won't let him in."

"You're engaging in behavior that, I promise you, has Sr. rolling over in his grave," Palmer said.

"Leave my grandfather out of this. If he were here, he'd be after you with his two fists and his own lawyer. That rotten Cully, and you, have no say in my life, or my father's . . . not now, not ever. I'm warning you— stay away from us."

Cady backed up toward the door.

"Don't be a fool, girl . . . you're headed down a dead-end street without a legal leg to stand on, and you're cutting off your nose to spite your pretty little face."

"No, Hal Palmer, you're wrong on all counts, and you'll do well to keep that solid fact in mind before you go one step further trying to intimidate me," she said, backing out the door.

"So long, little lady," Palmer said. The perspiration was evident above his top lip.

⁓

"I'm afraid you're going to have to leave and leave soon. I'll drive you to Concho City to the airport. Get your things together and quick."

"What's going on?" Renata asked, holding Jonas's hand at the kitchen table.

"Trust me on this one. Just go pack up as quickly as you can. I'll explain in the car."

"Aw, you're not going, are you, Ren?"

"Don't worry," she answered, touching him gently on the shoulder. "We'll meet again. Remember that old song, dearest?"

"Sure do," Jonas said, smiling up at her.

They sang a few bars of the song together, then kissed and continued humming. Renata bent over and buried her head in Jonas's shoulder. He put his arms around her.

"I'm so sorry, my darling, for everything, for leaving you alone all these years," Renata told him. "Please forgive me."

"Everything's put right, Ren. I love you."

Cady broke in. "Dad, I'm sorry, but we have to leave now. I'll take you downtown on our way out of town so you can have lunch at the Lone Star while I'm gone. Just stay down there after you eat. It's going to be way too hot for you to walk home. I'll pick you up there when I get back. Okay?" Cady said, looking in her purse for her keys.

"Well, sure," he answered with a confused half-smile.

"Sweetheart, everything's going to be okay," Renata said.

"Sure it will, Monkey," he said.

Cady hurriedly put the dishes in the sink. She was moved by the way they had sung together, the tenderness between them, and her mother's singing voice. It had been almost as good as her piano performance in Chicago.

"Come on you two, we've got to go now."

"Don't rush me," Jonas said, putting his arms around Renata again.

"I'm sorry, Dad. Please help me out here."

"It's all right, Cady. Come on my dear," Renata said to Jonas. "We can talk in the car and we'll see each other again, just like the song says."

They said nothing on the way to the café, but she passed her arm through to the back seat and found his hand to hold while Cady ran into the café to ask the waitress to keep Jonas there until she returned.

He stood on the curb smiling at Renata as Cady drove the car away. Leaning on his cane, he waved until the car finally disappeared over the bridge. The waitress, watching from the window, went out to walk him inside, seating him at his favorite booth by the window.

⁓

"I didn't mention this on the way over to Pecan Valley the other day, but I hadn't been at that airport in Concho City since the day some private dick escorted me there," Renata told Cady who was driving well above the speed limit of sixty.

"What are you talking about?"

"That guy your grandfather hired to frame me. It landed me in jail. The judge would only let me go free if I agreed to go back to Atlanta and never return. That was forty years ago."

"Are you making this up?"

"No, of course I'm not making it up. I alluded to it in Chicago. Remember?"

"Whole thing sounds pretty far-fetched to me."

"Yes, it was pretty far-fetched what they did," Renata said. She stared out the window at the identical white farm houses dotting the fallow fields on the outskirts of Concho City. "Had I only known then what I know now."

Cady felt her heart thumping as the signs for St. Joseph's began appearing on the side of the road.

"Listen, you haven't asked again why the rush to get you out of town," Cady said, as she sped out toward the airport.

"I figured you'd tell me when and if you felt it best," Renata said.

"I got a call this morning from a lawyer in Pecan Valley who said Cully was aware you were in town. The lawyer was threatening me."

"Threatening you with *what* for God's sake?"

"With the fact that my grandfather would be seething about my bringing you here after having made it very clear that if I had anything to do with you, I'd be disowned. Did you know Cully very well?"

"Oh yeah, I knew him," Renata answered, looking away. "He's a far, far cry from your father. You needn't say more. You have to protect yourself and your father. It's best for you that I leave. Really, I understand. I can't blame your grandfather for wanting me out of the picture back then, but I sure wasn't the threat he and Frances believed I was . . . and I loved your father then as I love him now."

Cady pulled the car over and turned toward her mother.

"Park called me today too, and he wasn't entirely sure of your motives in coming here. Did you know him well?"

"Yes. He never liked me or approved of me I'm afraid . . . he was a decent sort, just kept to himself most of the time. I felt sorry for him."

"Why?"

"I'm not entirely sure, but I think it was because I felt empathy for him knowing that he felt like an outsider."

"Do you realize where we are?"

"I recognize very well where we are...we're pretty close to that St. Joseph's Hospital. I don't like to remember that time. I don't know if you understand how painful it is for me to be back here."

"No, I don't know how painful it is for you. That's your story to tell. I have my own," Cady said, turning the car back onto the road.

"My dear, there's nothing I can do about the past, or about what happened to you or to your father, but I can tell you that people are not perfect, and they make horrible mistakes, and they pay for them. I have paid in spades, and obviously your father has."

"And so have I, in case you might wonder."

"Yes," Renata answered in a soft voice. "I'm so sorry."

For the rest of the trip to the airport, Renata sat stoically in the passenger seat, massaging her forehead, trying to distract herself from the intense pain in her head. She remembered singing "We'll Meet Again" with Jonas just an hour before. When they got to the front door of the airport terminal, Cady stopped the car in the unloading area.

"I'm sorry, Renata, but I need to get back, so I'm not going in to see you off. There's a flight to Dallas in about an hour. You've got enough to buy your tickets back to Chicago, right?"

"Yes, I do. Don't worry. I understand." A young boy opened her car door and offered to carry her bag into the terminal. "I understand more than you think I do. Thank you for bringing me here to see Jonas. It was a wonderful thing for you to do—for us." She slipped off the front seat.

"Goodbye," Cady said, looking away.

"Goodbye, my darling. Take care of yourself and your father."

"I'm sorry, but I can't find words right now."

"It's all right. No words are needed."

Renata smiled faintly and followed the young boy away. Cady noticed a remarkable heaviness in her mother's gait as she disappeared through the terminal's revolving door. It left her feeling profoundly sad. She gripped the steering wheel and clinched her jaw to fortify herself for the drive away. She'd decided to take the route that was a little longer to avoid Blanton Street and St. Joseph's. "Gotta get home," she told herself, "Gotta get home." Thinking of Renata alone at the airport, Cady pulled over to the side of the road to gather her composure. "It's so sad, it's so incredibly sad," she said, dropping her head back against the seat.

Jonas was sitting inside by the front window of the Lone Star when Cady drove up. Several old men were sitting a table over, and had invited him to join them for dominoes in a back room of the café. Cady made arrangements to pick him up at 5:00, in time for supper.

She drove home and sat at the top of the back steps for a little while. She watched the birds flit nervously across the wide expanse of the back yard while a few clouds gathered. When she heard the clear call of a mourning dove from the direction of the poplars by the alley, she rested her head in her hands and inhaled deeply.

She then thought of Renata, the heaviness of her step at the airport, and how her own felt heavy as she climbed the sixteen steps to her bedroom. She then spotted something lying at the head of her bed, on the pillow—a sealed white envelope with the following message neatly printed by hand on the front:

Cady, I am asking you to keep this envelope safely hidden and unopened until, God bless him, Jonas departs this world. At that sad event, hopefully a long time from now, open and read the letter inside immediately. You'll understand why I have asked this of you when the day comes. Until then, I thank you for respecting my wishes. I'll love you always, whether you can believe that or not. Your mother, RRR.

Cady turned the envelope over several times, ran her fingers over it, and held it to her chest. After several minutes of fighting the strong urge to ignore her mother's wishes, to rip it open, she instead dropped it into the old hatbox of Frances's, that was stored in the top of her closet, and pushed the lid down tight. She'd pick up Jonas at the café in a little less than an hour.

The weight of the day had taken its toll. She curled up on her bed and began drifting off to sleep. The phone ringing awakened her. She flew out of bed and down the stairs. "I've *got* to install a phone upstairs," she said, out of breath. She yanked the receiver off the hook in Jonas's room. The nervous caller could hardly speak. There were voices in the background, frantic. Jonas had collapsed at the café.

35

Same day—late afternoon

Cady rode in the back of the ambulance holding Jonas's hand. He was resting easy after collapsing in the bathroom at the Lone Star. Getting the call from one of the domino players, she'd managed to get down to the café before the ambulance arrived. The old men had all talked at once, trying to tell her what had happened: Jonas had seemed out of sorts and had gone to the bathroom. They were used to his taking a long time so didn't go check on him for quite awhile. Finally, when they called through the door and he didn't answer, a couple of them popped the hook lock to find him on the floor, sitting up against the wall, breathing heavily, his face pale and gray.

One of the men was cradling Jonas's head in his lap when Cady arrived. The emergency crew arrived shortly thereafter and loaded him into the back of the ambulance.

"Dad, how are you feeling?" Cady asked, as the ambulance sped down the highway toward Concho City.

"Fine, just fine," Jonas mumbled under the oxygen mask, his eyes crinkled up in a smile.

"Are we going to Regional?" Cady asked one of the attendants.

"Yes ma'am. There's a lot of construction going on inside St. Joe's, or we'd stop there, but I think he's stable enough to go the extra couple miles to Regional. They've got an excellent cardiac unit there."

"So you think he's had a heart attack?"

"I'd say so, but we'll leave it to the docs at Regional to make that call."

When they got to the underpass on Blanton, Cady shuddered. Jonas looked at her intently.

"I'm okay," he told her. "I'm just fine."

"Of course you are, Poppy. Of course you are."

⌒

"Oh Nancy, I told you I had brought a pestilence on our home. I'm afraid bringing my mother here was too much for him," Cady said, calling from the phone booth in the hospital lobby.

"Cady stop that kind of talk. Listen, I don't think you should be there alone. I'm gonna drive over."

"Oh Nancy, what would I do without you?"

"No better than I'd do without *you*, Cady Randolph. Everything's going to be okay, hear me? I ought to be there in about an hour, so hang tight."

"Okay. I'll see you soon. Bye . . . drive safely."

There was a light rap on the phone booth door just as Cady hung up the phone.

"Ms. Randolph, the doctor would like to speak with you," a nurse said.

Cady hurried with the nurse to Jonas's room. The doctor was standing outside in the hall.

"Ms. Randolph? I'm Michael Lawson, a cardiologist here at Regional."

"Yes, hello," Cady said, shaking his hand.

"Well, your father's had a mild heart attack, nothing I don't think he'll recover from quite nicely without surgery. Given his history, surgery wouldn't be advisable anyway. I'd like to keep him here for a couple of days to make sure he's strong enough to go home."

"Yes, of course, whatever you think."

"We suspect he's been moving toward this event for quite some time. Is there any history of cardiovascular disease in your family, with his parents, siblings?"

"Yes, both my father's parents died of heart attacks before their time."

"I see. Well, at this point, I think with proper diet, exercise and medication, he'll have some more good years."

"Could an emotional upset have caused this?" Cady asked, afraid of the answer.

"Well, of course, it's better not to have undue stress on top of any heart condition, but I think what you're seeing here was inevitable, just a matter of time before the underlying disease manifested."

"Do you think he knows what's going on?"

"Yes indeed, I do…matter-of-fact, he diagnosed *himself* and darn accurately. He still knows his stuff. Some of the staff here worked with him years ago, before his head injury . . . and, from what I hear, this town was fortunate to have snagged such a talented surgeon . . . and a good man."

"Yes, thank you. I know he left a good impression."

"Yes, ma'am, he sure did. Now, try not to worry, and get yourself a good night's sleep. I'll check on your dad later tonight and tomorrow." The doctor touched her lightly on the shoulder.

Jonas was snoring when Cady entered his room. She held his hand. It was warm. The nurse had given Cady both of Jonas's rings in a plastic bag. Jonas opened his eyes.

"Well, hello there beautiful," he said.

"Papa, you're supposed to be resting."

"Oh, I'm fine," he said, reaching for her hand, noticing his missing ring. "Where's my grandfather's ring! It's gone!" He attempted to sit up. His pulse was pounding through the depression in his forehead.

"Dad, be still. It's ok. I have it," she said, holding up the plastic bag to show him. "Your finger was swelling so badly, they felt they had to remove it. Please don't worry. It's safe with me."

"Oh, good," Jonas said. "I promised my grandfather I'd take good care of it always. I know you'll help me keep that promise."

"Of course I will . . . and I have your wedding ring too."

"Good, I know both are in safe hands." He then relaxed enough to drift back to sleep.

"Goodnight, papa, sleep tight. See you when the sun comes up." She kissed his hand and sat with him until his pulse and breathing slowed.

Fortunately, Jonas's room was directly across from the nurses' station, so she felt comfortable to go to the first-floor snack bar.

One of the fluorescent lights in the snack bar blinked and buzzed overhead. She took her father's signet ring out of the plastic bag and carefully examined the fracture in the band. Before it was cut from Jonas's finger, Jonas had begged the emergency worker to be careful, reciting the whole story of the ring. The fellow had been able to make a clean cut through the band without injuring Jonas's finger. "I'm pretty sure your daddy would rather have lost his finger than that ring," the man told Cady. She would measure Jonas's finger, as soon as the swelling went down, and have the band soldered back together.

"Nancy, over here," Cady said, waving to Nancy.

"I'm sorry it took me so long," Nancy said, giving Cady a kiss on the cheek. "I had to throw some food together for John Earl before I left. He's hopeless in the kitchen."

"Yeah, I know. You're a saint. I hope he appreciates you."

"Aw, he does, in his own peculiar way. How's your daddy doin?"

"He's sleeping. The doctor says he'll be okay, thank God."

"Have you had anything to eat?"

"No, but I'm really not hungry," Cady answered, slipping the ring back into her purse.

"Too bad 'cause we're going across the street to get some food in you, like it or not. Come on."

"Okay, but you better plan to spend the night over here," Cady said. She looked at her watch. "It'll be too late for you to drive back."

"Yes, I agree. I told John Earl I might stay over. I'll call him from the room later to let him know."

"Okay, sounds good. The Angler's Inn is only two blocks over. I can be back over here in less than a minute if need be. The nurses tell me he's stable, so I think I can feel comfortable leaving."

There was a knock on the door at the Inn. Cady had fallen asleep.

"Who's there?" Nancy called through the door.

"It's Park Randolph. Is this Cady Randolph's room?"

"Hang on a minute."

Nancy shook Cady awake. Cady slipped on a robe and, half-asleep, opened the door. "How'd you know I was here?" Cady asked, still groggy.

"I went to the house in Pecan Valley and the neighbor lady saw me and told me Jonas was in the hospital. I went by there first and the nurse told me you were staying here . . . drove straight over. Sorry to be knocking on your door so late and waking you up."

"It's all right. Come on in. I'm sorry. I forgot to call you. You remember my old friend Nancy? She came over to keep me company."

"Yes I sure do remember you, Nancy. It's been a long time. How are you?"

"Doin' fine . . . sorry about your brother."

"Yes, I am too, thank you."

"How about I get dressed and meet you down in the lobby in a few minutes, Uncle Park," Cady said.

"Sure, I'll go on down. Take your time. Good seeing you, Nancy."

"Yes sir, good seeing you too."

Cady leaned against the door a few moments after Park left.

"You be okay if I go talk with him a little while?" Cady asked.

"Sure. I'll be fine . . . you all right?"

"Oh sure, I will be. Don't worry."

"Wake me up when you get back."

The lobby was empty, except for the young man tending the front desk who was busy talking on the phone. Insects swarmed around the outside lights.

"First, how's Jonas doing?" Park asked.

"I called about an hour ago and the nurse said he was resting very comfortably. The doctor thinks he'll be in the hospital a couple more days."

"I'd like to go see him tomorrow morning if it's all right with you," Park said.

"Of course it is. Why would you ask?"

"For all I knew, you'd never want to see me again after I'd stayed away so long. I've been a terrible uncle and a terrible brother. I can't undo the past, but I can try to do the right thing now."

"Better late than never . . . I've wondered about you, where you were, why you hadn't been to see Dad over all these years. It didn't seem like you."

"As I told you on the phone, I was in trouble, didn't know what to do. Not a good excuse, but the only one I've got. I have to admit that I was afraid to see Jonas, that I wouldn't know how to be with him, you know. But, I don't want to miss the chance to see him now . . . to tell him how much he's meant to me. He deserves much more than he's gotten from me."

"It will mean the world to Dad to hear those things from you, and he certainly *does* deserve that. He's so kind and forgiving and, lucky for him, he won't remember how long it's been. If it makes you feel any better, he's never said an unkind word about you, only what a wonderful brother you are. I have to admit that I am not so forgiving."

"I don't blame you. I'm not deserving of your forgiveness or Jonas's devotion, but maybe I can make it up to you and him a little by telling you what I know about Cully. First thing is that I didn't find out about Cully selling off that land 'til a couple of years ago, by a pure fluke. I met the guy he sold it to down in the Valley while I was there trying to do some business. When the guy heard my name and where I was from, he asked if I was kin to Cully. Then he just ran off at the mouth about his business with Cully. He was hesitant at first, but after a couple of whiskeys, he spilled the beans about what he paid Cully for the land. That's how I learned about the $300,000 I told you about on the phone."

"I'm going to get an attorney to see what can be done," Cady said. "Would you be willing to talk with whomever, and tell them what you know?"

"Yes, of course. There's no doubt a statute of limitation for getting remedy for this sort of thing, and after thirteen years, any court will question why you've waited so long to file a complaint . . . but I think there could be a way around it."

"How?" Cady asked.

"I think if you can prove that you just discovered wrongdoings that you weren't aware of at the time, then no matter how much time's gone by, the statute of limitation can be overridden."

"You realize that you may end up having to testify against Cully and Palmer?" she asked.

"Yes I do, and I will if I have to."

"Well, you know, this is just too much for me to fully absorb right now. I need time to let it sink in, and I really need to get some sleep so I can go over to see Dad first thing."

"Yes, of course. Jonas comes first."

"I'm sure Dad will be glad to see you after all this time, and as I said, it's lucky for both him and you that he won't realize how long it's been."

Nancy was deeply asleep when Cady got back to the room. She didn't have the heart to wake her. She set the alarm for 5:00 a.m. They'd already planned to have breakfast together before Nancy headed back to Pecan Valley.

Jonas was eating his breakfast, joking with a nurse who was opening the blinds in his room to a bright sun.

"Let me go in first, Uncle Park. I don't want to startle Dad. I'll tell him you're here."

"Good morning, Poppy." She gave him a kiss and a hug. "Guess who's here to see you?"

"Well, the most important person in the world is standing right in front of me."

"Thank you, Papa, but I'm talking about Park."

"You mean my *brother* Park?"

"Yes sir, I mean your brother Park."

Jonas looked eagerly toward the door. "Well that's wonderful. Is he coming now?"

Cady called to Park. "Somebody we know is real happy you're here," she told him.

Park hesitated at the door. At least fifteen years had passed since he'd seen Jonas. The signs of Jonas's accident were still visible: the facial scars, the depression in his forehead, the drifting eye, but even more apparent, the missing signet ring from his finger. Park hesitated before speaking. "Jonas, how good to see you," he said, gently shaking his brother's hand.

"It's wonderful to see you, Park. Would you like some breakfast? I can ask the nurse to bring another tray."

"Oh, no thanks, but you go ahead and finish yours up. I'm in no hurry. Say, brother, what happened to grandfather's ring? I've never seen you without it."

"I have it," Cady interrupted. "Dad, don't worry," she said, when she saw the look of confusion on her father's face. "I have it."

"Oh yes," Jonas said.

Park asked to see the ring. Cady pulled the plastic bag from her purse to show him. He reached for the bag but she quickly pushed it back down into her purse. A nurse appeared at the door and asked Cady to come out in the hall.

"Yes, ma'am," Cady said, clutching her purse to her chest when she left the room.

"There's an older fellow in the waiting room who was asking about your father, wondering if he was the same Dr. Randolph who was hurt in that accident. I didn't feel at liberty to say much, but told him that I'd check to see if someone could talk with him," the nurse said.

"Okay, I'll run down there. Did he say who he was?"

"Said his name was Bill, didn't catch his last name, but I remember it sounded kind of different," the nurse said. "He's in the small waiting room by the elevators."

She left Park and her dad to visit with each other and told them that she'd return shortly.

She looked first in the waiting room. No one was there. She then saw an older gentleman standing by the elevator. He seemed nervous.

"Excuse me, sir, would you be the gentleman asking about Dr. Randolph?"

The man hesitated before speaking. "Uh . . . yes, ma'am, I sure am, but to tell you the truth, I started thinking maybe I shouldn't be interrupting you all. Fact is, I thought I better just hop on this elevator and leave you folks to your peace."

"Oh it's okay, sir. I'm Dr. Randolph's daughter, Cady," she said, extending her hand.

"Well, yes ma'am, very happy to meet you. My name's Bill. Bill Armand. I was just askin' the nurses if your daddy was the same Dr. Randolph that was in that terrible wreck way back."

"Yes sir, one in the same. Did you know him?"

"I sure feel like I did. I, uh . . . well, I was the first one come up on that wreck . . . I mean before anybody else showed up."

Cady's heart began beating hard and fast. "Excuse me, sir, but what was your name again?" It sounded so familiar to her.

"Armand, Bill Armand. Well, actually William Armand, but people call me Bill. I know Armand's different soundin' for 'round here. My people were Cajun from down in Louisiana. Armand's French for Herman. I don't know why they didn't just go by Herman."

"I was born in Louisiana, New Orleans as a matter-of-fact," Cady said.

"Well I'll be," he said.

"I hope you understand that it's more than surprising meeting you, Mr. Armand."

"Yes, ma'am, I sure can imagine. I dern sure don't want to upset you any. My wife's up here sick, and I heard the nurses talkin' about a Dr. Randolph bein' on this floor, and I just had to ask if . . . well, you know."

Cady took a deep breath when it dawned on her that it might have been his name that she had seen scribbled on her grandfather's notepad, just under the phone number for her Aunt Miriam in Atlanta.

"So you were the first person at the scene? That's remarkable. Can you tell me about it...I mean, I know it's been so long that it might be hard to remember details, but—"

"Oh, no ma'am . . . I remember everything like it was yesterday. I was scared plum out of my wits. He was starin' straight ahead. There was a big rain storm and water everywhere, I remember that . . . and I remember the radio was still playin' in his car. That was real strange. I even remember the song that was playin'."

"What song was that?"

"It was that song real popular back then . . . that nice married couple sung it...had a Spanish name about goin' with God, somethin' like that. I was just thinkin' that was forty years ago . . . you was probably still just a twinkle in your daddy's eye when that song come out. It was my wife's favorite. She liked it so much we bought the record . . . she still plays it."

"Yes, sir, I know what song you're talking about. It was called "Vaya con Dios," and that means go with God in Spanish. I was only six then, but I remember hearing it on the radio."

"Yes ma'am, that sure is the name of it. Well . . . anyways, when the cop started talking to me and askin' me questions, I remembered that I'd seen him, I mean your daddy, earlier that night."

"Seen him? Seen him where?"

"At Burney's is what it was called back then. It closed down a long time ago now. It was a real popular hamburger joint back then. I was the cook there . . . and I fixed him a burger that night. I remember it was rainin' cats and dogs."

Cady turned and moved into the small lounge to sit down. Armand followed her and sat across from her.

"You awright, miss?" he asked, seeing she had turned pale.

"I think so. It's just that I'd always wondered if he really went out for a burger that night . . . or if I just made that up . . . and here I am, meeting the man who made the burger."

"Well, yes ma'am, I sure did."

"Please tell me about that night, she said, leaning toward him.

"Well, I remember how busy it was, and your daddy, well, he was in a big hurry . . . said somethin' about his wife bein' out in the hospital.

Anyway, he seemed real grateful that I got the burger cooked up so fast. And then, well, awhile later, I get off work and, me and my wife, we get to our turnoff at the exact same time your daddy's car come a'spinnin' down the underpass . . . didn't recognize him at first. It took awhile."

"And then what happened, Mr. Armand?" she asked, feeling oddly elated and completely entranced with every word he spoke.

"Well, like I was tellin' you, the song was still playin' in his car, kinda echoin' and it was still rainin' pretty good, but the overpass was keepin' it from rainin' on us under there. I remember he was lookin' straight ahead... not sayin' a word."

"He was conscious?" she asked, "Vaya Con Dios" playing loudly in her head. She hadn't told Armand that it was one of her favorite songs, that she knew every word.

"Well, looked like it, but he wasn't sayin' a word. Not a day's gone by that I haven't thought about your daddy. Anyway, I told the cop that night that I'd sold him a burger, that I recognized his suit coat, but the officer didn't make too much of it, didn't seem to matter much to him."

"Well, it matters to *me,* sir. I can't tell you how much."

She invited Mr. Armand to visit Jonas. She'd go and get him and bring him to her father's room after Park left. Mr. Armand said he felt "right proud" that he was going to get to see Dr. Randolph again. He told Cady that he'd kept all the newspaper clippings about the accident and that he'd always felt responsible for Jonas, like he would have for his own brother.

～

"Nancy, you'll never guess in a million years what just happened over at the hospital . . . the strangest, most unbelievable thing."

"What?" Nancy asked, holding her hand over her mouth.

"I met the man who sold the hamburger, *the* hamburger, to Dad the night of the accident. And not only that, but he was there with Dad at the scene of the accident...the *first* person there."

"What? Oh my God. That is impossible! Start over again here."

"Yes, impossible, but true. And you should have seen Dad's face when I took Mr. Armand in to see him. I think Dad remembered him. They talked and joked for a good thirty minutes. Mr. Armand cried . . . it was moving."

"*I'll* say. The hair's standing straight up on the back of my neck, Cady. I mean, what is it they say? It's somethin' about somethin' being weirder than fiction? I know how important this is to you."

"You're thinking about the truth being stranger than fiction . . . and yes, I know you know how important it is . . . no one else would. It's serendipitous, or divine, or maybe both. Ok, listen Nancy, I'm so glad you answered so I could tell you, but I'd better go for now. Thanks again so much for coming over and staying with me. I'll see you soon. Okay? Love you."

"Okay, bye. Love you too . . . but one thing before we hang up?"

"Uh huh, shoot," Cady said.

"Don't ever doubt yourself again."

Park had headed back to Austin. Cady had much to do—to get the ring repaired, get Jonas well enough to go home, and then to find a good lawyer. She felt invincible. She rifled through her grandfather's file. There it was, plain as day: William "Bill" Armand, printed neatly in her grandfather's hand—*A witness at the scene,* he'd written.

"Cully, you better plan on getting your ass up here sooner than later," Palmer told him. "That niece of yours is plenty riled up, talking some strong stuff to me about you and me cheatin' her."

"Cool it, Hal. There's nothing she can do . . . not a damned thing."

"I'm telling you again, I think you better plan on getting up here. I don't have a good feeling about this."

36

Houston—October 1, 1993

Cully turned the key in the lock. Turner was a few feet behind him, gawking at the crystal sconces and Persian runners in the hallway of Cully's Houston high-rise. He followed Cully inside.

"Man, this is some kinda pad," Turner said, looking around Cully's 3,500 square foot apartment.

"Make yourself at home. Wanna beer?" Cully said, opening a fully stocked refrigerator.

"Yeah . . . sure. So where am I bunking?"

"You're not. We're leaving here as soon as I finish up a couple of things," Cully answered, tossing Turner a beer.

"Hey, man, I just got off that flying tin can. What's the hurry?"

"What's the hurry you ask? Are you kidding me? It took me a week to find you and we're due in Pecan Valley at the attorney's office tomorrow morning at 8:00 a.m. sharp. We've got a nine hour drive ahead of us."

"Fuck it, man. Why so early?"

"You better zip that mouth of yours shut when we get out to Pecan Valley," Cully said, wiping the counter where the sweat from Turner's beer had left a ring. "Folks out in the hinterland don't take too kindly to rough language, especially from a Northerner. Not that I give a shit about offending them, but I don't want you drawin' attention."

Turner stared, mouth open, at a life-size painting of a cowboy standing beside a horse at the far end of the cavernous living room. He took a gulp of beer. "Yeah, ok, so where'd you get all this dough?"

Cully was hurriedly gathering up a stack of paper from his desk by a tall window thirty floors up. The lights of Houston were spread out below like a carpet of diamonds as far as the eye could see.

"I got all this dough using my head . . . plain and simple," Cully said of the apartment Frances had bought outright, in his name, the year before her death. He smirked, no less cocky and acerbic at seventy-four than he'd been at thirty-four.

"Call me crazy, but that cowboy dude in that big picture looks a lot like you," Turner said.

"It *is* me, dope. Impresses those big money boys in Houston . . . gets me into the right places. Lot of 'em are Yankees, so they're easy to pull the wool over. Truth is, never been on a horse in my life, but I paid this artist guy big bucks to make it look like I was born on one." He winked at Turner. "Now get your ass in gear . . . we've gotta hit the road."

On his way to his room to get his bag, Cully averted his eyes from the enormous floor-to-ceiling mirror that had been strategically placed by an interior designer at the end of the long hall. The designer had insisted that the hall be given what he called a "palatial depth." To add to the illusion, three chandeliers were hung the hall's length. The first time Cully saw how small he appeared in the mirror, he began holding his hand in front of his eyes to avoid the disturbing image. "Soon as I get back, that goddamned thing goes," he grumbled to himself.

Turner continued staring at the painting of Cully in a cowboy hat, boots, chaps, spurs, belt buckle in the shape of Texas, with his hand up on the saddle. The image left Turner shaking his head in amazement.

Cully had decided driving was necessary to get the box, full of files, to Hal Palmer's office. The thirty-nine-year-old Turner had flown nervously for the first time in his life that day, and was relieved to hear they'd be driving the rest of the way.

They made it to Pecan Valley just before midnight and checked into the Silver Spur Motel on Main. When Cully hit the pillow, Turner walked over the couple of blocks to the all-night Lone Star Café.

"Well, good mornin' there, Turner is it?" bellowed Hal Palmer, extending a knotty hand to the younger man.

"Yeah, hey," Turner answered, shaking Palmer's hand tentatively, wiping his hand on his jeans when Palmer turned toward Cully.

"Mornin' Hal," Cully said, slapping Palmer on the shoulder.

"So, fellas, how about we get started?" Palmer said. "Want some coffee, either one of ya?"

"Nah," Turner answered.

"Well, might as well get right to it. I've drawn up a new Will for Jonas to sign that names you as a legatee."

"What's that?" Turner asked.

"It means you are named as an heir to his estate, that you're entitled to some of it," Palmer told him.

"So when am I gonna get the money?"

"We're going to give you the money today," Palmer answered. "Remember what we talked about?"

"You got cash, right?" Turner asked.

"Yes, cash in a bank bag," Cully answered. "Hal, you got that paper ready?"

"Yep, it's right here and a nice new pen right on top. You can keep the pen after, son," Palmer said, sticking his chest out.

"Am I supposed to read this whole thing?" Turner asked.

"No, you don't have to. We've already explained to you how this works. After you sign, you'll get the $10,000. You'll get another $10,000 from Jonas's life insurance policy whenever he passes. Simple as that," Palmer said.

"So how's the old man feeling?" Turner asked, attempting to make a joke.

"Well, Cully, apparently you haven't told him about Jonas's heart trouble?"

"For real?" Turner asked.

"Mild heart attack about a month ago," Cully answered, looking over at Palmer. "That sister of yours bringin' your mama back on the scene, stirrin' things up, is more than likely what brought it on. But don't get too excited. He's not dyin' anytime soon. The doctors say he'll be fine long as he keeps it simple."

"Okay, so give me the money and I'll sign the paper," Turner said.

"We've gotta wait on a notary. She's on her way over," Palmer told him.

"What's that?" Turner asked.

Palmer winked at Cully. "Somebody who verifies that you are the one who's actually signin' the document," he said.

"Well, who the hell *else* would I be?"

"Don't try to figure it out, son. It's just the way things work," Palmer said.

The notary arrived at that very moment. Being a good friend of Palmer's, she'd agreed to come over on a Saturday.

"Well, fellas, got seal, can notarize," she said, her lips opening wide to reveal rabbit-like front teeth. "Ya'll ready for me?"

"We sure are," Palmer told her. "Okay son, here's where you sign."

"Hold your horses, cowboys," Turner said. "I wanna see the money before I sign anything."

"All right . . . come on back here," Palmer said, looking over at Cully. Palmer opened a zippered bank bag full of bills that he pulled out of a drawer. "You can be sure there are one hundred C-Notes in here, but if you don't believe me, count 'em for yourself."

Turner laboriously counted every bill. When he was satisfied all the money was there, Palmer placed the bag back in the drawer.

"What's today?" Turner asked, with his pen poised to sign the document.

"It's Saturday, October 2, 1993," the notary answered. She signed and sealed the document and talked outside with Palmer while Cully went over his plan with Turner again.

"I don't think I really want to meet the retard," Turner said. "Can't you just sign that Will for him?"

"Jesus H. Christ, man. Keep your ignorance to yourself, okay?" Cully said.

Turner rubbed the back of his neck nervously. "Okay, so when are we gonna get this crap over with?"

"We'll pick him up in a couple of hours. He goes downtown by himself everyday about 11:00, eats lunch, and just sits around drinking coffee afterwards until he gets picked up. It won't be hard to find him," Cully said. "He's been at the same routine for years . . . nothin' else for him to do."

"What if that Cady girl shows up?" Turner asked.

"She won't be around to get him until later. She'll never know we were here because he won't remember he was with us," Cully said, exchanging a sideways glance with Palmer who had walked back in.

"She's gonna hate your guts someday, boy, when she does find out. You know that, don't you?" Palmer asked.

"What for? I never did anything to her."

"Oh, yes you have done somethin' to her, son, just bein' alive."

"What?"

"Come on, you can't be that dense," Cully said. "She stands to lose a lot of money with you coming in on the scene."

"You're making it sound like I'm stealing from her."

"Bingo. You're *finally* getting the picture. As far as she'll be concerned, you will be stealing from her, but that's not your problem," Cully said.

"But it may be *your* problem, Cully. She already thinks you've stolen from her," Palmer said.

Cully grinned and lit a cigarette. Palmer asked him to put it out. He ignored the request.

"Uh, don't forget that you told me you'd give me some extra for that airplane ticket I had to buy," Turner said.

"You gotta be kidding me," Cully said. "You're rolling in dough now, boy. You don't need lousy airfare."

"A deal's a deal," Turner said, his eyes narrowing in a warning.

"Go on and give it to him, Cully," Palmer said.

"No. No way. He's got plenty enough."

Turner startled them both when he hit the table hard with his fist and demanded the money. Cully pulled a one hundred dollar bill from his wallet and told him that he was lucky to be getting that much. Turner yanked the hundred out of Cully's hand and asked for the bank bag with the $10,000. Palmer gave the bag to Cully, who locked it in his attaché case, claiming it would be safer there until they got to Houston. Turner reluctantly agreed.

~

It was mid-morning by the time Cully and Turner got back to the motel. The tension between them was high. Cully pulled into the fifteen-room motel's parking lot. It was empty. It had been full of pickup trucks the night before. They'd gotten the last room, on the end. They'd seen an odd assortment of cowboys, dove hunters, and oilfield workers driving in and out. It was already hot, close to eighty degrees. The weatherman on the Concho City television station said the temperature was expected to reach the nineties by mid-afternoon. A couple of skinny cats were sitting by the garbage cans, and the smell of curry was strong from the direction of the motel office.

"Jesus H. Christ, this place is weird," Turner said. "I've never seen so many ass cracks and toothpicks in all my life," Turner said, carrying in the box from Cully's car.

"You're a fine one to talk. Keep eating those chicken-fried steaks and drinking that beer, you'll be sporting a pretty good one yourself," Cully said.

"Trixie used to talk about chicken-fried steaks a lot when I was a kid . . . said everything in Texas was chicken-fried, even the dirt," Turner said. "Speaking of, I'm getting hungry."

"Who the hell's Trixie?" Cully asked.

"It's what I call my old lady. She hates it."

"No love lost, sounds to me," Cully said.

"Probably so," Turner said, walking outside, feeling heat in his face.

"Get on back in here," Cully told him. "Somebody might see you."

"So, who cares, man? Nobody knows who I am around here."

"That's the smartest thing you've said all day," Cully answered.

Turner would have punched Cully out by then if it hadn't been that he wanted to get that additional $10,000 insurance money someday. He pulled at his short hair. Cutting off his pony tail had been a requirement for getting the money. "Any man with a pony tail in Pecan Valley would be as obvious as balls on a tall dog . . . and suspect," Cully had told him.

"I'm hungry, man," Turner said. "I'm going over to that café to get some chow."

"Bring me back something," Cully said, handing Turner a ten-dollar bill. "I don't care what you get. Just keep your mouth shut while you're over there. Not a word about your old man, or me, or who you are, or where you're from. Hear?"

"*He's* the retard. Not me. You don't have to keep tellin' me that shit," Turner said, slamming the door shut.

⟨∼⟩

"Papa, I'm going to run over to Concho City, but I'll be back to get you around 3:00. Okay?" Cady told Jonas, as she backed out of the driveway.

"You bet," he answered from the passenger seat.

"It's going to be a hot one, so stay inside until I come to get you."

She left Jonas at the Lone Star, and then drove over to get Nancy. They'd have lunch in Concho City and run a few errands. Nancy had wanted to go the next day, but it would be the 3rd of October, and the fortieth anniversary of the accident. Cady wanted to spend that day quietly and reverently with Jonas.

37

Noon—October 2, 1993

Cully sat in his car in the motel parking lot watching Cady drop Jonas off at the Lone Star. He then followed her car over the bridge until she sped out of sight on the highway toward Concho City. "Perfect," he thought to himself. He turned around at the cemetery and hightailed it back to the motel.

"Come on, get your ass up and turn off that television. I'm going over to the café right now to get him. I'll be back in a few," Cully told Turner.

"Ok, man, I'll be ready. Go on and get him so we can get this thing over with."

Cully drove the two blocks to the café and parked in front. Jonas was sitting in the window booth talking to the waitress. The café was full. "San Antonio Rose" was playing on the Juke Box.

Cully slid into the booth across from Jonas. "Hello, Jonas old boy," he said.

"Cully!" Jonas said, breaking into a wide smile.

"You ordered lunch yet?" Cully asked.

"No, I was just about to ask him what he wanted," the waitress said, overhearing the conversation. "Ain't you Cully Randolph?" she asked.

"Yeah, that's right."

"You probably don't remember me. I was in school same time as you, but you never paid me no never mind . . . can't say as I blame ya. I was nothin' much to squeal about."

"I don't remember you at all," Cully said, lighting a cigarette.

"Well, I see ain't nothin' much changed. What can I get ya?" she asked, with her pencil poised to take his order. "I already know what Doc wants. Right, Doc?" she said, smiling.

"That's right, beautiful."

Cully rolled his eyes. "Well, you're gonna have to hold off on that order . . . we've got a little business to take care before he eats lunch," Cully said. "Come on, Jonas, I'll get you back here in a flash if you play your cards right."

"I'm pretty hungry now, Cully. I think I just better stay here."

"Here's a little somethin' for your trouble," Cully told the waitress, ignoring Jonas. He slapped two ones on the table. "Come on, Jonas, the sooner we get outta here, the faster you get your grub."

"Doc's used to eatin' right about now," the waitress said. "Right, Doc?"

"Absolutely," Jonas answered.

"Be that as it may, we're going. Come on, Jonas, let's go," Cully said.

Jonas looked up pleadingly at the waitress. There was nothing she could do but assure him that she'd keep his plate good and hot and make a fresh pot of coffee for his return. That seemed to settle him down somewhat. Cully held the door impatiently as Jonas made his way slowly out of the café and into the front seat of Cully's car.

"That just don't seem right," the waitress told the other waitress while she watched Jonas being driven away. "And Cady didn't say nothin' to me about Doc havin' family comin' in. I'll bet she don't know that brat brother's in town," she said, shaking her head. She saw Cully's car pull into the parking lot of the motel a few blocks down.

"Reckon we oughta call Cady and tell her he took Doc off?" the other waitress asked.

"Aw, let's just see if he gets on back here before long. I can tell her when she picks him up, but it sure does make me nervous for Doc to be took off by that good for nothin' sorry excuse for a brother. I think I better go call her after all."

The waitress went into the back, got Cady's number off the bulletin board, and called. There was no answer.

"All right, Jonas, take a seat. I've got some papers I need you to sign," Cully said.

"Who's this handsome young gentleman with you?" Jonas asked, looking over at Turner.

"Well, you wanna tell him or do you want me to?" Cully asked Turner.

Turner seemed stunned. No one had ever called him handsome, or a gentleman. "*You* tell him," Turner answered.

"He's your kid, Jonas," Cully said. "And that's the business we need to take care of. Renata had him the summer after your accident. I guess the old man didn't tell you."

"Don't call our father 'the old man.' He wouldn't like that and I don't like it. It's not respectful."

"Did you even hear what I said?" Cully closed in on Jonas's face. "That handsome young gentleman, as you call him, is your flesh and blood."

"Cady's my child," Jonas said, pulling away.

"Well, you have two now. You don't remember, but Renata got pregnant with him just before you got slammed in the head. He's not in your Will, so Hal Palmer drew up a new one to include him. That's only right, don't you think?" Cully asked.

"We need to call Cady. She'll know what to do," Jonas said. He was upset and confused, looking around the room as if searching for help.

"No, we do not need to call her. She has no say about this. The lawyers say that you're a ward of the state, man, and I'm applying for a guardianship over you. Do you know what that means? It means that *I'm* in control, not her."

"Stop it, man," Turner said. "Can't you see you're scaring him . . . he's old. Just leave him alone. Sign the damned thing yourself like you have everything else of his. Let him go."

Jonas's face had turned crimson, his neck taut. He kept asking for Cady, pleading with Cully to call her.

"Sign the goddamned thing, Jonas!" Cully yelled, holding his fist up.

"I said leave him the hell alone, you asshole," Turner said, grabbing Cully's arm. "Can't you see he's scared shitless? What if he dies right here? *Then* what?"

"Oh, so now you're so concerned? What a joke!" Cully said to Turner. "Go on and get outta here, you fool," Cully told Jonas, with a dismissive flip of his hand. "You can walk your hungry ass back to the café and eat yourself into oblivion for all I care."

"Go on, old man. Just go back where you came from. You know how to get there, don't you? It's just a couple of blocks that way," Turner said, pointing the direction of the café.

Jonas nodded his head yes. His breathing had become labored. He was having a hard time standing. "I need to go to the bathroom," he said.

"You can use the one at the café . . . now, go on, git. I'm fed up with you," Cully said.

Jonas managed to stand, smiled at Turner, and walked unsteadily out into an intensely hot sun. He hurried, faltering on the uneven sidewalk. The concrete sent up a suffocating blast of heat. He stopped suddenly. The pain in his chest overwhelmed him. He reached for a lamp post, but crumpled into a heap on the sidewalk about half a block from the café. A couple of men driving by in a pickup saw him fall and stopped. One of them ran into the nearest business to call for help while the other attempted to revive him. The ambulance was there in a matter of minutes. The two men told the emergency crew who Jonas was and that they'd attempt to reach his daughter to let her know. It was 1:15 when the ambulance arrived at Regional.

The news had gotten around town fairly quickly. One of the men had gone into the café, telling everyone in there that it was Jonas the ambulance had carried away. The waitress had tried numerous times to reach Cady, but still no answer.

Cully had decided they would spend the night and leave for Houston before 9:00 the next morning. He had already taken the forged signature on the Will to Palmer and had thrown a copy of it, along with a copy of the forged change of beneficiary on Jonas's life insurance policy, into the box of legal papers that sat in the corner of the motel room. Watching television, with the air conditioner on high, neither he nor Turner had heard the siren.

Cady and Nancy reminisced and laughed on the way back to Pecan Valley. When they got to the cemetery, they drove by the Randolph plot. It was 2:45 and Cady still had a little time before she was to pick up Jonas at 3:00. There were a couple of ladies watering a severely wilted bush the next plot over. Cady and Nancy quickly pulled a few weeds from around the headstones. They then drove back to Rachel's plot and did the same. Nancy's people were all buried in Coldstone, about ninety miles from Pecan Valley.

It was a couple of minutes after 3:00 when they pulled up in front of the café. Jonas wasn't standing outside, as usual. Cady went inside to get him.

"Oh Cady, honey, I've been callin' and callin'," the waitress said, wringing her hands.

"I was over in Concho City doin' some shopping with Nancy. What's wrong, June Ann?"

"Well, honey, they took your daddy to the hospital. Couple of men found him down on the sidewalk just up the street. They called the ambulance."

"Oh my God, why was he out on the street?"

"Honey, now sit down," the waitress said.

"No, I can't. I've got to go find my dad. Oh Jesus, where'd they take him, do you know?"

"I think I heard them fellas say that they took him to Regional over to Concho City. I just got to tell you before you go that Cully Randolph come in here and took your daddy outta here before he could even eat, took him over to the Silver Spur Motel. I tried to call you. Anyhow, I watched 'em get outta the car over there and go in that last room on the end by the garbage cans. Doc musta been tryin' to get back over to here when he blacked out. It was awful hot out there."

"Wait a minute, June Ann, *Cully's* here?" Cady said.

"Yeah, he's here and Rhonda said some younger guy is stayin' with him over to the motel. I gotta tell ya that Cully was kinda ugly with your daddy. I didn't like that one bit. Wouldn't even let Doc have his lunch, said somethin' about gettin' some business done and then he'd bring Doc back over here to eat, but he never did. Like I said, I tried and tried callin' you. I sure didn't like Cully takin' your daddy off like that, but I didn't think it was my place to get in between 'em, Cully bein' family and all."

"It's all right, June Ann. You didn't know."

"One more thing, Cady, this younger guy with Cully come over here not two hours ago, and was braggin' to Rhonda that he wasn't leavin' 'til tomorrow mornin' and did she wanna meet him tonight."

"What was Cully driving, do you remember?"

"Yeah, sure do. It was this real fancy powder blue Caddy, one-a-them long 'uns."

"Okay, I've gotta go now but, please, if Cully or that other one comes back in here, you and Rhonda don't say anything about what's happened to Dad or that I know they're here. That's real important, okay?" Cady figured that the young guy must be Turner.

"Sure, okay. You know we're here for ya, girl, so, bless your heart, we just feel awful bad for you and Doc. We're prayin' for ya'll, honey."

Cady nodded her head and ran out to the car.

Nancy insisted on driving. It was all Cady could do to breathe.

When they got to the hospital, Nancy ran to a phone booth to call John Earl collect. She now wished she had brought the mobile phone John Earl had just bought, but it weighed a good two pounds and she wasn't yet comfortable using it.

"Where is Dr. Jonas Randolph . . . he's a patient here. I'm his daughter," Cady said.

"Let's see," the receptionist said. "Looks like he's in the intensive care unit up on the third floor," the desk lady told Cady.

Cady held herself in the elevator, talked to herself: "Stop it, Cady," she said out loud. "Everything's going to be okay. Dad's going to be okay. I promise. Okay?"

The elevator was slow. She wanted to pry open the doors with her bare hands. Mercifully, they opened. She ran to the nurses' station. Her mouth was so dry that her tongue was sticking to the roof of her mouth. "My father, Dr. Randolph, where is he? I've got to see him."

The nurses looked at one another. One spoke. "I'll take you to him, but please understand that he's suffered a massive heart attack and is not able to speak."

"Just take me to him," Cady said.

The room had been darkened. He was hooked up to a cardiac monitor, had lines in both arms. His face was deathly pale and swollen. Cady stood by his side, speaking softly to him.

"Dad, I'm here. I got here as soon as I could. I'm by your side and I won't leave, not even for a minute. I love you so much. Oh God, I'm so sorry I wasn't there to protect you." Cady cupped her hands carefully over his right hand to warm it. "Do you think the A/C is too cold for him? His hand's so cold," Cady said, looking up at the nurse.

"I think it's more than likely his circulation, honey," she said. "We're doing our best to keep him comfortable, and I believe he is."

Cady knew what it all meant. Jonas was dying. "Could I have some time alone with my dad?" Cady asked.

"Yes, of course. I'll be right outside if you need me."

She pulled a chair over next to Jonas's bed and put her head down beside his. "Daddy, I don't know if you can hear me. Can you squeeze my hand if you can?" There was no response.

"Ms. Randolph?" the nurse asked.

"Yes?" Cady answered. She was still groggy from having drifted off. "What time is it?"

"Let's see . . . it's about 7:15."

"At night? Why didn't you wake me?"

"Honey, it's okay. You obviously needed the rest. You're drained emotionally. We've been monitoring your daddy closely. There's been no change. We've been checking on you too. It's good you got some rest . . . listen, sweetheart, your friend Nancy's down in the waiting area and wants to see you, but I told her that no one but family's allowed in the room."

"She *is* family to us. Can't she please come in?"

"Let me check. I'll be right back," the nurse replied.

It seemed forever before the nurse returned. "It'll be all right for your friend to visit for a little while, but please keep your conversation to a minimum, and very quiet."

When Nancy saw Jonas, she couldn't hold back the tears. "I'm sorry, Cady, but I just can't stand to see Doc like this and . . . what you must be going through . . . " She hesitated. "Are you all right?"

"I don't know."

"Now listen, you're the strongest person I know." Nancy put her arm around Cady's shoulder. "The nurse said I couldn't stay but a minute, but John Earl and I are in the waiting area right down the hall and we're not leaving . . . it's real comfortable in there. You just tell the nurse to come get me if you need me."

They embraced. Nancy touched Jonas's shoulder as she left the room.

"Poppy, Nancy was just here. Did you know?"

No response.

She moved close to his ear.

"Dad, I'm so sorry for those times when I was unkind . . . after the accident, when you first came home. I was so angry with you and I didn't understand why then. But I'm pretty sure now that I thought you had left me. I know now you would never leave me on purpose." She positioned her head closer to his and felt a faint breath on her cheek. "I know you were a great surgeon, no denying that, and I know how much you missed a career you loved . . . but, Dad, Rachel told me you had a powerful lot to teach me, and she was right. I've seen you do so much good since the accident. Remember that homely waitress over in Concho City, the one who was always scowling and throwing the customers' plates at them like two-pound Frisbees? Remember that time she was acting nastier than usual and you told her she was beautiful and smiled that beautiful smile of *yours* at her? I couldn't believe you told her that. *I* didn't see one bit of truth in it. But, *she* did. Her face changed right then and there, and she smiled back at you, and she actually looked pretty. I was floored, and you just kept eating your dinner like nothing at all unusual had happened. Remember? She was bouncing all over the restaurant, asking people if she could do this or that for them, thanking them for coming in . . . unbelievable. I overheard the man in the booth behind us say something like, "she musta finally snagged some ole boy didn't know any better." And then someone else said, "Yeah, or maybe some fairy godmother come and knocked her over the head with a two-by-four." But, Dad, you know what she *herself* told me later? She told me that you had saved her life that night. Those were her exact words—saved her life, and you know what I think about that? You did that without a scalpel, Poppy. Don't you see how important that was? How important *you* are?"

Jonas opened his eyes just long enough to find hers, and with a gauzy stare, as if from somewhere very far away, he whispered the two words that best defined him—"Thank you."

At just past midnight, the 3rd of October, 1993, he drifted away in her arms. The nurse said that his had been a good death, that the slight smile on his face was proof.

Nancy and John Earl stayed in the room with her while the nurses disconnected the leads and removed the lines. They then left so that Cady could be alone with him for a little while.

She folded the sheet and blanket neatly over his chest, pulling both up just under his chin, the way he liked it. Through a flood of tears, with her hand on his forehead, she managed to hum the first line of "Always" before saying goodbye.

~

The ambulance wouldn't be there until 8:00 a.m. to take him back to Pecan Valley. The nurses assured her that they'd watch over him in the meantime, that he wouldn't be left alone. A couple of older doctors and an older nurse, who had once worked with him at St. Joe's, came in to tell her how much they had admired him.

There were two things that came into Cady's sharp focus on the drive back to Pecan Valley with Nancy and John Earl: the letter from Renata, and confronting Cully. She'd be at the funeral home to greet Jonas's body in just six hours, and in the meantime would fiercely defend his honor.

Nancy and John Earl had insisted on staying with her that night and would sleep in the guest room upstairs. While Nancy washed a few dishes in the kitchen, John Earl brought a beer in from the car, and Cady went up to her closet to get the letter from Renata out of the hatbox. She tore open the envelope. Nancy and John Earl came to tell her goodnight. She didn't tell them about the letter.

"We love you, Cady. Now try to get some sleep if you can. You have a lot to do tomorrow." She and Nancy hugged goodnight, and when she heard the guestroom door close, she began to read her mother's letter:

Chicago, August 30, 1993

My Dearest Cady,

As I write, I'm somewhere between excited and terrified at returning to Texas tomorrow to see you again, and to see Jonas again, after all these years. Since I have asked you not to read this until something happens to your father, that sad event will have occurred, so I know how you must feel at this moment. For all the years that you cared for him, as I should have, thank you. How I wish I could in some way ease your pain right now.

Instead, this letter will be an added blow. I regret that to my core. As you read it, you'll probably wonder how I could ever have loved your father. Ironically, It's because I did and do love him, and you, that I write it.

Cady went to the window seat and cranked the window wide open. Her heart pounding, she continued to read:

I found a letter addressed to my son, Turner, from a lawyer in Pecan Valley named Halford Palmer (the original is attached). In short, it says that as

Jonas's son, Turner is a "rightful heir" to your father's estate. Turner will receive $10,000 for signing a document that conveys to Cully any residual interest he, Turner, is "entitled" to from Jonas's estate at the time of Jonas's death. There's only one thing that is more wrong and deceitful:

Turner is not your father's son. The night after Jonas's accident, I did a terrible thing. I was intimate with Cully. Park knew. He showed up the next morning while Cully was still in the house. My son, Turner Mitchell Randolph, was born nine months later. He could be no one else's but Cully's because 1) I had slept with no one but Cully. Your father and I had shared no intimacy for more than three months before his accident. I was prone to using alienation of affection when I didn't get my way—to hurt Jonas. I was selfish, unkind, and believe it or not, at times even naïve; 2) My blood type is O+, your father's is AB+ and Turner's is O+. This further eliminates Jonas as Turner's father (the lab reports are also attached).

Knowing what I know of Cully's scheme, I can't continue the ruse. I am glad Jonas won't know the cruel blow of this double betrayal. Sparing you that blow would harm you more. I hope you will retain the services of a good attorney and use this letter, and its attachments, to completely thwart any plan Cully has.

Forgive me, if you can, and I hope you can find it in your heart not to judge Turner too harshly. He too has been wronged—brought up in the back rooms of cheap bars, and deprived of a good father. You all deserved far better from me.

This letter and my signature, as you can see by its seal, is officially witnessed and notarized. Therefore, there can be no question as to the letter's authenticity and its author's, my, identity. I will love you always—of that you can be assured.

Your mother,
Renata Rose Collins Randolph

38

≈

3:00 a.m.—October 3, 1993

Cady knocked on the guestroom door first, before opening it a crack. "Sorry to wake you two but I've just read something, and have got to get down to the Silver Spur Motel right now."

Nancy and John Earl shot up in bed and turned on their bedside lamps, blinking against the harshness of the light. Cady handed the letter to Nancy. She shook off her sleep and read it with one hand over her mouth while John Earl read it over her shoulder.

"Good God, Cady. What are you going to *do?*" Nancy asked.

"I'm gonna go down to the Silver Spur right now to confront Cully, and that so-called brother of mine, before they get out of town."

"That's too scary," Nancy said. "Cully's wicked, and who knows about that other one? They could hurt you. Don't you think we ought to call the police?" Nancy asked.

"And what are they going to do?" John Earl broke in. "They don't have any reason to arrest Cully. Look, I'll go down there with you, Cady, but first thing we're going to do is stop by City Hall and make copies of this stuff. The dispatcher's a friend of mine and she works graveyard. She won't ask any questions."

"I'm going with you," Nancy said.

"No, somebody's gotta stay here. If you haven't heard from us in an hour, *then* call the police. Don't worry, honey," John Earl told her. "We'll be fine. Just keep the doors locked and we'll be back soon as we can."

It was almost 3:30 a.m. when Cady and John Earl pulled into the garishly lit parking lot at the Silver Spur. The air was warm, and it was quiet, except for the crackle-buzz of flying night creatures getting zapped on the bug traps hanging at each motel room door. Thoughts of her father swam in and out of Cady's head. John Earl pulled the car over by the garbage cans. Cady held the copies of the documents in her hand. John Earl knocked on the door. They heard Cully cursing before he opened the door.

"What the hell are you doing here, waking me up at this hour?" Cully snapped.

"And what the hell are *you* doing in Pecan Valley?" Cady asked.

"Well, last time I checked, this was a free country, and where I go in it is none of your goddamned business."

"It's *all* of my business, you miserable bastard, when you kidnap my dad from the café and he collapses on the street!"

"What the hell are you talking about . . . and who the hell's the clown?" Cully asked, pointing at John Earl.

"I'm a friend, a very good friend," John Earl answered in a steely voice.

"What the hell's going on?" Turner asked, waking up fully clothed on one of the twin beds.

"Your lovely sister and her boyfriend decided to pay us a visit. Oh but my manners are slipping. Do come in."

Cady stepped tentatively inside, John Earl behind her. They stayed by the door of the cramped room that housed one chair, two twin beds, a dresser with a television on top, and a coat rack.

"So now tell me again the reason for this intrusion, Miss Randolph?" a shirtless Cully asked.

"You took my dad away from the café today. The waitress at the Lone Star told me what happened. He collapsed on the street near this motel. What did you do to him?"

"*Do* to him? I brought him over here to introduce him to his son, Miss Randolph. It was high time they met." At that, Turner sat up on the edge of the bed.

"You killed my father the same as if you'd stabbed him in the heart!" Cady yelled.

"Just you wait a goddamned minute, lady. What are you flapping your jaws about?" Cully asked.

"He's dead . . . collapsed on the sidewalk near this motel."

"Wow . . . dead? He shook his head and grinned. "Wow . . . Well, better off, I'd say. What kind of life did he have anyway?"

Cady rushed toward him, her hand raised to slap him. Cully blocked it. She tried again. John Earl stopped her. "A far better life than *you'll* ever have, you sorry bastard," she yelled, turning toward Turner. "I'm here to tell you that I hold in my hand documents that prove that my father is *not* your father. Fact is, *that* sorry excuse for a human over there is your father," she said, pointing at Cully. "And he's using you to steal money from *my* father."

"What the hell are you talking about?" Turner asked, rising from the bed, moving toward Cady.

"Not another step closer, fella," John Earl said, holding up his hand to stop Turner's advance.

"Here's the proof. Read the letter yourself," Cady said, handing the letter to Turner. "And by the way, it's a copy, and there are other copies . . . and of course the originals are safely locked away. Others know about this, so don't try anything funny."

Cully grabbed the letter away from Turner and took a seat in the room's only chair. John Earl quickly produced another copy from his jacket and handed it to Turner. Turner began reading it slowly and carefully.

"Is this true, man?" Turner asked Cully. "Did you sleep with my mother?"

Cully folded his arms and tilted back in the chair. "Even if I did, this piece of garbage doesn't prove a damned thing," he said, wadding up his copy and throwing it in the waste can. "What did we tell you? She'll do anything to keep you from getting even a penny of hers. She wrote that letter herself. I can guarantee it."

Turner looked at the letter again. Bewildered, he looked back at Cady.

"You are *not* my father's child," Cady repeated. "Cully is using you, and so is that slimy lawyer of his. I'm sorry, but it's true. Look at your blood type and look what your mother's disclosing about *herself.* It must have been really hard for her to do this. She knows you're a pawn. Can't you see what's happening?"

Turner turned pale. His eyes, spewing fire, left Cady's and darted around the room. He began pacing nervously, running his hands through his hair.

Cully propped his feet up on the bed. "You're screwing yourself if you don't tell that sister of yours to fuck off," Cully said.

Turner sank down on the bed. Cully stood, picked up a book of matches, and pulled one free to light his cigarette. Turner then pulled Cully's loaded Ruger from the bedside table and, without hesitation, shot Cully once in the neck and then in the gut before the match was struck. Cully fell head first into the dresser. Cady and John Earl fell to the floor.

"No!" Cady screamed.

"Shhh," John Earl whispered, covering her mouth with his hand.

"Be quiet, damn it, I'm not going to hurt you," Turner said, grabbing Cully's car keys and the locked attaché case containing the $10,000. He locked eyes with Cady before running out the door to Cully's car. It all happened in a matter of seconds.

"No wait, John Earl. Let him go!" Cady cried out, grabbing John Earl by the arm as he started out the door after Turner. "He's got a gun!"

They heard tires squealing as Turner sped away. John Earl found the Ruger on the pavement.

Cady stood staring at Cully who was unconscious and bleeding on the floor, one arm caught in the rungs of the chair, a deep gash across his forehead, his face and trunk covered in blood.

"John Earl . . . quick! Take that box out to the car before anyone gets here," Cady said, pointing to the file box in the corner. "I'll explain later."

They could hear motel room doors opening, voices outside. John Earl slipped around the corner of the motel and slid the box onto the back seat of his car. A couple of men from nearby rooms were standing outside their doors, one of them holding a rifle.

"It's all right," John Earl told them, holding his hands up. "I'm an off-duty reserve cop. The Sheriff's on his way."

The guest with the rifle was peering through the door of Cully's room. "You all right, little lady?" he asked Cady.

"I'm fine," she answered calmly.

She then joined John Earl and the growing number of motel guests who had gathered on the sidewalk. All she could think about was Jonas and how she'd be meeting the hearse in just a few hours. She looked back into the room, at the bloody scene. She felt nothing.

"What the hell happened here, John Earl?" the Sheriff asked as he stepped inside the motel room, his deputy behind him. "I'm downright flummoxed by this whole deal."

"I can explain everything, Bart," John Earl told him.

"Sure sorry to hear about Doc, Cady," the Sheriff said, removing his hat to hold it across his chest. "And now this . . . your uncle all shot up," the Sheriff said, shaking his head.

"Thank you, Bart," she answered stoically.

Bart Symons and John Earl were old high school friends, and John Earl was a volunteer ride-along cop, so his word was gold with law enforcement in the county. John Earl told Bart the whole story while Cady stood against the wall, staring at Cully and the pool of blood inching out across the carpet. The Deputy put out an APB on Cully's Cadillac and called an ambulance.

When the ambulance and emergency crew arrived a few minutes later, Cully was still breathing. Cady was caught somewhere between hoping he'd die and hoping he'd live, so that he and Palmer would have to pay for what they'd done. Cully's box of legal papers, safely stowed away in the back seat of John Earl's car, would go a long way in getting that accomplished.

The Deputy had taken a couple of photographs of Cully before the EMTs put him on the gurney and into the ambulance. It took less than an hour for John Earl and Cady to give their statements while the Deputy talked with the other guests to get theirs. The Sheriff assured Cady that she was safe, that Turner would not be coming back to Pecan Valley. Something about the way Turner had looked at her before he took off, had told her that she had nothing to fear from him.

A few hours after dawn, the 3rd of October, the long white hearse drove over the bump into the back drive of the funeral home. Cady watched her father's body being wheeled up the ramp through the back door. The final hours with him, her mother's letter, and the ordeal with Cully and Turner had prohibited sleep. It would be the next day before Jonas's body would be ready for viewing she was told. She'd bring his suit, shirt, and tie from the house the next afternoon. She'd then meet with the funeral director to go over the arrangements. He had assured her that, in the meantime, they'd take good care of Jonas.

She drove home especially slowly, over the big dip in the road, past the Victorian houses, and into the driveway at 161. A member of the newest generation of yellow cats from next door greeted her on the back steps. She sat with him a little while. Like the generations before him, he sidled up to her and purred. "This one I'll adopt," she thought, stroking his head while she looked out at the poplars. "No mourning doves today," she told the cat. "It's fitting. Nothing's okay about today."

Nancy came over to answer calls, and the door, while Cady rested. The neighbors brought food, and the preacher stopped by. Cady went to check on Jonas, out of habit. Reality hit when she reached the bottom stair. It took all her courage to open his bedroom door to see his empty bed and his favorite medical book by his chair, and to smell a hint of Old Spice coming from his bathroom. She shut his door and pulled Renata's letter out of her pocket to read it once again. It was a matter of amazement that she couldn't stop reading it.

Nancy went home. The police dropped by to check on her. She then found herself completely alone in the house for the first time in her life.

She made her way past the mural, ran her hand over one of the painted dogs in the scene, and walked through the living room to the kitchen. It had taken another large amount of courage to sit in her grandmother's chair for the first time in her life. The streetlight near the alley illuminated the poplars and the pecan tree. How different the kitchen looked from that chair—it was wider and bigger than she'd ever seen it. She could see into the television room, another view she'd never had. It seemed wrong somehow to read her mother's letter from Frances's chair, so she moved back to her own to read it again. When tiredness overcame her, she climbed the sixteen steps back up to her room taking Jonas's bottle of Old Spice with her.

At 10:00 the next morning the police called to tell her that Cully's car had been found seventy-five miles away in Greenwood; no trace of Turner. Cady had tried reaching Renata in Chicago. The number had had been disconnected. She tried the number twice more and got the same recording.

Turner got the last seat on the bus from Greenwood to Cleeryville. He'd been on the run enough in the past to know how to cover his tracks. He'd change buses and head back south to San Antonio. No one would suspect that he'd back track through Pecan Valley on the way. He'd paid for the bus ticket with the small amount of cash in his wallet.

When the bus rolled away, he was finally able to pull the bank bag out of Cully's attaché case, to count again his small fortune. He had broken the lock on the case in a bathroom stall in the bus station before boarding the bus. He held the thick wad of money down inside the case to hide it from any prying eyes. He began counting. His heart sank. There was a stack of one dollar bills sandwiched between two one hundred dollar notes, rubber-banded together. He counted the bills over and over again, hoping that the $10,000 would miraculously appear. Instead, there was barely enough to get him back to Chicago. He'd left his jacket, with the $100 bill he'd demanded from Cully, at the motel in Pecan Valley. "That goddamned lawyer switched bags on me when I was signing that paper," he thought to himself. "They had it planned all along . . . and if that sorry son-of-a-bitch Cully dies, I'll be on the run the rest of my life for this measly $298.00 in my pocket. Jesus Christ, now what?"

The bus took nine hours to reach San Antonio. When he boarded the plane to Chicago, he had $19.43 left to his name. That Renata had lied to him all those years left him numb; that Cully was his father left him forlorn.

Cully was expected to live. Miraculously, he would recover fully from the two bullets fired from his Ruger. The hit to the head, however, was a different matter. He couldn't speak, nor could he see. He mumbled incoherently. Park had gone to the hospital to see him. Cully hadn't recognized him.

The lawyers had assured Cady that there was more than enough evidence to indict Palmer and Cully. Palmer and his wife had left town, on an extended trip, the neighbors said. There was no warrant out for Palmer's arrest. It would take some time, and it was too early to tell if Cully would ever be able to stand trial.

39

Concho City—October 5, 1993

Cady had never wanted to return to Bobwhite Lane until then. She hadn't told one soul where she was going—not even Nancy or John Earl, or Dell Wayne Wilson when he called that morning to say he was in town and would be attending Jonas's funeral. He wanted to see her, but Cady made excuses to avoid having to tell him that the desire was not mutual. Her sense of time had vanished, so before she knew it, she was on the outskirts of Concho City.

When she approached the T in the road at Bobwhite Lane, there it stood—No. 8—looking much smaller than she remembered. The whole neighborhood seemed to have shrunk, except for the live oak the men had come and planted the morning after Jonas's accident. It had grown tall and wide.

She stopped alongside the curb in front, got out, and leaned against the car door, pressing her belly tightly against its warmth. She looked over at the house where Sweezer had lived. It was dilapidated and abandoned-looking, and the red shutters at Miss Alice's old place were faded and peeling. She then settled her gaze somewhat reluctantly back on No. 8. The things that Jonas had disliked the most about the house—the red and green tiles that flanked the front door—were still there.

The front step caught her eye and she grabbed her notepad and pen. She hadn't written a solitary thing for three years until then. She scribbled:

Sunlight sneaks down through the thick boughs of the live oak Daddy had planted, leaving lacy images on the spot where we sat together that night, talking about the stars and the train ride. And then we sang "Always" and I danced on his shoe tops—before it all happened.

Pausing and twirling the pen between her fingers, Cady noticed a figure moving toward her on the walk. A plumpish older woman was approaching, wiping her hands on her apron.

"Hi there," the woman said, a friendly smile spreading across her face. "Lookin' for somebody?" she asked in a heavy Texas drawl, squinting against the glare from the windshield of Cady's car.

"Uh . . . no ma'am. Actually, I used to live in your house and just wanted to come have a look at it and the old neighborhood . . . if you don't mind."

"Don't mind at all. Glad you came by. My name's Harriet, Harriet Reed," the lady said, extending a blue-veined hand to Cady, her other hand shading her eyes. "How long's it been since ya lived here?"

"It's been a long time. Forty years to be exact," Cady answered, shaking the lady's hand.

"Gracious me, that's hard to believe. You don't look that old."

"Well, thank you for the compliment, but I'm every bit of forty-six."

"My word," the lady replied, shaking her head. "So where 'bouts do you live now?"

"Over in Pecan Valley."

"Oh that Pecan Valley's such a pretty little town. Listen, my husband's not due home for awhile, so how would you like to come in and have a look around?"

"I'd like that very much if you're sure it's no trouble."

"Oh law, no trouble at all."

Cady followed Mrs. Reed up the walk where she and her father had danced. "How long have you and Mr. Reed lived here?"

"Honey, we've been here so dang long I've plum forgot the exact day, but it was back in '66, not too long after our youngest ran off and got married. Neighbors told us it'd been a rent house for a long time before we bought it."

Cady felt her anticipation building as she stepped onto the front step where the sunlight was dancing its shimmery jig. She hesitated when the spectacle slipped over the tops of her shoes. She wanted to linger there, to pay homage to the spot, but Mrs. Reed was holding the screen door open. She politely moved inside, but felt cheated.

Despite forty years of multiple inhabitants, and just as many coats of paint, the house had the same peculiar, not unpleasant, smell it had then— of oil-cloth, dust, and mothballs. With the exception of a bay window that the owners had installed in the living room, where the old picture window had been, the layout was the same. She looked through the kitchen, past the family room, and into the back yard where her mourning dove had lived. She remembered the imperial cats that had held nightly court in the alley, and she remembered those mysterious strobe lights, high in the sky, when she was barely seven.

Mrs. Reed invited her to roam around freely while she herself disappeared into the kitchen to make a pitcher of tea. Cady made her way down the hall to her parents' old bedroom. The thought crossed her mind that it might have been there that Cully and her mother had betrayed Jonas. She quickly opened the closet door to satisfy her memory that there was a trap door in the closet floor. It was indeed there. She then went to her old bedroom to find the once-lavender walls slathered in white and covered with religious depictions. There was a sewing machine table where her bed had once been, where her blonde-headed doll had slept with her every night. She still had the doll, in a box, in Pecan Valley. She took one last look before stopping at the hall bath to find the same green bathtub where the alligator had lived. Mrs. Reed called to her from the kitchen. She made her way to the living room, remembering where all the furniture had been, and the spot on the living room floor where she'd covered her mother with the blanket. The telephone stand by the garage door held nothing but a messy stack of magazines where the phone had once been. How different life would have been, she thought, had her father not answered the call that night, or gone for the burger. Before those thoughts could get too tight a grip, Mrs. Reed offered her a glass of tea.

She joined Mrs. Reed at the kitchen table that sat exactly where theirs had, where her mother had served that last inedible vodka-soaked meal. Sipping tall glasses of syrupy-sweet tea, Mrs. Reed talked to Cady about how Concho City had grown, about the weather, and about her grown children, until Cady announced that it was time to go.

She glanced one last time at the back yard through the glass door. The bush where she and Jonas had found the injured dove was gone. She asked Mrs. Reed about it. "Oh honey, don't recollect that one right off, but Mr. Reed did get rid of several old bushes out there, poisoned 'em matter-a-fact, said they were nothin' but weeds, and that gettin' rid of 'em would give him more room to make the patio bigger which a'course he's never got 'round to doin'," she said, winking at Cady.

Cady felt ill. "Do you ever hear any mourning doves out back, Mrs. Reed?"

"Come to think of it, can't recall hearin' any," she said, with a curious tilt of her head.

At that, Cady started for the front door in such a hurry to leave that she hadn't noticed that the dancing sunlight had vanished from the front step. She and Mrs. Reed talked outside just long enough for Cady to learn that there had been a series of renters living in Sweezer's old place, and that a widow lady had bought Alice Bock's house. Mrs. Reed had never met any of them and knew no one who had. They said their goodbyes. When she left, she didn't look back.

Cady drove the car by the side back of Alice's old place, where Alice had kept her De Soto, and from where she'd escaped with Sweezer and Alice that desperate night. She remembered "Always" coming through Alice's front windows that other fateful night, when the worn leather of her father's shoes had given way under her feet, squeaking a little as they danced. For the first time since Jonas's death just two days before, she wept without reserve.

⁓

The forty-minute drive back to Pecan Valley went by far too quickly, and the time before the funeral as well. She hadn't been alone. Nancy had stayed close by. There would no doubt be a good showing at the visitation that night and at the funeral the next day.

The other cars flew past her on the highway while she watched a swirling dust devil spin and skip like a top across a brown field. Dark clouds gathered on the horizon toward Rowan where the tall steeple of its landmark church would soon signal only a few more miles to go before crossing over the Corona River into Pecan Valley. Cady looked over at the empty passenger seat, where her father had so often sat, and could hear him say, "We're almost home." She would pass the cemetery soon, the one they'd so often passed together, the one where they'd pulled weeds and watered together, where Frances and Jonas Sr. and the other ancestors were buried, where Rachel was buried, and where he would join them the next day.

In fifteen minutes she'd meet with the funeral director. She'd make sure her father's hair was combed just the way he preferred. And then, for the last time, she'd whisk away the sure-to-be sprinkles of dandruff from the shoulders of his dark blue suit coat, the one reserved for church and special occasions. That Jonas's death came on the fortieth anniversary of his accident was downright eerie to some, strangely coincidental to others, but to Cady it seemed ordained.

When she got to the funeral home in Pecan Valley, she stopped in front and turned off the engine. She looked at what she'd written just a couple of hours before—about the sunlight on the step at No. 8. She carefully tore the page from her notebook. In a few minutes, she would slip it into her father's breast pocket along with their unused train tickets.

40

~

Pecan Valley—October 6, 1993

There was a thick stack of unopened sympathy cards on the front entry table across from the mural. Cady hadn't had the heart to read them. The visitation the night before had exhausted her. There were people there she'd never met. "Where have they been all these years?" she whispered under her breath. She kept steady watch over her father's coffin. The chatter all around him, as he lay motionless, had made his absence all the more apparent. Flowers filled the parlor. It would take two pickup loads, the funeral director said, to get them to the church and grave site.

"Cady, honey," Nancy said. "We need to leave in about fifteen minutes . . . you 'bout ready?"

"As ready as I'll ever be I guess."

"How 'bout we go sit out back to wait for John Earl. It's such a pretty day. It'll be good for you to get some sun, and maybe the little yellow cat will come over? Wouldn't that be nice?"

"I guess so," Cady answered, wishing Marlon could come back to sit on her lap for just a little while.

The sky was that deep cerulean blue that only autumn produces. There were touches of red and yellow in the trees and bushes. It would be much cooler that day than it had been—a high of seventy-five. "Perfect weather," Cady thought, looking up at the sky. There wasn't a cloud to be seen. Nancy and Cady sat side-by-side on the bench out by the little house.

"I never saw so many beautiful flowers in my life as I did at the funeral home last night," Nancy said. "Even Richard and his wife sent some from New York, and your old news agency in D.C., and oh, I forgot to tell you, your friend Leigh in Maryland sent a beautiful arrangement."

"That's nice. Leigh must have gotten in touch with the others," Cady said, dropping her forehead into her hand. She had a raging headache.

"Those bronze mums you ordered for the casket are particularly spectacular," Nancy said, noticing that Cady's hands were trembling. "You feelin' all right, sweetheart?"

"I feel like my head's exploding . . . probably from tryin' to find a hiding place for these thoughts that won't leave me alone. Her throat was tightening. She squinted against the bright sun. "I haven't heard one single mourning dove all day, not one, and of all days. They're probably hiding from the hunters out after them. God, I hate thinking about that."

"Then try not to, sweetheart. They'll be okay."

John Earl pulled into the driveway. The three of them drove the short distance to the church. The funeral service would begin at 1:00. It was 12:00 noon when they arrived. Lynn Simms, the old friend and neighbor of the Randolphs, was carrying food into the church hall, including a plate of the cinnamon rolls that Jonas loved so much. Other women followed, carrying their own contributions to the lunch for family, close friends, and church members. Dell Wayne showed up to eat; his aunt was serving. There wasn't much of an exchange between Cady and him, just a few pleasantries. It was a strange and awkward meeting. Park was nowhere to be seen.

After lunch, Cady, Nancy, and John Earl climbed the interior steps to the sanctuary, and took their places on the reserved front pew. The church was filled beyond capacity. Folding chairs had been brought up from the basement for the overflow of people. Cady saw Dell Wayne out of the corner of her eye. He had positioned himself prominently at the front of the sanctuary, leaning against the wall as the preacher began the service. She settled her gaze back on Jonas's casket a couple of feet in front of her, and reached for his signet ring, holding it tightly in her hand. She'd put it on a chain around her neck to keep it safe and close. The pressure in her head began to lessen.

It was a good service, folks told her, one they were sure Jonas would have liked. Taking the long walk up the aisle to leave the sanctuary, Cady spotted Bill Armand at the back. They nodded to one another, an all-knowing kind of nod. She then caught sight of Park sitting with his former love Marjorie, who had driven up from Austin with her grown daughter. Cady hardly recognized Park in his dark glasses, and hadn't seen Marjorie since Jonas Sr.'s funeral thirty-one years before. When Park rose to embrace her, Cady whispered in his ear, "Why didn't you sit with us?" He just shook his head. She somehow understood and continued walking toward the front doors of the church with Nancy and John Earl close behind.

They descended the front steps and climbed into the back of the funeral home's only limousine. Park had declined an offer to ride with them to the cemetery, said that he'd ride out with Marjorie. It was no time for arguing. Cady let it be. Dell Wayne was nowhere to be seen. Someone said they saw him leave out the side door of the church, and then drive off the opposite direction of the cemetery in his father's old pickup.

The procession to the cemetery was the longest the Sheriff said he ever remembered seeing. "Doc's is even longer than Mr. and Mrs. Randolph's, and those were big 'uns," he'd told one of the funeral-goers. The cars on the highway followed the long-held tradition of stopping along the shoulder, not budging until the last car in the funeral procession had passed through the cemetery gates; it took a full fifteen minutes that day.

"Cady, honey" Nancy said, "I don't want to upset you any more than you already are, but I've just gotta say it . . . I can't *believe* the preacher brought that evil Cully up, even *praying* for him, right over your daddy's coffin . . . just blew my mind."

"Yes, I know . . . but he doesn't have a clue what Cully did and, even if he did, I suppose he'd be held to a higher standard than we are. Can you believe how many people came?" Cady said, changing the subject.

⁓

The tent was set up with enough chairs for family and those too infirm to stand. The rest huddled in as close as they could get to the coffin. A green cloth, passing poorly for grass, covered the red dirt that would soon become Jonas's eternal blanket. The crowd was quiet. A little wind rustled through the tops of the sycamore trees, and the cars were making clacking sounds along the highway again. The ceremony was short, at Cady's request. The preacher announced that there would be no reception after, but that Cady appreciated all the good wishes and support. Most left quietly. A few stayed to pay their respects, Nancy and John Earl stood by, and the grave diggers waited in the distance for their moment.

Park stood off by himself in a tall tree's shadow. He waited until Cady stood alone before approaching her. "Cady, I want you to know that I loved and admired Jonas. He was nothing but good to me, and I'll always regret having not been there for him when he needed me most. I'm deeply sorry."

Cady stood silent for a moment and, in a spontaneous act that surprised even her, she lifted the chain that held Jonas's ring over her head, slipped the ring off, and handed it to Park. "Please, I think Dad would want you to have his ring. He thought a great deal of you, Park, and I believe that the ring will mean as much to you as it did to him."

Park held it in his palm, staring at it in disbelief. He looked at her for confirmation that it was indeed to be his. She signaled "yes" with a nod. He slipped the ring on his finger. It was still warm, and a perfect fit. The look on his face defied adequate description but, suffice it to say, he appeared weightless.

"Thank you, Cady. You have no idea what this means to me."

"I think I do. Wear it in peace."

Park hugged her, got into Marjorie's car, and waved goodbye as they drove away.

Cady waved back until the car disappeared down the highway.

"No, Nancy, I'm going to stay here awhile. You and John Earl go on home. I need to see this through."

"Are you sure, Cady? I hate leaving you out here all alone."

"I'm all right, Nancy. It's important for me to be here by myself for awhile."

"Okay, then, we'll go, but please call me as soon as you get home, okay? And I've just got to ask . . . what did Park say to you?"

"I'll tell you later, okay? Don't worry about me. I'm fine."

The limousine left with Nancy and John Earl, and would return to get Cady. The grave diggers loomed large in the distance.

Cady sat alone under the tent, looking over at the rusted iron crib that had marked a nearby grave for almost a century. She had stood at that grave as a child, sad for the baby, for all the years lost to it. Her attention returned to her father's casket. She was numb. That her note and the train tickets were with him offered some amount of comfort.

And then, it came—the five-note song of a mourning dove. Shivering with a surge of adrenaline, she looked up to see the bird perched high on a branch of the giant sycamore tree that towered over the Randolph plot. She could make out the heft of his pinkish breast through a spray of fall leaves. "Thank you, Papa . . . thank you," she whispered. Resting one hand on his casket, and the other over her eyes, she listened.

And then, a voice called to her from behind. "Cady?"

Startled, she turned around to see a very tall, quite handsome, and beautifully-dressed man standing at the back of the tent.

"Hello," she said. "I didn't know anyone was here. Did you attend my father's service today?"

"Yes, it was a wonderful service I thought," he said, moving toward her. Cady shook her head in the affirmative.

"You don't know who I am, do you?" he asked.

"No, I'm sorry I don't. Were you a friend of my father's?"

He didn't answer. Instead, he pulled a smooth oval-shaped rock from his pocket and handed it to her.

Cady stared at it, turning it over. She could make out the faded lettering on one side. "Sweezer, is it really you?" she asked, closing her eyes, afraid he'd say no.

"No one's called me that in many years," he said. "It sure sounds good."

She opened her eyes and sank into one of the chairs under the tent, holding the rock to her chest. "I always hoped I'd see you again," she said.

"It's the strangest thing . . . I don't understand how I can be this supremely happy at probably the saddest moment of my life." She looked up at the sycamore. The dove was gone. She looked back at Sweezer.

"I know what you mean . . . I feel the same. Your father meant the very world to me," he said, sitting down next to her. "I've handled that rock so much over the years that I've just about rubbed the paint off. It's been kind of a good luck charm . . . always with me."

"How did you find out? About Dad I mean."

"I've kept a friend in Concho City all these years, an old school chum. She knew how important your father was to me. She called to tell me."

"It's been forty years . . . do you realize that? Did you come a long way?" she asked.

"Yes, it's been a very long time . . . and yes, I've come a long way in more ways than one. I live in Brooklyn, and have since . . . oh, we can talk about all that later. I plan to be around for a couple of days."

"Funny thing . . . I lived in New York too for awhile," Cady told him.

Their conversation was interrupted by two men approaching the tent. "Excuse me, folks," one of them said. "Mind if we get started?"

Cady's heart began beating hard and fast. "I guess so," she said.

"Would you like me to stay?" Sweezer asked, touching her lightly on the shoulder.

"Yes, please," she said, still clutching the rock to her chest.

They sat together quietly while the men lowered Jonas's casket into the ground. Then using a small back-hoe, they began filling the grave with the sandy red earth. Cady had removed two bronze mums from the casket. She gave one to Sweezer. He took it from her as if it were a piece of fragile glass.

"I'll keep it always," he told her, as he slipped the stem into his breast pocket.

"I have no doubt you will . . . like you've kept this rock," she said, handing it back to him. He slipped it into his coat pocket.

The funeral director had just returned to get Cady. "You about ready to go home?" he asked.

"I'll take her home," Sweezer said.

Cady watched the workers place the flowers on Jonas's grave, being careful not to cover up one arrangement with another.

"Have we met?" the funeral director asked, extending his hand.

"No, sir, we haven't. My name's Carl, Carl Riley. Cady and I, and her father . . . we go back a long way."

"Pleasure to meet you, sir . . . you from around here?"

"A long time ago I was. I live in New York now."

"You mean the Big Apple?"

"Yes . . . Brooklyn actually."

"Boy howdy, that's a far piece from West Texas."

"Yes sir, a very far piece."

"Well, nice to meet ya, Carl," the funeral director said. "Let us know if there's anything more we can do for ya, Cady," he added, tipping the brim of his hat to her, nodding to Sweezer.

Cady took a last look back as they drove away in Sweezer's rental car. She hadn't needed to give him directions to the house. He remembered the route taken forty years before when he'd driven her there to safety in Miss Alice's De Soto. She stared at him as he drove, able to resurrect in his profile the freckle-faced boy he'd once been. He returned her glance a couple of times, with a smile.

~

"Cady, I have some things I want to share with you that I think might have meaning for you," he said, sipping coffee from one of the living room's wingback chairs.

He went to the car and returned with a sack, the contents of which he placed carefully on the coffee table: a worn silky garment holding an old 78 record that he unwrapped from some tattered tissue paper, a thoroughly used edition of *The Little Prince*, and a small candle glued to a yellowed note.

"You remember those Friday nights when Miss Alice played her music?"

"Yes, of course I do. She played "Always" the night Dad was hurt. We danced to it on the sidewalk . . . until it started raining."

"Well, this is the record, I mean *the* record, Cady. And *The Little Prince* is *the* book you gave me so long ago. It was left on my porch not long after you went away."

Cady picked up the book without opening it and began reciting her inscription. "Hi Sweezer, it's me Cady . . . "

"Remember how you asked me to say hi to your mourning dove?" he asked.

"Yes, I do."

"Well, it might interest you to know that I *did*," he said.

"Really?"

"Yes. And to this day, I can't hear a mourning dove without saying hello," he said, grinning. "And this candle? It's the very one from that cupcake that you asked me to save for your dad that awful day. It's glued here to the note he wrote to me telling me about the rock. Remember?"

Cady buried her face in her hands. "Oh Sweezer, your birthday was the 3rd of October . . . how could I have forgotten? I'm so sorry."

"It's really okay. I don't celebrate my birthday . . . haven't since, well, you know."

"If he'd known, that would have made Dad very sad."

"Look Cady, I turned thirteen the day he was hurt . . . and turned fifty-three on the day he died. How could I *ever* celebrate such a day?"

"Of course you couldn't. I'm sure I'd feel the very same . . . but yet you've kept these reminders of that day all these years?"

"Yes I have...because they've meant more to me than anything I've been fortunate enough to accumulate over the years . . . much more."

"How on earth did you get the record?"

"Miss Alice. I promised I'd take care of it for her. It was left to me when she died."

"What a story, Sweezer . . . my grandmother's old phonograph still works. Could we play it?"

"Wonderful idea," he answered.

They sat together in the dim light of the living room. It was close to dusk. They listened. Cady shut her eyes and remembered. Sweezer did the same. She played the record through once more and then told him about Bill Armand, about returning to Bobwhite Lane the day before, and about going through her old house and seeing his and Miss Alice's. It turned out that he too had returned to the old neighborhood the day before. They had just missed each other.

"I want to hear everything, Sweezer, everything about you, where you've been all these years, *how* you've been."

"Mine's a long story, as yours must be. I want to hear everything about you too."

"I'll bet you're hungry," she said. "And I'm starved. How about we go down to the Lone Star Café and get a bite? The food's pretty good."

"That's a great idea. Let's go."

The Lone Star was slow that night. Luckily, June Ann was working. Cady chose the booth in the front window where Jonas had often sat.

"Tell me more about Miss Alice, Sweezer. I remember her being on the gruff side."

"Well, yes I suppose she was a little gruff, but I think it was because she was afraid of letting her guard down to get hurt again. Her husband left her with no explanation. She had no one. And well, I didn't either after you and Dr. Randolph left. I guess she and I became family. She paid my way through undergraduate and medical school. There was even enough to help me through my internship and residency."

"A doctor, Sweezer," Cady said with a sigh. "Dad would be so pleased."

He looked down, and then back up at her with a small, sad smile. "Because of him, I didn't want to become anything *but*." He paused. "Anyway, Cady, Alice Bock made it all possible. The short story is that I kept the house on Bobwhite Lane for awhile after Joe, my father, died. I returned only once—when Miss Alice became ill. After she died a short time later, I sold my house and hers, and never returned . . . until now."

"What a story. I could have sworn I saw you in Concho City back in the 60s."

"You could have. I was there in '65 for a short while when Miss Alice passed."

Cady knew then that it had indeed been Sweezer she'd seen in the department store that day.

"What about a wife, kids, that sort of thing?" she asked.

"I have a daughter, Faith, named after my mother. She's twenty-four now, living in Manhattan, working hard. Her mother died a few years ago. We were divorced before she passed."

"I'm so sorry to hear that."

"Thank you, but it's all right. I've come to peace with it."

There was a long silence before the conversation continued.

"You said you live in Brooklyn?" Cady asked.

"Yes, Brooklyn Heights, for the last eight years or so. I found a great place there to hang my hat, and what about you, Cady? You mentioned you'd lived in New York?"

"Yes I was there for awhile, in the 70s, in the Village around the corner from Your Father's Mustache . . . did you know that place?"

"Yes indeed. I went there often. The lead banjo player was a very good friend of mine."

"You're kidding! It was one of my favorite spots . . . hated to see it close."

"Yes, that was a sad event. I was actually there that last night. I suppose you're going to tell me that you were too?"

Cady smiled. "I absolutely *was!*"

They laughed at the absurdity of having been in the same room, possibly sharing one of the club's long tables, having no idea that the other was there. June Ann came along about that time to warm up their coffees.

"Tell me, Cady, did you get to meet the wizard, as you once told me you would . . . marry, have kids, a career? And that uncle of yours in the hospital . . . the one the minister mentioned during the service today? I've got a thousand questions," he asked in one long breath.

"Oh, let's talk about all that later. I only want to talk about good things right now," she said, taking a sip of coffee.

Just then, June Ann plunked down two steaming-hot plates of food.

"Yes, good things, like this delicious-smelling food," he said, smiling up at the waitress.

It was 3:30 a.m. when they left the Lone Star and strolled toward the car. The stars overhead were plentiful and bright. A puffy cloud raced across them, back-lit by the moon.

"Cady, you really must come visit me in Brooklyn."

"Are there any mourning doves in Brooklyn? I don't recall," she said, looking up at the sky.

"Yes indeed, but you'll just have to come listen for yourself."

From the Author

~

Thank you for adding *Listen for the Mourning Dove* to your library, and for becoming a part of the life of this book.

I hope that you enjoyed reading it as much I enjoyed writing it over the course of more than seven years—a true labor of love most of the time, and of blood, sweat, and tears just as often.

I invite you to contact me with any questions or comments about the book at my email address: *pearcesantafe@gmail.com*. Please visit *www.bookleafpress.com* for additional information.

I look forward to hearing from you,

Acknowledgments

For their various and invaluable contributions to the end result of this book, I thank the following individuals:

Ellis Aronson, Steven Baker, Pam Bladine, Pamela (Elle) Boers, Fred L. and Peggy Campbell, Diana Ceres, Nick E. Chavez Jr., Veronica Copeland, Jayne Cotten, Kathie Cox, Kelly Davis, Gary Denny, Florence Everts, Carol Ann White Fahrner, Carol Beth Ford, Joyce Fox, Ann Gholami, Stephanie Harding, Jeanie Harris, Ann Hodge, Julie Kelly, Peggy King, Joyce Knight, Kakie Love, Robert Mathes, Michelle Mills, Andy Pearce Myer, Bill Newroe, Nancy Newsom, Michele M. Jacquez-Ortiz, Annie Osburn, Carol Otto Pearce, John Y. Pearce III, Margaret E. Pearce, Sibyl Saam, Maxine Sanchez, D.S., Melissa Selsor, Polly Summar, Alison Sykes, Betty Timlen, Lynne Velasco, Greg Weber, Louise Williams, Christopher Wyndham.

Special thanks to Dr. David Gregory for his painstaking and expert perusals of the book's early drafts, to Susan Mansell for lending her true artistry to the cover, and to Jack Wright for having endowed the book with unwavering enthusiasm and a generous spirit.

I'm grateful for my dear departed dog and cat companions, Leo and Sugarbear, who made a warm place at my feet during a good bit of the writing of this book, and for my cat Sweezer who took up where they left off.